T0105509

A RELUCTANT ASSASSIN

✦

C. E. Wilcox

iUniverse, Inc.
Bloomington

A Reluctant Assassin

iUniverse books may be ordered through booksellers or by contacting:

iUniverse
1663 Liberty Drive
Bloomington, IN 47403
www.iuniverse.com
1-800-Authors (1-800-288-4677)

Because of the dynamic nature of the Internet, any Web addresses or links contained in this book may have changed since publication and may no longer be valid. The views expressed in this work are solely those of the author and do not necessarily reflect the views of the publisher, and the publisher hereby disclaims any responsibility for them.

ISBN: 978-1-4502-5780-0 (pbk)
ISBN: 978-1-4502-5781-7 (cloth)
ISBN: 978-1-4502-5782-4 (ebk)

Printed in the United States of America

iUniverse rev. date: 12/3/2010

Library of Congress Control Number: 2010913322

Cover design by Glenn Wilcox

For
Rita Wilcox
Harvey H. Wilcox
Robert A. Gould

Chapter 1

There are six of us shrouded in the pitch-black, practically claustrophobic darkness of a Marine Corps CH-53S Sea Dragon helicopter heading to a drop zone close to the Afghanistan-Pakistan border for deployment. We are each on a special solo scout/sniper assignment, assignments the Pentagon in Washington DC projects to have less than a 10 percent survival rate. For this night, this moment in time, we have prepared extensively to jump into the cold, black night air of Afghanistan, parachuting into what appears to be a dark bottomless pit, as nothing illuminated on the ground gives us a clue as to our location or even the elevation of our helicopter.

I only knew the other five by their code names, having learned them as we trained together during the past four months in the deserts of central California. Individual assignments assured that we were deployed separately. To maintain utmost secrecy, no discussion of our missions had been allowed— not among ourselves, not with our immediate supervisors, and definitely not with anyone outside the military. We did know that all of our missions were a response to 9/11, which made their successful completion seem that much more important.

The Sea Dragon S—S for stealth—was required to fly at some twelve thousand feet for this mission, which was unusual for the aircraft. The standard CH-53 is primarily a troop transport and support helicopter. The Sea Dragon CH-53S is a top-secret stealth, or silent-operating, helicopter. The stealth technology, originally developed during the Vietnam War to silently insert and retrieve special operations personnel from behind enemy lines, results in a maximum achievable ceiling of approximately twelve to fourteen thousand feet. The high altitude we were using provided the silent insertion necessary for our mission. Our enemies, the Taliban and al-Qaeda, were equipped with advanced technology for detecting any lower-level insertion into what they considered their space, whether land or air.

When a CH-53S Sea Dragon navigator identifies a drop zone, a small red light comes on in the troop compartment of the helicopter. When this light pops on, all six of us will have approximately one minute to exit through the back ramp. As we prepare to jump, the Sea Dragon starts a dead drop: the engines are cut back to idle, and the aircraft free-falls for two thousand feet. The reason for this descent is to reduce any engine sound the enemy might hear. Once we parachute out the back, the helicopter continues to descend with its engines idling for at least another forty to fifty miles from the drop zone. This greatly reduces the possibility of al-Qaeda or the Taliban detecting deployment.

I, Sergeant Oscar Wylton, a six-foot-two, 196-pound Marine, was assigned position number four in the lineup to exit the rear door.

My fifty-plus pounds of combat gear included two gallons of water. The water was strapped to my body by bladder-type tanks; this would eliminate sloshing as I moved about. My assignment required me to be on the ground for at least two weeks, and my research of the drop zone and target area had revealed not a single source of water. My water supply had to be used sparingly. The Pentagon had planned for us to be picked up precisely two weeks from the initial drop, at the same location, at the same time—the water had to last through that duration.

I checked my chute and all my gear—everything was set and ready to go. Everything except my nerves, which were a little frazzled. This was my tenth mission—the previous nine all in dangerous territories—yet there was no way my mind could relax and not race with thoughts of injury, capture, or death. Each one of us undoubtedly dealt with the same emotions.

After several hours of flight, the light finally blinked on.

The night air at ten thousand feet proved to be cool with low humidity. The drop zone could not be seen in the moonless night, as my descent allowed only a view of the mountain peaks silhouetted against the black sky. Having no idea how close to the ground I was, I checked the only method available: a small Doppler device attached to my parachute harness that required my continuous attention in order to determine my position relative to the ground. Dropping at a pretty steady rate, I knew to pull up on the chute as the ground approached, causing my descent to slow. At two hundred feet, I pulled the cords attached to the chute to reduce my descent. This still did not prevent a hard landing, as the ground proved much closer than two hundred feet, more likely one hundred.

Shit, a helluva way to start the mission.

Bouncing and rolling for about thirty feet, my aching body finally came to rest on the hard sandy surface. My right leg and my right elbow had been skinned. Fortunately, my Marine Corps-issued cammies (camouflaged utility uniform) demonstrated more resilience than my tender skin. With the wind blowing at about twelve to fifteen knots, I knew I had to collapse the chute. If not, it could quickly fill with the blowing wind and drag my tender ass across half of Afghanistan, probably ending up in some poor unsuspecting sheepherder's outhouse—assuming they had outhouses.

Once I collapsed my parachute, it had to be disposed of. Burning it would produce a flame that could be seen for miles, so I proceeded to dig a hole. Ever try digging a hole in concrete with a knife? When we practiced this mission in the California desert, the surface consisted mostly of loose sand, so burying the chute hadn't been a big deal. Laboring for two hours with my KA-BAR (a military knife comparable to a hunting knife), I finally produced a hole deep enough to bury the parachute. Covering and smoothing the surface over with some weeds and brush that lay nearby, I concealed the burial site of my dead parachute; in this case, there would be no grave marker.

I glanced at my watch, finding it to be about one thirty bravo time or about three thirty in the morning local time. Bravo time is a single worldwide military time zone used so all operations are in the same timeframe. I had to get my ass in gear, needing to travel at least six miles before sunup, while allowing myself time to establish a hide. A hide is a totally camouflaged position that provides a Marine with sufficient concealment so that a person standing within two feet cannot know of the Marine's presence in any way. Establishing a proper hide for the day was critical to the success of my mission, as travels could only be at night to avoid any possible detection.

Although it was hotter than a witch's tit, being encased head to foot in infrared avoidance clothing reduced the heat generated by my body. This necessary garment, a special covering somewhat like pantyhose, provided the technology to avoid detection by an infrared scope at night; however, it hadn't been fully tested, and this mission would be its first combat use.

I checked to be sure that all of my gear, weapons, water, and provisions remained in my possession following my little encounter with the ground. Everything seemed intact and ready to roll. With fifty-plus pounds of weight being humped across the plain, maintaining the average walking pace established for the mission would prove to be difficult. Despite the oppressive heat and humidity, the need to cover at least six miles before sunup required a blistering pace.

The GPS system, which included a topographical map screen, required checking to determine my position. Before boarding the helicopter for the flight, the GPS had been calibrated for this mission. The GPS screen indicated my current position, the mission destination, and the distance I had to cover each night before developing my hide for the day. The total distance to the target was calculated to be approximately thirty miles, meaning that I must cover a minimum of six miles each day in order to accomplish the mission and return to the drop/pickup zone with little time to spare.

I had confidence in being able to hump the twenty-nine miles to the critical point. The critical point, a location approximately a quarter mile from my final hide, was where I would take out my target. That last quarter mile would take at least a full day to complete. My final day's movement to the critical point could only be made at night and had to be accomplished on a belly-crawl, using my fingers and toes to move myself slowly across the ground. During the day, a ghillie suit would provide my hide. A ghillie suit is special camouflage clothing developed by a Scottish hunter prior to the First World War. The British successfully adapted the suit during the First World War and subsequent wars for use by their trained snipers. The United States started to use the suit during the Second World War. Yet, despite the ghillie suit, I would have to remain alert and move sparingly and only as necessary.

Even though anti-infrared stockings covered my body, the Taliban or al-Qaeda still had night vision equipment. Such equipment could spot any movement within their protected area. The protected area extended radially outward approximately two thousand yards from their base camp. To be within my firing range, which was a 99.9 percent probability of a hit on the target, I had to be inside a radius of twelve hundred yards of the base camp. That fell well within the night vision capabilities of my adversaries. My movement inside the final five hundred yards to my final hide position had to be painfully slow so as not to be detected. The final hide position, from which the fatal shot would be fired, had been carefully selected through research and topographical maps.

The hard ground had a loose, sandy covering. My location was on a plain with a low growth of shrubs, grass, and the occasional dwarf tree. Mountain ranges completely surrounded the plain. The twelve- to fifteen-knot winds quickly blew the loose soil over any tracks I might have left. I took a sip of water and looked at my GPS to ensure my heading was in the right direction. Carefully checking the GPS topographical setting to determine if any drop-offs or cliffs existed, I further assured myself that the chosen direction would take me to the correct location. My eyes had adjusted to the almost-total darkness, but I could only see about ten to fifteen feet ahead of me. I set off at the pace I knew I had to maintain to reach my first night's objective.

Not even thirty steps into the hike, sweat began to pour down my face and my back. At this point, my extensive and strenuous conditioning really paid off. At the California desert training camp, Gunnery Sergeant Mike Turner pushed us every day to maximize our conditioning. We were up at five in the morning doing push-ups, squats, jumping jacks, and an assortment of other physical tortures designed to condition our bodies for this mission.

Gunnery Turner, himself in exceptional condition, made sure we were in excellent physical condition as well.

In addition to the morning physical training (PT), we took long hikes every day with full packs, including scoped rifles and Glock P38 (pistol) sidearms, all fully loaded, to further harden our bodies. The forced marches, as we referred to them, covered twenty miles per day, ten out and ten back. The temperature, always in the triple digit range and often exceeding 110 degrees, prepared us for the heat of the deserts in Afghanistan, but not the oppressive humidity.

To add to our daily physical preparedness, we spent numerous hours on the rifle and pistol range sharpening our skills as expert marksmen. Being equipped with the latest and best sniper rifles and scopes provided a potential edge against our adversaries. This equipment, developed by the Marine Corps Scout/Sniper School located in Camp Pendleton, California, included the M-14 with a 10x scope, technologically the most advanced rifle and scope available anywhere.

We trained and trained with our weapons until we could consistently hit a man's head at fifteen hundred yards. We had to hit the target every time, regardless of weather conditions, such as wind, rain, extreme heat, and extreme humidity, and were trained to look for telltale signs, such as the movement of grass or heat waves rising from the ground, any or all of which could distort the target image or the path of the projectile. The knowledge greatly improved our marksmanship. The rigorous training required our movement to Camp Pendleton in southern California, Camp Lejeune in South Carolina, and various other camps throughout the United States. All of this was to perfect our marksmanship with both the M-14 and with the Glock P38, as well as expose us to various climate extremes.

Not being the best recruit in boot camp or infantry training, I still ended up as one of the Marines selected for the scout/sniper program. Captain James Broody, who headed the school at Quantico, Virginia, personally selected each candidate. The initial selection could only be through volunteer placement. Next, Captain Jim, as we came to know him, put each candidate through a two-hour interview that covered every aspect of his or her life. The questioning focused on why one wanted to become a scout/sniper. After Captain Jim completed his interrogation, his staff would continue the interview process. The interview with the staff involved subterfuge, such as a candidate being misled to believe the interview was just a social gathering of fellow Marines in order to get the candidate's guard down. Captain Jim wanted the braggarts and "I-want-to-be-a-killer" types weeded out.

The final part of the candidate selection included a psychological evaluation. Scout/snipers need to have exceptional abilities, among them being able to lie in a single spot with limited movement for days at a time. They would have to defecate and piss in their pants and lay in the waste for days. One leading question concerned marriage or potential of marriage. Captain Jim preferred unmarried candidates—no one who had already been married, and those who were "about to be married" went to the bottom of the candidate list. He possessed skepticism of any candidate who carried pictures of his or her current "honey." But the most significant factor in the selection included the candidate's ability to look into the eyes of the victim and put a bullet into the body of that individual. The scout/sniper could not view his occupation as one of a vendetta or as an opportunity to get even. He or she mentally had to eliminate any personal feeling about the target; the job was to eliminate the designated target and move onto the next, period.

Not the best marksman in my boot camp platoon at Parris Island, South Carolina, my scores consistently ranked me somewhere from the middle to the bottom half of the shooters in the platoon. Psychologically, I'm very stable and tested high on IQ tests; while not a genius, I still placed in the top 10 percent of the candidates. I followed orders as given and maintained my equipment and uniforms in top condition. All things considered, I was a good fit for the scout/sniper program.

I volunteered for the program and fulfilled all the basic requirements, which resulted in my selection to the program. Next, I spent eight weeks training at Quantico, Virginia, and graduated in the middle of my class. After graduation, I had been assigned to the Second Marine Division at Camp Lejeune, North Carolina, India Company, Third Battalion, Eighth Marine Regiment. The first year of that assignment I spent snooping and pooping around the pine forests of Camp Lejeune. At times, my team would sneak up on unsuspecting grunts and put an imaginary round into them.

But I had no time to reminisce; the schedule had to be maintained. My topographical map indicated a small ridge of one hundred fifty feet that I had to scale before arriving at a plateau where my first day's hide would be. Arriving at the bottom of the ridge, pretty much on schedule, the climb up started in earnest and with the knowledge that it would significantly slow my pace. With the weight of my gear, the climb proved to be more difficult than anticipated. I began huffing, puffing, and sweating while attempting to maintain the pace. This proved to be unrealistic. Figuring the pace could be improved on the downside of the ridge, I slowed to a more manageable level.

After reaching the top of the ridge, the trek down the reverse slope came as a welcome change. The pace picked up and I started to catch up with the set schedule. Miscalculating my ability, my pace increased substantially while going down the descending side of the slope. The weight of the equipment and my upper body speed began to exceed the speed at which my legs could keep up. If my Parris Island drill instructor, Sergeant Morgan, saw me, he would be all over my ass. I felt like a circus clown. Finally, my legs could no longer keep up, and over I went, ass over teakettle spout, right onto my kisser. Sliding the last one hundred feet or so to the bottom of the ridge, I now had an abrasion on the right side of my face that matched the one on my outer thigh.

Righting myself with no time to reflect on or care for my injury, off I went to my first day's hide. The first hide was located approximately one hundred miles east of Kabul and some twenty-three to twenty-four miles from my target destination near the Afghanistan-Pakistan border. Arriving at the hide fifteen minutes behind schedule, I quickly dug in and camouflaged the position. Even though I was in a remote area with little chance of discovery, the hide had to be thorough.

As a scout/sniper, the ability to acquire adequate sleep while maintaining mental acuity is an essential skill. Through diligent practice, I had attained this skill. Quickly acclimating my hearing to the surrounding sounds, sleep proved a welcome relief.

After sleeping for several hours, an unusual sound woke me. Voices in an unknown language appeared to be approaching my hiding place. Had I been detected? Were these possibly Taliban or al-Qaeda operatives on their way to eliminate me? Listening attentively, the language could not be determined. Even after having studied Arabic for several weeks, not a single word they spoke seemed familiar to me.

Language is not my strong suit. During testing to determine my abilities, my speaking or understanding a foreign language didn't rate very high. Hell, even English is a problem.

Prior to my enlistment with the Marine Corps, I attended the University of California in Long Beach, majoring in computer science. In my second year, a very pretty Hispanic girl named Rosita Hernandez caught my attention. After numerous approaches, some of them rather simple-minded, she finally agreed to date me. Within a month or so, we saw each other on a regular basis. Sex had been fantastic—much better than the awkward experiences with my first few girlfriends. Things got so serious that understanding her culture and language became of paramount importance, mostly to Rosita.

Initially I added Spanish to my already-heavy credit load at the university. Struggling with a foreign language while taking calculus, physics, and chemistry sure didn't help my workload. Rosita became increasing annoyed at my lack of progress with the Spanish language, which she attempted to drill me in every night. Finally, she gave up on me, became increasingly distant, and didn't return phone calls. She ultimately dumped me unceremoniously, which broke my heart, and I moped around for months until eventually joining the Marine Corps to abate my poor suffering heart.

I was deployed to Sarajevo, Bosnia, and Herzegovina on highly secret missions as a scout/sniper. Being one of the few U.S. military personnel with this training and actual combat experience placed me in a very select group.

In November 1994, while home on leave from the Marine Corps, during a period just following my boot camp training and prior to the deployment to Sarajevo, I met a beautiful girl named Janet. Through a series of passionate encounters and the unplanned failure of a protective sex device, Janet became pregnant. Doing the right thing, we got married, shortly after which Janet gave birth to a beautiful baby girl, Emma.

Following our marriage, the birth of Emma, and my deployment to Sarajevo, I was discharged from the Marine Corps. Rather than immediately seeking work, we decided it was best that I return to college and complete a degree in computer science. Although there were numerous employment opportunities after graduating, Janet and I decided to set up our own business, the Wylton Computer Systems, Inc., which grew to a moderately successful firm.

Now my marriage—the desolation of it—continuously occupied my thoughts. Why had my marriage failed? Janet and I had started with such a serendipitous relationship; everything had come up roses. Where had it gone wrong? Together we had built a very successful computer support business. Two beautiful children, Emma and David, resulted from the marriage. There is an old axiom that undoubtedly provides the answer. *If you want to destroy a good friendship, go into business together.*

In recent years, I traveled extensively, searching out new customers, while still visiting current customers, to keep the business moving and growing. On numerous occasions, Janet had accused me of having affairs while on business travel. For me, a breaking point ultimately manifested. Since I was constantly accused of extramarital relations, and sex between us was absolutely nil, why not enjoy a little tryst?

While on a trip to Auburn, New York, a receptionist at the firm we dealt with felt sorry for me having to eat my meals alone. She offered to join me for dinner one evening. After dinner and a few drinks, the next stop was my hotel room and some fantastic sex. The physical sex exhausted us, so sleep soon overtook first her and then me. We slept until late the next morning, waking just in time to make a meeting at her company.

Breaking the ice, so to speak, it occurred to me that perhaps it is true that the first time you cheat on your spouse is the most difficult. After the first one the rest just seem to come as a matter of course. For me, months of agonizing over what had occurred in Auburn, New York, provided sufficient guilt that no further extramarital relationships interested me.

The obvious answer to the decline of my marriage had to be the pressures of being in business together. I constantly traveled, being the only one with the necessary technical knowledge, and Janet remained in Croton, New York, with the daily grind of the business and care of our children. Time became so demanding, with her taking care of the office and making sure our two children were properly cared for, that we hired an office assistant and receptionist to help.

But there still appeared to be a significant resentment and jealousy on Janet's part about my travel. She considered herself chained to the home and office, while I went off on my merry way wining, dining, and probably fucking all of our clients. For me, traveling proved to be a bitch in angel's clothing: a different sleazebag motel every night and diner food. It didn't strike me as a life of extreme pleasure.

Often, clients had difficulty with their systems and faulted me for any malfunctions. After all, our contract was to keep things operating. Client technical issues that cropped up while I was out of the office automatically came to me no matter my location or immediate involvement, even if that involvement concerned another client. Often my travels took me far from where a new client problem existed, requiring me to drop everything and fly or drive to the client's office. Handling everything became too much of a burden and had a detrimental effect on my health. I just couldn't be in two places at once, plus have the bombardment of technical issues and marital problem back in Croton.

To address the problem, we hired a computer technician who came straight out of the local community college. Fred Wallberg came highly recommended, had outstanding grades, and really knew his stuff—or so I thought. We hired him and trained him to respond to the less-severe emergency situations. From all indications, he did a good job, at least according to Janet.

Shortly after 9/11, a letter came addressed to me from the United States Marine Corps. In a nutshell, my country needed me in this tenuous, difficult situation. Given my MOS (Military Occupation Specialty) as a scout/sniper, my immediate reaction was, *Oh shit, what am I in for?* Given my training and skills, undoubtedly it would be a clandestine mission somewhere in enemy territory, wherever that might be.

What knocked me on my ass though, was Janet's response when I showed her the letter; she went ballistic.

"You fucking son of a bitch." She launched her anger into my shocked face. "How did you engineer this, you fuck? You want to go off and play soldier boy, well, fuck you. I'm getting a divorce, and there is nothing you can fucking do about it." She stood staring at me with piercing blue eyes. Her blonde hair was disheveled, and her ample bosom rose and fell as her anger intensified.

"Janet," I started in a soft, controlled voice, "our country needs me to help in the fight against terrorism. This is vital to us and our children, and I'm not about to try to weasel out of it." *That should pacify her,* I thought, but no such luck.

"No fucking shit." Her face turned red, her voice almost a screech. "There are umpteen millions of you fucking Marines that can handle this situation, why you? I think you are complicit in this, somehow you got hold of one of your fucking buddy boys and arranged to be activated." She had a full head of steam, ready to run me down.

"Janet," I said, still maintaining my cool, "there is no way I could have created this letter and had it sent here; that just doesn't make any sense. Why would I do such a thing?" I looked at her askance.

"Don't fucking bullshit me, Oscar, soldier boy." Spittle flew from her mouth as she raged on. "Whatever the fucking reason, I want a divorce. There is no way I will sit around here trying to keep this business and our family going while you're off having a good time." I couldn't reason with her, there was no sense in pursuing it any further, so I turned and walked away and out of my marriage—and possibly into the waiting arms of al-Qaeda or the Taliban.

Chapter 2

There was too much reminiscing and not enough concentration on the mission at hand. Such inattention to detail could easily result in a serious mistake that would compromise the mission and my life. And this maudlin self-pity was out of character and had to stop now.

The voices passed about twenty meters from my hide and faded away. Apparently, the hide was close to a pasture used by goats and goatherds.

Sleep eventually returned to me until late afternoon when I awakened to some birds singing and rustling in nearby shrubs. Movement on my part had to be very slow and meticulous in the event someone might be nearby. I carefully scanned the entire area; no one could be found within my sight radius. Satisfied that there would be no witness to my movements, I began to nourish the mechanism I considered to be my body. I opened a package of crackers and cheese and washed it down with only a half pint of water, consuming my supply very sparingly.

Darkness finally descended on the hide, and the night's goal lay before me. The mission was purposely scheduled during a moonless period. The sky, a clear and very dark blue, offered little illumination from the shimmering stars. This had to be the kind of night in which you would lie on your back and look up at the stars, perhaps noting the occasional interruption of an airplane passing through the night's sky. Even better would have been lying back home with an attractive, loving girlfriend in your arms—harboring thoughts other than just looking at the stars.

This territory belonged to al-Qaeda and the Taliban; caution had to be perpetually in my consciousness, as the slightest misstep could result in my death. Both groups undoubtedly had sentries posted within twenty miles of their combined training base. Approaching this base had to be methodical and slow, with every few steps requiring a pause and a careful search of the surrounding area. I used night vision binoculars to survey 360 degrees after every fifty or so steps, just enough to maintain my pace while giving some assurance that I wasn't walking into a trap. The next hide plotted on my map, whatever the physical demand might be, had to be reached before sunup.

The sky became indistinguishable from the horizon. I knew that a mountain range existed ahead of me, but it could not be differentiated from the darkness of the sky. Fortunately, this night's journey would be over the flat, hard plain, with no ridges to stumble over. My trail did require maneuvering among large boulders, outcroppings, shrubs, and small trees. A gentle breeze blew across the plain, which greatly improved my tolerance to the heat and humidity. The infrared avoidance garment sucked much of the heat and moisture from my body, forcing it to dissipate at the bottom of my camouflage trousers. By redirecting my body heat, my infrared profile could not be seen by any of the current scope technologies.

The night became so dark that even the night-vision binoculars proved useless. Plodding at a reasonable pace, I made the hide just as the sun began to lighten the eastern sky. Camouflage, made by digging a shallow hole in the hard soil and covering it with brush and twigs, concealed my position for the day. A complete lack of any motion on my part was essential to not being discovered by the al-Qaeda or Taliban sentries. Although I didn't drink much liquid or eat any food aside from the crackers and cheese, my body started to make me aware of the need to eliminate some waste. Very quietly, I disposed of the waste in my clothing. This would become a real bitch in a day or so—not just the wonderful aroma, but also the rash that the moist crap would produce on my body.

Complete silence and lack of any motion had to be maintained. Even passing gas could alert a nearby lookout to my presence. At this point, having not shaved or bathed and having pissed and shit in my pants, the odor emanating from my body would successfully compete with that of a homeless person or a woodsman of the old days. I hoped that the odor emanating from my body didn't reach the noses of the lookouts or goatherds—although they probably could successfully compete with me in terms of smell.

Settling down for a hot day's rest in my little hideaway hole, I entered my alert doze-off stage. After several hours of light sleep, something awoke me. Looking 360, I saw a young goadherder moving in my direction with an expression of curiosity in his eyes. It became obvious that one of his goats nibbling on my hide was attracting him. This quickly developed into a very delicate situation. Firing at him with my rifle or pistol could surely alert others in the area. Additionally, killing him with a rifle or pistol shot could produce an international situation.

On the other hand, if he discovered and reported his findings to other villagers, it would disrupt or terminate my mission and probably me. Having the foresight to pack a silencer for my Glock 34 9 mm pistol, I slowly removed it from my breast pocket and withdrew the Glock from the fast-draw holster, screwing the silencer onto the muzzle.

My hope against hope that the young goatherd would be satisfied with his investigation and back away was not fulfilled. As he began to remove some of the brush from my cover, waiting any longer made no sense. The small pop from the pistol produced a noise no louder than a rock dropping. The 9 mm round hit him in the sternum; he dropped like a rag doll, with his arms falling loosely by his sides, and sinking to his knees, he gradually rolled over on his right side.

Now came the perplexing situation of what to do with the body. Obviously, it could not be left close to my hide, as the body would attract anyone who might be in the area. Cautiously moving from the hide, I lifted and carried the body to a nearby tree. Looking into the boy's face, I saw the innocence of his eyes glazed over with an unnerving stare into space, the stare of death. This had to be the worst thing I have ever done, and the worst thing I would ever do. I hoped that the mission would in fact save many lives, including young children like this one.

Slowly making my way back to the hide, tears obstructed my view. Settling into the hide, I waited for nightfall. What had occurred had to be a distant memory; total concentration on the mission must be my sole focus. Perhaps the boy's family would discover him and believe the Taliban or al-Qaeda had killed him.

Nightfall brought cooler temperatures and, again, total darkness. The starlight did not provide sufficient illumination to see the terrain, to distinguish plain from mountain or mountain from sky. My progress was now exceedingly slow, as constant surveillance of the surroundings became necessary after every few yards of movement. A mountain ridge between my target and my current position provided some assurance that the enemy could not see me. Not far from there, however, the Taliban and al-Qaeda wandered many of the same hills and paths as I.

This night, being uneventful much to my satisfaction, allowed me the opportunity to maintain my blistering schedule. Before sunrise, I had settled into my hide, ready for a day of rest. Wearing a ghillie suit designed for this terrain provided adequate concealment for the day.

Although physically and mentally alert, I began to relax and settle into my half-sleep, half-wake mode. The day progressed slowly, and, as normal for this area of the earth, it remained extremely hot even in my sheltered hide. At various times I would slowly raise my head and scan the terrain in search of possible intruders. I endured various crawling creatures, resisting the urge to smack one, as such movement might alert an unwanted observer. The day passed without incident—I heard no one, nothing, not even a goat.

By nightfall, my body was drenched with sweat, but otherwise I was rested and anxious to move on. Consulting the GPS, I assured myself of my current position and decided what had to be accomplished for the day. It's best to know the day's objective before setting out. From now on, the pace had to be extremely cautious and, of necessity, slow. The stars appeared but only provided sufficient light to see perhaps ten yards in front of me. The lack of light made it difficult to determine if anyone could observe my movement. Night vision enhancement binoculars possibly could pick me up from several hundred yards away. I frequently employed mine to determine if anyone might be within my sight radius, the imaginary circle with my body at the center, in which night-vision goggles can detect any moving object.

The base of the mountain, which I needed to climb, came into sight somewhat past midnight, confirming I was on schedule. During the planning stage of this mission, I had carefully identified and recorded on my GPS unit specific points and when they needed to be achieved to assure my progress was on or close to the preset schedule. The base of the mountain was one of these points. The climb proved to be difficult and exceedingly slow, but the decrease in my pace had been calculated into the timing of my mission. Climbing several hundred yards by daybreak and finding and establishing a hide to settle in for the day became essential. The morning glow of a rising sun could expose me to Taliban or al-Qaeda sentries, reasonably assumed to be guarding their training camp. Once again, my camouflage, the ghillie suit, provided the necessary concealment for the day.

I dug down a foot or so in an attempt to provide some cover from the day's intense heat. The fresh dirt surrounding my hide would dry quickly and blend with the soil of the area. Half awake and half asleep, my day passed without incident. Not even an airplane passed overhead—what a desolate area. As had become my usual habit, I would awake every half hour or so and scan the area with my binoculars. Satisfied that no one had appeared in the area, I returned to my rest position.

As the ink-black darkness enveloped the area, my night's journey began. Climbing the mountain once again proved difficult. Striving to remain on schedule, the need to stop and do a full search with the night vision binoculars consumed much of my time, but had its reward. Around three o'clock, at approximately three hundred yards in the distance, a Taliban or al-Qaeda terrorist sentry appeared on a nearby ridge.

What distinguished this from the goatherds or farmers of this territory was the fact that he carried a rifle and appeared to be searching the area with his binoculars. Hopefully, the binoculars did not have night vision or infrared capabilities. I gradually lowered myself to a kneeling and then prone position so as not to project an obvious silhouette or create a distraction by a sudden movement. After watching him for some fifteen to twenty minutes, it became evident that he had not spotted me—or that he knew how to put on a good act.

After a half hour or so passed, he moved off the ridge. Assuming that the sentry soldier had moved off to either bed down for the balance of the night or go off in another direction to continue his night watch, I began to move out.

So that the night's journey could continue, I took several cautious minutes to stand erect. Having lost almost an hour of my schedule, the possibility of reaching the planned hide became increasingly unattainable. Although in exceptionally good physical condition, my body could only tolerate so much stress, physically and mentally, and that point evidently had been achieved.

Deciding to rest for a few minutes, I took out the night-vision-enhanced binoculars, which proved to be a very fortunate decision. Just below me climbing fast, unencumbered by all the equipment that impeded my progress, appeared a friendly neighborhood terrorist. My Glock with the silencer had to be my tool of choice, and I withdrew the weapon silently from the quick-draw holster under my left arm and attached the silencer. Concealing myself as much as possible behind an outcropping of boulders, I awaited my prey.

In the back of my mind, this seemed too easy: my enemy walking toward me, ready to be shot, just didn't seem logical. Several small stones bouncing off my head and back interrupted my deep thought and concentration on the Taliban approaching from below. This without a doubt had to be a squeeze play: one above and one below. My major concern now was how they communicated. Was it by radio? If each had maintained awareness through walkie-talkies of the other's location and movements, my mission surely would be in jeopardy, and my ass would be cooked.

Crouching low and waiting, I wondered who would get it first, the uphill one or the downhill one? The first had to be a quiet kill so as not to alert the other. The downhill guy came first, as he stopped and stood inches from my position. Withdrawing the KA-BAR, a hunting knife carried by marines to deal with just such a situation, I made the kill a quick and easy one: a throat slice, a little gurgle, and he departed for unknown heavens. Not having time to search him for radios or weapons, I pulled his body off the trail and out of sight. Mister uphill came huffing and puffing up the path. As he approached my position, the Glock completed the task at hand, dropping him with a single quiet shot to the head.

First, both bodies had to be removed from the trail and any evidence removed or covered up. This especially applied to blood that saturated the ground where each victim lay. Undoubtedly, the bodies would bake, bloat, and smell in the heat of the day. Plenty of wild animals in the area could make a quick meal of them once the odor migrated to their nostrils.

Completing the cover up, I prepared a grave sufficiently far enough off the trail so as not to be discovered by another terrorist. I thoroughly searched both bodies, finding no radios, just an AK-47 and several clips of ammo on each. The lack of a radio somewhat settled my nerves but then raised the question, how did the second guy know of my being on the trail and my climbing the mountain?

Had the first one somehow alerted the base camp of my presence, thereby negating my mission? Perhaps, by chance, the second Taliban or al-Qaeda had descended the mountain on a late night stroll—fat chance. Whatever the situation, mulling it over at this point made no sense; I had to keep moving.

At the top of the ridge, a search for a good hide needed to be conducted since the sun started to lighten the eastern sky. Off to the left of the trail, I found several large boulders behind which a good hide could be established. Moving as rapidly as possible, I secured myself between the boulders. The location provided excellent visibility of the trail uphill and downhill. Consuming crackers, cheese, and water somewhat diminished my rabid hunger. This meal tasted better than a steak dinner at any fancy New York restaurant. Food tastes so much better when you are truly hungry, believe me; I have suffered from hunger pains.

The next item on the menu was rest, even though maintaining alertness was still extremely critical given my proximity to the target. Al-Qaeda surely had implemented some method of keeping watch over the surrounding territory. Falling into a light slumber, the hours began to idle away. Suddenly awakened by a movement on the trail, I gradually moved my head around to obtain a clear view of the trail above and below me. There, some twenty yards distant, a parade of mountain goats traveled, apparently on their way to distant pastures. After a brief few moments to relax my nerves, sleep gradually returned.

It's funny how one is usually awakened by the sunlight; however, in this case, I woke at sunset. One more night's journey would bring me to my final, strategic destination, a hide with an overlook of the al-Qaeda camp. This proved to be a difficult situation, as the camp actually existed across the border in Pakistan. My sighting and firing of *one shot one kill*—the marine scout/ sniper code meaning that for every shot taken, one adversary is eliminated— actually would occur from the Afghanistan side of the border.

The border is internationally known as the Durand Line, named after Sir Mortimer Durand, an Englishman who established the line in 1893; but it was not my concern. Fortunately for me, the line is not formerly recognized by the people on either immediate side of the line, and therefore technically

I could be in either Pakistan or Afghanistan. Given this inability of the locals to decide on a definitive border, I decided the target must, in fact, be in Afghanistan. The target, however, assumed his presence to be in Pakistan, poor fellow.

Behind schedule, but refreshed and relaxed, the night's journey would be a quick one. I reached the ridge within a few hours. Quickly I determined my position on the GPS and checked the GPS mapping of the route to the hide. The hide, as planned, overlooked the al-Qaeda camp and the intended target. Being in position well before sunrise allowed me time to prepare the hide for what could be a long wait.

The ground provided a pleasantly cool bed to recline in, which had not been the case in the previous hides. I dug down about half a yard, placing the excavated soil around the base of the surrounding boulders. The 20x spotting scope and the riflescope were set up and camouflaged. This last step was an extremely important one, since any reflection off either lens would alert the intended target of my presence. I had enough water, cheese, and crackers to last several days.

The odor from my body had begun to be offensive, even to me, and I was sure I smelled like the local goatherd or, more likely, his goat.

As golden light rays of the morning sun were casting long shadows over the camp, I started to scope out the area. This definitely was a military training camp, as all of the necessary ingredients were present: obstacle courses, firing ranges, a kind of parade field, and about twenty-five to thirty barracks. The barracks actually were large canvas-covered, wood-framed buildings. A few guards were noted, casually walking about, undoubtedly feeling secure in the knowledge that because of the obscurity of the location, no one would invade their camp.

Reveille or wake-up call at the camp sounded more like a call to worship. At least that was my perception, given my limited knowledge of the Muslim faith. Some two hundred or so black-clad terrorists-in-training soon formed in two ranks on the parade field. From there, they moved off to what I assumed to be a meal hall. Several minutes later, they all emerged from the chow hall and commenced the daily activities. Activities consisted of some physical exercise to limber up, followed by groups breaking off and either going to the obstacle course or the firing range.

I began to use the 20x spotting scope, searching the individual group leaders to determine if the target was in the camp. After several hours without success, I settled back and relaxed. Evidently, the individual commander would only be in the open for some special occasion. Every few minutes I would scan the camp but still could not pick out the mission's target.

The target, a young Muslim believed to be dressed in a military-style uniform, had the reputation of being the primary and singular contributor to the success of this particular camp. The uniform would distinguish him from all the others in the camp. He would be in his mid-twenties with a black, full-length beard and a military cap similar to the one worn by Fidel Castro.

This routine of scope-watching continued for several days. Some frustration settled in, though my experience as a scout/sniper prevailed. On the third day, out of the main office building, an individual dressed in a military-style uniform emerged. Having spotted the terrorist leader with the 20x spotter scope and confirming his identity with photos in my possession, I quickly moved to my M 40A weapon system to zero in on the target. Normally, Marine Corps scout/snipers operate in pairs, with one Marine on the spotting scope and the second on the rifle. In this case, this had to be a solo operation.

Marine Corps marksmanship training and scout/sniper training school both taught the mantra *deep breath, half out, cross hairs on target, squeeze trigger.* Whenever sighting a weapon on a target, there is both unintended movement of the weapon (from breathing or just simple body movement) and movement of the target (unless the target is fixed). In order to hit the target each time the crosshairs are actually on it, the trigger is squeezed slowly, as squeezing the trigger too rapidly causes the muzzle of the weapon to be jerked. Repeating that mantra until the weapon is fired and the target hit ensures a successful shot.

My rifle system now all set up, I just needed to point and shoot. This would be a head shot to ensure death. Closely following the long-established practice of the sniper, I took in a deep breath and let it half out.

Hold my breath, scope crosshairs on target, squeeze.

Chapter 3

The M 40A weapon system kicked back into my shoulder; I quickly moved to the spotting scope.

The general population has the impression that when people are shot in the head they just drop, but this is not the case. Most often, the nerves and muscles in the body contract and expand, causing the victim—or terrorist in this case—to be propelled, bouncing from place to place, frequently covering ten to fifteen feet. Indeed, this is exactly what occurred with my target: his body jumped and rolled some ten feet or more.

Taking advantage of the confusion and disarray in the terrorist camp, I quickly packed up and prepared to move out. Suddenly, puffs of dirt with the telltale zing and buzz of bullets bouncing off the ground were before me. Shit! How could the terrorists pick out my hide so quickly? Attempting to move out of the hide, something on the left side of my belt snagged, preventing my movement. Rolling to the left to determine what arrested the shifting of my position, I discovered the source of the rifle fire.

On a ridge one hundred feet away, stood a terrorist sentry aimlessly firing an AK-47. He was too distant to hit with the Glock 9 mm pistol, so my rifle now became the only hope of killing him before he killed me with one of his random shots. Evidently, he had no idea where I was hidden, but he had heard the rifle fire and decided to unload a few clips. Without a doubt, panic had set in as the camp realized that a sniper actually positioned himself close enough to fire a shot and kill their supreme leader. The senior officers of the Taliban or al-Qaeda organizations would be a little more than just upset—somebody's ass would part for the promised land.

Moving with great caution so as not to alert him of my position, I moved the rifle to my right shoulder. Being in an awkward position, I had to shoot from the hip, so to speak. There must be something of the Old West in me since the shot hit him in the torso, sending him bouncing back against the cliff. He dropped slowly to a sitting position with his back against the cliff, his dulled eyes staring off into space.

My new urgent task: move as quickly as possible to the pick-up zone. The zone was a minimum of a four-and-a-half-day hike away, with the pickup scheduled in five and a half days. I had to catch that plane—the last one, and only one out of town. A number of impediments stood in my way. First, all of the equipment that came in must go out; I couldn't leave a scrap of evidence to my presence in the area. Second, my body had become exhausted, physically and mentally. This area would soon be crawling with terrorists ready to drop my ass on sight.

Fortunately, mentally, I had had the wherewithal to plan several escape routes. At the planning stage of this mission, three routes of egress or escape were included. First, return the way I came in; second, climb to a higher-level ridge and proceed down a different route to the valley below; and third, take a route that ran close to the camp where my target used to reside. Unfortunately, both two and three required almost a half day of additional time. My water situation also entered into the equation, being a significant factor for a decision to take the shortest route. An extra half day would mean added physical stress, requiring more water consumption. I had no choice but to return the way I had come in. This would be extremely treacherous, as this route would also be the most likely one considered by the al-Qaeda and Taliban to be my logical escape route.

Having selected the route, moving fast became critical. Not wishing to fall on my face again, I made sure my head did not move ahead of my feet. The loaded pack containing ammo, food, and water had become considerably lighter. The provisions were now just sufficient to get me to the pickup site.

I proceeded quickly but cautiously down the path I had come up a few days earlier. One serious problem in selecting this route was the two tribesmen I had killed on the way up. Surely, someone must be looking for them. Approaching the location where the bodies had been concealed off the path, I stopped and surveyed the area, first with just my eyes and then through my binoculars. Seeing no one in the area, a quick search of the location and the grave revealed that both bodies were missing. Someone or some group had dug up and removed the bodies, definitely not a good sign.

The steepness of the trail became troublesome; going downhill can be as strenuous as going uphill. The only significant change is that a different set of muscles are employed, which ensured that all of my leg muscles would end up aching. Of particular concern were my feet. Although the boots issued to me had been fitted to my feet, my foot would slide forward as I descended the mountain. The constant pounding of my big toes, cramped up against the front of the boot, soon produced painful throbbing with each step. No doubt, one or both of the large toenails would be lost because of this constant pounding.

After devoting most of the day to descending the mountain, the bottom finally came into view by late afternoon. Following several more hours of hiking, and judging from the GPS, my day's target had been achieved. An extended rest would reinvigorate my body. Moving off the trail about thirty yards, I spread the ghillie out over my tired body. This would provide good cover in the event anyone should pass by on the trail.

Sleep came quickly and deeply. The half-awake, half-asleep mode normally used for these rest periods had to be set aside, forgotten this night. Sleeping soundly for about six and a half hours, some movement close to my hide woke me. There was not a wisp of wind—a pitch-black night, but cool and dry. Slowly turning to observe the area around me, the source of the movement became apparent: a lone goat feeding about eight feet from my hide. Gradually moving the ghillie suit so as not to alarm the goat and possibly the goatherd, I stood up. The goat continued to feed, not paying much heed to my movement. No goatherds were in sight, just the single goat, which must have wondered off from the herd.

Back on the trail, being rested and anxious to keep moving, I set off for my day's objective. Setting a good pace and an achievable goal would ensure I made it to the pickup site in time. The first few hours passed quickly with my pace actually much better than expected. At this speed, reaching the pickup site became less and less of a problem. The sun rose over my right shoulder, casting a reddish glow on the sand and rocks surrounding the trail. I could feel the heat on the nape of my neck; this would be a scorcher of a day. The sky, a clear blue with not a cloud to be seen, added to my newfound invigoration. The mountain ranges surrounding me on all sides were clearly visible and appeared to be stark, bare cliffs—no trees, just rocks and cliffs.

Tramping along for three to four hours, I noticed some movement about twelve hundred feet ahead. I bolted off the trail and crouched behind some brush and large boulders.

Deploying my binoculars, I observed five or six men in turbans and cloaks walking the trail in my direction. Using the ghillie suit again as a hide, I hid some forty feet off the trail and waited for the men to pass by. About forty-five minutes passed before I heard the voices coming along the trail. It sounded as if they were engaged in a heated discussion about something. Being in a foreign language, which, of course, I did not understand, I had no way of knowing what the fuck the discussion was about. Waiting patiently and without motion, I was exercising extreme caution, wanting to be certain all the tribesmen had passed by.

This delay consumed the time I had gained on the morning's hike, and now I barely maintained my schedule.

The trail appeared clear. Using my eyesight and binoculars, I couldn't see anything moving ahead of me. For about an hour, my pace remained brisk and steady. After a while, feeling comfortable with my progress and with the conditioning of my body, I began to relax as I moved along.

Rounding a slight turn in the trail, I heard some rustling of the brush just to my rear.

"Hold it right there, soldier boy," came an accented voice close behind me.

Coming to an abrupt stop, hoping the individual might be close enough to be disarmed, I waited his instruction.

"Turn around real slow," came his succinct command. "Keep your hands above your head."

Slowly turning around and keeping my hands on top of my head, I saw a bearded, rather short man wearing horn-rimmed glasses. He had on a black turban, a white cloak, and sandals on his feet. He also held a very large 38-caliber handgun, which I had no intention of arguing with.

"Sit over there," he instructed, motioning me to sit just off the trail on some low rocks. I did as directed. This turn of events directly resulted from my pushing the pace, hiking during the day, and not exercising sufficient caution. Being captured alive absolutely could not be an acceptable outcome. But for the time being, following the instruction appeared the most prudent approach to the situation.

"I am Imam Mohammad from the local Madras"—he waved the pistol as he spoke—"or school to you, soldier boy."

I nodded in acknowledgement, making sure my hands remained on top of my head and in plain sight. No sense in getting my sorry ass blown away at this point, especially by a bearded short guy with horn-rimmed glasses.

"I have a little message for your superiors, and I fully expect you to take this message to them." His glare was one of hate and apathy for my situation. "Do you understand and will you fulfill my instructions?" Imam Mohammad scowled at me while he spoke, waiting for an answer.

Again, a nod indicated my understanding. What the fuck else would he expect me to say?

"The only point in our allowing you to live and proceed is your assurance, as a soldier, that the message I am about to give you will be repeated to your superiors," he continued. "Do you agree to this arrangement?"

Once again, I nodded in agreement, the only acknowledgement on my part—although, the word "our" bothered me, as "our" obviously implied more than one person.

"You, meaning your soldiers and any other persons from your country or your associates, meaning Europe, South America, Canada, or what is known as the Western nations, are not welcome in this country or any Islamic country, for that matter. Why do you, you Westerners, think you are so superior to others that you can invade our countries and disrupt our social and religious structures? You, once again, are on a crusade to change Islam, the way of our lives for thousands of years. You corrupt our women, our children, and particularly our young adults. You mean to destroy our religious culture, to change the way we live. We do not need you to change our ideology." The imam continued, glaring at me with every word.

"We are happy with our lives, which may be backward by your standards, but nonetheless are satisfying and content by ours. Our men do not wish to change, our women are happy as they are, and our children, although impressionable, do not need to change. Look at your society with the drugs and crime, with children who do not heed their parents, with women who would rather work than become wives and mothers; you want us to be like that?" Imam Mohammad paused, frowning at me as if waiting for a reply.

I am a soldier, a marine, actually; my duty is to my country and to the Corps. My country, to me, is the freest form of government available anywhere. My country has evolved as a democracy over some five hundred years. Everyone can pretty much live the way he or she wants without fear of reprisal. Granted, we may have higher crime than other societies, but perhaps this is a necessary negative of freedom. How much of our freedom would we be willing to give up, to ensure a society completely without any crime? However, being in no position to enter into a debate with the imam, as I was sure it would only lead to getting my tender ass shot, I elected not to reply but only nod in agreement.

The imam continued, "You cannot win this war, this crusade of yours. We have millions of our faithful who will gladly sacrifice their lives in order to preserve our Islamic heritage, our religious society. We have already infiltrated your country and your associate countries. We have infiltrated every level of your society, your government, your legal system, and your religious organizations. Should you not heed this warning, we will simultaneously destroy every aspect of your life. Leave us be, that is all we ask. Leave our countries; take your military out of our countries. If it is oil you want, we will provide that to you. I have no more to say. You may be on your way with our message."

With that, the imam turned and walked away, leaving me sitting there with my hands on top of my head.

After a few moments, I lowered my hands, gained control of my thoughts and emotions, and moved on down the road. Precious time had been lost listening to the imam, not that there had been a choice. Exercising more caution became a necessity, despite the fact that much ground had to be covered in a short time.

After my encounter with the imam, my pace picked up, making up for some of the lost time. Perhaps what he had said to me gave me motivation to move a little faster. Approximately three and a half hours after leaving the imam, I finally paused for a drink of warm, actually hot, water. Regardless of the temperature, the water tasted quite good, almost as refreshing as a cold beer on a hot, humid day.

As I sat enjoying my warm drink, I mulled over what the imam had to say. Perhaps there was some truth in his little speech, but that the women of Islam enjoyed being subjected to their husbands to the extent that they could not make any decisions on their own I found somewhat doubtful. They couldn't fall in love with anyone of their choosing or go out of their home without being accompanied by their husband or a male blood relative. Just considering this limited view of their culture assured me that being westernized, to my way of thinking, was by far the preferable way to live.

As I took my third sip, I heard a strange moaning sound, something like a wounded animal. Could it be an animal stalking me as I moved along the trail? This was a real possibility, as mountain lions and wild dogs lived in the area. Listening more intently, the sound seemed human and came from a short distance off the trail, somewhere east of my position. Like a fool, my curiosity overruled my need to be cautious.

Some thirty feet in off the trail, I found what looked like a pile of black cloth. *What the hell, could this possibly be—?* Kneeling down, I moved some of the black rags, and there before me lay a young girl, perhaps fourteen or fifteen years old, with a bruised, cut, and swollen face. Despite her condition, she appeared quite pretty, with beautiful brown, almost black, eyes. Her head was covered with a black cloth that concealed most of her face. Dark hair curled up in wisps against her cheeks, which even through the blood and bruising had a soft olive tone.

For a few moments, I thought of my daughter, Emma, and the deteriorating condition of my marriage. Dwelling on this subject only brought sorrow and anguish. Quickly putting those thoughts to the back of my mind, I returned my attention to the situation before me.

She spoke to me in an unknown language. I shook my head, indicating my lack of understanding. She tried to sit up, and with some help from me, she managed a cross-legged position. In my pack, a small first aid kit provided some provisions for treating her wounds, including a few Tylenol 3 to ease the pain. From the pack, I produced gauze, first aid cream, and bandages, which would be of limited help. After tending to her injuries to the best that my limited medical knowledge would permit, I put a half of canteen water next to her and proceeded to leave.

Almost immediately, she cried out. Returning to her side, the obvious pleading in her eyes tore at my heart.

"If you leave me, I will be killed," she said in halting English.

"Why?" I asked, perplexed as to why anyone would do harm to this young, beautiful girl.

"Because I have sinned against my father, my mother, and the Islam religion," she replied in a whimper. "I am pregnant; I'm not married," she continued in a very soft voice, almost a whisper, "which is a crime punishable by death." She looked from me to the ground as if I too would punish her.

What the fuck could I do, perform an abortion or something?

"Please take me with you," she begged, the anguish showing in her face as tears streamed from eyes and down her chin. Her voice was much stronger as she pleaded for her life.

"Fat fucking chance of that," I mumbled to myself.

No question, this put me in deep fucking shit; just going off the trail to help an injured person, no matter what the circumstance, violated every possible regulation of the United States Marine Corps, not to mention the holy grail of the scout/snipers. To move this poor young injured girl only further violated my charter as a bloodthirsty, battle-hardened, cutthroat warrior. Not to mention it totally ignored my specific orders for this mission, much like orders from God himself.

But the mission had been completed, finished when the target died at my hands. *What the hell,* I thought. Maybe there was a soft spot in my mean heart, or else I'm just a sympathetic fool rescuing a damsel in distress. I looked into her eyes, eyes of pain, of need—wanting and pleading eyes. My emotions began to flood over me as I thought of my daughter, Emma, safe in the United States.

Maybe this seemed an opportunity to balance the killing of the goatherd boy. There was no choice; I had to kill the boy. But circumstances were different with this young girl—saving her did not jeopardize the mission.

Digging a hole deep enough with my knife so that most of my gear could be buried, I dumped unnecessary equipment into the hole. Once my load was sufficiently lightened, the hole covered over, and excess soil spread around to conceal the spot, I prepared to carry my young ward to safety and medical help. Fashioning a sling with one of my belts and covering little miss what's-her-name, I gingerly hoisted her onto my back. Despite every effort to avoid aggravating her injuries, she cried in muffled pain at every motion made to secure her to my back. She was obviously intelligent enough to bury her face into her clothing so as not to make loud cries. A loud cry would be carried by the breeze to unintended and dangerous ears. Once I had her secured, we headed for the pickup area. She proved to be relatively light, definitely lighter than the load I carried in on this mission.

By nightfall, we stood at the bottom of the ridge that had presented such a problem for me on the first night of the mission. For the most part, the scratches received from the little tumble caused by my miscalculation of weight versus speed on a downhill slope had pretty much healed. The ridge would be about two hundred yards up and some three hundred yards down on the opposite side.

On our walk—or ride for Little Miss Muffet—we had begun a little conversation. Her name was Nadira, and she came from a small village in Afghanistan, which was pretty much ruled by the Taliban.

"The Taliban are very mean," she began. "If you do not live by their interpretation of the Koran, you will be severely punished. My people are simple farmers and goatherds; we just obey the directives of the local imam.

"My mother never instructed me on the facts of life, nothing about sex or relationships with boys. I fell in love with a boy from the next village; we had sex and I became pregnant. My father did not know what to do so he went to the imam for advice. The imam instructed him to bring me to the mosque in the village the next day, and my father obeyed.

"My father left me in the care of the imam, who is also a member of the Taliban. Once my father had left the village, the imam pushed me out the back door of the mosque where many of the village women were waiting. As I faced them, they threw stones and sticks at me until I fell down, and then they punched and kicked me until I became unconscious. The imam, assuming I was dead, had one of his, what you call altar boys, take me to the desert and dump me so wild beasts could consume my body. That is where you found me, thank God." Her sobs melted my heart as her tears ran down my neck and back.

Her talking proved a good antidote to her pain, as the talk took her mind off her wounds. Frequently, she would cry out when I took a halting step that jarred her body. Naturally, I made those as infrequently as possible.

Long shadows from the western sky descended over the ridge. I judged the distance to the pickup zone to be approximately one and a half days away, provided I maintained a decent pace.

Taking this ridge would require at least ten hours up one side and down the other. This would be no piece of cake. Even though I had crossed the ridge in a few hours coming from the drop zone, carrying Nadira and the deteriorating condition of my body now considerably slowed my pace. I could rest here and tackle it in the morning, but the slightest delay could mean missing the pickup. The ridge had to be completed this night. Up the hill we went.

The climb up proved to be rigorous and extremely demanding, especially with Nadira on my back; as light as a frail young girl could be, it almost was too much for me to handle. Early morning light produced a glaze-like effect on the valley floor below us as we reached the top of the ridge. A few hours of rest, after an examination of Nadira's wounds, would refresh us for the day's journey. We had to make the landing zone by nightfall and prepare for the pick up at first light, around five o'clock local time. As gently as possible, I sat Nadira down, but not gently enough, as at least six times she screamed out in pain. Despite her condition, she had the fortitude to continue to muffle her cries into her loose clothing. If she had not, surely by this time the Taliban would have been on our asses.

Removing her cloak while leaving her undergarments on, I assessed her injuries as best as my knowledge would permit. There appeared to be at least two or three broken bones. The bones had not penetrated the skin, but large lumps made it quite obvious that serious injury lay beneath. The bruising had turned black and blue and had swollen considerably since I first observed her injuries on the previous day. No water, especially cool water, was available to cleanse the wounds. I took two more Tylenol 3 tablets from my first-aid kit, and with a small cup of water, had her swallow them.

Using the first aid cream, I cleansed the wounds as best as possible. Someone or some group had certainly used Nadira as a punching bag and a target for a stone-throwing contest. At this point, the decision to carry her had, without a doubt, been the correct choice. She would not have survived the night and certainly not the day if she'd been left on her own.

After cleaning and redressing Nadira's wounds, she lay back in my lap and fell into a deep deserving sleep. Covering her with my body and the ghillie suit, I also fell into a deep exhausted sleep. About midday, I was jolted awake by someone pushing on my back. Had we been discovered? Maybe the little shit of an imam had followed us and decided I had broken our agreement by saving Nadira. Or perhaps Nadira's enemies tracked us down with the intent of finishing their job, with me thrown in for good measure. Rolling back, I found a little goat nibbling on the ghillie suit. Go figure—hope he enjoyed the sweat-soaked rags; probably the salt and moisture appealed to him. Three times these little fuckers casually strolled up to the big strong Marine and took a little nibble out of his cover. Fortunately for me, and, of course, Nadira, they weren't part of the al-Qaeda or Taliban terrorist groups.

Nadira woke with a start and a scream. I cuddled her and rocked her back and forth, trying to comfort her, which seemed to work. She settled down. Explaining the need to keep moving, I mounted her onto my back with some difficulty, just as I had the previous day. The Tylenol 3 helped to relieve some of her pain. Off we went, downhill, with a great deal of caution.

The downward slope consisted of hard-packed soil with loose sand on the top. The loose sand presented a serious slipping hazard, so each step had to be taken with care. The slope, sparsely covered with low brush, provided a good brake when I began to slip. The brush also provided food for the goats, wild or from local herds, as much of it had been chewed back, making the protruding ends sharp. The precious cargo constantly needed protection and care, particularly from the sharp ends of the brush. We made the bottom of the ridge in less than six hours, not an especially good time but sufficient to make it to the pickup zone by morning.

Although the ground seemed relatively level, the going became tedious as my conditioning began to desert me and each step seemed to require an inordinate amount of energy. My Marine Corps training had always conditioned me to push my endurance to the limit and beyond, and that philosophy certainly paid off now. Being mentally and physically exhausted hardly described the current situation—"running on an empty tank" seemed better fitted to these circumstances. Only the extensive training and conditioning of the past gave me the necessary stamina to make it to the pickup zone.

At least the night air remained cool, making the going a little easier than the hike up and down the ridge. The terrain now became a flat plain, still covered with low brush and scrub with the sharp ends left by the goats, which tended to impeded my progress. I began to move as a robot, with GPS keeping me on track and my legs just moving as directed by the electronic technology of the GPS unit. My brain seemly had shut down, acting only as a vision mechanism to avoid hazards on the trail. Although the night shrouded us in a very dark moonless sky, the surrounding mountain ridges could be distinguished by a very soft dark blue glow. We had about two pints of water left, with no water source available in this arid land. Just a flat endless plain lay ahead of us with goats, all kinds of wild animals, and other unknown hazards.

Chapter 4

Finally, we made it to the pickup zone. We had to remain secluded in a brush area behind some large boulders, as sitting in the open could expose us to unwanted eyes. We also had to remain vigilant and alert, as allowing any sleep on my part could result in missing our ride out of this shit hole. My watch had an alarm feature, but the possibility of my sleeping through the small sound emitted by it presented too great of a risk.

Right at five o'clock, the CH-53S Sea Dragon helicopter appeared on the western skyline. With Nadira on my back, I cautiously made my way to the landing zone. In the soft glow of the morning light, several of my fellow scout/snipers could be seen emerging from the surrounding landscape of brush and boulders. The chopper's spinning blades kicked up an enormous swirl of sand, temporarily stinging any exposed part of our body and blinding us as we closed our eyes tightly to prevent sand from getting in. Making my way up the rear ramp of the chopper provided unimaginable pleasure. After the past few weeks of living on the edge, entering the enclosed body of the helicopter, a semi-safe section, now proved absolutely exhilarating.

Only three others of the original six scout/snipers returned to the waiting aircraft. What happened to the other two would remain a mystery. This type of scout/sniper operation, being highly classified, would remain top secret for many years to come, in all probability, never again seeing the light of day. The ability of the United States to launch clandestine scout/sniper operations was essential to maintaining secret assassinations of terrorists who were hard to locate and eliminate.

Entering the cargo area of the CH-53S Sea Dragon, I gently lowered Nadira onto the floor. On board, a medic had been assigned to evaluate any injuries that might have befallen us on our missions. The medic, William Gunderson, and I had become somewhat friendly during my training in California.

"Hey, Honcho, what you carrying, your roadkill?" Gunderson exclaimed as I set Nadira down on the floor. Honcho is a nickname he gave me during the California exercise.

"Just a little care package." I looked over at him, hoping he wouldn't be too pissed off. "I would like you to take a look at her."

Gunderson came over and looked down at Nadira. "Jesus Christ." His facial expression indicated the shock of seeing the young girl. "What the fuck have you brought back with you? Are you out of your fucking mind?" he exclaimed.

Explaining why Nadira needed protection took some embellishment on my part. "She's pregnant with a child out of wedlock, which is a sin punishable by death in the Islamic world." In search of his sympathetic side, if in fact he had one, I continued, "If I had not carried her out, wild animals would surely have killed and eaten her. If, by chance she made it back to the village, she would have been stoned and beaten to death." This openly displayed my deep concern and, now affection, for Nadira.

Reluctantly, Gunderson began looking at Nadira's wounds, which were many. He found three broken bones and wondered aloud how she had survived both the stoning and the journey out. He administered some morphine and then set the broken bones, carefully bandaging the areas so they would heal properly. Then, Gunderson looked extensively at the bruises and scrapes on her body. In order to do this he had to disrobe her. Being pretty much out of it from the morphine, she had no cause to be embarrassed. He administered an ointment solution to the scraped areas to aid in healing and then applied bandages to the wounds he considered most severe. After almost an hour of examination and medicinal application, Gunderson sat back and stared at me.

"You know this is totally against all regulation," he began to admonish me, "and particularly the directives of the scout/sniper battalion." Although we were close associates, his message came across as very direct and very stern.

"What the hell would you do, throw her out of the plane?" I responded almost in anger to his reprimand.

"Shit, man," he backpedaled, responding to the anger evident in my voice, "I'm only saying you're in deep shit, that's all." Gunderson sat back, a little apologetic. "You know the battalion, or even the division for that matter, has no provisions to care for her. I mean, what the fuck are they going to do with her?"

I knew what he said only provided ample warning of what I faced back at the Marine base. Shit, no way would I leave this poor soul on the plains to die. Surely, there had to be some way of caring for her. Perhaps she could be transferred to the Afghanistan government. Although turning her over to the

Afghanistan authorities could land her back at her village and eventually lead to her death; that would not come to pass. Her care and ultimate disposition would require some research, plus a deep commitment to her future well-being on my part.

The CH-53S Sea Dragon landed at our battalion base just southeast of Kabul, Afghanistan. Kabul is the capitol of the country and the most populated area. Gunderson had radioed ahead to have a stretcher available to carry Nadira off the plane. She remained heavily sedated, not aware of her surroundings. She would be transported to the base hospital and admitted there for medical care.

Heading to my quarters, I reflected on the situation. Gunny Abramson would be my first hurdle. "Gunny" referred to his rank, which was a gunnery sergeant, a high NCO ranking in the Marine Corps. Anyway, I knew I would be "invited" to his office once he found out about Nadira. Oh well, we are responsible for our actions, and I clearly violated every regulation imaginable. Don't get me wrong, I am very proud to be a Marine and especially a scout/sniper. But being a human and sensitive to the difficult situations others find themselves in is a good trait to have. This was especially true in the case of Nadira. As expected, interrupting my thoughts, word came down to report to Gunny Abramson posthaste.

Gunny sat in his office behind a large metal desk with the trademark cigar in his mouth, puffing away and filling the room with a haze of acrid smoke. Gunny Abramson was a big guy, six foot three or four, mostly muscle, with a balding head and broken nose—definitely not a guy to fool with. Without a doubt, Gunny was quite annoyed as he chomped and puffed away on the cigar.

"What the hell were you thinking, Sergeant Wylton? You land on your head when you parachuted from the plane?" He made no effort to remove the cigar from his mouth as he spoke, letting each syllable emerge in a blast of smoke and spittle. "Something has really scorched your brain, you fucking imbecile. I honestly don't know what the fuck I'm going to do with you or that young girl you ferried in here." His eyes showed his contempt for my poor judgment, or at least what he considered to be poor judgment.

Gunny and I went back a few years to Bosnia and Herzegovina. He generally tolerated me, as this was not my first fuckup. "Consider yourself on report"—he half rose from his desk to emphasize his point—"and you are not to leave the scout/sniper compound. Is that clear to you? Does that penetrate your eggshell head?" He slammed his fist on the desk, producing a thud that must have made a significant dent.

"Yes, Gunny," the only logical reply.

Gunny stood up and began puffing furiously on his cigar like an old locomotive building up a head of steam. He paced up and down while I stood at parade rest in front of his desk.

"I know you have a soft spot in that head of yours"—he seemed to be easing up for some reason—"but a soft spot in your heart has no place in the Marine Corps and particularly not in the scout/sniper battalion." He removed the cigar as he looked over at me. Could it be I actually saw softness in his otherwise intensely glaring eyes?

"Once Lt. Commander Nickerson hears about this"—I knew Gunny had no love for Nick the Prick, but as a good marine, he respected rank—"your ass is going to be ground up and spread over the entire base, if not all of Afghanistan. For now, you are to return to your quarters. Get cleaned up and prepared to see the CO." The CO, or commanding officer in this case was Lt. Colonel Nickerson. "Hang loose until you are directed up to his office. Dismissed, you stupid fuck."

Well, the first admonishment came pretty much as expected. Seeing Lt. Colonel Nickerson, Nick the Prick as he was known throughout the battalion, would be another matter. Gunny, in his own way, was one of us, having served as a field scout/sniper in Sarajevo, Yugoslavia. We all had tremendous respect for him. Gunny had been wounded several times, including shrapnel in his back from friendly fire. An exceptional leader, the Corps couldn't have picked a better lead NCO (noncommissioned officer). Nick the Prick, however, was a totally different subject. He had graduated from some highfalutin eastern Ivy League college and felt himself to be far superior to anyone of lesser rank, especially enlisted men and women. Lt. Colonel Nickerson felt enlisted personnel were dispensable, totally disposable, particularly in combat situations. He rarely left his office, issuing orders through his orderlies and various officers under his command. I was not looking forward to any face-to-face meeting with him.

After returning to my quarters, I showered, shaved, and put on fresh cammies, my camouflage uniform that had been nicely starched and pressed for this special occasion. Waiting proved to be 60 percent of the stress. Hours passed before a battalion runner showed up to instruct me to report to the lt. colonel immediately.

During the time I waited to hear from Nick the Prick's office, thoughts of my return to civilian life began to flood my brain. Janet, my ex-wife, had become a major issue. In a sense, my love for her still pervaded my sorry heart. The first year or so of our marriage had been blissful, full of love and sex, and then almost overnight she became more distant. I didn't have a clue as to why. Two fantastic children, Emma and David, resulted from the marriage, even though in both cases they had been unplanned pregnancies.

Living alone, there was nothing for me to return home to except a job at the company Janet and I had built together.

Lt. Colonel's little shit of an orderly interrupted my thoughts. "Lt. Colonel Nickerson wants to see you right away," he whined. Off I went to the command center.

Nick the Prick's office flunky sat in the outer office, smirking as I entered.

"Have a seat and relax," he gloated over at me, "if you can, Sergeant Wylton," the little shit instructed me. "The lieutenant colonel will be with you as soon as he has a few moments," he added. I always wanted to kick this little fuck's ass. He thought he came from a higher social class than the rest of us because he screened all of the lieutenant colonel's visitors and communications. Some day this little shit might see combat, and I would bet a year's pay he would shit in his fucking pants, he and his asshole commanding officer, Lt. Colonel Nickerson.

For two and a half hours I sat in the lieutenant colonel's outer office, waiting patiently to have my ass chewed out. Undoubtedly, Nick the Prick intentionally let me cool my heels, knowing it would stress me out. Finally, as the sun began to set over the row of tents at the western edge of the military base, the little shit orderly ushered me into the inner office.

"Sergeant Wylton, reporting as ordered, sir." I expressed myself in my best Marine Corps bark while snapping to attention in front of the lieutenant colonel's desk.

"Stand at ease, Sergeant," the lieutenant colonel instructed. "Well, Sergeant Wysecock, is it?" He obviously erred intentionally.

The lieutenant colonel, like his orderly sweetheart, was a little shit of a guy with broad shoulders and a face with a permanent frown imbedded in it. He probably stood all of five foot eight inches but had to weigh close to two hundred pounds. He had piercing steel blue eyes and a Marine Corps regulation brush cut. I couldn't tell the color of his hair, as it was cropped very close to his head. He wore horn-rimmed glasses, which emphasized his appearance as a prick.

"Sergeant Wylton, sir," I corrected, a very bad move.

"Whatever." He motioned with his hand as if to brush the remark aside. "You're a total fuckup, aren't you, Sergeant Wyseass?"

"No sir," I responded, best to keep my responses short and to the point.

"You're actually fucking dreaming"—he glared at me over his glasses—"if you don't consider yourself the major fuckup of this battalion, of the division, and probably of the entire Corps. You are a worthless piece of shit." This required no response, so, none given.

"From now on," he continued to growl, "you will be Private Wysinhimer, who is restricted to the battalion compound with zero privileges." He half rose from his seat behind the desk to emphasize his instructions. "Is that sufficiently clear to you, Private?"

"Yes, sir," I said, keeping my response short and safe.

"You are not to visit that cunt you brought in under any circumstances." I thought he had finished, but that only proved to be wishful thinking. "I have arranged a meeting with a local Afghanistan official to determine what is to be done with her. My best guess is that she will be returned to her village and her family." He apparently had concluded, but I could not let it pass.

"Sir, if she is returned to her family and her village, she will be killed," I stated as emphatically as possible.

"That is neither your concern nor mine, Private." He rose from his desk and leaned forward to emphasize his point. "Take this to heart, Private Shithead, stay clear of her and have nothing to do with her. Put her totally out of your fucking mind and return to your duties. Reestablish your reputation as a valued member of this battalion and of the scout/snipers. Any additional fuckups and you will spend the rest of your tour in the brig and end up with a dishonorable discharge. Sinking in, fucking meathead? You are, for now, dismissed. Return to your quarters."

"Yes, sir," again, the only logical reply to Nick the Prick. Best to move on—although, some ideas began to percolate in my head, shame on me.

A trip to the chow hall seemed in order as soon as Nick the Prick dismissed me. Christ, I had hunger pains, not having had a decent meal in more than two weeks. Steak, eggs, and home fries really fit the bill. After wolfing down two steaks and half-dozen eggs, I headed back to my quarters.

Once there, a little scheme began to take shape in my head. First, I contacted Gunderson, the corpsman. He was out of his quarters when I called so I left a message for him to contact me once he returned. At about eight o'clock, he returned my call.

"I need a contact at the hospital, a softhearted doctor. Do you know of one?" As usual, Gunderson stonewalled me, reluctant to get involved, especially in one of my little episodes. After prodding him for another fifteen minutes, he gave in.

"Yeah, I know a doctor at the hospital who has a soft touch. He's a real outspoken liberal—one who criticizes just about everything, especially anything concerning military operation in Afghanistan. Fortunately for him, he is a real outstanding surgeon; otherwise he would be back in the States." Gunderson had come through for me.

Lt. Colonel Mike Collins, a graduate of Yale Medical, had an outstanding career as a chief surgeon at a Philadelphia hospital before being called up for the Afghanistan invasion. He didn't appreciate being called to active duty and let everyone know about his feelings. Gunderson arranged to have him meet me at Gunderson's quarters.

After some brief introductions and small talk about Philadelphia, I got to the point. "Listen, Doc, mind if I call you 'Doc'?" He nodded okay.

"A very difficult situation has developed with one of your patients," I began.

"I'm listening," Doc acknowledged.

"You have an Afghanistan girl by the name of Nadira in your care who is in serious danger of losing her life." I put my heart and soul into every word. "If she is released to the Afghanistan government, as planned by Lt. Colonel Nickerson, she will be returned to her village. Once there, she will be subjected to an honor killing.

"She fell in love with a goatherd," I continued in earnest, "from a different village. Since neither one of them had any understanding of sex, he got her pregnant. According to Islamic law, she is, therefore, guilty of an unforgivable sin. The law is unpardonable, and she will be stoned and beaten to death by the women of her village, a village controlled by the Taliban. They already attempted to kill her once. All I'm asking you to do is prevent her from being moved for at least several days—a few days so I can make arrangements for her to be transferred to a more protective environment. Can you prevent her from being moved?"

Doc appeared perplexed and paced around the office for a few minutes, finally coming to a decision. "I'm reluctant to become involved with local customs and laws. However, sending this girl to certain death does not at all appeal to me." He evidently bought my story and began to soften up. What a relief.

"I will have her sedated"—he motioned with his hand—"and instruct my staff that she is not to be moved without my authorization. In addition, I will constantly monitor her situation so no one can counter my instructions. I can only accommodate you for a few days at the most. Please move quickly with whatever plan you have in mind." His concern and humility were obvious by his facial expressions.

"Thanks, Doc, I couldn't ask for more." My reply indicated the relief I felt. If he had been a woman, any woman, I would have given him a big hug and a kiss, but hugging a guy at this juncture just didn't seem to be the Marine thing to do. In fact, kissing a guy under any circumstances just didn't set with me.

I moved on to the second part of my plan: finding a reporter receptive to my idea. This could be a real challenge. Going to the information officer at headquarters would only alert Lt. Colonel Nickerson that I had cultivated a plan to place Nadira in a protective environment, an environment in which

Afghanistan could not take custody of her. My first stop had to be Gunny Abramson, since I knew of his reliability in resolving almost any problem. Somehow, he had to be convinced that protecting the girl would be the noble thing to do. Fortunately, Gunny had a soft spot.

Going to him and laying all my cards on the table proved to be the right call.

"Gunny, the girl, Nadira, who I carried in from the field is in grave danger." I pled my case. "If the medics follow Lt. Colonel Nickerson's directions, she will be turned over to the Afghan government." I paused for a response but probably should have continued.

"So what the fuck do you expect me to do?" The cigar might be absent but his temper certainly hadn't dissipated.

I knew he had a couple of teenage girls back in the States whom he was very proud of. I had to play on that sentiment, knowing he would never allow anything untoward to happen to those girls.

"If Nadira is returned to the Afghans, she will be sent back to her village—the village where she had been beaten, stoned, and left in the desert for wild animals to feast on. If I hadn't stumbled on her, she would surely be dead at this point."

I emphasized the fact that by following Nickerson's directive, she would be turned over to Afghanistan officials and certain death. This did not appeal to him at all. After my detailed explanation of what I planned to do, he reluctantly gave me the name and location of a well-known TV reporter.

The reporter, Alex Mathews, was embedded with the First Marine Division. The division headquarters were out of bounds for me, since Nickerson had restricted me to quarters. Once again, my good buddy Gunderson would come in handy. Explaining to him my need to see the reporter elicited a not-unexpected response.

"Jesus Christ, Wylton, I wish you would forget I exist," he grimaced. "Christ, you're going to get me involved in shit up to my eyeballs, and we'll be drummed out together. This is the last of my fucking involvement in this thing with that girl. Do you understand?" Off Gunderson went to the division headquarters.

About an hour and a half later, a Humvee pulled up outside my quarters, and four or five men dressed in civilian clothes emerged. Shit, this surely would alert Nick the Prick or one of his flunkies that something was going on. Quickly, I rushed outside and herded the group in, instructing the driver to move the Humvee around to the back of the building. Alex Mathews I could easily pick out after seeing him on the TV news many times back in the States. He greeted me with a warm smile and a firm handshake.

"What's this I hear about a girl being stoned and beaten because she is pregnant out of marriage?" he asked.

I went through the entire story, concluding with how Lt. Colonel Nickerson wanted to turn her over to the local Afghanistan officials.

"Where is she now?" he asked, almost a demand.

"She is at the base hospital under the care of Dr. Mike Collins," I explained. "He can only keep her there for another day or so, and then she is to be released to the Afghanistan government." The situation at the hospital only intrigued him that much more.

"Let's go!" he instructed his entourage. Off they went, to do what could be anybody's guess. Being confined to quarters, I didn't have the liberty of joining them. I sat back and waited for the result, which came faster than anticipated.

"Lt. Colonel Nickerson wants to see you immediately, Private Wylton," came the annoying voice of the little shit orderly. No waiting in the outer office this time: Nickerson sat behind his desk glowing as red as a beet—maybe more like a deep purple.

"You fucking little shit of a person." Definitely his most amiable greeting. "Who do you fucking think you're fucking with? Your days as a Marine are over as of today, as of this minute, as of this very second. Not sergeant, not private, just a little shit in civilian clothes with a fucking dishonorable discharge." He turned increasingly redder, spit flew from his mouth, and his fucking little horn-rimmed glasses began to steam up. For all I knew, he might be having a heart attack. Standing there, staring at him, made me think of a person who had totally lost it.

"Sorry, sir, I have no idea what has upset you, sir," this being my best bewildered response.

"You engineered that little human interest thing"—spittle flew from his mouth and across the desk in my direction as he spoke—"with that cunt you bought with you. What kind of dummy do you fucking take me for, private—make that *civilian*—Wylton?"

"I'm sorry sir, but I don't know of any human interest thing with Nadira." What a liar, straight-faced at that.

"I'm researching this, Private Wylton Shithead, and once I have all the facts, you're dead meat. Get the fuck out of my office; you're still restricted to quarters, you civilian shit." I have never seen Lt. Colonel Nickerson so red. His blood pressure could give him a heart attack, not that I would wish that on him.

On the way back, I stopped off at the mess hall for a nice, big helping of steak, potatoes with gravy, and to keep things on the healthy side, some mixed vegetables.

Back at my quarters, noise coming from the recreation room—shouting and whooping—became almost deafening.

"Hey, you got to see this, Wylton," several of the other Marines called out.

The guys surrounded the television set. There, on the evening news, transmitted from New York to our base television system, stood Alex Mathews reporting from Afghanistan with a human-interest story. Mathews did one hell of a job that would bring tears to the most hardened Marine. His spot ran almost five minutes, and it included every detail he had been provided with by the hospital staff and me.

Mission accomplished, came my immediate thought. Still, Lt. Colonel Nickerson had to be considered, as Alex Mathews had disclosed that I had saved this girl. With the Marine Corps wanting to present the best image to the general public, the probability that I would be drummed out seemed to fade. As a matter of fact, several days later my rank had been restored. In addition, Division Command summed me to headquarters to receive a special commendation by General William "Bulldog" Emerson. All this, of course, televised from Afghanistan with Nadira standing alongside me. She now had new caretakers, a couple of nurses who took her under their wings. With Nadira safe, I could start to relax.

Much to Nick the Prick's consternation, my tour came to an end; so it was back to the States for me. I sure had pride in my accomplishments. After returning to the Marine base at Quantico, Virginia, I sent a letter to my local congressman detailing the meeting I had with the imam. This fulfilled my obligations as a soldier and citizen—and I moved on, to a different life for me.

Chapter 5

Along with a few other Marines and special forces Army personnel, I flew from the airport just outside of Kabul, Afghanistan, to Langley Air Force Base near Washington DC. From Langley, a bus took me to Marine Corps Base Quantico. At Quantico, my new assignment as an instructor for new scout/snipers trainees provided a new perspective of the Corps. Apparently, the Marine Corps deemed me too old for combat assignments, but considering my experience in Sarajevo and Afghanistan, the Corps decided I could serve by imparting my extensive knowledge to new young recruits. At least they awarded my experience and efforts with a promotion to warrant officer.

It had long been a dream of mine to wear the Marine Corps officer's uniform. The day, if not the minute, my promotion came through, I headed to the nearest authorized uniform supply store. It would take several days for my uniforms to be ready; in the meantime, I removed the sergeant insignia from my cammies and replaced them with the warrant officer's bar. This being a proud occasion for me, it only seemed natural to share it with Janet and my kids. As I prepared to phone her, it occurred to me that I had not received a single letter from her since my deployment. In contrast, I had sent a letter almost every week, except when on the secret mission in Afghanistan. The plan for a phone call had to be dismissed out of hand.

Instead of sharing the excitement with Janet and possibly my children, I brought my dampened excitement to my mom and dad. Dad, especially, seemed excited, an emotion he rarely exhibited; proud to hear of my promotion, he wanted pictures of me in uniform sent by e-mail to him as soon as possible. I'm sure he wanted to show me off to all his friends at work and the country club. The dress uniform, "dress blues" in Marine Corps parlance, finally arrived several days later. I rushed back to my quarters, which now was a private room, and put the uniform on. I took several photos of myself with a digital camera and sent them to Dad before heading out to the officers' club. This would be my first ever opportunity to have a drink at the Quantico

Marine Officers' Club. Several officers at the club, who I knew from training programs around the base, each bought me a drink in recognition of my recent promotion. They all kidded me about wearing the dress blues to the club but understood my enthusiasm, as they had had the same enthusiasm when first receiving their officer's bars.

I took my responsibilities as a scout/sniper training officer very seriously. I devoted a great deal of my time researching history and literature on scouts and snipers with specific concentration on recent developments in the art of camouflage and concealment. This being my specialty, it required my total commitment. I had received numerous letters of recognition from all branches of the service. Of particular pride were the citations received from the U. S. Army Special Operations Command and from the U. S. Navy Seals.

My training of prospective scout/snipers for the Marine Corps had to be diligent and thorough. The life of the program's graduate depended on the techniques and disciplines acquired in this training. All applicants had to be thoroughly screened prior to their assignment to the program. Applicants came from the best of the best, primarily from the Marine Corps regiments. Of those, approximately 30 percent would ultimately graduate. The program, by its very nature, had to be very rigorous, both physically and mentally.

I took great pride on graduation day watching the individuals who had completed the training and marched in review. Most graduation ceremonies were well attended by Marine Corps brass and admiring families and friends. Following the graduation, the individual Marines returned to their respective organizations.

My stint as a Marine Corps officer proved to be short-lived. In early May 2002, a change of command notice arrived, addressed to me. As of June, my tour of duty with the United States Marine Corps would be up, and I would return to civilian life. The one consolation from the change of command letter was my transfer to inactive reserve status as a chief warrant officer. This promotion certainly recognized the time and effort I had put in to help develop the scout/sniper training program. Younger, seasoned Marines returning from combat assignments in Afghanistan needed to be posted as instructors, and I, after all, was getting on in age, although I had hoped to retire rather than be discharged.

My return to Croton proved uneventful. My parents had a little block party for me with a number of relatives and some friends from the neighborhood. Notably absent were the Armstrongs, Janet's mother and father, and of course my children, which proved to be a major disappointment for me; I would have enjoyed sharing this event with my children. The party broke up early, and I hit the sack at my parents' house by ten that night. I stayed with my parents, at least temporarily, as there were no other options available. I had no home to speak of—maybe a hotel or motel room, but Mom would have none of that.

The next two weeks were spent looking for apartments nearby, devoting some time to the purchase of civilian clothes. Janet had given all my clothes away to the Salvation Army or other charitable organizations. Once she completed all the divorce papers, out on my ass I went, lock, stock, and barrel. The judge who administered the divorce concluded that I lacked responsibility. Apparently, the court had sent numerous notices to my Marine Corps address, and having not received a response, they considered me to be irresponsible. Dad had retained an attorney to represent my interests before the court but to no avail. Not only did the house go to Janet, but sole custody of the children also went to her. The judge proved to be completely unresponsive to my attorney's documentation, including proof that I had been assigned to a special operation, would be out of the country, and, because of the secrecy of my mission, would be unavailable to respond to the court's directives.

Once an apartment had been located and furnished and a new wardrobe picked out, tailored, and delivered, I wanted to return to work, naturally to Wylton Computer Systems, Inc. On the Monday after July 4, 2002, I returned to the office with a pent-up passion for work. Well, sort of. To my dismay, a new receptionist guarded the front, and someone named Freddy occupied my old office.

As I walked through the doors to the office, the new receptionist confronted me.

"May I help you, sir?" came her terse greeting.

Trying to be as pleasant as possible, I said, "I'm Oscar Wylton," thinking my name might elicit some recognition, "an owner of this business along with Janet Wylton."

"I'm sorry, sir," she continued in her most stern voice, "but there is no Oscar Wylton or Janet Wylton owning any part of this business. Janet Wallberg is the president, and Mr. Fred Wallberg is technical director."

"I see," I remarked as I moved toward my old office. "As soon as Janet is here, this all will be straightened out."

Shit, Janet not only dumped me, she married that incompetent technician Fred whatever-his-name-is. I supposed he was living in my house, being a daddy to my children.

She moved to block me from walking back to the office area. "I'm again sorry, sir, but you will have to wait until Janet Wallberg arrives and says it is okay for you to go back to the offices." She reminded me of some of the football linemen of my high school days. A big burly woman, she had dark hair with gray speckles; I estimated her to be in her early forties. "You can remain here in the waiting area until she arrives." She motioned to the seating area by the front door.

At five after eleven, Janet and Freddy what's-his-name entered the office by the front door. Janet stopped short and stared at me. Her appearance had dramatically changed since the last time I saw her. Her hair was no longer the well-kept, shoulder-length blonde but a short, dark blonde, almost unkempt. The clothing she wore looked like something out of consignment shop. I almost jumped with joy that we were no longer a married couple.

"What are you doing here?" she demanded without a flinch, just a cold stare.

"Returning to our company, ready to resume my position and responsibilities," I curtly responded.

"You must be kidding," Janet chuckled, annoying the shit out of me.

"Why would I kid about such a serious matter?" I demanded to know.

"You don't have a job here," she said, glowering at me. "You certainly are no longer employed by this company, period," she responded.

"Who says so?" I asked, showing some surprise in my voice.

"The company charter and agreement you signed when we incorporated the business." She pursed her lips and continued to stare at me. "If you have questions, take them to the attorney. I have work to do and no time to spend explaining things to you. Now get out." She turned and walked to the back with Freddy following her with a shit-eating grin on his face.

The law firm that had set up the incorporation of the business had offices in White Plains, New York, about a half-hour drive away. Determined to find out what the fuck happened with the business, I jumped into my parents' car—graciously loaned to me—and drove to the law office. Undoubtedly, it would have been wise to phone first, but I had a head of steam and wanted to get to the bottom of this fast.

Announcing my name and purpose in being there to the receptionist at the law office took almost fifteen minutes. Finally, she disappeared into the thick-carpeted, mahogany-paneled office corridor, apparently in search of an attorney who could address my issues. Time rolled by, calculated by the large grandfather clock ticking away in the well-appointed reception area. The clock sat in a framed glass enclosure apparently in deference to its age.

At last, an attorney introduced himself as Jack Billings, a junior partner with the firm.

"I'm Oscar Wylton of the Wylton Computer Service Corporation of Croton-on-Hudson, New York," I, very businesslike, presented myself, "and I would like to go over the papers that incorporated our firm several years ago."

"For what particular purpose do you need to see the papers?" he inquired.

"If you are a party to the incorporation, why don't you have copies?" A good question.

"Well, Jack, it's a long story, and I don't want to take up your valuable time. There is one particular clause that is of specific interest to me. That clause has to do with my being eliminated from the corporation for some reason," continuing to be equally as pleasant.

"Give me a few moments," Jack requested as he turned and walked down the hallway he had entered from. The receptionist had returned and kindly offered me a drink: coffee or tea but definitely not her. I accepted the offer of tea. Something a little stronger would have settled my nerves.

Jack returned, all smiles, with several documents in his hands.

"The clause you are looking for is an unusual one," he began to explain as only a lawyer knows how to address a dissatisfied client, "and it is only put in at the insistence of the incorporating parties. Essentially, what the clause stipulates is that if one or more of the incorporating parties cannot participate in the day-to-day activities of the company for a specified period of time, two months in this case, the remaining parties assume full responsibilities for the corporation. The absent party or parties are permanently barred from any further participation in any of the corporation operations or decisions. In other words, the absent party or parties are no longer part of the corporation."

I stood there dumbstruck. That sneaky bitch had put one over on me. Having totally trusted her, I had signed the fucking documents without reading them. How stupid could one person be? I left without another word, leaving Jack, the junior partner, standing there, obviously wondering what had just transpired.

The drive back to my apartment was a very depressing ride. What had been done, what could be done? I had signed the goddamned papers without reading them. Christ, would that ever stand up in court? Everything favored Janet, no question about it. I was livid, even contemplated killing her, but that would really have been another dumb ass idea. I seemed to be loaded with them. Thinking of my kids growing up without a mother and with their father wasting away in prison, I cast that thought aside fast.

I could consult with an attorney, but that would eat up what I had left of my meager savings—best to swallow hard and get on with my life. Back at the apartment, a stack of mail sat in my mailbox. Funny, I had totally forgotten about mail since none had been addressed to me in such a long time. Among the pile of unpaid bills and junk mail appeared a letter from Wylton Computer Services, Inc. Must be the letter terminating my position as president; how kind of them to inform me.

I sat and stared at the letter from my former company. Why should I be so reluctant to open it? Curiosity eventually ruled, so I picked it up and gradually, almost painfully, opened the letter with the sharp edge of my penknife. Something fell out and landed on the floor. I paid no attention but went to read the letter.

The letter was obviously written by an attorney, probably my friend Jack Sprat what's-his-name from the White Plains firm. The letter stated that in compliance with the agreement of incorporation signed by me, I would no longer be associated with the firm; in other words, an ignominious firing from my employment.

However, in consideration of my years of employment with the firm, especially the technical support and establishment of a sizable client base, the firm had decided to award me one hundred and fifty thousand dollars in severance. Knock me over with a feather, could this really be true? Perhaps Janet wasn't such a bitch after all. Maybe she would even let me see our children. I felt rich for ten seconds or so. Anyway, at least I had some money to live on while searching for employment elsewhere.

There was a caveat, however: cashing the check meant that I agreed to abide by the letter of agreement included in the incorporation. That letter specifically stated that I would not compete in any way with the corporation, and I would not attempt to take any clients, present or future, from the corporation. Well, shit. Was I being bought off? You bet.

Sleeping on it overnight, literally under my pillow, the next day I took the check to the Bank of Ossining, located in the City of Ossining, a community about six miles south of Croton, and deposited it all into my savings account. The interest rate wouldn't keep me in beer, but I needed to get this over and done with. I had plenty of time to contemplate where to put the funds to earn more money. For now, things were somewhat set; I could relax a little and look for a good job in the computer industry.

I wanted to treat myself to a good night out, maybe even get laid. A nice steak dinner at one of the more fashionable restaurants in the area would start the evening off just right. Dressing in one of my new suits, shirt, and tie, I headed out for the evening. After the steak dinner, I decided to hit some of the old haunts where there might be some loose women. To my dismay, the great old haunts were either gone or were populated by a bunch of young singles, none of whom seemed interested in an old former Marine. No way of getting laid, not this night anyway.

Over the next few days, I spent most of my time planning and devising a method for gaining employment somewhere in the computer industry, in a position with an organization that did not compete with Wylton Computers. There were several online job search portals available. On just about every site there were multiple positions listed, and many appeared to be a match for my education and experience. E-mailing copies of my resume with a cover letter would surely elicit a quick response. For the next several days, I followed the same procedure: online search, find matches, and respond with a cover letter and a resume. This took about three hours a day, and the rest of the time I could do whatever I wanted; great life.

For the next four weeks, I followed the same procedure every day. Not a single nibble, nothing, nada. Disappointment and frustration were settling in. I never really had to search for employment before. What a shitty experience. I needed a different approach, one that had some promise to it. Several of my friends in the past had used job search firms with considerable success; perhaps that would expedite my finding a good position. For positions in the local area, the yellow pages seemed the best place to start. Firms that specialized in the computer industry logically would be the best bet. I found several in White Plains, phoned, and set appointments for the next day.

At the first firm, a young woman by the name of Patricia looked at my resume and interviewed me. My education and experience were now dated, as most companies would be looking for recent college graduates who had two or three years of hands-on experience.

"Look," I said, "I set up a thriving business from scratch with an excellent clientele base."

"Why aren't you still with that company?" she asked.

"That, unfortunately, is a long story—associated with a divorce." My comeback seemed a little lame, but the truth be told, embellishing on my tale of a divorce might serve a useful purpose.

"I see." She looked down, avoiding eye contact. "We don't have anything matching your education or experience at this time, but we will keep your resume on file and phone you when something develops." A well-practiced brush-off; out the fucking door I went.

The next two search firms essentially gave the same worn response. "Nothing available at this time, but your resume will be kept on file and we will phone you as soon as something develops." Shit, they must go to a seminar or something to learn that phrase; they all had it down pat.

There had to be another way. Nothing much was available locally; I needed to expand my search area. New York City had to be one of the best cities in the world for employment; surely there would be something there for me. The next day I began my extended search in New York City with phone calls and interview appointments. Several large placement firms that specialized in technology accepted my request for an interview. Hell, my father had commuted by train for years, no reason I couldn't.

The next morning, I hopped the early train headed for the big city with five interviews scheduled for that day. The first interview was located just off Fifth Avenue, not far from Grand Central Terminal, the train station. The office of the placement firm seemed to be a busy one with people on phones and secretaries running around with stacks of papers in their hands. A Mr. Rodgers would be my interviewer. He proved to be a very happy, smiley person, delighted to see me, and knew we would have a long and meaningful relationship; it sounded more like a date than a placement interview.

Rodgers studied my resume intently, only periodically glancing up and nodding with a little hum that indicated he had a great deal of interest in what he read.

"Mr. Wylton, I know we are going to find something that absolutely matches your education and your experience," he began with a smile and a nod.

"What needs to be done at this point," Rodgers said in a very decisive tone, "is to get the paperwork in motion so our search department can come up with a match for you. As I'm sure you are aware, conducting these searches is time-consuming and expensive, and, as such, we ask a commitment on your part by providing some funds up front." I hadn't expected this. Funds up front? I'm out of fucking work, and they want funds up front?

"These funds will be returned to you," Rodgers continued in his well-rehearsed recitation, "by your future employer as soon as you accept employment with them. Do you have any problem in making that type of commitment to our firm?" He frowned as he looked askance at me.

To be honest, surprise could hardly explain my reaction. Why would they want funds from me? What the fuck, if it would expedite my employment, why not?

"How much are we talking about here?" showing my lack of knowledge on how this process worked. "How long would the search take?" starting to indicate some understanding in such an agreement—this from a guy who just got screwed out of the company he created.

"Well, Mr. Wylton," Rodgers continued with what I assumed to be the corporate answer to such questions, "we ask our clients for five hundred dollars up front to defray the cost of an employment search. The search will take about three weeks; however, with your qualifications I figure about one or two weeks, tops." This guy would make a good used car salesman. Bullshit, bullshit, and more bullshit, the business world is definitely propelled by tons and tons of bullshit. I should have been a lawyer, go figure.

I popped out my trusty checkbook and began to fill in the name and numbers. Rodgers, obviously pleased, proceeded to get one of the secretaries to prepare the contract agreement, an agreement I would thoroughly read before signing. Rodgers assured me that the agreement was a standard boilerplate agreement used throughout the industry. Nonetheless, it would be carefully read before being signed. After I paid them, I packed up and headed to the next firm.

The next firm, Sperling Associates, seemed honest and somewhat reassuring. Jason Sperling introduced himself as one of the principles of the company and seemed very interested in my resume, especially my education and in particular my experience with a start-up of a small computer servicing company. Jason appeared to be very honest and forthright about my prospects for employment in the computer field. He said their firm received between ten and twenty resumes every day. The resumes and cover letters ranged from recent college graduates to individuals with more than fifteen years in the field, which, on the surface appeared to be encouraging news. Doing a quick calculation for my friend Rodger's company, they had to be hauling in five to ten Gs a day just in that field. *Wonder if I can make a stop payment on the check?*

Jason continued. "In contrast, we receive requests for maybe five positions per week in the computer field, most of which are for recent graduates." He paused for effect.

This was really getting depressing. "However," Jason emphasized with a wave of his hand, "your background and education are exceptional, and, as such, we here at Sperling would do a search for you." He seemed to be waiting for my reaction, great, another five hundred in the tank.

"How much money do I have to provide up front?" I asked.

Jason's reply was a very refreshing and unexpected one. "Sperling only receives payment from the employing firm once we have placed you." What a relief. I left all my information with Jason and moved on to my next appointment.

The rest of the day proved to be a waste. The remaining three employment firms that interviewed me either said I didn't have the necessary qualifications or wanted funds up front. Up front funds ranged anywhere from five hundred to several thousand dollars. No way would I hand out any more of my precious money.

Before leaving the city, I thought a trip to Rodger's firm might be a smart move. Once there, the lovely receptionist informed me that Rodger was not available. Seems he had been booked with interviews for the balance of the day. What a waste. The next day I went to the Bank of Ossining and stopped payment on the check.

For the next six months, I continued to send out resumes with cover letters, in response, nothing, not a phone call, not even a letter acknowledging the receipt of my cover letter and resume. Nothing to indicate I didn't meet the company's requirements or even that they would keep my resume on file for future reference. Each day, each week, each month was the same, and depression began to set in. After sending out the daily allotment of resumes, I began to hang out at a local bar, which became my primary daily activity. Not exactly the best place to do a job search, but at least there were other losers to share my cares and tribulations with.

Unfortunately, this led to some experimentation with drugs, particularly with marijuana. At least this experimentation didn't lead to addiction. But Janet somehow got wind of my alcoholic consumption and smoking weed. She went back to the judge, who seemed to be taken with Janet. The judge immediately sent me a notice of restraint prohibiting any contact with my children.

In the last six months, I had gone through fifty thousand dollars, leaving one hundred Gs in my accounts. Something had to be done about my employment. Nothing resulted from my efforts, not even an interview. I lowered my expectation with a willingness to take a position even as a technician; still nothing. Depression began setting in, deep depression for the first time in my life. No way could I continue without any prospect of employment; something had to be done and done soon.

Of all the dangerous situations I had encountered in the Marine Corps, nothing had depressed me to the extent of this sense of worthlessness that now enveloped my everyday existence. Without employment, and especially with no prospect of employment, my life had no value. The fact that I couldn't see or be around my children—definitely of my own doing—just added to my loss of self-worth. Contemplating suicide actually entered my brain, my alcohol- and marijuana-soused brain, but was quickly pushed aside; there were still many positive aspects to my life.

What were my options? Nothing came to mind. Being a policeman or a fireman appeared to be out, just too old. To get a position with any municipality required political contacts, which I didn't have. Talking to my father proved to be no help, as he had to struggle to hang on to his job in the defense industry. The defense industry was in a recession, so they were laying off right and left. Along with depression, desperation began to take hold. Christ, I actually started to feel sorry for myself; how desperate could I become?

I might as well get drunk and sleep it off—one day just like the next.

Chapter 6

In April 1994, President Clinton had decided to secretly deploy U.S. forces to Sarajevo, Bosnia, and Herzegovina to counter the devastating effects Serbian snipers were having on the citizens of Sarajevo. Crossing the main boulevard of the city provided the only method to obtain fresh water. Citizens crossing the boulevard to replenish their water supply were literally putting their lives in danger. Serbian snipers hiding in the hills and buildings surrounding the city effectively dissuaded the citizens from venturing across the boulevard for water by indiscriminately killing them.

To contain the Serbian sniper activity, U.S. forces concealed themselves in various office and apartment buildings. I had been assigned to the Second Corps Expeditionary Battalion, which consisted of both U.S. Army and Marine snipers. Our job: spot the Serbian snipers and take them out, which hopefully would discourage them from killing the civilians. What angered us the most was the population here consisted primarily of children and the elderly. The elderly had to rely on the children to fetch water resuting in many of the children being shot. The children were much faster and could avoid some of the rifle fire. Sadly, many did not, and their bodies would lie for days, bloating and decaying on the boulevard, as the families could not safely retrieve the bodies for a decent burial. Compounding the criminal activity of the Serbian sniper was the killing of any family member or friend trying to retrieve the dead body.

Our deployment into the city had to be under the cover of darkness and without the knowledge of the citizenry, since we didn't know who to trust. Corporal Anthony Ramos of the Army and I located ourselves in a high-rise building with a commanding view of the boulevard. Corporal Ramos would be the spotter, and I would be the sniper, or shooter. The building we situated ourselves in had been bombed out and blackened by fire outside and inside. We elected to position ourselves one story down from the roof, on the tenth floor of an eleven-story building. Being equipped with both an infrared scope and a night-vision scope provided us with the ability to monitor the surrounding area 24-7.

The first few days consisted of shooting fish in a barrel. The Serbs, not expecting any response from the citizens of Sarajevo, did not conceal themselves very well. Within the first hour, Ramos had spotted fourteen and I had dropped fourteen, a 100 percent success rate. The Serbs became suspicious and started searching the area with their binoculars, often standing up or hanging out windows. The next hour we dropped ten more. At this juncture, the Serbian sniper activity had greatly diminished.

The next day proved more difficult. The Serbs were becoming aware of the opposing sniper activity from somewhere in Sarajevo. It took us all day to drop four more. They increased their nighttime activity, since many of the people of Sarajevo tried to retrieve water under cover of darkness. Of course, we were prepared for their change in tactics, knocking off another six that night.

By dawn on the third day, the sniping along the boulevard had declined significantly. On the fourth day, as we watched in dismay, the remaining Serbian snipers, evidently being a more professional group, began to successfully kill numerous civilians. Citizens died in large numbers, shot down either carrying empty containers to the water source or returning with containers filled with water. Spotting became extremely difficult. The snipers in the hills dug in, and the ones in the building knew to remain hidden well back in the rooms they occupied.

We estimated there were approximately twenty Serbian snipers left, which would take us time to locate and eliminate. Even though the Serb snipers concealed themselves by hiding in the rear of the rooms in the buildings or by camouflage in the hills, we could spot them with our infrared 20x scopes. Once Corporal Ramos spotted one hiding in the hills or the rear of a room, I could pick up the sniper with my less-powerful riflescope and take him out.

There are cardinal rules for scout/snipers. First, never underestimate your opponent. Second, never take more than one shot from a hide position. Once you have taken a shot, whether or not it is successful, never take a second from that location. Always move to a new location. At a new sight, establish at least three methods of exiting your location or escaping. Lastly, never become emotionally involved with the target. Complete the mission and move on.

Corporal Ramos and I violated just about every one of the rules, starting with not underestimating the capability of our opponents. We assumed they didn't have the training, skills, or technology we had. Particularly, we thought the Serb snipers didn't even have night-vision scopes or infrared equipment.

From the get-go, we became emotionally involved. Looking out at the boulevard, six hundred feet from of our position, we could see the bodies of young children, defenseless women, and a few old men lying where they had been shot to death. How could one look at this and not feel some emotion? Ignoring another rule, we had taken all of our shots from the same location through the same window opening. Lastly, we had not bothered to establish an exit strategy, thinking we would go back out the way we came in.

Corporal Ramos sat cross-legged on the floor, looking through the spotting scope, and I lay on the floor next to him, ready to take a shot as soon as he located a target. Suddenly, Ramos flew back several feet from his position. Turning to my left and raising from my position, I felt a severe pain just below my right shoulder. My body jerked backward, and I landed next to Ramos, toward the rear of the room. My immediate reaction was that a Serb sniper, with luck, had put a round through me. Examination of my shoulder revealed an indentation in my flak jacket inches below my right shoulder. Standing up and turning to the left had saved my life.

Ramos, unfortunately, had taken a direct hit. A single shot hit him on the right side of his neck, and blood oozed and spurted out, covering the floor next to his head. I had never witnessed so much blood being expelled so quickly from a person. Grabbing our radio, I summed either an army medic or a Marine Corps corpsman. Several minutes later, I could hear them coming up the stairs.

"In here. In here," I shouted in desperation.

The "medical assistance" came charging through the door, weapon lowered and ready to fire. Not a medic or a corpsman but a Serb soldier prepared to end my existence. My rifle lay several feet away, near the window we had been using to fire through. The Marine Corps had issued me a 9 mm sidearm, which I quickly drew from its holster. The Serb, armed with an AK-47, sprayed the room hoping one of the rounds would finds its mark. Luckily, none of the shots hit Ramos or me. Taking careful aim and firing a single shot, my round found its mark. Down went the Serb; and none too soon, as right behind him came another Serb. Before he could spot me, I got a shot off, hitting him just below his neck, and down he went. Fuck, those hours, days, and months of training with a pistol now paid off.

Next through the door came a real Marine Corpsman; I had a round chambered and ready to go. Recognizing the Marine Corps cammies, I returned the pistol to its holster. The corpsman went to Ramos's aid but nothing could be done; he couldn't be saved. I had developed a likeness for Ramos in the short time we had been together. He came from East Los Angeles, California, and grew up in a neighborhood of gangs and drugs. The Army had given him a way out, and Ramos took full advantage of the opportunity, becoming an exemplary soldier, successfully shaking his past. He died a hero, defending the poor civilians of Sarajevo. Sadly, few would remember him. I surely would though.

My shoulder had become inflamed and quite sore. The doctors back at our base in Ancona, Italy, said the severe bruising of the chest area would take a while to heal and prescribed painkillers and rest. Relaxing for a while helped relieve some portion of the trauma that resulted from the death of Ramos and of witnessing the criminal activities of the Serb snipers in Sarajevo. Although having killed some twenty or more of the Serbian snipers, I had never witnessed someone killed close up like that, especially someone I had established male bonding with.

Reflecting on my mission with Corporal Ramos, I recalled my first kill. Ramos took the spotter position and I took the shooter, primarily because of my skill as a marksman and my extensive training with the Marine Corps scout/sniper program. When we took out the first Serb, my shot hit him in the neck, resulting in blood and guts spurting all over the place. Through my scope not much could be made out, but Ramos, on the more powerful spotter scope, could see every detail. He got up, went into one of the back corners, and threw up. It is not a satisfying feeling to kill another person, no matter how much you might hate him or his ideology.

As soon as I could get near a phone, I called Janet. My mission was top secret so nothing about my location or activity could be divulged. Janet pressed for information but accepted the explanation about being top secret. We soon settled into talking about us, including our daughter, Emma, and our future as a family. How much I wished I could be there, sharing the growth of our child, Emma. She had already put on weight. Explaining to Janet my feelings seemed very difficult, although I tried, and I think she understood.

I apologized for not being able to write, since I know how much her letters meant to me. Surely, she looked forward to hearing from me. She understood I had a job to do, and that I wasn't in a position where writing would be feasible.

I felt an obligation, a duty, and a fervent desire to correspond with Corporal Ramos's family and let them know how he had died, what the circumstances were, and about his dedication to his assignment as a soldier. After recuperating for several days, a trip to our battalion headquarters produced his family's address in Los Angeles. I spent hours agonizing over how to write the letter. After numerous fitful starts, I finally put something together—not an outstanding piece of literature, but for me, something heartfelt and special. Perhaps someday I could follow it up with a personal visit.

A chaplain came by to check up on me, and he counseled me on the circumstances of conflicts. Losing close associates to wounds or death was an unwelcome aspect of war. In time, the feelings I experienced would fade but would never be forgotten. He wished me well and left. My time in Sarajevo now finished, I headed back to the States.

Over the years, I had maintained a correspondence with Ramos's mother, Elaina, and his younger sister, Raquel. We wrote each other several times a year, mostly on holidays and on the anniversary of Anthony's death.

They had used the fifty thousand dollars from Anthony's military death benefit to purchase a home in Orange County, California. They had been living in an apartment in East Los Angeles, a gang-infested area. Their letters reflected their joy at leaving East Los Angeles. Over time, I noted their enthusiasm for Santa Ana, a city in Orange County where they had relocated, gradually diminished with subtle hints of a growing gang presence in that city. I vowed to one day take the time to go and visit them.

I woke with a start, sitting up in bed, still with my clothes on and drenched in sweat. What had happened, where was I? Looking around my bedroom in an effort to orient myself, gradually reality began to return. I now sat in my bed in Croton, not Sarajevo. Why had this dream occurred now? The first human being I had killed had not traumatized me at the time. But this dream had not been about the killing; my background and experience as a scout/sniper clearly had been the focus of the dream.

This might be a solution to my dilemma: adopting the training and skills learned in the Marine Corps for a civilian life. Why not? In a sense, I had become jaded. Like many returning veterans, especially those who experienced direct combat with an enemy, upon returning to civilian life there seemed to be no recognition of our service to the country. Perhaps my thoughts were unfair to society, but my expectations were to be treated differently, as someone a little more special—like being given the first shot at employment opportunities. Although recognition and employment opportunities were given political lip service, the facts were that receiving special treatment had proven to be only wishful thinking. Superficially, such thoughts were considered unreasonable, but somewhere deep in my psyche these concerns remained.

Millions of men and women had chosen service to our country; should I be treated any differently? Troops had returned from Vietnam only to be ostracized and spit upon; that definitely was not my case. I was extremely proud of being a U.S. Marine, especially the specialized training I received and my promotion to a warrant officer—that in itself was more than sufficient recognition; I needed nothing more.

The thought of adapting the sniper skills to my current life began to moderate my depression. I took an inventory of my skills. What parts of my training could be modified to civilian life? Where would my experience, education, and background be the strongest? Computers out, technician out, fireman out, policeman out, everything seemed to be out. How about janitor? What possibly remained for me to do? Veteran's associations did have support groups, but they had a certain stigma to them. Scout/sniper? Fat chance of going back in the Corps at my age. What the hell was there to do?

That night I went to sleep with all these questions on my mind. Probably because of the concentration on my scout/sniper abilities and my dream from the previous night, another strange dream materialized. In this dream, a private firm hired me to assassinate one of their executives. I contemplated a plan for how best to approach such a situation. The plan had to do with acquiring the necessary equipment: rifle, ammunition, scopes, and ghillie suit. On the first two attempts to take out the target, I had been discovered and almost caught, eluding capture at the last possible moment. Before waking, I finally eliminated the target, and when I returned home, a nice check sat in my mailbox.

The dream gave pause for thought. Could it at all be possible for me to become some kind of hit man? It seemed ridiculous, but as time passed and my inability to find work, even the most mundane type of work, continued, the idea gained traction. Why not? The skills acquired in the past certainly could be applied to the present.

This would be a dangerous undertaking and a significant change in my life, going from relative comfort as a civilian to one of great danger. The level of uncertainty would depend on the target and on how well I planned to take that target out. The detail, every possible situation that could occur, every i dotted, every t crossed, all being absolutely necessary for a satisfactory outcome.

Gradually, the idea took shape. How would a potential client be contacted? I couldn't hang out a shingle or go online and advertise. Some method that would ensure my not being discovered had to be hatched. How would payment be made? Any transfer of large sums of money or deposits of large sums of money to my account would raise questions. How would the tools of the trade be acquired—the rifle, scopes, ammunition, and infrared and night vision equipment?

I sat down and began to list everything needed to carry out this plan. First, a rifle could not be purchased on the open market. The weapon, unfortunately, would not be an M 35 system like the one used by the Marine Corps. The forerunner of the M 35, developed by the Marine Corps scout/sniper, was a World War I rifle. This weapon, U.S. Rifle 1903, also known as the Springfield 30 06 or the Springfield 03, could be picked up at just about any gun show.

Ammunition would be a problem, since even with the Springfield rifle, special competition ammunition had to be obtained, namely a .308-diameter,

175-grain competition round. A reasonable expectation that an online search would turn up the necessary ammunition addressed that concern for the time being. A Glock 9 mm semi-automatic pistol would satisfy the required sidearm. Nine-millimeter ammunition could readily be obtained at any sporting goods store. I could undoubtedly purchase the Springfield at a gun show, no questions asked. An alternate source would be online, using a computer that could not be traced to me. A Unertl scope, the best scope/rifle match-up for this weapon, would serve my purpose. The scope would be available for purchase online, at a gun show, or even at a swap meet.

With the equipment requirements satisfied, at least on paper, the next project had to be a method for determining potential clients. What would define an entity as needing my proposed service? How would I initiate a contact once the potential client had been identified?

One of the most difficult aspects of fulfilling a contract was finding a method of payment that could not be traceable to either the client or me. This required considerable thought and planning. For several weeks, I mulled over various scenarios that might meet my strict needs.

By the end of the third week, with a fictitious identification developed by using some blank driver license forms downloaded from several Web sites, I started visiting gun shows. Additionally, online computer access at a local library facilitated my search for a rifle, scope, and ammunition. Purchasing anywhere in the New York area had to be out of the question, and it was best to travel to states with the least stringent regulations involving the sale and purchase of a weapon.

Virginia had become notorious for their lax laws on weapon purchases. By the end of the fifth week, a Glock 9 mm pistol, Springfield rifle, scope, and ammunition had all been purchased and locked away in the trunk of my car. Additionally, a special quick-release holster for the Glock had been procured.

Silencers for both the rifle and the pistol were added to my list of required items. I located a swap meet that specialized in weapons and weapons accessories through a computerized Web search. It meant a day's drive to western Pennsylvania, but it was best to purchase my needs a good distance from my home. My trip there produced the remaining two pieces of equipment necessary to complete the inventory.

The Springfield with the scope and silencer mounted and the Glock pistol with the silencer had to be test-fired and aligned before they could be used. To accomplish this, I needed a secluded, out-of-the-way location.

An old friend had a place in the Adirondack Mountains in upstate New York. The location proved ideal, as a small cabin at the end of a two-mile dirt drive provided ample seclusion. The location lay well off any main highway and far enough from any inhabited area, so the firing of the weapons could not be heard.

For two days, I fired both the Springfield and the Glock without silencers and then with silencers, assuring myself that the weapons were indeed perfect for my purpose. I repeatedly disassembled and reassembled the rifle, assuring myself that the disassembly and reassembly did not affect the sighting of the weapon. My strict standards met, my equipment was now set and ready to go.

Chapter 7

At my apartment in Croton, I began a computer search of articles from every possible newspaper I could find throughout the country. The search criteria: a case where someone had been defrauded or swindled out of a large sum of money, or a high-stakes divorce case where one of the parties lost a substantial amount of money in the settlement. In the case of fraud or swindle, the case had to be one where the plaintiff lost the judgment because of a technicality or inadequate legal representation. In the option of a high-stakes divorce, the losing party had to lose because of outright manipulation of the legal procedures or total bias on the part of the court.

A divorce case in Cleveland, Ohio, piqued my interest. The divorce had been acrimonious and worked its way through the courts for more than two years. The husband, a wealthy and powerful local doctor and businessman, Dr. Gerald Able, had elected to dump his first wife and marry a secretary who worked in his office. Over the years, the doctor had garnered many friends in the political and legal community of the city. Using his connections, he manipulated the local legal system to achieve a divorce settlement that gave his first wife only about 5 percent of his estate. The first wife, Elisabeth Able, received two million as final settlement, an insignificant portion of Dr. Able's net worth, which was estimated to be more than one hundred million dollars.

Elisabeth exhausted every legal means available trying to elicit more money from her husband. Her efforts resulted in an annual stipend of two hundred thousand dollars with the understanding that she could no longer pursue legal action against the doctor. She agreed to the terms of the award. This, however, did not dampen her anger. One night, she attempted to run Gerald off the road and ended up spending several days in jail. On another occasion, she was apprehended on Gerald's property carrying a loaded revolver. This time she spent several weeks in jail. These circumstances certainly appeared to meet criteria I had established to carry out the structure of my plan. With the information in hand, I arranged a trip to Cleveland, Ohio.

First, I considered it prudent not to use my own vehicle; a different one had to be purchased under a false name. To accomplish this, using the name identification forged from the Internet—a facsimile of a New York driver's license—I took the train from Croton to Albany and purchased a car. The car, an older Toyota, I considered to be reliable, at least sufficiently reliable for my purposes. From Albany, my new and dangerous life began.

On my way to Cleveland, I stopped off at several large national commercial outlets that sold electronic gear, TVs, surround sound systems, and other such products. My primary interest was to purchase cell phones, the type you purchase and add minutes to as needed, rather than a phone with a plan where you had to give out personal information. These phones could be sold to whoever wanted one, no questions asked and no financial obligations other than the initial payment for the phone and a pay-as-you-go card. Not even a legitimate name was required. Telling the salesperson I planned them as a surprise for my family, I bought four cell phones and several pay-as-you-go cards.

Dr. Gerald Able located his estate in the Clifton Park section of Lakewood, Ohio, a wealthy suburb of Cleveland. His medical practice and a business he had founded, Medical Research Labs, Inc., he had established in Cleveland. The estate, situated on approximately four acres, sat on a somewhat secluded country road just inside the town limits of Lakewood.

By contrast, Elisabeth Able lived in a Cleveland high-rise condominium complex overlooking the Cuyahoga River and Lake Erie. The condominiums mostly catered to the well-heeled locals, and as such, they were some of the best apartment condominiums in the city.

From the 1960s through the late 1980s, Cleveland had fallen on hard times with white flight to the suburbs and the decline of manufacturing and steel production in the area. More recently, the city had been experiencing a renaissance with new high-rise offices and condominiums in the downtown area. Many successful people began returning to the city. Their return resurrected the culture of the city, namely museums, concert halls, off-Broadway productions, and similar developments. Dr. Able, being an extreme extrovert, savored the limelight, involving himself extensively in most of these developments. He and his new wife frequently had their names and pictures in the local papers, particularly the society section.

First, I had to find temporary lodging, perhaps a monthly rooming house or a cheap hotel, preferably not far from Lakewood or Cleveland. A run-down motel just off West 250th Street in Cleveland would serve my purpose. I spent the first night settling in, acclimating myself to this new temporary home and its surroundings along with finding places nearby to eat. Some small family restaurants and a number of fast food outlets were within easy walking distance. I opted for the fast food, taking it back to the motel room.

The next day I drove around, observing Dr. Able's estate in Lakewood and Elisabeth Able's condominium in Cleveland. Dr. Able's residence could not be seen from the local road passing by his front gate, as a heavily wooded area surrounded his home. Down the road about a half mile past his estate, the city of Lakewood maintained a park, which overlooked Lake Erie and was surrounded by a public forest.

Obviously, I couldn't stop in front of the doctor's property and start to reconnoiter the area. However, stopping in the city park definitely proved a viable option. Checking the park out a little more carefully crushed my optimism, as a posted sign stated that the park was exclusively for residents of Lakewood. My optimism returned when another sign close by indicated that a public bus ran through the area.

Returning to the no-tell motel by about six o'clock, I began to put my plan into action. Using one of the pay-as-you-go cell phones, I placed a call to Ms. Able. She picked up on the fourth ring.

"Is this Ms. Able, formerly Dr. Able's wife?" I spoke with some caution into the receiver of the little phone.

"Who would like to know?" was her not too unpleasant but demanding response.

"My name doesn't matter," I spoke in hushed tones. "I have been referred to you by a mutual acquaintance whose name I cannot divulge. This has to do with resolving your problem with your former husband." I followed my short disclosure with a protracted, almost uncomfortable, long pause.

"I'm not sure what you're talking about," she replied. She had to be cagey, but it was definitely a positive sign that she didn't dismiss my call out of hand.

"Your former husband has caused you grief and sorrow you have not deserved," I continued in my hushed tone. "Eliminating that from your life could relieve a great deal of stress."

"Yes, but I don't know who you are," she continued, hedging. "I cannot discuss anything to do with my former husband without some references or some knowledge of who you are." She became hesitant; but she definitely had some interest or she would have hung up by now.

"Elisabeth—I hope you don't mind my calling you Elisabeth—if you think about it, it's best for both of us if you don't know who I am." I launched into my sales pitch. "Should something befall your husband, the police would certainly suspect you. Any ties they can make between you and me would disclose our arrangements. Therefore, it is best that you do not know who I am." My logical explanation was followed by a long pause.

"Perhaps you would like some time to think about this situation." I intended to hang up.

"Wait." Some excitement became evident in her voice. I waited. "I guess what you say makes sense, but I'm afraid of being trapped by the police. You understand?" She remained reluctant.

"Elisabeth"—something began to gel—"the police or any law enforcement agency cannot phone you with such a proposition and expect you to agree to it since it would be entrapment. Entrapment is specifically against the law; no law enforcement organization in the country uses it."

"You know, you're right." Her voice changed and became pleasant and excited. "Can I think about it and phone you back?" she asked.

"You won't be able to contact me, but I will give you two days to consider the offer," I said, exercising caution on my part. "I will phone you back at this time in two days. And, Elisabeth, be warned, do not contact any law enforcement agency, as it could jeopardize your life," I concluded.

"Okay, I'll hear from you in two days. And don't worry, the local law enforcement and I do not get along. I look forward to hearing from you." She hung up.

Well, things evidently were coming together almost to plan. Could it possibly be this easy? Only time would tell. For the next two days, I familiarized myself with the Cleveland area. Being late fall, the leaves were turning their autumn colors, especially in the surrounding country. The soft breeze came off Lake Erie, a cold blow, but steady and refreshing.

To further pass my time, I tried one of the more upscale hotels, first buttonholing a bell captain to see if there might be any local girls of interest. He gave me a phone number as I checked in. Later that evening, I phoned the number he had given me; a sultry female voice announced herself as Sandra. Explaining that I had come to Cleveland on a business matter and the bell captain at the hotel had provided me with her number elicited a kind of purring.

"Yes. When would you like me to come by?"

"Anytime that's convenient for you," I answered.

"Okay, see you about seven." She hung up.

At quarter to seven, I went to a little lounge area just down the hall from my room, an area that provided a clear view of the door to my room. At seven, a very shapely and attractive brunette stepped off the elevator. She walked to my room and knocked. I hurried down the hallway to meet her.

"Hi. Sorry I was out for a few minutes, please come in." Without a doubt this girl, woman, had to be one of the most beautiful in Cleveland and probably within a fifty-mile radius.

Once in the room, she asked. "What would you like from me?" What a lead-in.

"I think just a little hugging and kissing and some nice warm sex," I said, tripping over my words.

"You're kind of new at this, aren't you?" she asked. I nodded in agreement, not knowing what words to choose and afraid that if I opened my mouth only mumble jumble would come spilling out.

"I'll just go in the bathroom and freshen up." She motioned toward the still made-up bed. "Why don't you get undressed and hop into bed and be all ready for me." Who would argue with such a beauty, especially with all kinds of sexual fantasies filling my head? Besides, a very obvious bulge began to appear in my pants.

I undressed and hopped into bed, pulling the sheet over me. When Sandra emerged from the bathroom, she had on a negligee and, of course, appeared as an absolutely gorgeous goddess of love.

Christ, I'm getting over stimulated, I thought. Not good to drop a load even before she got into the bed.

"You really are new to this," she laughed. "Why are you covered with a sheet; are you ashamed to show me something?"

Needless to say, I was embarrassed. I threw the sheet off me. My body could use some shaping up, but I still maintained a pretty good firmness for someone my age. Right at this point, I had to concentrate on reducing my sexual excitement, or as soon as Sandra touched my erect organ there would be an enormous volcanic eruption.

Sandra hopped into bed, and we began to kiss and caress. This would be my first sex since the divorce, the divorce initiated by Janet. The sex proved to be very pleasurable and somewhat fulfilling but lacked the intimacy of a true, loving relationship. Surprisingly, it all came to an end by eight forty-five. Sandra received two hundred dollars, which seemed a lot, but what more could I ask for?

After Sandra left, I showered, dressed, and got in my car. Driving East on Interstate 80 to Interstate 86, and exiting at Jamestown, New York, I found a shopping mall situated near the exit. A Radio Shack located in the mall provided four more pay-as-you-go cell phones. The additional phones would prevent any repercussions in the event that law enforcement checked Elisabeth's phone records. On two of the phones, the clerk, a sharp, technical individual, set up business accounts with 866 numbers. Should law enforcement ask Elisabeth about the phone calls, she could claim they were unsolicited sales calls.

Returning to the hotel, I rewarded myself with a good movie and a couple of shots from the minibar. Sleeping late in the morning didn't present a problem, since I had no plans for the day. This time I headed West on Interstate 90 toward Toledo, Ohio, where I could spend some time relaxing before phoning Elisabeth. At the appointed time, I called her using one of the cell phones purchased in Jamestown. She must have been sitting by the phone, as the first ring had not even finished when she picked up the receiver.

"Hello," she spoke softly but with noticeable excitement into the receiver.

"Hi, this is the assassin, but you can call me Bill," I replied.

"I've been waiting for your call. I'm sorry; I am so excited," which her breathing made quite obvious. "I have to calm down, give me a minute." She had been breathing into the receiver in short gasps. As she calmed down somewhat, her breathing became steady.

"This situation with my former asshole husband, excuse me," she began, "completely occupies all of my waking minutes and most of my nightly nightmares." Her extreme bitterness toward her former husband was evident in every word she virtually spat into the phone.

The situation with her husband had indeed occupied her time and continued to depress her, and she went into great detail.

"For eight years, I supported that son of a bitch while he was pursuing his medical degree. During that time, whenever he got frustrated he would drink and end up using me as a punching bag. I don't know why I stayed with him. Once he had his medical degree he continued to struggle to find a hospital he could intern with. In his frustration, he would get drunk, come home to our shabby little apartment, beat the shit out of me, and rape me.

"The only positive result from that difficult marriage was two wonderful children. We did nothing together, nothing as a family, but at least I have memories with the children. Gerald and I never did anything memorable.

"I don't think we were ever in love, not at least in the passionate way most young couples seem to start their marriage. Directly out of college Gerald interned at Cleveland General and was always at the hospital, only occasionally coming home—mostly to abuse me. He was never happy with my homemaking; nothing pleased him.

"There was no question of his brilliance. After finishing his internship, he was invited to join one of the more successful medical organizations in Cleveland. It didn't take long for him to become president of the firm. Once he became successful, the first thing he did was to take up with a young secretary in his office.

"We had joined a country club, not to relax and enjoy the socializing, but so Gerald could make contacts with the political power structure of Cleveland. Ultimately, Gerald formed his own company, designing and manufacturing medical equipment based on his concepts. I devoted all my time to working shoulder to shoulder with him, helping to build the business. I attended to the administrative necessities, so he could concentrate on the design.

"But the designs, prototypes, and production of the equipment were not all Gerald's; my software training and experience, not to mention my efforts in obtaining all the legal requirements and patents, equally contributed to the success of the company.

"Once the company was up and running successfully, I devoted my time to the home, raising our two children and making a comfortable, attractive home so Gerald could entertain associates and twist arms for programs he had a special financial interest in.

"I tolerated his abuse and his womanizing, and then he decided to dump me—and instead of sharing his wealth, wealth I helped him acquire, he virtually cut me off with only a small percentage of his net worth. To top things off, he manipulated the judicial system using his contacts and cronies. You bet, I am stressed.

"Since you contacted me, I think you are right in saying it would be entrapment if you were, in fact, from law enforcement. That being said, I am prepared to offer you one hundred thousand dollars to take care of the situation for me, is that enough?" She seemed hesitant, hoping she had hit on the right number.

"That is an agreeable number," I said, my voice calm. Christ, it was twice what I had expected. "However, any payment you make to me cannot be traced to either of us, do you understand?"

"I have set aside that sum of money for emergencies." Her words became matter-of-fact, and she sounded comfortable discussing the elimination of her ex-husband. "It's all in cash, unmarked bills, hundreds." Her excitement continued to show as she again took very short and erratic breaths. "I just never thought this would come to fruition. Now you, out of the blue, like a white knight, have come to my salvation. I am too hopeful, just feeling that everything is a mirage." She remained breathless.

"I will phone you tomorrow night at this time and give you information on how to transfer half the funds. The balance can be arranged at the completion of the contract." An exchange that was not directly linked to me had to be established. "Also, write down every idiosyncrasy you can think of about your ex-husband." I needed definitive information on the good doctor's movements, to know what his weakest point might be. "Any time he might be alone outside of his home, not anywhere in Cleveland. If he takes walks in the morning or evening, anything you can think of that isolates him. Okay?"

"Yes, I understand, and I will prepare a written dossier on Gerald." She willingly followed my instructions. "I know quite a bit about him that will surely help you. And thank you for coming to my salvation; I don't know what would have happened to me without you. I just hope and pray you are real," she said, still breathing erratically into the phone.

"I will talk to you tomorrow." I hung up, drove back to the upscale hotel, and took the phone into the bathroom, smashed it into a million little pieces, and flushed them down the toilet. I stood there watching every little piece swirl down the drain. Could it be this easy? In a few days, I could be dead. In the Marines, every time we were engaged in combat and things seemed to be going too easy was when everything went wrong. As they say, "Caution is the better part of valor." Just slow down and check every detail.

A detailed checklist of necessities. I wrote down every step, everything I could think of, anything or anyone that could jeopardize this mission. What else hadn't I thought of? A big, open—what? The list ended up being three pages long and in great detail. It took me more than four hours, and when it was finished, I slept on it.

The next morning I packed everything up, checked out, hopped into my smooth-running Toyota, and headed back to the no-tell motel. This was an exceptionally beautiful day: bright and sunny day, a purely lazy day, definitely a day where nothing could go wrong. Well, almost nothing. When I got to my room at the motel, the door stood open, and several people were wandering around inside.

"What the fuck is going on here?" I demanded to know.

Everyone looked up, startled.

"Ah, well, you didn't come back last night, and we thought maybe you skipped out on the bill." I recognized the desk clerk.

"Goddamn it, I paid up to the end of the week. Don't you keep any records?" I scolded him.

"Sorry, man. You know, people skip out all the time without checking out or paying their bills. Okay, guys, everyone out," he instructed the others.

After they left, a careful inventory of my clothes was necessary. Everything seemed to be there. Fortunately for me, my rifle, pistol, scopes, silencers, and ammo were all locked safely in the trunk of my car. Also, the cell phones were all in the glove compartment, except of course the ones I had used and destroyed.

I had left nothing in the room that could suggest illegal activity, but I moved most of my stuff to the car, just to be marginally safer. In this neighborhood, could anything be safe? The car had an alarm system, and it was parked right outside my window.

That evening, I decided to dress up and go out on the town to relax my nerves, unwind, and maybe have an early celebration. It could be my last celebration of anything, except getting out of prison.

Let the chips fall where they may, came to mind. Cleveland had some really nice restaurants, including a few exceptional steak houses. A rare filet mignon with a vintage bottle of wine satisfied my lust for an exceptional meal. I followed my gourmet overindulgence with an excellent cigar.

The next day, I looked up a mailbox service center located in downtown Cleveland. At the center, I contracted two large mailboxes for a month. Once I provided the clerk with all the necessary (and fraudulent) information, I asked if he could do me a personal favor. He agreed, provided it wasn't illegal or anything unethical, whatever that meant. Being assured nothing illegal or unethical would transpire from my request, he agreed to move any item coming into the first mailbox automatically to the second mailbox. Once he had agreed, I tipped him twenty bucks with a commitment for twenty more at the conclusion of the project.

The reason for doing this had two purposes. First, to determine if Elisabeth was being followed, and second, to determine if she was being straight with me, for if she was cooperating with the authorities, they would be watching box number one and not number two. I planned on parking nearby so I could keep an eye out for what might be unusual activity around the mailbox place. If some law enforcement types should show up, I could observe them. In any event, it would leave me free and clear to either leave town or complete the contract.

At six o'clock sharp, from a fifty-mile-distant location west of Cleveland, the call went to Elizabeth with instructions to deposit the money in a plain brown package, along with the dossier, into box one at the mailbox store. I gave her the address. She said she had everything ready and would leave right away for the mailbox store, which sounded good to me.

An hour and forty-five minutes later, Elizabeth showed up with the package and an envelope in her hands. I knew what she looked like after going through multiple pictures of her during my research. She entered the mailbox store, remained inside about two minutes, and then got into a Mercedes-Benz and drove away. For the next three hours, I watched the street to see if any suspicious vehicles showed up. None did. Several other people went in and out of the store, but nothing suspicious happened. The store closed at eleven at night. At ten minutes before eleven, I got out of the car and walked to the store. Only the clerk was inside. He nodded as I entered. Going directly to box number two, I removed the package and the envelope, tipped the clerk another twenty dollars, and returned to my car.

Sitting there for several more hours was necessary to determine if anyone had followed me. Additionally, being extremely careful in accordance with my checklist, the package had to be opened and sorted through to determine if any marked bills were present. A small black-light (ultraviolet) pen had been purchased specifically for this purpose. No marked bills were found. In addition, the package had to be checked for any tracking devices. An electronic instrument, purchased along with the black light, would detect any electronic tracking devices hidden in the packs of one hundred dollar bills. Nothing suspicious turned up in any of the fifty packages or in the package containing the dossier. Breathing a heavy sigh of relief, I started the car and headed back to the motel.

The dossier that Elisabeth provided obviously had been painstakingly composed, given the extensive detail given on Dr. Able. The twenty-first page of the fifty-page profile indicated there was a dirt track, or ATV track, that ran for several miles from behind Gerald's home to the park. Most mornings, according to Elisabeth, Gerald jogged along this path.

The next morning I moved my base of operations. Things were getting a little too unsettled here. After all, this section of the city didn't particularly make one feel safe and secure, especially when storing fifty thousand dollars in the trunk of a car. Going to a local bank and checking out a safety-deposit box certainly wasn't the best approach either. Loading the car and checking out, with an intention of moving to a safer section of the city, only took an hour or so.

Leaving the car in a secure garage in downtown Cleveland, I took a bus to the park in Lakewood, a travel time of two hours and twenty minutes. Exiting the bus at the park, I strolled through the park to the shore of Lake Erie, just to be sure no one would check my residency and ask me to leave the park. Although there were numerous people in the park, some dressed in coveralls who were assumed to be Lakewood employees, none asked for proof of residency. To assure myself that at some point I wouldn't be accosted by someone in authority, I initiated conversations with several of the coverall people—conversations about the location of the men's room or if there was a lifeguard on duty. No one asked for proof of residency, and I guessed I was home safe.

Sitting on a bench, looking out, Lake Erie reminded me of the Atlantic Ocean, a truly magnificent sight, especially for someone who has never seen one the Great Lakes. The water, unfortunately, had a dirty, greenish-brown color, with the waves rolling in on a dark, sandy beach. In comparison to the clear aqua blue waves that rolled in along the Florida coast, this reminded me of the articles I read some years ago about the polluting of the Great Lakes—how sad.

After sitting for several hours, I walked along the shore toward Gerald's house to see if the ATV trail Elizabeth wrote about could be located. At the East end of the park, a two-track trail emerged from the woods entering into the park through two old wooden posts. Undoubtedly, this was the trail she had alluded to. So as not to raise any suspicions, I walked back to the bus stop and boarded the bus back to Cleveland.

After locating and settling into a new, more luxurious motel, I began to lay out a plan. From Gerald's estate to the park covered approximately two and half miles. From the main road to the ATV trail and to Dr. Able's house included close to six square miles of good, heavy undergrowth and woods, ideal for concealment. The area needed to be reconnoitered before a definite plan could be laid out in any detail, and, as assuredly as a royal flush beats all, the area had to be patrolled at night. Since my car could not be left anywhere in or near the park, the only option was the bus.

Taking the last bus out dropped me at the park about eleven thirty that evening. The moonless, pitch-black night offered an element of security, but falling and breaking a bone just didn't sit well with the mission or with me. I could not use a light of any type, except for that on the GPS. The GPS provided the only reference to my topographic position in the woods.

After my eyesight adjusted to the darkness, I made my way down to the shore and the ATV trail. A night-vision scope made things a lot easier. Following the ATV trail to where it went behind Gerald's property and laying out every detail on a notepad took me several hours. There were several spots that would be ideal for hides, and carefully selecting the right one was paramount to the success of this mission.

Another several hours were devoted to thoroughly envisioning the target from each of the possible hides. A selective process of elimination helped me choose a hide nearly midway between Gerald's property and the park. The hide would be about three hundred feet in from the ATV trail and just elevated enough to provide excellent surveillance of the trail and the surrounding area. All the information was carefully recorded on the GPS so it could be recalled as needed.

Deciding the first bus back might raise some suspicions, I waited until the snack bar got busy. As park employees and park visitors started to order breakfast meals, I ordered an egg sandwich and coffee. I sat at one of the picnic tables and enjoyed the meal, which hit the spot, especially after sleeping in the woods with the mosquitoes and ticks. An odorless repellent had helped, but a few welts were materializing on various parts of my anatomy. Unfortunately, some of the welts occurred in areas that could not be scratched in public.

The bus ride back to Cleveland took more than two and a half hours, with the bus dropping me two blocks from my new motel. The neighborhood here proved to be much better than the no-tell motel's neighborhood, especially in that no seedy-looking characters were hanging about. My mind kept racing over all the things that could go wrong. Despite thorough, careful planning and attempting to think of every detail, something always cropped up unexpectedly.

At the motel, I retrieved the equipment from the car. Taking everything to my room, I began to pack in preparation for my first contract. Was I really going through with this? Could there be some trepidation? No, the decision had been made; the first contract would be fulfilled. That had to be my mindset—no further thoughts, period.

The Springfield rifle could be broken down into three sections so that the total length ended up as twenty inches. It would easily fit into the canvas gym bag that I had purchased for the occasion. Emphasis was placed on going over the checklist again and again to ensure everything had been accounted for and properly packed and every movement had been considered in detail. Staying totally focused on the checklist presented problems in itself. Such a focus could result in my missing some simple item, failure to observe an obstacle—any number of details that could totally jeopardize the plan.

At the car, I stored the canvas bag in the trunk, got in, and drove to Lakewood Park. Just before the park, a heavily wooded area previously marked on the GPS provided an ideal hiding place for the canvas bag. At night, I had found this area to be very quiet, nothing moving and no sounds except for the soulful cries of birds, toads, and other night creatures. Again, no moon, so the woods were pitch black. Reluctantly, a flashlight had to be employed to assist in the concealment of the gym bag.

There also had to be some obvious locator on the GPS so the next night the canvas bag could be found without any difficulty. I was able to triangulate the position using two telephone poles and a road marker; these would be a backup to the GPS reading.

The drive back to the motel proved kind of foreboding, particularly when passing Gerald Able's estate. A few lights were on, but all appeared to be peaceful. In that house lived a man whose life I was about to take. If Elisabeth's story and description of her former husband, Dr. Gerald Able was, for the most part, the truth, perhaps this person, at least in Elisabeth's eyes, deserved to die. No further thoughts of this individual, whether he deserved to die or not, occupied my deliberations. *No personal involvement*—a cardinal rule that I had to follow for the rest of my career, my career as an assassin, in order to be successful as a hired hit man.

The next morning, a nice late breakfast before taking the bus out to Lakewood Park at least started the day on the right foot. The day passed slowly as I sat by the shore watching the pretty girls in bathing suits go in and out of the water. The temperature for the past few days had been unusually warm. The girls were taking advantage of this extended summer, sunning themselves on colorful blankets, laughing, and enjoying each other's company. A day and a scene of life as it should be.

For me, it was a very relaxing day, but a day that would digress into a night that would change my life forever. By this time tomorrow, truth be told, I would be a much different person. What would tomorrow bring, a jail cell or a new life? There could be no doubt about what was being undertaken.

Chapter 8

Finding the canvas gym bag was not a problem, because the triangulation along with the GPS positioning worked out perfectly. The hide had been triangulated too, but was deeper in the woods, about a two-mile hike from the gym bag. The hide took more than three hours to reach. Once there, preparations were made to ensure I had judiciously readied all the equipment to complete the contract. I assembled the rifle, loaded it, and checked it out. Water and provisions were set nearby in the hide to be certain they were readily available without much motion on my part. The ghillie suit was prepared and put on. I crawled into the hide and waited for morning light, lightly dosing through the remainder of the night and early morning.

At about six thirty-three in the morning, a jogger came down the road from the direction of Gerald's estate. Watching closely through the scope, I could easily identify him as Dr. Gerald Able, soon to be my first victim of a contract killing. It seemed so cold, looking at things in that perspective, but at some point I had to be honest with myself. I waited and watched as he passed, checking his image with a recent picture Elisabeth had provided. About a half hour to forty-five minutes later, he reappeared, jogging in the opposite direction. Again, caution was the best approach. Be absolutely sure of the target, and make absolutely certain no other human activity occurred in the area. Not a sound could be heard except for birds and squirrels chirping and chattering.

I lay in the hide throughout the day, periodically checking the surrounding area for any human activity. Nothing happened of any note. Night fell, casting a dark shroud over the wooded area. Through the night I slept, waking every half hour or so to again check my surroundings for any evidence of human activity. Nothing occurred within earshot; all remained quiet except for the occasion chatters or chirps of wildlife. The next day, Gerald took his morning jog past the hide, again returning about a half hour later from the other direction. Once again, no other human activity developed during that day or the following night. *All is ready*, I thought.

The next morning at six thirty, there came Gerald, jogging toward me. I waited, riflescope sighted on his forehead. He came closer, no problem, like taking candy from a baby. Slowly, *deep breath, let half out, crosshairs on target—*

Then, panting close to the right side, what the hell could that be? Then, digging to my right, a damn dog began to dig into my hide. In my right-side hip pocket, I had a small plastic water pistol with ammonia that had become part of my equipment since the episode with the goat in Afghanistan.

"Maggie, get over here," I heard shouted off to my right.

"Hey, Jair, is that you?" came another shout.

"Yeah, Paul, what's up?" coming from Gerald as he stopped his morning run to look over to his friend or acquaintance.

"Sorry to interrupt your run, just a quick question." Paul, or whoever he was, walked over toward Gerald, with Maggie at his heel.

Their muffled conversation could not be heard from my hide. After ten or fifteen minutes, Paul turned and said something about Maggie finding something in the woods that needed investigating. Shit, I thought, this presented a possibility of my being discovered. Maggie began to trot in my direction. I zeroed in the riflescope on Gerald's head, and squeezed off a round, hitting him flush on the forehead. Gerald did not bounce or make a sound; he just fell in place on the trail where he had been standing.

The silencer did its work; not the slightest sign that Paul heard anything. Maggie, however, stopped for a few moments and glanced around to see if her master had noticed anything.

"What's the matter ole girl, a squirrel outfox you?" Paul said, directing the comments to his dog.

I moved the riflescope onto Paul's forehead, and within seconds of the first shot that had killed Gerald, Paul dropped to the forest floor. Maggie again stopped and looked over at her master. My final shot killed Maggie, a decision made almost in a vacuum. Leave no traces, no witnesses, regardless of who they might be. Maggie would have stayed by her master until I emerged from the hide. At that point, she would have either attacked me or started to raise hell attracting someone's attention, a risk that could not be taken.

I left the hide and checked the area completely, using my 20x and an infrared scope. Nothing, no one anywhere near. I dragged Gerald's body off to the opposite side of the road and covered it with brush. From there, Maggie and Paul were concealed in the hide I had vacated. My mission could not be completed until I made it safely back to Cleveland—or, actually, out of Cleveland.

Using the GPS, I started the trek south toward the main road, the road going into Lakewood Park, about three and a half miles distant. After hiking roughly two miles, I began to look up into the trees, wanting to find two trees growing closely together. It took me fifteen minutes to spot trees situated close enough together for my purpose. From the base of the first tree, I set off in a southerly direction toward the main road. A half mile from the base of the tree there was an old logging trail now used as an ATV trail by locals. At the trail, I turned, and using the GPS, retraced exactly my steps back to the base of the tree I had previously selected.

At the base of the tree, I urinated. Next, a rope, which had been packed in with my equipment, was produced from a side pocket of my backpack and looped over a strong, low-lying limb. Careful not to damage the bark and not to drop any of my equipment, I climbed the tree. Once up in the tree I jumped to a strong limb in the adjoining tree. The limb cracked but held long enough for me to crawl to the trunk of the tree. Employing this method of going tree to tree, and using the GPS, I traveled more than three hundred yards without ever touching the ground.

Dropping to the ground near a clearing, I spent a few minutes packing all my equipment into the canvas bag. Again using the GPS, the location I previously used as a drop-off point for the canvas bag was located, and the canvas bag safely hidden away. A brisk walk to the park and a two-and-a-half-hour ride back to the motel on the bus, relieved some of my stress. At the motel, I got my car from the garage and drove it back to the wooded area where the canvas gym bag had been hidden. The road here was quite straight and any traffic or any individual coming from either direction could easily be seen. I quickly grabbed the bag, put it in the trunk, and drove back to the motel.

At the motel, once the car had been securely parked in the garage, I opened the little food and beverage cabinet in my room and poured myself a good belt of whiskey. It really didn't matter what kind of whiskey I drank, it gave a warm, reassuring feeling as it passed down my esophagus into my stomach, seemingly settling my jangled nerves. It's funny; the two guys didn't bother me as much as Maggie. Just a really nice dog that happened to be a little curious and as a result got her and her master killed. The killing of Maggie proved very troubling and continued to bother me until I fell asleep at two or three in the morning.

There is a small element of the population that finds personal pleasure and excitement in taking the life of another; serial killers immediately come to mind. Even my stint in the Marine Corps exposed me to individuals who essentially salivated at the prospect of going to war and killing. I am not one of these people; killing under any circumstance bothers me. Have I, by chance, chosen the correct profession?

Elisabeth had arranged to be away for several weeks visiting some friends in California. She had provided me with her friend's phone number in the event that she had to be contacted. The next evening, I randomly drove some sixty miles west of Cleveland, and then using one of the phones purchased in Jamestown, New York, I called her at her friend's.

"Is Elisabeth Able there?" I asked.

"Just a moment please," was the reply from a soft female voice on the other end of the phone.

"Hello." Definitely Elisabeth.

"Your contract has been fulfilled," I stated, without any emotion. Again, a long pause, and almost a sob came in reply.

"Thank you." I could hear the relief in her voice. "I can't thank you enough. I can't believe how much of a relief it is to hear that at last that bastard has paid the price. Thank you, from the bottom of my heart. I want to give you a bonus." Elisabeth seemed overjoyed.

"It's not necessary; the compensation for the completion of the contract is more than sufficient. Leave the balance at the same location as the first payment. That will conclude any contact you have with me. Stay at your friend's for another few weeks before you come home. The police undoubtedly will want to question you. No more contact. I must say goodbye." I had to be emphatic.

"Okay," she replied, and Elisabeth left my life forever.

Staying in Cleveland could prove beneficial, just to see if any news popped up. I didn't have to wait long. Two days later, on the evening news, there it was, two men and their dog found shot to death in Lakewood. They were described as a prominent local physician and a land speculator. The police were questioning anyone who happened to be in the area, but as of yet, had no leads.

The story continued, saying that the doctor had been the focus of the local media before regarding his involvement in an acrimonious divorce a few years ago. During the divorce, his former wife had attempted to run him off the road, and on another occasion she was discovered on the doctor's estate carrying a pistol. His former wife, Elisabeth, was a person of interest; however, she was currently out of town, visiting friends in California. Police had requested her immediate return, which she had agreed to.

The other individual, a Paul McCarthy, had a home close to Dr. Able's estate in the very upscale Clifton Park section of Lakewood. Both were recently divorced and remarried to younger women. They were known to be close associates in some land speculation. Mr. McCarthy had been taken to court on a number of occasions by disgruntled investors, but he had always won. Updates would be provided on any new developments in the deaths of the two men.

Well, had my first contract been accomplished without any trace to me? Without a doubt, law enforcement would be combing those woods with every technical device available to them. Bloodhounds would be the best, oldest, and most reliable method of searching for a lead. Hopefully, my little ruse of going from tree to tree would undermine the capabilities of the dogs.

The next few days brought no new news; authorities were still searching the wooded area where the bodies had been found. Elisabeth had been questioned but was no longer considered a suspect since nothing had been discovered tying her to the crime. The bloodhounds had tracked what possibly might be the killer or killers' trail, from the site of the killing to an ATV trail nearby in the wooded area.

At this point, I started to consider packing it up and heading out of town, but the last night brought some welcome news. Paul McCarthy had been a heavy gambler, and investigating detectives found he had some serious gambling debts, to local mob characters as well as online gambling casinos. The police now considered the killings to be enforcement by underworld contract killers. To further these current findings, the police were looking into his creditors. Dr. Gerald Able was now considered to be a person who happened to be in the wrong place at the wrong time. It looked like Elisabeth and I had lucked out.

I had to conclude my business in Cleveland; I packed everything into the car and prepared to leave. The last item on my list was to close the two mailboxes. At the mailbox facility, I checked the boxes before closing them out. A different service clerk was on duty so he did not recognize me. As expected, the first box had nothing in it; the second had the package supposedly containing my final payment; however, the package was much larger than expected, plus a letter addressed to "Bill" was in the box.

Christ, now what? I thought. There had to be a mistake. Removing the package and letter, it was evident these were intended for me, as the package had been addressed to "Bill in box number one."

Shit, I thought to myself. If Elisabeth dropped off the package and letter, she might have been followed. I stuffed them under my jacket and informed the clerk that the two mailboxes would no longer be needed.

I set the package and letter on the passenger seat, started the car, and left Cleveland. Being extremely sensitive to the possibility of being followed, I drove around in a large circle, constantly watching the traffic behind me. Of course, if the package had a tracking device, driving around would do me no good. The sensing instrument used to determine if a tracking device was in the package was packed in the trunk of the car. Eventually, I saw a motel just off the main highway where I could spend the night and have time to check the package and the letter.

Once settled in the motel room, I used the tracking device sensor from the trunk of my car to scan the package and letter. No indication of any tracking devices. The letter was addressed "Dear Bill," which of course was me. The letter thanked me for my services and indicated that package contained a bonus—which I was more than deserving of, according to Elisabeth. She assured me that the package, the letter, and its contents could not be traced to her. The letter, being nondescript, only referenced Bill, so it could not be traced to the sender or the recipient. She had had a friend's son deliver the package to the mailbox store.

This did not conclude the letter. Elisabeth provided the name and phone number of a close friend of hers who needed the type of service I provided. The situation, however, seemed somewhat different. Her friend, an Alice Goodhue, had made a substantial investment with a person she considered to be a trusted friend. The friend advised the woman that the money had been lost. The loss of her money was attributed to an investment in a local business, a business that subsequently failed.

Alice had no proof of the investment, not even a receipt; she had placed full confidence in the friend. Now, the trusted friend had a life of luxury and extravagance, a lifestyle with a new home, expensive cars, and a membership in an exclusive country club, plus frequent trips to Argentina. Alice had consulted with an attorney who advised her that there being no proof the trusted friend had embezzled any money, he could not be prosecuted or sued. Absolutely nothing legally could be done for Alice; she had lost the money. The enormous stress caused by the situation seriously affected her health.

The package contained one hundred thousand dollars in one hundred dollar bills. Funny, all I could think of was Maggie. The thought of having killed her greatly saddened me. The next day I loaded the car, gassed up, and headed back to Croton.

Chapter 9

A contract referral, could this possibly be so easy? I couldn't allow myself to become complacent; no question the first contract had been a resounding success; however, my guard had to be constantly up. One slip and my little foray into a questionable lifestyle would come to a screeching halt, and I would spend the rest of my life in prison or end up on a cold slab in some pathology lab.

Driving offered me time to reflect and enjoy the scenery. Route 17, West of the Hudson River Valley, is undoubtedly some of the most picturesque land in the country. The highway winds through valleys, rolling hills, small villages, and along small rivers and brooks. The area offers some of the best trout fishing—comparable to that found in the Rocky Mountain states, such as Wyoming and Colorado, to name but two.

Now while I continued my drive down New York Route 17, my mind wandered to a more current and meaningful problem: what I could do with all that money. This would be an absolutely fun problem to solve.

Yet, it still remained a perplexing issue. The money could not be deposited into any bank because of the federal government's policy of tracking amounts over ten thousand dollars, and obviously I couldn't account for the source. There was no logical explanation for me to have that much money. Claiming the money came from some business venture would leave me open to an audit by the IRS, which, believe me, I had no lasting desire to ever deal with. For the time being, the best place for the money would be in a safety-deposit box.

Before going to Croton, the car had to be disposed of. Stopping in Poughkeepsie, New York, I found a small-time used car lot; I sold the car for a very low price, but who cared. Taking a train from Poughkeepsie to Croton provided an opportunity to look out at the Hudson River and across to Storm King Mountain. Some say the view along this part of the river is similar to a cruise on the Blue Danube in Germany. It is spectacular scenery, and every time I either drive along the river, take a boat ride, or take the train, the beauty of the scenery consumes my thoughts—a wistful place to escape to.

Before returning to my home, a safety-deposit box was purchased at the Bank of Ossining where I had my savings and checking account. For now, the money would be safely hidden from any prying eyes. From time to time, I could dip into it for small sums but had to keep them below ten thousand dollars in any one year.

Once I returned to Croton, a short walk from the train station brought me to my apartment. My phone answering system lights flashed indicating the answering capacity had been exceeded, overloaded with messages. Before doing anything else, I needed to listen to the messages. Two were from a job placement firm in New York City. The first came from a placement agency with a possible job offer, the second to inform me that I waited too long to apply for the position. The other ten or so messages were, naturally, from Janet. Where was I? She needed to talk to me but no one knew where I had gone—not my mother or father, not anyone. It sure sounded urgent. The most recent message from Janet came in this morning.

Best to find out what was so urgent, so I dialed Janet's number and let it ring for several minutes before her answering system picked up.

"This is Oscar," I began, "I just took a little trip to Atlantic City to get some of the bugs out of my head. Sorry no one knew where I went, but it didn't seem important to let anyone know. Anyway, I'm home, so if you want to give me a call, wait about a half hour and phone back. I'll be in the shower for about a half hour or so." Hanging up, I headed for the shower.

I turned the shower hot handle up as high as it could be tolerated, hot, but refreshing and very cleansing, which my body definitely needed. Returning to the living room, the light on the telephone voice mail flashed away. I hit the speaker button and then the play button.

"Where in the fuck have you been?" Janet's angry voice came out of the speaker. "We have been trying to reach you for days. Not even your mother or father knew where you were. What fool goes off without letting anyone know where he went? Anyway, it is important you call me back as soon as possible." Slam went the receiver.

Jesus, that could have punctured my ear drum, passed through my mind.

Obviously, Janet had truly missed me, how nice. Should a call be made right away or should I let her cool her fat ass for a little while? What the hell could be so important? Curiosity got the better part of my judgment, so I picked up the phone and phoned Janet back.

She picked up on the first ring. "Oscar, that fucking better be you."

No nice hello-how-are-you or other platitudes? Pausing for a few minutes seemed a good plan, but unfortunately, Janet had other ideas.

"Answer me, you fucking son of a bitch." It was so nice of her to talk about my mother that way.

"Yeah, this is the one and only Oscar"—I spoke pleasantly, so as not to appear aggravated by her anger—"the missing person who everyone is looking for. Notice, notice, all points bulletin for Oscar Wylton, arrest on sight."

"Very fucking funny, where in the fuck have you been?" she demanded to know.

"Left you a message, didn't you listen to it?" I asked.

"Mister Freedom, take off whenever you want, go wherever you want, don't let anyone know." She was definitely on the warpath.

"You know, Janet, for months no one bothers to phone me, ask me how I'm doing, if I'm okay—nothing, not a word. I go away for a couple of weeks, and all hell breaks loose." I started explaining myself; I had no idea why. "To fulfill your needs we get divorced, you get the kids, the house, a new husband, and the business. I get shit. Now all of a sudden you want to know what I'm doing. You know, lady, get fucked, I no longer have to answer to you." I slammed the receiver down.

Not three seconds passed before the phone began to ring. Eight rings seemed sufficient. "Hello, this is Oscar. How may I help you?" Being polite was always the way to answer the phone, you never know who it might be. It even might be a beautiful blonde or brunette phoning to offer me a spectacular date with an evening of unbridled sex, although somehow I doubted that.

"Okay, Oscar, I'm sorry, but we are in a desperate situation here." She sounded frustrated and at loose ends. "Do you remember the manufacturing firm up in Auburn you set up an account for?" she asked pleasantly. What a refreshing change.

"Yes, I remember. Auburn Systems. What's the problem?" I asked, continuing to be my really nice, normal self. I had no trouble remembering this little company, as it was the one where I had the little overnight affair with the receptionist. She had been a remarkably nice piece of ass, as I remember.

"We can't find their files or the contract you signed with them." She now almost pleaded for help.

Tough shit, I thought, expressing my frustrations to myself. "Janet, when I left to go overseas all those files were properly stored on the computer system, with backup hard files in the office filing system." I wanted to be as emphatic as possible. They misplaced them along with God only knows how many other files. That asshole she brought in and married lacked any formal background in computer technology despite his two-year degree in computer science. He certainly had no background in running a business. Why should I bail them out?

"I know, Oscar, but we can't find anything on the computer system or in the hard files." She sounded like she was going to burst into tears. "I hope you can help us find them," now the real pleading. Apparently, someone inadvertently erased those files off the computer system. In addition, the hard copies were probably misfiled in the file cabinets.

"Has Freddy searched the backup hard drives on the servers for the file?" I asked.

"I had our secretary go through all the file cabinets in the office to see if the file had been misfiled. No luck. I asked Fred, not Freddy, to look in all the hard drives. He assures me they aren't in any of them," she explained.

"That is not what I am asking, Janet. Did Freddy, or whatever his name is, search all the hard drives and backup drives for erased files with the name Auburn Systems?" I started to get really annoyed. I put things direct, suspecting Freddy baby didn't have a clue how to search for an erased file on the hard drives or the backup server.

"He said he did. But could you come over and look?" She sounded relieved I would be able to bail them out. "You could spend some time with the kids and maybe take them out for dinner. They would like that." Sounded like the old Janet of bygone years. Payback for my efforts in locating the files. No way, baby, you're going to pay dearly for those files.

"Janet, I'm not going to work for free," now to dropping the other shoe. "To do a file search, which could take me anywhere from an hour to several hours, I want three hundred dollars up front." Surely, that would only be fair for the use of my expertise.

"That sounds high, Oscar." She sounded a little annoyed because they were over a barrel, financially.

"Look, Janet, if you contract an outside firm to do an erased-file search, it will cost you more than a thousand dollars. You're getting off cheap." No bullshit here, just factual information. "If you don't believe me, phone any of the file recovery firms in the yellow pages and see what they quote you."

"I already did that, and yes, they are expensive." Score one for Oscar. "I just thought that this having been your contract, you might take a personal interest in seeing it properly administered." Bullshit comes in all forms, and this one was packaged very nicely, or at least it used to be.

"If you continue to con me, Janet, the price will only go up. At this point, it's last call for three hundred up front dollars." I meant it.

"Okay, okay, I'll cut a check and have it ready when you get here." She gave in.

"Sorry, Janet, three hundred dollars in cash only." I remained adamant.

"Christ, Oscar, what the hell's the difference between a check and cash?" she asked.

"I prefer cash, that's all."

"Okay, I'll have cash for you when you get here," she acquiesced.

"I'm on my way." I hung up. Shit, how did one search for erased files? Looking through my library of computer tech books, I found the one on operating systems and a little refresher jarred my memory.

On the way over, my thoughts turned to my children. Not having seen them in a while inspired some consideration of how I would greet them. Going empty handed was not a good idea. Stopping at a local shopping mall and searching for some nice gifts seemed like a smart thing to do and it wouldn't take long. Images of Maggie began to dominate my thought process. Sure would be nice to show up with a golden retriever puppy. Not a good idea though, without consulting with Janet and, of course, Freddy. Instead, I purchased a couple of DVD movies that the kids would possibly enjoy. If they already had seen my selection, they could exchange them.

The office of Wylton Computer Systems, Inc. was located in a small office park near the Croton-Harmon railroad station. The building, a gray, nondescript, one-story with several small glass windows and a glass door facing a parking lot, had a number of small business located in it. I parked the car in front of the office and walked to the door.

The day was a bright one, with a few wispy clouds floating along in an otherwise clear blue sky. Light breezes blew in off the Hudson River with a slight hint of fall. A day I would have preferred to be sitting out on my deck absorbing the sun and knocking down a few beers while enjoying a vintage cigar, but circumstances dictated otherwise.

Entering the offices of Wylton Computer Systems proved to be a shock. It looked like the place hadn't been cleaned in years. There were books and files piled all over the place, including in the reception area. The receptionist, some young girl with multi-colored hair who chewed gum and slouched in the chair behind the reception desk, obviously wanted to be somewhere else. She seemed to be deeply engrossed in a movie magazine, and my entrance annoyed her.

"What do you need?" was her curt question as I came through the front door.

"I'm here to see Janet," I replied.

"Okay." She turned toward the back of the building.

"Hey, Janet, there's some guy out here to see you," she hollered down the hallway.

"If it's Oscar, send him back to my office, otherwise have whoever it is wait, I'll be out," came Janet's reply, shouted back from down the hallway. Guess the intercom wasn't working, among other things.

"Are you Oscar?" the receptionist asked.

"Yes."

"Okay, then go back down the hall—" I cut her short with a wave of my hand and headed down the hall.

There were stacks of papers, files, books, and all kinds of junk in the hallway leading to Janet's office.

"Hi," I greeted Janet on entering her office.

"Good, you're here. Can't thank you enough for coming and helping us out, even though you are being handsomely paid." She seemed genuinely appreciative.

After pocketing the money, I asked, "Like to get right to work. Where can I access the system?" No time for small talk.

"You can use Fred's office, he is out of town." *Hope he is doing something worthwhile,* I thought.

In Freddy's office, it took me less than a half hour to retrieve the file. The file apparently had inadvertently been erased several months ago. Everything was intact except for the file name, which had been deleted. Not wanting to appear like I hadn't earned my three bills, I spent a little time browsing around some of the company's files that piqued my interest.

Things were far worse than just the junk piled in the hallways and offices. Most of the files were corrupt and definitely not current. The Auburn file hadn't been updated since the time I had been with the company.

Really impressive, I remarked to myself.

After wasting an hour or so in Freddy's office, I informed Janet the file had been retrieved. She thanked me and gave me a key to their house. The kids were in school and would be home around three, which gave me a couple of hours to waste.

The house, originally Janet's and my home, was located in a nice area of the Harmon section of Croton, an excellent area for children. A spacious two-story colonial, it sat on a well-manicured, half-acre lot. Nice and level, well-maintained yard of plush green grass, and neat, clipped shrubbery. A two-car attached garage with a finished room above served as a very comfortable study—a place to escape to when I lived there. In the back, an enormous yard with swings, sand boxes, and a small wading pool was ideal for Emma and David. Just off the house was a covered patio with lounge chairs, picnic table, and my favorite: a large gas-fired charcoal cooker, undoubtedly now Freddy's plaything.

Inside the house, to my surprise and dismay, was a mess equal to, if not exceeding, that of Wylton Computer System's office. Finding anything here or at the office would take a magician with extraordinary skills. What a shame the children had to be raised in this atmosphere, but there was nothing I could do about it.

The kids came home at three and the reunion was one filled with tears of joy, hugs, and kisses galore. Both Emma and David were excited about the DVD movies I had purchased for them and wanted to watch them right away. Instead, we pulled some games out from stacks of junk on the living room bookshelves. It became a game of them versus me, and being a really smart dad, I let them win most of the time.

To my surprise, both of the kids had grown substantially in a little over a month. Emma, a beautiful, blue-eyed girl with blonde hair who loved swirly dresses, stood almost four and half feet. She liked to twirl around so the dresses would swirl out. David liked sports, all kinds of sports, and spent much of his free time watching sporting events on television.

At six o'clock, it was dinnertime, and we needed to select somewhere to go. The kids wanted fast food, what else? Using some adult negotiating skills, we chose a nice family restaurant. During dinner, the kids talked excitedly about school, friends, sports, and projects they were involved in. They talked so fast, they stepped on each other's sentences, and so a lot of what they were saying had to be repeated for clarity. By nine o'clock, they were back home and in the care of their mother. As quickly as possible, I exited the house, avoiding any confrontation with Janet, pleasant or otherwise, and headed to my apartment.

Chapter 10

The next morning after showering, shaving, and eating a light breakfast, I realized that my mail had piled up on the dining room table, unopened. Grabbing a hot cup of coffee and the small mound of accumulated mail, I plopped myself onto my favorite living room chair, fully prepared to assault the junk mail. For the most part, the mail had to be junk, as no one I could think of would be writing to me. A quickly devised method of sorting junk from letters of significance rendered three letters.

The first letter came from the search firm in New York City where I had cancelled the payment of my check. Needless to say, their financial department was irate and extremely threatening, a squad of Texas Rangers backed by Canadian Mounted Police had been dispatched to do justice and ensure full payment would be forthcoming from me immediately. I properly disposed of the letter by tearing it up and throwing it, without ceremony, into the garbage.

The second letter came from my former classmates of Croton-Harmon High School; they would like me to join their group planning a twenty-year reunion. I mean really, there is no way I have been out of high school for twenty years. They must have me confused with someone else. The letter required an acknowledgement; my category fell into one of two classifications: nonresponsive, local deadbeat, or enthusiastic, get-involved participant. The letter, for the time being, went into the perhaps-in-the-future-respond pile.

The final letter came from the apartment management company. The building had been approved by the Town of Croton Planning Commission to be converted into condominiums. As a renter resident, I had first choice of either purchasing my apartment or vacating within the next ninety days. The proviso, they had to know within thirty days. No shit, that left me with less than a week and a half or ten days to decide. The price bordered on gouging—one hundred thirty-three thousand. Most single-family homes in the area were going for less than a hundred thousand.

I still had close to a hundred thousand in my savings, which could be fudged with nine thousand from my little enterprise of killing unsavory characters. Possibly Mom and Dad could lend me the balance plus any closing costs.

Within the week, through all the financial manipulations, loans from my parents, and favors from high school friends who had become successful lawyers, the property was purchased and in my name. At the conclusion of the closing, Mom, Dad, and I went out for a plush dinner, after which I retired to the upper deck of my new home with a Jack Daniels on ice and a vintage cigar.

The next morning, it was time to start planning a new mission. Before contacting Alice Goodhue, Elisabeth's friend, several steps needed to be completed. Once again, a different identity was a necessity, and a new residence had to be registered under the new assumed identity. The best approach for the identity was to borrow one from some down-and-out individual, temporary identity theft. Instead of New York City, which was just too close to home, a different city, Los Angeles, came to mind. I considered LA, just not out of hand, but with the intent of looking up the Ramos family to see how they were doing.

With the decision made, I quickly made arrangements and was on my way.

Skid row in Los Angeles is a run-down, six-block area around the LA mission on the East side of the city. Finding a likely candidate for identity theft, as that is what it is, was a difficult venture. I spent several weeks on the streets, sleeping in local parks, and getting mugged and beat up on numerous occasions. I had just about had it, ready to give up and pack it in, when I made a friend one night at the LA Mission. John Murdock, in his previous life, had been a successful talent agent but had involved himself in drugs. First, he became addicted and then began selling to support his habit. Fortunately, he had no family or close relatives to carry around as extra baggage, which left him pretty much a loner.

Making up a story similar to John's tale of woe won him over, and we soon became close associates. Hanging out with John did not present an opportunity to breach the subject of his social security number. Each time I brought the subject up, John quickly changed it to something else. Finally, one day we took a journey up to MacArthur Park, located in a predominately Hispanic section of LA. On the way, we purchased a six-pack of cheap beer and sat under a tree to consume it.

After several hours of drinking and talking, John said he had to take a leak. Urinating in public is not a good idea. There are several public restrooms in the park; however, John explained that going into one with any money on you was very risky. He asked me to hold his wallet while he went to take a leak, which I agreed to do. Jonathon C. Murdock was the name on the social security card. I wrote down the name and number and returned the card to his wallet just as he emerged from the restroom.

"Any problem?" I asked.

"None, no one in there," John replied.

Handing him my wallet minus any identification, I went into the men's restroom. A couple of Hispanics followed me in and were talking about something in Spanish. After I finished urinating into a smelly toilet, I turned to leave. One of the guys blocked the doorway, and getting past him was impossible without pushing him aside. He had his hands in his pockets, probably on a knife, so shoving him would result in an unwanted response. No question in my mind as to what these two had in mind for me. The single element on my side that could save my ass was surprise. They had no idea what I would or could do, so a little execution of my defense mechanism worked flawlessly. A beautiful sucker-punch clocked the door-blocker, and I quickly exited before either one of them could react.

Once outside, I grabbed John and headed to the subway just south of the park. I filled John in on the events in the men's room and our need to leave the area as quickly as possible. We hopped on the subway and headed south to the LA Mission and the questionable safety of our fellow homeless acquaintances.

Hanging out with John for a while longer possibly would moderate any suspicions of my true purpose in befriending him. Several weeks were spent in John's company, sleeping in the LA Mission and hanging out on the streets, drinking beer during the day and, in general, just being a bum. This activity caused me to neglect my body; once I was back in New York, a good exercise regimen would be necessary to get back in shape.

Leaving John was a sad event. He had become somewhat attached and valued my friendship. When initially informed of my plans to leave, he almost turned to tears. What a wonderful friendship we had established, such a close compatibility is extremely rare. To soften our separation, I explained pressing family matters had to be attended to and possibly once finished, I would return.

Before returning to New York, I had to establish a local address in order to apply for and receive a California driver's license. A sleazebag hotel on the East side of Los Angeles would serve as a temporary place of residence. There was no problem there, as slipping the proprietor a twenty assured me he would state to anyone calling that I had lived there for the past five years.

At one of Los Angeles's motor vehicle departments, applying for and receiving a valid driver's license, took all of an hour and a half. I even had my clean-shaven face on the ID. The only problem was the date of issue. A sharp individual in the New York Department of Motor Vehicles would notice the date and wonder about the sudden relocation to New York.

In the seamier areas of LA, there are any number of shifty characters who make a living producing counterfeit credentials. Locating one proved to be less of a challenge than anticipated. Within half a day, I had a new driver's license with my picture and all necessary information, including a new issue date five years prior to the original date of issue.

Before returning to Croton, I had a little business to take care of, something I had promised myself several years ago. That little business was to visit Sergeant Ramos's family in Santa Ana. Santa Ana is a sprawling city about thirty miles south of Los Angeles and situated in Orange County, a rather affluent California county. Newport Beach, Laguna Beach, San Clemente, Irvine, Anaheim, and San Juan Capistrano are some of the larger cities situated in this county. Newport Beach is viewed as one of the most affluent cities in the country.

The Ramos's house was located in what appeared to be a nice residential neighborhood of mostly small one-story stucco homes. For the most part the homes were well maintained, with clipped hedges and green, cut lawns. The Ramos's house, a one story with a small porch on the front, with several chairs placed on it so one could relax and watch any activity on the street, appeared to be a well-kept home.

Mrs. Elaina Ramos and her daughter, Raquel Ramos, were expecting me and sat waiting on the porch of the home. As I walked up, they stood to greet me. The meeting was a very emotional one—for Elaina Ramos in particular, given the fact that I had been the last person to see her son alive. She hugged me and thanked me for taking the time to come by and see them.

"I hope you can stay for a little while and talk with us, maybe have dinner with us," Elaina said in almost a whisper.

She was a short woman—she only came up to my shoulders—and was attractive, probably in her early-to-mid-fifties. Elaina wore her dark, gray-speckled hair short and brushed back on the sides. Her appearance and mannerism made me feel comfortable right away. She wore a long, neat, colorfully patterned housedress, buttoned fully to the neck.

Raquel almost immediately caught my eye and imagination for all the wrong reasons. A stunning beauty, much more than anything I had anticipated, anything my sick mind could conjure up. I stood momentarily affixed on her beauty and had to emotionally suppress my sexual thoughts, thoughts that had instinctively swamped my pea brain. All I needed was for my johnson to become erect and produce a very evident lump in the front of my pants. In addition to the front of my pants sticking out, she would surely feel my hard, throbbing dick pressed against her stomach when we did a little introductory embrace. She had short, black hair, piercing dark eyes, and a body and face *Playboy* magazine would die for. I just had to be sure my drooling wasn't too evident. Raquel wore an attractive light-colored skirt, which had been tastily selected, being just tight enough to show off her striking figure. She had on an off-white blouse, buttoned to slightly above her breasts to give a small peek of her cleavage. Tony, my friend, you have one gorgeous, younger sister.

"Please come in where it is a little cooler," Raquel said.

I followed them in and found a very pleasant and cool living room. Most of the furniture appeared to be new and carefully selected. The patterns were a medium to light tan. The drapes around the windows had colorful, matching patterns. Each window had a Venetian blind that could be closed at night to discourage any peeping toms. I sat on the couch next to Raquel, and Elaina sat in one of the cushioned chairs facing us.

"Can you tell us a little bit about Anthony?" Elaine asked with a very soulful tone. "I know it has been a while, but any news you can provide will be greatly appreciated."

Looking over at a small fireplace, situated on the wall opposite where Raquel and I sat, slightly off to the right of Elaine, I noticed several pictures on the mantel and a large wooden cross just above them.

I embellished a tale of my association with Elaina's son, Anthony. The situation as it existed in Sarajevo at that time, I explained in detail, including why we were there and what we had accomplished. It became evident that Elaina must be a devoted Catholic, a conclusion made obvious by the wood cross and various other symbols indicative of a religious family. Raquel evidently had a more avant-garde mindset.

The killing of the snipers in Sarajevo had to be downplayed so that Elaina wouldn't think of her son as a cold-blooded killer. I phrased the story as a life-saving situation for the citizens of the city. This painted Tony as the person finding the killers, so I could prevent them from firing on the poor children and elderly people. Elaina seemed quite satisfied with the stories I told of her son and of his being a hero to the people of Sarajevo.

Mrs. Elaina Ramos got up from her chair. "I'm terribly sorry, perhaps you think me rude for not offering you something to drink," she said, very apologetically. "Would you like something refreshing, perhaps some iced tea or even a beer?"

"Thank you; you are not the least bit rude." I began trying to make her feel comfortable with my presence. "Iced tea would be just fine for me."

Elaina went to the kitchen to get the iced tea and probably some crackers and cheese or something else to nosh on.

"Mother is much too stressed," Raquel said, looking over at me. "We moved here from East LA thinking it would be a nice safe area for us, but unfortunately that is not the case." She looked down at her lap and folded hands. "This had been a nice residential street, but then undocumented immigrants began to arrive and a gang started to form. Soon the area and the neighborhood became overrun and controlled by the gang.

"Within a short time, the gang developed drug sales and addiction, prostitution of the young girls, and general criminal activity throughout the neighborhood. Now it is not safe to be on the streets at nights. Every week we have shootings, mostly drive-by shootings. At first, we tried to form a citizen's group, but that ended in failure, as fear gripped the area and people became intimidated by the gang. We have pleaded with the police, but to no avail; they say their hands are tied. No one will come forward and identity any of the gang members or any of the individuals involved in the shootings. We are at a loss; we don't know what to do.

"I'm so sorry for dumping this on you; I realize you cannot do anything. I guess I just needed to vent to someone who is willing to listen." She looked up at me momentarily and then back down at her folded hands. I could see tears in her eyes.

"I'm so sorry to hear of your situation." Shit, why was I being so dumb as to think something could be done, something by me? "Perhaps we could meet somewhere outside your home so we could talk a little more. Maybe there is some way I can help. Please don't get your hopes up though, but listening to you may give me some ideas." Ole johnson sure had complete control of my stupid fucking brain.

"Oscar, I really didn't mean to get you involved." Her moist dark eyes stared at me, unblinking for several minutes. "I shouldn't have vented our problems at you. It is kind of you to offer help, but I honestly doubt you could do anything to help us." She again looked down at her folded hands.

"Raquel, there is a good possibility that I can help." Ah, the asshole hero to the rescue, *Hi ho, Silver, away.* "I have seen similar situations where just the right actions can eliminate the problem. Tony's and my operation in Sarajevo was an action that eliminated an otherwise hopeless situation." I kept my eyes on her, waiting for a reaction. It took a few minutes, but finally Raquel responded.

"I guess it wouldn't hurt to hear you out. It would be such a Godsend if you could help us." As she looked at me, her face showed a sense of relief. To be perfectly honest, I was not really just thinking through my johnson, although the ole pecker had an active role in this. My main motivation was to protect the family of a close, deceased associate, Tony. If he were here, without a doubt, he would take care of this situation, and now I would be his surrogate.

Raquel worked in a law office in the nearby community of Irvine. She gave me the address and phone number along with her cell phone number. We had just completed our conversation when Elaina came back from the kitchen with a tray containing glasses of iced tea and cookies. I spent the balance of the afternoon and early evening sharing stories, particularly of my recent life and divorce. We had a very pleasant dinner of Mexican-style roast chicken, followed by apple pie. By ten o'clock, I was headed back to my hotel in LA.

Mid morning on the next day, I phoned Raquel at her work. Following a pleasant conversation, I suggested we meet at a nice restaurant in the Irvine area near her office. She accepted the idea and suggested the Orwell Restaurant and Bar in the Irvine Spectrum. Irvine Spectrum is an upscale outdoor mall in south Irvine. We were to meet at seven o'clock that evening.

Leaving my hotel in LA early proved to be a smart move, as the traffic going south was incredibly heavy. Arriving at the mall just a few minutes before seven, I located a directory and found the restaurant without any difficulty. Raquel sat waiting for me just outside the main entrance.

"I'm sorry to be late, but I wasn't aware the traffic would be quite so heavy," I apologized.

"No apology necessary, I'm glad you were able to find the restaurant without any difficulty." She wore a beautiful light gray suit and high-heeled shoes. Yesterday she had been attractive in street clothes, but today she really stood out. "The first time I was to meet a group here I got lost, and by the time I found them they had almost finished lunch," she laughed.

We went in, and the maître d' directed us to a small booth near the back of the restaurant. He must have thought we were secret lovers cheating on our significant others, as the lighting had been turned so low that I had trouble reading the menu. After a short while, my eyes dilated, adjusting to the darkness so the menu was readable, and better yet, I could fully take in the beauty of Raquel. I just hoped Tony didn't look down from the heavens and read my rather risqué thoughts of his younger sister. Well, actually somewhat beyond risqué, more toward the perverted side.

"You are such a beautiful girl, how is it that you are not married or don't have a boyfriend?" I asked, prying into some personal aspects of her life. "You can just tell me to buzz off if I am asking too much about your personal life."

"No, Oscar, I don't mind you asking." She showed me a very pleasant smile. "I am not married. All the young men at my office are married, as are the older ones. I just have not been able to find anyone who appeals to me. Mother would like me to marry a nice Hispanic boy, but there just aren't any I know who are educated or employed in a professional occupation. Without education, the Mexican men, or boys, who live around our area will never be successful, and I want a successful man. I really don't think my expectations are too high. After all, I have worked very hard to get where I am, and I don't want to give it up just to pump out babies." Man, I sure hit a hot topic here, perhaps the conversation should be steered in different direction, but before I could redirect, she asked, "Oscar, what about you?"

Now came her turn to pry as she looked across the table with those soft brown eyes. "You said you were divorced and living alone. Have you any love interest? And what do you do for a living?" Shit, I wanted to be forthright but not disclose too much about me, so I told her that my love life, for the most part, didn't exist, and my trip to LA was a potential employment opportunity.

"I've been quite busy since being discharged from the Marine Corps, and haven't had time to attend to my love life." Not really lying. "One of the reasons I am in LA is for a job interview. My background is in computers; I have a degree in computer science." Well, not everything could be accurate, but hey, how could I explain the true nature of my trip was to acquire someone's identification, illegally?

"Wow, computer science," she said as her face lit up. "That is a very impressive degree. We have an IT person at the law office who makes more than most of the lawyers. I guess you have to be pretty smart to graduate with a degree in computer science. I am honestly very impressed. I wouldn't think you would have any problem finding work." Shit, I should have said I was unemployed and let it go at that. She literally beamed across the table. Had I set myself up here?

"Well, normally my degree is in demand, but the economy is not very good, and I am a little rusty," I said, glancing down at my half-empty glass of Jack Daniels as I spoke. "Being in the Marine Corps is not necessarily a good reference. In addition, I graduated some years ago and firms like to hire a computer engineer right out of college. In theory, recent graduates are more up-to-date on technology and computer technology advances very rapidly." For the most part everything told to Raquel came without deceit; there was no point in my not being truthful to her. The main point being that the true purpose for my trip to LA need not be disclosed.

"Raquel, the reason I asked you to meet me for dinner is to discuss the situation with the gang and how they are holding your residential area in their grip," I said, diverting the conversation to the true purpose of our meeting. "How much do you know about the gang? Who are the leaders, and to what degree do the leaders hold sway over the membership?" I looked across the table; she sat staring down at her drink, apparently thinking of a reply.

"Oscar, do you mind if we postpone any discussion about that until later?" She continued to look down at her drink. "I would just like to relax and to get to know you better. Tony wrote Mom about you all the time, and his letters praised you and said how lucky he was to be paired up with you. Talking to you somehow makes me feel closer to my brother. Is that okay?" Her eyes fixed on me, pupils dilated, making them appear almost black, a very beautiful black.

I could feel my pecker begin to rise under the table. Christ, I wanted to taste her. She was definitely pussy-eating good-looking. Tony, I am so sorry to have such a desire for your sister. It would be much better for me if we talked about the gang, it would get my thoughts off Raquel's body, but her wish was my command.

"Sure, I understand, it would be nice to get to know each other better," that being a lie, but who was keeping track? "At the time Tony and I were paired as a sniper team in Sarajevo, I had just gotten married." At that time, all my conversations revolved around my marriage and how much I had been in love with Janet.

Over the next two and a half hours, we told stories about our former and current lives. As we talked, we continued to consume alcohol, getting a real buzz on. When we left the restaurant, without much thought I put my arm around Raquel's shoulder. There was no objection on her part as she snuggled up to me.

"Is there somewhere nearby where we can sit and talk about the gang?" The subject had to be broached. "Somewhere quiet, maybe back at your mom's place?" *A nice comfortable motel room would be nice, a room where I could get you out of your clothes and into bed*, a reasonably pleasant thought, under the circumstances.

"I don't stay with Mom except on weekends or when she needs someone around." She put her arm around my waist and gave a squeeze. "I have a small apartment just across the street from the Spectrum; we could go there, it is very quiet." She began to steer me in that direction, and who am I to question where we were going.

"That sounds good to me." My heart had definitely picked up a few beats.

Her apartment building, a recently built two-story structure located in a complex of two-story apartment buildings, appeared to be a nice place to make a comfortable home. Raquel pointed out her place of work, a new, modern, fourteen-story office building that was close by. The layout of the complex appeared to offer everything one needed, all within walking distance.

Raquel's apartment was a large unit, consisting of a living room, dining area, kitchen, study, and a large bedroom with a queen-size bed. The walls of the rooms were painted in soft shades of greens and beiges with contrasting walls of a darker green. The furniture seemed recently purchased, as it had that new feel to it. The chairs and couch were all soft Italian leather that one would sink in when sitting down. The dining room had a modern table with four light-green, fabric-covered chairs. The floors were wood, covered with a large, light-brown rug, which left only a one-foot boarder around three sides of it. The fourth sided opened into the dining area.

"You have a very nice home, tastefully furnished," I commented, making a quick assessment after glancing around.

"Thank you." She seemed genuinely appreciative of my observation. "I selected everything myself, well, with a little help from a friend who is an interior decorator. Make yourself comfortable. Can I get you something to drink?" She walked toward the kitchen as I sank into the leather couch, although the bed would definitely be more comfortable.

"Ah, Jack Daniels, if you have it." I didn't want to change my drink, just not a good idea. "Or just plain whisky if you don't have any Jack." I heard the clinking of ice in a glass, kind of a refreshing sound.

"Jack it is," she said as she came bouncing out the kitchen carrying two drinks. She had taken off the jacket of her business suit and now wore just a tight white blouse and an equally tight skirt. The drool began to run out of both sides of my mouth as my eyes scanned from the top of her lovely face to her bare feet and then back up. My pecker rose in unison with the upward scan. I couldn't help but wonder if she knew how much danger she had put her lovely ass in.

She sat next to me on the couch, placing the drinks on the coffee table in front of us. She turned to me, asking, "Where to from here?"

"I think we need to get this gang thing out." I stumbled over my words as any effort at staying focused disappeared along with my effort to restrain my sexual desires. "So I can think of any possibilities of ridding your mother's neighborhood of this constant threat," concluding, with my voice trailing off as I noticed her erect nipples protruded under the tight white blouse.

"That can wait a little longer." She actually seemed to be purring—at least that was my perception. A serious question just happened to pop into my foggy brain: now who wanted to seduce whom here? She moved next to me so the warmth of her hot body pressed against mine.

"Do you like me, I mean, my appearance and everything?" she cooed into my ear in a soft and extremely sexually enticing tone. Man, she had to be kidding; did I like her? From the time we had first met until now, my dick turned hard every time a thought of her crossed my mind, which seemed to be most of the time.

"I, ah, ah, Raquel, you have to be the most attractive woman I have ever met. I'm not just saying that to please you, but I'm saying that because it is

God's honest truth." Always pays to stutter a little to show you are in charge. No question I had everything under control here.

I had barely finished the last sentence when in one fluid motion Raquel moved on to my lap, her arms around my neck and her open mouth pressed against mine with her tongue searching for an opening in my lips. Her tongue, the key to unlocking my pent-up sexual desires, immediately found a receptive parting of my lips. Wrapping my arms around her and pulling her tight to my chest, my tongue began to duel with hers, while my hands began to explore other areas of her body. Her ass was so round and so very firm, almost muscular, like a dancer's.

I unbuttoned her skirt and pulled the zipper down at the back. She got on her knees while still keeping her arms around my neck and her tongue in my mouth. Her skirt slid down over her legs, exposing a pair of white silk panties. From there I worked up to her blouse, unbuttoning, with trembling hands, from the bottom up. She let the blouse slide down her arms and drop to the floor.

Raquel broke away from our embrace and began to unbutton my shirt, pulling it from my body and dropping it on the floor. She undid my belt, unzipped my pants, and pulled them down. Ole pecker popped right through the opening in my shorts, and Raquel took it in her mouth and began to move up and down on it while firmly sucking with each motion. Being overstimulated, I almost climaxed; however, at just the right moment I recalled articles previously read in *Playboy* magazine on how to avoid premature ejaculation. At that moment in time, I successfully applied those methods, saving my pent-up desire for a long evening and night of fantastic sex.

Picking her up and kicking my shoes and pants off, I carried her into the bedroom. In the bedroom, my shorts and socks were quickly dispensed with. Once on the bed, she removed her bra and panties, disclosing small but firm breasts with hard, erect nipples. At the V where her legs and her pussy met, was a small patch of black hair and hairless pussy ready for my anxious lips and tongue.

Rolling her over, I began to work my way down her back, passing my tongue through the crevasses of her ass as it found her very moist vagina. Raquel rolled over as my tongue moved between her thighs. It must have been some time since she last had sex, as to my knowledge she climaxed several time from my licking, sucking, and pressing my tongue into her.

She rolled away from me, rose to her knees, and pushed me down. Raquel caressed my neck, chest, and stomach as she worked her way down my body. She took my hardened cock in her mouth and sucked hard without moving. Her tongue flicked over the head of my cock, causing a unique stimulation that quickly resulted in an almost violent climax. My ejaculation into her mouth seemed unending as every bit of cum in my body emptied into her.

Throughout the night, we made love and had sex over and over, getting it right every single time. By early morning, we fell asleep in each other's arms in total exhaustion.

At six thirty in the morning, a loud, unwanted ringing in my right ear jolted me awake. Raquel moved across my back to the nightstand where a clock radio began to blare the morning news. Just what I needed to wake up to.

"Oscar, lover, I am so sorry. I forgot to turn the alarm off on my radio." She mounted me with a leg on either side of my butt and her pussy pressed against the crack of my ass. Gently, Raquel began to massage my back. She moved down my back until she got to my ass. She licked down my crack, which brought me to an extreme level of excitement. Raquel rolled me over on my back, took my erection in her mouth, and sucked on me, and for the umpteenth time, I ejaculated.

"That should hold you for a little while," she laughed as she sat up on the edge of the bed. "You seem to be running low on your cum." She looked over at me smiling.

"I think my tank is almost empty." I lay on the bed with my hands behind my head and looked over at her exquisite body. A beautiful body proportioned just right as far as I was concerned, a definite ten. "We should get dressed and go over to the Spectrum for breakfast," I continued. "Are there any food joints over there that serve breakfast?"

"Yes, there are several." Raquel looked off toward the bedroom door. I couldn't tell what was going through her mind. In the back of my mind, a nascent thought took hold. *Now is not a good time to get involved in a prolonged relationship.* Raquel, while sexually appealing, probably was socially a very nice, thoughtful person too; however, at this point in my life, I couldn't see anything beyond a brief sexual relationship.

"You know, Oscar"—she lay face down on the bed next to me—"if you lived closer, we could have a nice sexual relationship, you know, no commitments, just spending time with each other and fucking a weekend or an evening away." She stared off into space, not at me. This struck me as a strange way of addressing another person, particularly regarding such a sensitive subject, but I let it go.

"There is a remote possibility I might be working in California." I didn't want to make any commitment or give her hope. "Even without employment here, I will be traveling here every few months or so. For some reason, I doubt if a girl as attractive as you, with your intelligence, will last as a single girl.

Some lucky guy will zero in on you." I sat up on her side of the bed and looked down at her for a reaction, but none was forthcoming.

"I'm famished." She perked up, jumping up off the bed. "Let's go get something to eat. All this exercise has really developed some hunger pains." She smiled at me as she grabbed some clothes and headed into the bathroom.

I put on my shorts and waited for her to finish up. When she finished, I borrowed a razor, shaved, showered, and dressed. It was time for breakfast. We walked over to the Spectrum, and as we walked conversation ensued, just talk about funny things that had happened to us. We found a small diner where we could sit in the back, away from the morning rush of office people.

"We really need to discuss the situation with the gang in your mother's neighborhood." I looked into her eyes, conveying the seriousness of my commitment to helping resolve the problem. "Perhaps there is something I can help with. At least I have an idea what Tony would do in this situation," I concluded and waited for a response from Raquel.

Chapter 11

She looked out the window for several minutes without replying. "I'm sorry, Oscar." She turned and faced me with an intent look on her face that I hadn't seen before. "I have been avoiding this topic because I'm very reluctant to get you involved; however, there is my mother to consider. I know Tony would have done something to rid the neighborhood of the gang; if you are able to help, I will describe to you what I know. You can listen to a brief explanation, and I'll let you decide if you want to commit yourself to this very dangerous environment." The joy and affection evident in her face just moments ago had been replaced by sadness, with a note of fear in her voice.

"I just cannot come here and witness the conditions around your mother's home without at least evaluating the situation," I said, my voice also filled with serious intent. "Give me a cursory description of the circumstances surrounding the gang structure in your mother's neighborhood." I sat watching her as she continued to stare out the window.

After a few minutes, she turned and faced me. "This gang in the Santa Ana neighborhood is very, very dangerous. Killing someone in another gang is nothing to them. It is a constant war for supremacy of the neighborhoods. They force the girls of the area to be prostitutes and to service the gang as sex slaves. The young boys of the area are all expected to join the gang; no one is exempt. Each member is expected to sell a certain amount of drugs; methamphetamine, marijuana, cocaine, and any other drug they get hold of, each week. If the member doesn't sell his weekly quota, he has to shell out of his own pocket enough money to pay for their weekly quota." She paused, looking at me with saddened eyes. This was very difficult for her, but I needed to know all the details.

"Each female member has to provide the gang with a set amount of money from prostitution every week. If she does not meet the financial needs of the gang, they rape her, knowing that the fear of being raped again will ensure a commitment to the earning money." She no longer looked at me, just stared down at the cup of coffee that had been placed in front of her.

I didn't want to pry into what, if anything, had occurred between her and the gang. Perhaps it would come out as she continued to tell me some of the gang's history and the methods of keeping members in line. Raquel looked up at me. "Over the past four years, my mother and I have accumulated a lot of information about the local gang. On numerous occasions, we have taken our information to the police, but to no avail." She looked down at her hands and continued. "According to the police, there is little they can do unless they catch the gang actually involved in a crime."

Raquel paused and stared out the window for several minutes to get her thoughts together. "The police have not been able to penetrate the gang, since the gang is mostly made up of Hispanics who all come from the same area of South America, often from the same village. There is a strict code of silence that is backed up by beatings and even the dismemberment of a finger or a whole hand."

Our food arrived. "Why don't we enjoy our food and each other's company while we eat?" I suggested.

"Thank you, Oscar." She smiled over at me. "I guess you can tell that talking about the gang is emotionally draining for me."

"You know, if you have all the data, why don't you just give that to me, and I will go through it," I suggested.

"There are things that are not in the files, but let's wait until later when we are all fucked out." She laughed.

What a nice change to see her brighten up again. Raquel had worn her hair drawn back in a ponytail. Many women wear ponytails, but most are not very attractive. On Raquel, the ponytail—although a short one—was very attractive. She was dressed in a light orange blouse and snug black slacks. The slacks certainly showed off her shapely figure, especially her nicely formed ass.

For the rest of our breakfast, we engaged in lighter topics of discussion, such as my children and the type of work she did and the type of work I did. After breakfast, we wandered around the outdoor mall, going in and out of shops, and by late afternoon we returned to her apartment.

It didn't take us long to exhaust ourselves with perpetual sexual gratification. Sore tongues, sore dick, sore pussy, and sore lips brought the fulfillment of all our sexual fantasies. As I lay on the bed, Raquel snuggled in a tight little ball against my body. Sleep soon overtook us. Several hours into a deep sleep, the motion and crying of Raquel woke me. She wasn't awake; however, a traumatizing dream had invaded her sleep, causing her to scream out in pain.

Putting both of my arms around her and holding her tight brought Raquel out of the dream. She shook and sobbed. For the moment, holding her tightly to me helped to settle her down, and soon she realized she lay safe in my arms. For fifteen minutes, she wept and whimpered, finally relaxing and laying still. She rolled out of my embrace and onto her back so she could face me.

"I am so sorry, Oscar," she spoke in a very subdued voice. "Talking about the gang brings back horrible memories for me. I wasn't going to tell you about it, but my encounter with the gang was a terrible experience.

"When mother and I first moved to Santa Ana, the area consisted of a mixture of whites, Hispanics, and a few black families. Everyone got along really well.

"Then, a few years ago, the immigrants began to arrive. Don't get me wrong, by far most of the immigrants are friendly, hard-working families. But a lot of the young men had families in Central and South America. They came here for work so they could send money back to their families. When the economy provided employment opportunities, the gang had no purpose, but when the economy turned bad, many people, particularly the illegals, couldn't find work and the gang began to form.

"The guys started hanging out, hoping someone would come by and offer them work. They crowded into rental homes and apartments with sometimes over twenty people in a two-bedroom home. Often, to find money to pay their share of the rent, they would rob people on the street or hold up small stores or gas stations. As the gang coalesced, they turned to selling drugs to provide income.

"The only people safe in the area were the gang members. They would wear orange scarves to distinguish themselves from everyone else. If you were caught wearing orange and not a member of the gang, you ended up getting severely beaten. Whites and Hispanics with employment and money began to leave the area, followed by the black families. Soon, the entire neighborhood ended up under the control of the gang. Mom and I didn't have any money; everything went into our home. I made just enough for food, clothing, and the mortgage payment, with a little left for fun things. After I received a promotion and a significant salary increase, we had enough to move, but Mom said this is her home, the one Tony bought for her, and she wasn't going to let any gang drive her out. She knew Tony would have dealt with the gang, but Tony died serving his country and the home she lived in.

"Mom and I started putting together a complete dossier of the gang leaders. When we felt we had all the information, we went to the police who informed us that the information was good, but they couldn't pursue anything without witnesses.

"The gang found out what we had done. One night they came to our home, broke in, and repeatedly raped Mother and me. When they left, they told us that if we went to the police or anyone else and complained, they would be back and finish what they had started. Since then, we haven't done anything to upset them. The rape and the beating only hardened Mother's resolve to remain in her home; she won't budge.

"Now when I walk down the street, they whistle and make suggestive comments. Oscar, I am afraid for my mother and for me. I honestly fear you will endanger your life if you get involved." Tears continued to flow down her cheeks, wetting the satin pale-pink pillow cover where her head lay.

"Let me look at the dossier you have put together," I softly instructed her, "I can determine if anything can be done without endangering your mother or you." I continued trying to placate some of her concern, "I have been in extremely dangerous situations, both in the Marine Corps and since. From a simple humanitarian viewpoint, something has to be done." Inside I felt the burn of anger. In any society, there always seems to be an element that wants to bully everyone else. This is a classic example that has permeated the poorer sections of our communities.

The rest of that evening and night were spent consoling Raquel. Having her pull up memories of the gang that traumatized her and her mother left me with a frustrating, burning desire to eliminate the cancer that had invaded their neighborhood and home. Whenever Raquel rolled over in her sleep, she would clutch me, pulling herself as close to my body as she could. Her body, hot and very sensual, which under normal circumstances would be sexually inviting, could not even enter into my thoughts.

The next morning we had breakfast at the same place as the previous day. Our conversation remained light and playful. We fully enjoyed each other's company. I couldn't help but wonder what things would be like if my home had been closer. That, though, would never happen. By noon I left, with the dossier neatly packed in the passenger seat next to me. Parting was difficult, but I made assurances that I would return in a few days after having had the chance to review the files.

Back at my hotel room in Los Angeles, I sat at a small desk and began to read through the information gathered by Raquel and her mother. They had accumulated over fifty pages of information including photos, home addresses, and gang meeting locations. Each gang leader was described in great detail—information that had been painstakingly compiled over at least the past four years.

Their conclusion at the end of the dossier was that the gang is a hierarchal structure in which the gang leader or senior member had unquestionable control. The gang leader, Enrico Garcia, maintained absolute control using three assistants, Pabla Sanchez, Tomas Rivera, and Chico Torres, who were known as *Auxiliar de Vigilante*. In addition to enforcement, each assistant was responsible for ensuring every young person in the neighborhood was a paying member of the gang.

Anyone refusing to join the gang and declare his or her allegiance to Enrico Garcia took the risk of being beaten and robbed, which 90 percent of the time is what happened to them.

Often, the gang members repeatedly raped the girls. This was a vicious and ruthless organization that controlled everything in the neighborhood through fear. The senior members were wealthy, earning money through dues paid by the membership, prostitution, protection for all the local merchants, and drug distribution and sales. They rode around the neighborhood in Cadillac SUVs, playing loud Hispanic music so everyone knew they were making their rounds. Their homes were the largest and most expensive. The gang leaders were definitely a malignancy on the neighborhood, one that had to be effectively and secretly eliminated. Only two people in the world would know of the plan and its, hopefully, its successful completion.

Occasionally, members would be arrested for drug sales, drug possession, or prostitution, but were ever sent to prison. The most time ever served by a gang member had been a short stay in the city jail. Going to jail was an honor; with all the younger members looking up to those who had completed jail time. All the senior members at one time or another had done jail time.

Tattoos were also a method the gang used to identify its members. Each member was expected to get a gothic cross on the back of the neck so that it was visible above shirts or blouses. Girls were not exempt from this requirement.

Raquel and her mother concluded at the end of the dossier that four senior members had virtual control of all the members and of every aspect of the neighborhood. If those four were somehow removed, maybe the gang would collapse. Their theory was predicated on some very sound observations and reasoning.

In the past, when Enrico was in jail, the gang's daily operations seemed to fall into limbo. Pabla, Tomas, or Chico did not enforce rules, and many of the rules were repeatedly broken. People moved around the neighborhood a little more relaxed, often spending late evenings on the street, out in front of their homes talking to neighbors. Dues were not collected on a punctual basis, and drug sales and prostitution lapsed.

For the next two days, I spent all my time in my hotel room rereading the dossier. The preliminaries of a plan began to develop in my mind. To reinforce the conceptual portion, I would frequently phone Raquel and discuss various aspects of the plan. After a brief conversation, we agreed to meet in person.

On the first ring of the bell, the door flew open and Raquel almost jumped into my arms. It was indeed a passionate reunion, as we went straight to the bedroom with hardly a word spoken between us, the entire night filled with out-of-control sex.

The following morning, I prepared to launch into a discussion on the gang with numerous questions about their operations. Before a word came out of my mouth, Raquel had something extremely important to say first.

"Oscar, "she began almost breathlessly, "there is something you need to know about me so I don't feel like I'm leading you on." This sounded strange, but I sat on the edge of the bed, receptive to whatever she felt had to be disclosed about herself.

"Since having been repeatedly raped and viciously beaten by the gang three years ago, I haven't had sex with anyone else, you are the first. It may seem strange that there is so much passion in me, passion that I only share with you." She sat looking down at the floor as she spoke and then moved her eyes up to mine.

"I absolutely adore you; you are the perfect man, and any woman would be grateful to have you in her life—as I am. Unfortunately for me, it stops there. I cannot marry anyone, my brain is too jumbled, and I have no desire to go to a shrink to straighten it out." She kept her soft brown eyes on me, occasionally blinking away some moisture that formed in the corners of her eyes. Little did Raquel know, this actually came as a relief for me to hear. The past few days I had developed a deep respect and love for her; however, given my current profession, a serious relationship made no sense. In a relationship, regardless of how devoted I would be, in no way would I be able or willing to disclose my activities.

"Raquel, I understand perfectly what you are saying; you have to understand that the way things are between us right now is just fine with me. You are the first woman I have had a relationship with since leaving the Marine Corps; actually, even before I left the Corps. The passion and affection we share will always be there, and no one else can match that feeling. It is unique, exceptional." I held her in my arms, and we lay back on the bed, falling into a deep sleep.

At breakfast the next day, I began to lay out my plan. Raquel would be the only person in the world to know me to be an assassin, but she didn't need to know any past or future contracts I might be involved in. At this juncture, she had to feel comfortable with the plan and, as such, be complicit in it. She would also have to be the spotter, to ensure the right gang leader would be assassinated.

In order for her to understand what I proposed, she had to know my background as a scout/sniper in the Marine Corps. She should also be made aware of my extensive training at Quantico, Virginia, my innate ability to conceal myself in any environment, and the actual details of how her brother, Tony, and I had killed Serb snipers in Sarajevo. These skills and abilities I possessed, and a willingness to utilize them to remove the scourge from her mother's neighborhood, should appease any doubts she might harbor. My plan would also settle a score with Enrico for raping Raquel.

At first, Raquel remained reluctant, but as my plans unfolded, she became convinced of its potential success. She was particularly happy with her involvement and the fact that her efforts would help her mother, along with other residents of the neighborhood. Of particular satisfaction, however, was the prospect of killing her rapist, an action she would be an intricate part of.

Over the next few weeks, we planned and carefully checked out areas of the neighborhood where I could hide and wait for the gang leader, Enrico. When we weren't planning, we spent time in bed, in the shower, and on the living room floor of Raquel's home, having sex and making love.

Most of the gang would hang around a convenience store on the corner of a thoroughfare that ran through the neighborhood. I purchased brown contact lenses, dyed my hair black, and stained my face and hands a light brown so my appearance was that of a Hispanic. Raquel got a big kick out of my new appearance, needling me about having a latent desire to be Mexican.

Across the street from the convenience store sat a small meat market. The entrance to it had a few steps going up into the market interior. I used a hooded sweatshirt, old jeans, and old sneakers to aid in my disguise as I sat on the steps watching the convenience store on the opposite side of the street. Raquel would follow the gang leader to the store and point him out so I could clearly identify him at the right time.

One night while sitting on the stoop, three young Hispanics came by and stopped in front of me. They began to laugh and point at me. Unfortunately, I had no idea what they were saying. One grabbed my arm and pulled me off the stoop, and the others began punching me. I tried to get away from them, but they formed a circle and were able to keep me in the center of it by pushing, kicking, and punching me. My initial instincts were to use my hand-to-hand training skills to punish them; however, such an action would give away my true identity.

When I fell on the pavement, the three started to kick and stomp on me. The only protection available was to roll into a ball and moan with each kick or stomp. After what seemed an eternity, they got bored and left. For fifteen minutes or so, I lay on the pavement in pain. Several people walked past me, giving me a wide berth, not wanting to get involved.

In considerable pain, I made my way to a bus stop and boarded a bus for a long ride to Raquel's home. At her door, at first she did not recognize me, and kept asking me why I was there. She began to close the door on me until my whimpering voice let her know of my identity. She took me in her arms and helped me inside and into her bedroom. She removed all my clothes, and in the dim light she could see the cuts and bruises all over my body.

Trying to speak only produced extreme pain in my throat. Raquel put her hand across my mouth, instructing me not to attempt to talk; we could talk when I sufficiently healed and regained my ability to speak without pain. She ran a hot bath and assisted me into it; a good hot soaking for a half hour or so relieved some of the pain. Raquel produced some Vicodin from her medicine cabinet, medication left from a prescription her dentist had given her. Two, taken painfully with a glass of water, sent me off to dreamland.

For the next few days, I remained in the loving care of Raquel. Using some subterfuge, she had the prescription for Vicodin refilled. She fed me chicken soup and crackers to wash down the pills. My system could only tolerate one Vicodin at a time or I totally zoned out. By the third day, most of my aches and pains had diminished. Now, having the ability to talk in a slightly raspy voice I started to fill Raquel in on what had happened. Her initial reaction was to cancel the mission to kill the gang leader, it being too dangerous. However, remaining firmly committed to my plan, and stressing that the run-in with the three Hispanics had nothing to do with our plans, changed her mind.

The following week, the time came to put our plan into action. Diagonally across the street from the convenience store sat a vacant mercantile store, actually located in the same building as the meat market. The only possible drawback to using this location was that a family lived on the second floor of the building. The family consisted of a mother and two young children, ages about eight and ten—no husband or boyfriend. The mother worked two jobs and left her children alone while she worked. Most days she didn't get home until after ten o'clock at night.

However, it checked out as the only location in the neighborhood that met my criteria for an acceptable hide. After extensive search of the area around the corner convenience store where the gang hung out, the vacant store proved to be the only possibility. Raquel parked her car a half block from the convenience store, and when she saw the gang leader go by, she would follow him to the store. At the front of the store, she signaled me with her hand, a wave for Enrico. Our primary selected target had to be Enrico, to determine if killing him resulted in the dissolution of the gang and its control over the neighborhood.

On the third day of our stakeout, a man came up the street, followed closely by Raquel. Near the front of the store, she raised her hand, signaling a wave for Enrico. What luck! The man walked past the front of the store and stopped at the far corner. There, he looked toward the street and put one foot back up on the building, took a pack of cigarettes out of his pocket, and lit one up.

This was a unique opportunity, a gift on a golden platter, and had to be undertaken this night; there just might not be another such chance. To take the shot, the front door of the store that served as my hide had to be open just enough to accommodate the barrel of my rifle, the barrel with the silencer. Taking a deep breath, letting half out, and slowly squeezing the trigger as the cross hairs rested on his forehead—a perfect headshot. The strike of the projectile caused Enrico's body to bounce uncontrollably around on the sidewalk and then out into the roadway. Just as he landed in the road, a car came by, screeched to a stop, but could not avoid Enrico and ran over his body.

The driver got out, a young woman, visibly shaken, her eyes searching the forming crowd for perhaps a familiar face, someone who could help her. People came out of the store, cars stopped, and the occupants got out. Soon a large crowd began to form. As I watched, I heard someone running on the floor just above me in the store, followed by a person quickly descending the stairs. At the bottom of the stairs, the person began to beat on the locked door, the door between the stair landing and the store. They continued to hammer, attempting to open the door; if they got in, without a question, I would be in deep shit.

How stupid of me. I had wasted valuable time lingering to witness my handiwork. In theory, I should have been long gone, but my performance as I aged and adapted to civilian life began to slip away. Grabbing all of my equipment, including the shell casing from the round just spent on Enrico, I looked around, making sure no evidence was left behind. Just as my quiet movement took me to rear of the store and my escape route, the side door from the stairs to the store burst open.

Moving rapidly toward the back door, I looked over my shoulder to see who might have entered the vacant store. Instead of watching my clumsy feet, my attention diverted on the person or persons holding a flashlight and looking around inside the store produced a very graceful swan dive. My equipment and I made a resounding two-point landing in the hard dirt yard at the rear of the building. My stealth abilities certainly left something to be desired. Perhaps I had to recognize that age, along with other considerations, just had to be factored into this assassin business. But at that moment, there simply was no time to pause and reflect on my life's occupation. I picked myself up and made my way to a small thicket of trees, some twenty feet to the rear of the building.

My pursuers, I'm sure just to make me feel better, also tripped into the back yard. The flashlight went sailing to one side as the individual fell, cussing and cursing, down on all fours with what sounded to be considerable pain. Good to know I'm not the only clumsy fuck in the area. The flashlight was apparently broken, as the pursuer used the Lord's name in vain but again, while crawling around and looking for the flashlight.

For me, time ticked away, and I had to keep moving or risk being discovered. Making my way to the side street, I cautiously moved to a vacant lot of overgrown grass, weeds, and trees. The plan from here on out called for me to hide there at least a few days until things settled down, at which point a phone call to Raquel would bring her over to pick me up.

From the hide, I could hear police sirens as they responded to the accident in front of the convenience store. The activity took place on the other side of the row of building out of my view; I had no way of knowing what transpired. Things seemed to die down after an hour or so. The remainder of the night I spent peacefully, eating crackers with cheese and peanut butter, washing it down with a cup of water and then sleeping soundly in my little hide.

At the end of the second day in the hide, I called Raquel.

"Hi, it's me, Oscar," I said in a muffled voice in case someone was within hearing distance.

"Oscar, Oscar," she cried into the phone, "are you okay?"

"Yes, everything is fine," I assured her. "Can you pick me up as planned, you know, the lot just down the street from the store?" I asked her.

"Yes, oh yes, Oscar, I will right there." She sounded upset, but right now I didn't have the time to get into a conversation. "Give me about twenty minutes, okay?"

"That's okay, don't rush, I will watch for you as we planned." I punched the disconnect button on my cell phone.

I made my way from the hide to a point closer to the street where Raquel's car could be more readily seen. Some twenty-five minutes later, a car stopped in front of the lot. Exercising caution, without question the driver had to be Raquel, I moved with deliberate slowness to the passenger side of the car. Raquel leaned over and opened the door so I could get in.

"Oscar, it was so terrible." She was visibly upset. "The poor woman who ran over Enrico was so upset they had to give her injections and take her to the hospital. The car ran over Enrico's head, crushing it." Raquel had the shakes but would soon get over them. I smiled to myself, knowing that if his head had been run over there might be a chance that the coroner would not find evidence of a gunshot wound. Given Enrico was a local gangster and out of the police's hair, there also existed the chance there wouldn't be much of an investigation.

At Raquel's, we sat and talked for a while. We talked extensively about the successful execution of our plan and how it possibly would relieve the neighborhood of the gang's influence. As we talked, Raquel became more and more comfortable with us having killed another human being. She actually began to feel a sense of self-esteem from having had an integral part in killing the person who had raped and beaten her and her mother years before.

That night, we lay together naked in her bed. We had no sex, not even any thought of sex, just a closeness two people feel when they are totally comfortable with each other. In the morning, we went over to the Spectrum for breakfast and lingered until late afternoon. From the restaurant we strolled through the mall and actually did a little shopping; she bought some shoes and clothing and I bought some shirts.

That evening we had passionate sex frequently and with great satisfaction. The next day Raquel had to go back to work, and I returned to my hotel room in LA. Over the next three weeks, I kept an eye on gang developments in Elaina's neighborhood. The killing of Enrico appeared to be paying off. Some open warfare between Pabla Sanchez and Tomas Rivera ended with Pabla killing Tomas. Pabla went to prison, leaving only Chico Torres. Chico didn't have the magnetism of Enrico and soon left the area.

With the collapse of the gangs, the neighborhood took on its old life and people felt comfortable walking around at any time, day or night, venturing out more frequently. Vacant stores were soon rented out to small businesses. Raquel and I got together a few more times, but eventually we had to say goodbye, and I headed back to Croton.

Chapter 12

On returning to Croton, New York, checking in with Janet seemed a prudent undertaking. I dialed the office number for Wylton Computer Systems. As usual, a new receptionist answered the phone with a tired, disinterested greeting.

"Hello, can I help you?"

"Is this Wylton Computer Systems?" I enquired in a more cheerful but businesslike voice.

"Yeah, this is it," came the surly reply. "What do you want?"

"Can I please speak with Janet?" She cut me short. I could hear her banging the phone headset around, followed by a complete disregard for employer-employee etiquette as she hollered down the hall, "Janet, there is some guy on the phone who wants to talk to you."

It was followed by, "Who is it?" a pause then, "Please find out," evidently coming from Janet.

"Yeah, oh, hello, this is Wylton Computers, Who's this?" came a disinterested response to my business phone call.

"This is Oscar Wylton, and I would like to speak with Janet." Isn't that something, I couldn't remember Janet's new last name, go figure.

"Is it for business or is this a personal call?" Finally showing some professionalism.

"This is a business call from Oscar Wylton," was my rather terse response.

"Hold on a minute, buddy, I'll see if she is taking calls." She disconnected before I could say anything.

"Where the fuck have you been?" She launched into her usual greeting, "Mister I'm-not-responsible-to-anyone, nice of you to check in."

"Janet, it's none of your fucking business where I have been." What the hell, at heart, I'm really a nice guy. "As you may recall, you and Freddy dumped me out of my home and out of my business. I'm no longer responsible to you and have no plans on keeping you informed of my whereabouts. And, Janet, this is the last fucking time I'm going to say that. Next time, I'll simply hang up and take another vacation somewhere far away from here." For the time being, that settled things, at least as far as I was concerned.

"Now that we have that straightened out, I would like to see my children." I really tried to be pleasant as possible, given the situation. "Is it okay if I have them for the long weekend coming up? That should give you and Freddy some time alone," I said, trying to wave a little olive branch.

"It is okay for you to have the kids." She obviously wanted to be pleasant too. She probably wanted Freddy to fuck her all weekend. "Just please keep me informed as to where you are taking them and when you will be back."

Since this would be a long weekend away for the kids and me, we could do something special. When I stopped by to pick them up, they were anxiously waiting by the front door. Both were dressed in jeans, sneakers, and sweat shirts and had little suitcases ready to spend the weekend out with good ole dad. I had to marvel at their appearance. They were well kept, had bright and shiny faces, and were a joy to behold.

"Where would you guys like to go?" I asked, wanting to give them an opportunity to select a place they would enjoy visiting.

"Disneyland!" they shouted in unison.

Crap, Disneyland was in Florida and just too far to go in such a short period of time. I hated to disappoint them, but I explained how far we would have to travel to get there. Their faces fell with the unpleasant news, which, of course, made me feel like shit. What could possibly match Disneyland? There is an excellent amusement park in south New Jersey—perhaps that would fill the bill.

"I know of a wonderful amusement park in New Jersey we can go to," I said, trying to put some real excitement in my voice. "It is almost as good as Disneyland and it has all kinds of rides and things to do. We could spend a day there and also go to the New Jersey shore. What do you say?" I ended hopefully, expecting them to show some excitement about going to a new amusement park plus having a day or two at the New Jersey shore.

"Yeah!" came the response, again in unison. "Gee, Dad, that sounds like fun, and we know going to the Jersey shore is fun because we went there last year."

"Great, we'll leave at the crack of dawn tomorrow, so that we'll miss any traffic and get to the amusement park by noon. Okay?"

"Okay, Dad."

The time with the kids relieved all my stress. It also gave Janet and what's-his-name time to relax and enjoy themselves—and probably have a little sex.

Although quite tired from the whirlwind trip through New York and New Jersey, they showed their appreciation by providing good old dad with extensive hugs and kisses. Emma, in particular, seemed to not want to let go, and her clinging brought a feeling of guilt, even though I had not been the source of the separation and divorce. I felt bad about the effect it was having on Emma and David. The short times we had together were always special. The two of them were absolutely perfect children, well behaved and constantly demonstrating their love for me. At bedtime, I would make up little stories for them, and at the conclusion of the storytelling there were long hugs and affectionate kisses, particularly from Emma.

As I walked out the door after dropping them off, I could hear Emma and David enthusiastically telling Janet about our trip.

Returning to my condo, it didn't take me long to pack things up and head for Elmira, New York, where I established a new residence.

Once settled in Elmira, I took a trip to the department of motor vehicles and received a shiny, brand-new New York State driver's license. The next step was to purchase several pay-as-you-go cell phones. Using my head for something other than a hat rack, I had purchased three pay-as-you-go phones in the LA area. In several of the small towns surrounding Binghamton, New York, three separate stores were located and phones purchased. Binghamton is approximately forty miles east of Elmira.

That evening, I placed a phone call to Alice Goodhue. The phone rang at least five times before someone answered.

"Hello," answered the very soft but somehow very appealing voice of a woman on the other end.

"My name is Bill," I began in a hushed tone, "your name was given to me by Elizabeth Able—" That's as far as I got before Alice interrupted me.

"Oh god, Bill." She was almost too breathless to complete her sentence. "I have been waiting in such anticipation for your call. I was almost at the point where I thought you were an illusion of Elizabeth's mind. We both have been through so much pain inflicted by men we had grown to trust." She paused, but I couldn't tell if she had run out of things to say or needed to catch her breath.

"It is good to hear I come so highly recommended," I interjected. "I hope I can meet your expectations. What is it you require my services for?" I asked, sounding like a true businessman.

"Bill, I guess that is how I should refer to you," she continued, apparently having caught her breath, "I have covertly located and interviewed three potential assassins to carry out a contract for me." She paused, but this time I waited for her to continue. "All of them sounded like uneducated foreigners and, in my opinion, not up to the task. I had given up hope until Elizabeth, a very close and dear friend, informed me of the excellent results she obtained from you. You are truly a wish come true for me. I am prepared to pay you the same as she did if that is agreeable with you."

She sure wasn't looking to drive a hard bargain, possibly I could have asked for twice as much; she would undoubtedly have agreed to the terms. However, I had no interest or greed driving me to suck money out of this seemingly lovely person who had been financially deceived by a supposedly close and trusted friend. What she offered provided more than sufficient funds to fulfill the contract.

I knew from the extensive information provided to me by Elisabeth Able that Alice was a wealthy woman, having been married several times to very successful businessmen, all of whom had met untimely ends. One had died of a heart attack and the second of cancer. She now lived alone with a butler and a maid, both of whom she considered very trustworthy.

Several years ago, she had met a financial adviser through a mutual acquaintance. For over a year through this adviser, James McClarin, she had invested several million dollars. About six months following Alice's last large investment with McClarin, he informed her all the money had been lost on a real estate investment in Houston, Texas. He had some trumped-up papers indicating where the funds had been invested and what the amount was of the subsequent loss. She believed a real estate developer colluded with McClarin, also ending up with a substantial amount of money. Alice wasn't particularly interested in the developer, though, since she had never met or in any way dealt directly with him or her.

For the past year, her entire daily focus remained on the loss of the millions of dollars and James McClarin. Despite medical and psychiatric help, her depression became so severe that her health began to deteriorate. Something had to be done, and Alice prepared herself to spare almost no expense.

"Bill, I guess I am actually begging you to come to my rescue. If this matter is not resolved shortly, I'm afraid my health will take a turn for the worst." Her voice broke several times as she spoke. "I am more than willing to pay the quarter of a million, with half up front and the balance when the contract is completed." She waited anxiously for a reply, obviously hoping I would accept the contract. Naturally, my heart skipped a few beats after hearing of the quarter-million, but being cautious was extremely important, as this could be a trap.

"I am very interested in your proposal," I said, trying not to sound too optimistic, "and since some previous study of the situation has been conducted, I believe we can come to terms." My voice remained level and showed no hint of any of the excitement that rocketed through my feeble brain. Such excitement could quickly lead to a miscalculation or an unintended move, a move that could end my life.

"Oh Bill, that is so good to hear,"she said, the relief evident in her voice. "What do you require of me at this point?"

"I will need every bit of information you have available on Mr. McClarin." I began to instruct her while holding my level tone. "Anything at all that lets me know of his habits, associations, travel, family, anything at all."

"I have every bit of detail you can imagine about James," she exclaimed, "minute detail on all of his activities." With great patience and detailed care, Alice had clearly prepared for the possibility of finding an assassin to take Mr. McClarin out.

"In a few days I will phone you with instructions," I said, continuing in a somber tone. "You will need half of the money for the advance plus the dossier on James. The bills should be one hundreds, unmarked, and not traceable by any means. Place the bills in a nondescript package and await my instructions. Can you be ready in, say, two days?"

"Absolutely, I have set aside the quarter of a million in a safety-deposit box, all in hundreds and not traceable." She was indeed well prepared. "I also have all of the information about James McClarin ready to go." Her smile radiated through the phone.

"All right, I will phone you in a few days." I hung up. I now had two phones that needed to be trashed. I broke up each with a hammer and piece-by-piece the parts accumulated in one pile. The piles were then separated into two smaller piles and dropped into several different garbage bins near my place in Elmira.

A small insurance company operating out of a storefront on Water Street in Elmira provided car insurance. In a little-used car lot in Elmira I purchased, with cash, a reliable older car. The guy who sold me the car almost fell over when I produced thirty-six hundred dollars in one hundred dollar bills as full payment for the car. I hoped he shared it with his boss or at least quietly left town on the next bus.

The next morning, everything was packed and ready to go, including the Springfield, the scopes, the Glock, and all the accessories. The drive to Houston took two full days. By the time I found a mailbox store and had two mailboxes set up, I needed to find a motel. I found one in central Houston that served my purpose, so I registered with the front desk and received a two-night room rental. After checking in, I took a ride in my new car to a truck stop somewhere about sixty miles east of Houston. Once parked and settled, I placed a phone call to Alice Goodhue.

She was almost breathless on the phone. "Oh god, Bill, it is so good to hear from you. I thought you had deserted me. You are going to be my lifesaver, aren't you?"

"Sorry, it took me a while to get things set up." My voice, as usual, remained flat but provided assurance to relieve any stress she might be experiencing. "We're all set now, and yes, I will take care of things for you." I gave her the location of the mailbox and instructed her on how to deposit the money and the dossier into the box.

"I'm all ready. I'll do it tonight," she said—no doubt, she would.

There was no sense in staking out the mailbox store, as I had no idea what Alice looked like. I should have request a picture of her. No matter how thorough you think you are, there is always some little matter that slips through. Simple mistakes can lead to being captured, shot, or both. I had to be more thoughtful, especially when laying out an assignment. In the Corps, the assignments were much more straightforward, having been planned out by the intelligence department. We foot soldiers just had to move from point A to point B per instructions, take care of our assignment, and return to base—one, two, and three—simple.

The information provided by Alice proved to be very thorough, with over eighty pages of text, photos, and maps. James McClarin was indeed a character who didn't hide his fraudulent successes. He went from a semi-poor apartment complex in a lower income area of Houston to one of the more expensive high-rises in downtown Houston. The high-rise had all the amenities, including a swimming pool, workout room, steam bath, and concierge and included membership in a local upscale golf and country club. In addition, he had an estate in Argentina where he spent time in winter.

James had a young blonde or brunette on his arm whenever he entered the high-rise apartments. One could only guess what transpired once they were safely in his apartment home, but getting laid sure appeared to be the primary objective.

Without the least bit of doubt, a very difficult mission lay ahead of me. McClarin spent 99 percent of his time in the city of Houston. The other 1 percent he spent at the golf club. This guy just never stopped in a secluded spot where an easy shot would take him out. The golf club might provide a solution, though. My skills as an assassin, through my choice, strictly limited my methods too long distance rifle shooting, nothing else—no close-up pistol work or use of poison, knives, or similar killing devices. Always do what you are trained for, where your skills will provide the most likely positive outcome.

For several weeks, I surreptitiously followed James around, which proved pretty boring. He went from his high-rise to a small office he had in another high-rise in the Houston business district. From there he would go out to lunch, back to the office, out to dinner, and then home, usually with a different girl each night. The only possibility to take a shot might be from one of the smaller office or apartment buildings in the area.

The next day, I cased each of the buildings. There were twenty buildings that met the criteria that had I established. The process had to be painstakingly slow, as thoroughness was of paramount concern. On the first day, only two buildings were completed. The entire process took over two weeks.

With all of the information from each building compiled on individual sheets, a matrix was set up to determine which building would best meet my needs.

Two buildings filled almost all the requirements. One building, an apartment building located between his office and the restaurant where he usually had his dinner, appeared to be an ideal location. The second building, an office building located between the restaurant and his residence in the high-rise apartment building, also would ideally serve my needs. Further onsite study of each building became necessary before making a decision.

The next day I devoted to the apartment building. Fortunately no doorman or security of any type protected the building, one could walk in off the street and go anywhere in the building except into the apartments themselves. A directory, just inside the entrance doors where the mailboxes were located, listed the occupants of the building and their apartment numbers. One large name at the bottom, with a doorbell button next to it, indicated that apartment to belong to the superintendent of the building.

Surprisingly, access to the roof simply required going to the top of the stairs at the rear of the building, up fourteen stories, and then opening the door to the roof. Also, this being an older building, probably built in the 1930s, I found an airshaft and a garbage shoot. The airshaft faced the street and had small stairs so maintenance staff could easily walk up through the building.

Most appealing was the fact that the airshaft had windows at each level, though they were small and dirty. But the stairs were close to each window, making it difficult to hide from any peering eyes from the street, which in this case, proved to be a serious drawback. I gave this building an A-minus and returned to my motel room.

The next day I devoted to building number two, an architecturally old-style office building, again probably built in the 1930s. The building apparently had been modernized several years ago but the elevators, stairs, and doors remained antiquated. As I searched through the building, I had to keep in mind the need for at least three avenues of escape to be available once the target had been taken out. This particular day, along with the three avenues of escape, I had to find a good hide that would allow me to take the target out without creating any distraction. Once James McClarin was eliminated, I needed to leave the building without being detected.

Being an older building, it also had an airshaft facing the street with small windows at each landing. The building, a sixteen-story steel structure with marble slab facing, had adjacent buildings on each side with small alleyways separating them. In the rear, sat a small courtyard and behind that a modern four-story parking garage. I preferred the airshaft rather than the roof. The roof left too many problems in exiting the building once the target had been eliminated.

The stairs in the airshaft were close to the front of the building, but wide enough that I could stand at the back and not be seen from the street. The stairs had a firm metal handrail to prevent anyone from falling down the shaft.

Back at the motel, the matrix, now complete, gave the last office building an A—not a perfect A-plus, but good enough for this task. Three methods of exiting the building had been carefully determined. The first, go out the way I entered; the second, the fire escape in the back of the building; and lastly, in the event that a passerby noticed the termination of James McClarin and notified the police, I had picked a place to hide in the building. A fourth but dangerous alternative was to use a grapple hook and climber's rope to swing over to an adjoining building, which sat to the north side and had two stories less than the selected building.

A detailed procedure, precisely written out similar to the analysis for a computer program, listed each step with what-if decisions in an attempt to be proactive. Using this analytical process, hopefully all eventualities were considered as well as what actions to take to circumvent anything that obstructed the plan. Every possibility had been considered with the knowledge that despite all precautions, there was always a significant chance that something or someone could gum up the works. Trying to prepare for all circumstances was next to impossible, as only so much equipment could be carried into and out of the selected building at any one time.

I planned two trips to the building prior to assassinating McClarin. On the first trip, I stashed all the extra equipment, grapple, rope, etc. in a janitor's closet on the ninth floor. The closet looked like it hadn't been used in the past ten years. Day two I spent locating several additional hiding places in the building, in the event that a quick exit could not be made.

Day three was a go. To avoid any questions by any of the building occupants, I purchased coveralls with a heating and air-conditioning logo on the front and back. Under the coveralls, I wore business attire. Nervousness set in as I entered the building, not unexpected but to be avoided; I needed to settle down and concentrate on the task ahead. Part of the plan was to enter the building in the late afternoon when most of the business people had left for the day. When I entered the building after four thirty, I saw no one in the lobby or in the basement. In the basement, I entered the room the airshaft stairs were located. The airshaft stairs could only be accessed from the basement or the roof. There, I waited for nightfall.

James normally left the restaurant around nine o'clock at night, so a bit of a wait became necessary; at least the basement access room proved to be comfortable enough. At eight o'clock, I climbed the stairs to the ninth floor where the window had previously been opened. Moving to the back of the stair's landing, I scoped out the street on the opposite side from the building. The restaurant lay just up the street and well within range.

My nerves now less jangled, I started to settle down, the task before me my singular focus. I carefully scoped out each person leaving the restaurant—no sense in knocking off the wrong person. James ran late this evening, and the time ticked past nine thirty. Patience became my mantra. Finally, at nine fifty-one, Mr. McClarin emerged from the restaurant alone. Apparently, his inability to pick up a date delayed his departure from the restaurant. Better for me, I didn't care to drop him while he had a girl on his arm.

Giving myself plenty of time, I held the crosshairs on his head just above his left ear. Take a deep breath, let it halfway out, and squeeze. I was just about ready to let a round fly when something passed in front of the scope. Shit, I took a quick glance and saw someone going in the opposite direction. I again locked onto James. *Breathe, crosshairs, squeeze.* Perfect shot, dropped him in his tracks. No bouncing or jumping, just fell onto his face, *boom*.

Setting my rifle down and preparing to exit the building, noise on the street interrupted my plan. Looking out, the person who had just passed James to my surprise and dismay, had to be a cop. Shit, he now ran toward my building. Undoubtedly, he saw the rifle flash. I had to move quickly. I packed everything up and as quietly as possible made my way to the roof. My planning now paid off, the door from the roof to the main stairwell, as part of my preparation had the latch taped open so it could be opened from the roof side.

Rapidly removing the tape, I ran down the stairs from the roof to the top floor of the building. There I entered the men's room. This being a retrofitted building had the ceilings dropped with fiberglass ceiling tiles set into a metal grid. Removing one of the tiles in the back of a toilet stall, I pushed my equipment up inside the ceiling. Climbing on top of the toilet, I pulled myself up inside the false ceiling and dropped the ceiling tile carefully back in place.

None too soon, as the men's room door opened and two men came rushing in and started to slam and bang each bathroom stall door open to check into the stall, searching for the perpetrator, namely yours truly.

"Nothing here," one exclaimed. After a short pause, they left.

Sweat beaded on the back of my neck and my forehead, running down my back in torrents. Once again, getting to a relaxing mindset became extremely important. In a state of nervousness, significant errors can be made, and this was not the time to fuck up.

The ceiling tiles could not hold my weight; I had my body weight suspended across the top of the cement wall that separated the men's room from the women's room. Strange, any guy aware of the height limitation of the wall could climb up, loosen one of the ceiling tiles in the women's washroom and look in. What a dumb idea, but at least it calmed me down to let my mind wander a little.

More than an hour passed, and then the men's bathroom door again slammed open; as I peered through a small opening in one of the ceiling tiles I could see several armed police come in, probably part of a SWAT team. They banged around in the stalls, looking around.

"Nothing in here, whoever it was is long gone. We're just wasting our time searching this building over and over again and again," one of them exclaimed.

"Yeah, Ken, I think you're right," the other spoke in a raspy voice. "Let's get the fuck out of here." He slammed the door as they went out.

I waited until five in the morning but decided the building was probably under surveillance and thought it best to wait things out. In my pack I had several packages of cheese with crackers and peanut butter crackers. Retrieving them slowly and quietly, they sure tasted good. To be smart, the next two days were spent in my little hiding spot in the men's room. Only very late at night or very early in the morning did I venture down to get something to drink and to use the urinal, being careful not to flush anything. I also shaved, as beard stubble could be a dead giveaway, and I had no desire to be dead.

On day four at noon I lowered myself from the hiding place, washed my face, combed my hair, removed the coveralls, which were over the men's business suit, took the elevator to the lobby, and left the building without incident. That evening at the motel, I called Alice on one of the cell phones. She was ecstatic; she had seen it in the papers and on the TV news.

"You are truly a wonderful man, Bill, or whatever your name is." The excitement was evident in almost every word she spoke. "I honestly cannot thank you enough. A tremendous load has been removed from my mind. The last two days have been the most trouble free of my life. All my ills are disappearing, and I am able to sleep comfortably each night." She finally paused for some air.

"I am glad that I was able to fulfill your needs." My voice was a practiced flat and matter-of-fact tone. "I must move on before there is a more thorough investigation. Please take care of yourself, and enjoy the rest of your life." I laid it on a little thick, but what the hell.

"Thank you, Bill, and take care of yourself. Goodbye and good luck." She hung up.

For the time being, I had to leave my equipment in the building. Undoubtedly, the building would remain under surveillance for some time. Taking a tour of Houston and its environs would be a good way to pass off most of my excess time. Feeling somewhat wealthy, a moved to a more expensive hotel provided added comfort. I tried to bribe the bellboy at my new digs into furnishing me with a girl for the night, but he refused, so one had to be found using my own devices. Not being a golfer, there wasn't much else to do.

After three weeks, I became exasperated and decided it was time to pick up the equipment. Using an attaché case purchased for the purpose, I made three trips to pick up the equipment and other items left in the men's room ceiling. Removing all the items I had taken in, including the spent cartridge, hopefully eliminated all loose ends and lessened any possibilities of my ever being discovered.

The last item on the list, a very necessary detail, was to stop by the mailbox store to close out my account. I checked each box to be sure nothing had been placed in them except junk mail and my final payment. In the second box, there was a package and an envelope. I expected the package but not the envelope.

Putting the package and envelope under my jacket, I notified the clerk that the boxes wouldn't be needed any longer. In the car, I placed the package and envelope on the passenger seat. Heading out of town, I kept a close eye on the rearview mirror for any potential followers. Still nervous, I drove for eight hours before leaving the freeway and finding a place to stay for the night.

In my new motel room, I opened and read the letter. Alice provided three more contacts who were interested in retaining someone with my skills. Christ, was this becoming a referral business? The letter was set aside for future reference, but first I needed to get control of myself and decide where my life was headed. Being a hit man just didn't particularly appeal for the long haul. The longer I remained in this business, the greater the chance of being discovered, arrested, or shot, none of which were of particular interest.

I expected the package to contain the balance of the payment. Instead, it contained a quarter of a million in hundred dollar bills, all old bills and apparently unmarked. In a sense, I was wealthy, but nothing extravagant could be done with the money. Certainly it could not be claimed as income, as I couldn't tell the IRS that the money had been earned by knocking people off. Maybe they didn't give a shit as long as they got their cut. I needed to look into this and come up with a solution, but not this night.

The next day I drove back to Elmira, sold the car, and closed out the apartment. Amtrak provided train service to Croton, which took a while but provided time for introspection. More than eight hundred thousand, including some of the money remaining from Wylton Computer Systems, was nicely packed away in either my savings or checking account or my safety-deposit box. If only I could come up with some legal way of laundering the money without raising issues with the federal or state tax people or without involving the FBI. This required deep thought and planning. An old friend of mine had become a tax lawyer, perhaps he could help, though I hated to get anyone else involved.

Home in good old Croton, the telephone answering machine flashed like the lights of Broadway, and I bet one guess would disclose who would be calling me. Actually one message came from my mom, wondering where I had gotten myself off to; I should really keep her informed. Another originated from the apartment management company who needed access to my apartment to repair some plumbing. A quick search revealed no significant leaks anywhere. The rest of the messages, of course, came from Janet.

Janet's messages ranged from the sweet girl who had come into my life some twelve or so years ago to the wretch she had become.

The final message: "Where the fuck are you?" Ah, the voice of love and affection. Her voice seemed actually raspy and almost incoherent. "I'm tired of talking to your fucking answering machine. Don't you pick up your fucking calls, you asshole? Phone me when you can find time from whatever you fucking do." God, she was in good form.

Fuck it. Tomorrow will be fine to return calls. Today I'm going to shower, freshen up, and relax. Maybe I'll just sit and count money.

Chapter 13

Home again, home again, but who cared, other than me, and hopefully my children? As usual, I had to phone Wylton Computer Systems to see what new urgency had developed during my short absences. A new receptionist answered the phone. Big surprise there, guess they couldn't hang on to the charming one who answered last time I phoned.

"Good morning, Wylton Computer Systems, how may I direct your call?" What a surprise, someone actually answering the phones courteously—a real human being—well, just knock my socks off.

"Could I speak to Janet please?" I requested in a very dignified manner.

"Just a moment please, sir; I will see if she is available." She sounded very pleasant. I wonder if she was as attractive as her phone etiquette indicated.

"Yes, this is Janet," she said, also pleasantly. I guess she didn't know who phoned her. The one shortcoming of the new receptionist: she forgot to ask my name or the purpose of my call.

"Hi, it's me," my equally pleasant response.

"No shit, it's about time we heard from you. Where the fuck have you been?" No more pleasantries here, no doubt she knew who had phoned her now. "As usual you come waltzing back in to our lives whenever it occurs to you that you have a family."

"Janet, if you're going to be a pain in the ass I'm going to hang up. As I told you before, and it apparently needs repeating to penetrate your thick, fucking head, where I have been or what I have been doing is none of your concern. Remember, we're divorced. A divorce resulting from me going off to risk my life for our country and you getting everything except a measly hundred thousand dollars you so graciously gave me. You know what else is the proverbial shaft deep up the ass? This was all because you had to have a new dick inside you. Now, what the fuck do you want?" I guess I could be unpleasant too.

119

"You son of a bitch, you don't talk to me like that." Now I had really pissed her off, good.

"Nice talking to you." I gently placed the receiver down on the phone.

Let's see how long it would take her to calm down and phone back. I figured at least half an hour, maybe longer. In the meantime, a call to the apartment management company had to be made. A very nice receptionist answered the phone and asked me a few questions in order to determine where to send my call. Two rings later, another thoughtful woman answered the phone and asked a few questions.

"Yes, we were trying to get a hold of you to gain access to your apartment. However, that was several weeks ago. We located the problem in the common area of the complex and made the necessary repairs, so we don't need to access your apartment. However, Mr. Wylton, in the future, we should have someone on file to contact in the event that we can't locate you." I gave her my mom and dad's phone number as a backup, thanked her, and hung up.

Next, I made a small deposit to my safety-deposit box at the Bank of Ossining. I had already rented the largest box available on an annual basis. However, it now had reached capacity so another large one needed to be rented to accommodate all the one hundred dollar bills. The manager of the bank, who I slightly knew from high school days, looked like she wanted to ask why I needed so many large safety-deposit boxes. She apparently decided not to ask any questions though, and she left me alone in one of those little rooms just outside the walk-in safe. Man, what a lot of moola. *Semper fidelis*, thank you, U.S. Marines, particularly the scout/sniper schooling.

I had purchased the upscale apartment in the northwest section of Croton. The apartment, really a condominium, was in a six-unit complex with garages underneath and additional parking spaces to the rear of the building. Three apartments faced the rear, looking out over the parking lot and onto New York State Route 9 and further to the distant Hudson River. On the other side was Riverside Avenue, the north-south main drag through Croton. My apartment, on the southwest corner of the building, without a doubt had to be the best in the complex. The unit consisted of two stories with the living room, dinette area, and kitchen on the first floor. The second floor had one large master bedroom and a very up-to-date bathroom. Also, on the second floor, was a relatively large second bedroom that for now served as an office for my computer, files, and other junk.

Both the living room and the bedroom had majestic views of the Hudson River. The view of Croton Point in particular presented a panoramic setting to the river. Croton Point is a peninsula that juts out a half mile or so into the river. Croton Point is not a part of the village of Croton but is owned by the county of Westchester in which Croton is a small village. The county abused its ownership of the point for years, using it as a garbage dumping ground. Finally, by the 1970s Croton convinced the county to stop dumping garbage there. Of course, the garbage already dumped could not be removed so it had to be capped.

Often during summer months, before the county finally capped the garbage mound, the rubbish would catch fire and provide the village with a real treat. The prevailing winds of the Hudson would carry the smoke and the scent of burning garbage across the entire village and as far as the wealthier areas of Mount Airy.

Few people are aware that Croton is also noted for having the largest man-made masonry structure in the United States. Croton Dam, not actually in the village of Croton, is part of the New York City reservoir system. It is also one of the largest man-made masonry structures in the world, second only to the pyramids of Egypt.

Train travelers are familiar with Croton, as the Harmon section station is a mandatory stop for all trains going from and into New York City. Back in the nineteenth century, wood- and coal-burning trains going into New York City caused many New York City residents to complain of the smell of the smoke and the cinders that came from the smoke stacks of the trains. Ultimately, it was decided that all trains going into and out of New York City had to be powered by electricity. The Harmon section of Croton was the hub for the change of steam to electric, thus all trains stopped there and continue to do so today despite the use of diesel instead of coal-fired steam. There is also a large roundhouse at this location. Here, the diesel and electric locomotives and the passenger cars are maintained. The Harmon yard employs many of Croton's residents.

Entering my condo, I found my phone ringing off the hook. Oh well, might as well deal with the last of my immediate tasks.

"Hello," I picked up and softly spoke into the phone.

"Oscar, I apologize for yelling at you before, but damn it, there is a crisis here." The harshness of her voice changed to a mellower pleading one. There still remained a level of annoyance but at least not that demanding bullshit. "You may no longer be part of Wylton Computer Systems, but the income from this business supports your children. I have never asked you for a dime in support." She had a point there, one I had failed to consider.

I needed to let that one ride though, as she and asshole Freddy had taken away my means of support. Besides if I could manage in any way to share my newfound wealth with my children, without question it would be done.

"Just a little consideration is all I am requesting." Now came the butter-up time. "When a crisis hits here, I need your knowledge to resolve it. Please pick up your messages when you are away, and contact me as soon as your time permits. Is that asking too much?" Janet asked. I guess Freddy Sweetie couldn't cut the mustard, and wondered how he handled her in bed.

"I guess that could be agreed to under certain circumstances. I am not always in a position where either picking up messages or returning calls is possible. Sometimes it may be five or more days before even access to a cell phone is possible. When an emergency arises, and I am on a job, your business has to pay all expenses." I needed to get that on the table. "Is that agreeable with you?"

"I suppose we have no other choice but to pay your expenses." Janet sounded a little contrite; perhaps she started to recognize the way she and Freddy had treated me hadn't been very fair.

"Now, what is the problem?" There was almost a note of demand in my voice.

"A couple more files can't be located. We'll pay you the same as last time, three hundred for the job." I'm glad she didn't know how much I had stashed away. "Is that okay; and how soon can you get over here?" She sounded panicked, and a little understanding on my part would undoubtedly be appreciated.

"I'll be over within the hour," giving me a little extra time to prepare for another trip to my old company. "Also, I would like to take the kids out for dinner. I will have them home early, by eight." I hung up without waiting for a response.

This trip to Wylton Computer Systems brought back unpleasant memories. The divorce from Janet had not been easy. Changing from a comfortable, successful life with my own business and a nice young family to one of a lonely, unemployed bachelor just did not exactly fulfill my life's ambitions and neither did shooting people. My new job eliminated any prospect of establishing a meaningful relationship with a woman or even a close friendship with any of my former buddies in Croton.

At Wylton, the reception proved to be ten times better than on my previous visit. However, now computer printouts were stacked in every nook and cranny. When a little area might have been missed, some kind of reference book had been crammed into the void. I couldn't imagine a customer coming into this area and not turning around and walking out.

The young receptionist looked like a part-timer who hadn't yet finished high school.

"Can I help you?" She showed some professionalism, at least.

"Yes, I am here to see Janet. My name is Oscar." That should be sufficient.

She picked up the phone and punched a number. "There is an Oscar here to see you." She seemed nervous; perhaps Janet had become a wretch around the office too.

"She said you know your way, just head back there." She smiled a very pretty smile.

"Thank you for your courtesy and your professionalism," I said, pausing in front of the receptionist desk to let her know how much I appreciated her. She smiled and thanked me.

Walking back through the hall reminded me of a time I entered a dark hallway during counterinsurgency training in the Marine Corps. Every inch of space had been piled high with files and books, on both sides of the hallway. The piles actually blocked the lighting. If OSHA ever came in here, they would have a field day. However, this did not concern me, so I continued back to Janet's office.

"Oscar, thank you so much for coming so quickly." Janet jumped up and embraced me. She hadn't even shaken my hand in years. What a change, but why? She didn't particularly present an appealing appearance, either. Her hair had become ratty with gray streaks and looked like it hadn't been combed for a long time. In addition, she wore a frumpy housedress.

When we initially set up the business together, we had established a rule for office wear. Always be professional, as you never knew when a potential new customer or an existing customer would walk through the front door. For the men, this required a minimum of a shirt and tie, with neatly pressed dress pants and shined shoes; plus a sport coat should always be handy. I guess all that went in the shitter with every other rule we had established. It no longer worried me, so fuck it.

"Just give me the information, and send me in the right direction," I said, indicating I wanted to get on with the business at hand. "I'll see if I can recover the information for you," I added, lightly returning her embrace. I didn't want to be overly receptive to her apparent reaching out, on the other hand being a cold slop didn't cut it either.

She gave me the names of the two files and directed me to Freddy Baby's office, which appeared to be more of a storage room than an office. Recovering the files took all of a half hour. Not wanting the task to appear to be such a simple one, I decided to hang out for a while in Fred's office. Almost immediately, I noted the files piled in his office were in no particular order; how could anyone find anything in here? Not only that, his drawers had been stuffed with all kinds of pink phone call receipts. If he hadn't responded to any of the customer's needs, without a doubt the business was in dire straits. Enough, enough, it just could not be any of my business.

I went to Janet, got $300 in cash, and reminded her that all funds paid to me should be entered as expenses from the general fund. This was very important, as there could be no trace of payments being made to me. That is why everything had to be in cash. Ducking the IRS was not a good idea, but somehow I would eventually make it up.

From there, I went to Janet's house to get the kids. "Hi guys, how is everything going?" I said, greeting them.

"Great, Dad, we were looking forward to seeing you." They were cheering and jumping up and down. We went to a nice little Italian family restaurant in the business district of Croton. The kids had picked it out, saying it had become their favorite place because of the pizza. We ordered two large pies and stuffed ourselves, though apparently not too much, as the kids wanted ice cream before going back to Janet's.

During the course of the meal at the restaurant, the kids surprised me by talking about their mom and Freddy. Apparently Fred wasn't around very much and rarely slept at Janet's at all. What the hell could this be all about? Did I really want to know? Now why would the kids confront me by talking about their mother's arrangements with Fred? I decided it was best to move on to other topics.

After dropping the kids off and starting to back out of the driveway, Janet came running out of the house waving her arms. *Now what?* I asked myself.

"Oscar, can we talk for a few minutes when the kids are asleep?" she almost pleaded.

"Yeah, okay," came my rather weak response. I thought, *Shit, what am I getting into?*

I went in and sat quietly in the living room while Janet put the kids to bed. She made sure they didn't know that their father had come back into the house. I guess there must be some big secret she didn't want them to know about.

She came in and sat in a chair to my right. She looked frazzled. Janet actually looked like she had aged fifteen years since the last time I saw her. "Oscar, things are not going very well at our business," she started. Our business? What fuck is *our* business?

"I had to let Fred go about a week ago," she continued. "There were too many complaints about him from customers. He wasn't returning phone calls, and he couldn't seem to solve the problems that were developing with the files and with the system. I have been looking for a replacement but haven't been able to find anyone competent or experienced enough for the position. We desperately need someone to help out. I was wondering if you might find it in your heart to help us at least long enough for us to find a good replacement."

Christ, if she got down on her knees it wouldn't have surprise me in the least.

"Jesus, Janet, you know you dumped me." I stared at her in disbelief. She looked down at her hands, not wanting to face me. "Not only from the business, but also from our marriage. I really don't know if I want to get involved, especially after seeing the condition of that office. My life is going really good now and to change at this point would be extremely difficult. Give me some time to think about it, okay?"

Shit, there was no need to get involved in whatever was going on between her and Fred, assuming they were still married. On second thought, there was no desire to get involved with Janet given the fact she had become a real wretch, but firing Freddy, that took some guts.

"How long do you have to think about it?" The pleading in her eyes was evident, even in the poor light of the living room. "Things are desperate; I'm afraid of the business going under. Right now a technical person who can answer customer's phone calls would really help out." She had tears in her eyes. Shit, if the waterworks were coming on, I needed to get the fuck out of there.

"Let me see what my schedule is for the next month or so," I said, trying to buy myself some time. Shit, I was easy. "I'll phone you before noon tomorrow. I'm sure something can be worked out." With that, I got up to leave.

"One more thing, Oscar." She stood and faced me her hands noticeably trembling. "Fred and I have split up. I don't know where he went, but he has nothing to do with the business or with the kids. I just wanted you to know." That did come as some vital information; funny though, I didn't feel the least bit sorry for her, only for our kids.

"Thanks," I said, almost mumbling, "and sorry to hear it. I'll call you tomorrow."

The front door closed quietly behind me. That gave some pause for thought. There was no way in hell I would ever go back into a marriage with Janet, not after she dumped me. Besides, she looked frumpy, unlike me who had maintained my condition. Every other day I spent keeping my body hard, which, of course was a necessary part of my business. Having sex with her just didn't appeal to me, even though I desperately needed a piece of ass, shit even a snake was starting to look like a good fuck.

Back in the apartment, my thoughts turned to my future. At least the three referrals should be looked into—one or more might just be worthwhile. Also, there, from the back of my mind, came the question of how the money could be accepted by the IRS. Personally, I preferred the term "washed," as it was certainly dirty money that needed cleaning.

At some point, extracting myself from the business had to be a major consideration. These two items had to be addressed as soon as possible. Remaining in my present business was impossible, since at some point, someone in either the FBI or the local law enforcement agency would put two and two together. Their addition would add up to a serial killer, which I did not want to be known as. Hired assassin would be a better moniker. Taking out the slime that slipped through our legal system, that is what I wanted to be known for.

Chapter 14

The next few days would require some answers to these two enigmas. Meanwhile, the issue of Janet and the business had to be addressed. No way would I spend any time on her problems, not until the three referrals were attended to. Six months seemed like a good guess.

The phone call to Janet the next morning proved pleasant but difficult. Janet cried continuously, talking about how much I was needed, and asking if I cared about the kids. She really pushed just about every button except sex, thank God.

"Janet, I have previous commitments that cannot be broken, period." I had to remain adamant. "For much of the next six months I will be away on personal business. I promise to pick up and respond to phone messages from you. Sorry, but that is it."

"Oscar, please try to make it sooner." She wouldn't give up on the pleading. "There is so much to be done, and I can't do it all. I have hired a nanny for the kids so at least our home is taken care of." She seemed finished, but the "our" bit more than puzzled me; somehow I had to come up with a definitive response so without a doubt Janet knew "our" did not exist in our relationship, except for our children.

"Janet, I'll do the best I can, I promise." With that, I hung up. At least that little piece of business was out of the way for the time being. Now at last, time for bed and a good night's sleep.

That night ended up to be a fitful one, with thoughts of Janet and the kids versus thoughts of finishing up my little business running through my head. The business won out, it had to be finished up, and that firmly had to remain my decision.

Next perplexing issue was how to extricate myself once the three contracts were fulfilled. Although I had pretty much kept my identity concealed, there existed the potential of my leaving some clue that ultimately would be traced to me. Even though my efforts to date should cover any potential trail to my door, I had to be certain; some subterfuge, a secretive plan known only to me had to be perfected. Nascent impressions of how to manage this issue began to form in my less-than-nimble head.

Before anything else, before continuing with any of the three individuals whose names had been supplied by Alice Goodhue, there had to be a method, a system to provide me with a foolproof escape from this life, my life as an assassin. There had to be a logical plan to extricate myself from the business. The best solution that came to mind, was to just dump everything on someone else's doorstep, so that the FBI, or whatever other agency that might be involved, suspected someone else. Good thought, but how to accomplish it?

On the surface, it seemed to be the best approach. The long-dormant analytical cells of my brain sprung into action to formulate a logical plan on how to dump all this on someone else's doorstep. Several months ago, I had been reading an article in a New York newspaper about some perceived bad blood between the New York Mafioso and another group from Italy known as the *Ndrangeta*. I decide to do a little research online and at the local library.

In a small district of Italy called Reggia di Calabria, approximately eighty years ago a poor group of farmers, having no way of scratching a living from the sandy soil, formed a group called Ndrangheta. In order to provide for their families, the group very successfully employed kidnapping and extortion to raise money. Ndrangeta, over the years, developed into an organization comparable to the Costra Nostra, the Mafia. Unlike the Costra Nostra, the Ndrangheta remained a very tightly knit, family-oriented organization. Only families from Calabria or their blood relatives could become members, thus keeping the overall organization small and manageable. The head member of each family met in Calabria each year to review the overall progress of all the various components of their businesses.

Over the years, they became financially successful, making money from drugs, prostitution, and other illegal activities. More recently, *The Organization*, which they became known as, started entering into legitimate businesses, such as restaurants, construction companies, pizza parlors, and supermarkets, where they could launder their illegally acquired money.

In the early 1980s, the Ndrangheta decided to expand to the United States. Unlike the Costa Nostra, the Ndrangheta did not center its business in the Little Italy section of New York City, but instead rented plush offices in midtown Manhattan.

Like any worthwhile criminal enterprise, someone had to enforce the rules, and The Organization was no different. Enforcement fell to an appointed member of each of the founding families. In the United States, one Ndrangheta family had sole responsibility for all operations. Operations included gambling, prostitution, drugs, and immigrant smuggling. The head of the family, one Ernesto Philipino, delegated all enforcement to his brother-in-law, Gino Francotti. Francotti mostly functioned on his own, carrying out enforcement activities assigned to him in monthly meetings. Meetings generally were held at Ernesto's estate just outside Saranac Lake, New York. Saranac Lake, located in the heart the Adirondack Mountains in upstate New York, catered to both summer and winter tourists, there being no true off season.

Gino liked New York City but avoided Little Italy, a section in the lower east side of Manhattan. Instead, Gino preferred midtown Manhattan, in particular an Italian restaurant called Mama Rotino's. Almost every evening, Gino would spend time at a table in the rear that normally was reserved for him. Mostly he dined alone, but occasionally he would have a lady friend with him.

The FBI and the NYPD were aware of Gino's activities but could never catch him or develop sufficient evidence to arrest him. Gino's methods of enforcing The Organization's codes uniquely followed the same pattern: victims just disappeared. On some occasions, a body would either float up in the East River or turn up in the New Jersey flatlands. On some relatively rare occasions, bodies would be found in the garbage dumps in New Jersey.

Numerous newspaper articles had been written about The Organization and Gino. One in particular covered a daylight killing in front of a pizza parlor in White Plains, New York. A car had stopped in front of the pizza parlor where several lunchtime customers were enjoying pizza at the outdoor tables. Four shots rang out, resulting in the death of three men.

Residents of White Plains were furious, wanting those responsible apprehended, tried, convicted, and incarcerated for the rest of their lives. The incident remained front-page news in the local papers for weeks, but gradually moved to the back pages, eventually disappearing all together. The three victims were thought to be recent illegal immigrants from Italy, apparently smuggled in by the Ndrangheta. They apparently violated a code of the Ndrangheta—like skimming money from the pizza operation—so as an example, they were executed. Gino, considered a person of interest, had a solid alibi and after extensive questioning left on a long visit to Las Vegas.

Gino became a person of interest for me too. Perhaps some way of using Gino to cover my covert assassinations just might deflect any suspicion off me. Photos of both Ernesto and Gino accompanied several of the newspaper articles, providing me with a good image of their appearance. I would need this information in order to identify Gino when I went to New York City to locate his hangout. Gino, a short, stocky individual about five foot eight, had black hair that he combed straight back. Of particular note, he had a distinctive scar on his right cheek.

By contrast, Ernesto was tall, about six one, and heavy set. The most recent photos of the two, especially the two together, had been taken several years ago. Gino, in particular, did not like his picture taken, and as a result, he avoided most public places. Ernesto, by contrast, dressed in expensive suits, expensive Italian shirts and ties, and frequented some of the more upscale restaurants and clubs around New York City. Ernesto had black, graying hair that he partially parted on the right side and combed straight back.

Every Friday, I would take the evening train to New York City and have dinner at Mama Rotoni's. Often I wore disguises so as not to raise questions or become known as a regular. For several weeks, I waited until Gino left, and then I got up to go to the men's room, snatching the wine glass off Gino's table as I passed by. In the men's room, I used special tape to lift fingerprints off of Gino's wine glass. On the way back, I placed the wine glass back on the table. If the table had been cleared, the glass would be placed on a separate table where the customers had departed but the table had not yet been cleared.

Fingerprints are actually an oily wax coating left when the fingers are pressed to any smooth surface, such as a glass. Fingerprints are unique to each person, therefore are successfully used to convict individuals who have left them at a crime scene.

But fingerprints alone would not be sufficient. Some personal items with DNA, such as skin, blood, or hair would be needed. How to acquire these items was a problem. In preparation, I went to a local hardware store in Croton and purchased a spool of half-inch, double-sided tape and a few small plastic vials.

For the next few days, all my time was devoted to following Gino in hopes of picking up some skin or hair. On the fourth day came a unique opportunity—Gino went to get his haircut.

I sat waiting my turn as Gino, being a special customer, went right to a chair and proceeded to get his hair trimmed. When the barber trimming Gino's hair removed the cloth used to cover Gino's clothing and shook out the loose hairs on to the floor, I made my move.

I had taped a piece of the double-sided tape to the front of my shoe. I got up and approached Gino's barber. As I walked, I slid the toe of my shoe through the hairs on the floor. On reaching the barber, I asked where the bathroom was. He directed me to the back of the shop.

At the rear of the shop was a dimly lit, cramped, unkempt bathroom. There was sufficient light so I could remove the tape and see that a significant amount of hair had attached to the tape. As the floor around each barber is swept between customers, most of the hair on the tape would be Gino's. Mission accomplished. I had picked up a number of hairs that obviously came from Gino's head.

Wanting a third source, I returned to my stakeout in Mama Rotoni's.

Late one afternoon, having completed his luncheon meal, Gino got up and walked to the rear of the restaurant, apparently going to the men's room. My patience was about to pay off. Waiting a few minutes, so as not to be too conspicuous, I followed him in.

As expected, he was in the men's room relieving himself into the single urinal. This was a small restroom: one urinal, one sink, and one booth, I stepped into the booth and stayed there until Gino left. Being the inconsiderate person I pegged him to be, Gino hadn't flushed. From my pocket, I removed a small plastic vial, previously purchased for this exact purpose, and used it to scoop some of Gino's piss from the urinal. I washed my hands, left the restroom, and walked past Gino's table and out of the restaurant—job done.

The information and evidence acquired on The Organization and Gino would be used to address my first dilemma, deflecting the responsibility for the assassinations onto someone else.

My second dilemma, how to launder all that money sitting in my two safety-deposit boxes at the Bank of Ossining, remained a dilemma, but it was not as pressing as how to extricate myself from the business.

To partially deal with dilemma number two, I set up a small business called O&W Consulting. This way, about five thousand per month could be processed as salary payable to me. All appropriate taxes and social security were paid, so everything appeared legal. This income, along with several thousand I also appropriately registered with the IRS, came from the hundred thousand or so from the Wylton Computer Systems severance. My total monthly net income ended up being a little more than seven thousand—not bad for an unemployed person.

Wanting to keep the remaining balance of the severance intact in case of an emergency, I needed to fund future income from the ill-gotten gains in the safety-deposit boxes. However, the income had to come from some legal source, or at least a source that appeared to be legal. I had to create the show of some means of actually earning money. If I didn't desperately need to do so, I wouldn't go through the subterfuge, but the money sitting in the safety-deposit box at the Bank of Ossining might prove too tempting.

I contacted a tourist agency in New York City that specialized in arranging travel to India and Pakistan. The agency obtained a visa from the Pakistan consulate in New York City and arranged a package that allowed me to travel freely about the country.

At considerable risk, I withdrew five thousand from the safety-deposit box, placed it in a money belt around my waist, and flew to Pakistan. Once situated in an upscale hotel in Karachi, Pakistan, I went to a local office of the Allied Bank of Pakistan.

At the bank, I met with a junior bank officer, Mr. Ghulam Abdful Hakim, who proved to be a very congenial, efficient, and helpful banker. In addition to Ghulam (as he preferred to be addressed) setting up a business checking and savings account, he advised me as to what steps were necessary to establish a small consulting business.

Over the next three to four days, we developed a remarkable friendship. Ghulam had spent four years in the United States living with a family member in Peekskill, New York, a small city about eight miles north of Croton. He had had a student visa to study in the United States and attended New York University. He had received a bachelor's degree in economics from the university but had to return to Pakistan since his student visa expired.

Ghulam went so far as to invite me to his modest home, which he shared with his very attractive wife and two small children. Rebeca, his wife, prepared some delicious, albeit spicy, meals. Following the meals, Ghulam and I shared many stories about of our lives in the Peekskill/Croton area. On my departure to return to the United States, Ghulam drove me to the airport. We had become rather fast friends and promised to stay in touch with each other.

Prior to leaving Pakistan, I arbitrarily wrote down the names and addresses of some fifty or so small business. These would serve as fictitious clients for my consulting business.

On returning the United States, I wrote a small check on my Pakistan account as a trial run. It took more than a week for the check to clear, but all was good with the Pakistan O&W Consulting business checking account. Next came the risky part: funding the Pakistan account. There were two options—a single trip with a large sum attached in a money belt around my waist, or five or more trips with a smaller amount, perhaps ten thousand. I opted for the second option, as making multiple trips would also appear I was actively engaged in the operation of my consulting business.

Although Ghulam did not question the funding of my account, I advised him the money was from an inheritance, and I didn't want to pay U.S. taxes on it. He was very obliging. Over time, I transferred one hundred thousand dollars to the Pakistan account. Now I could withdraw four to six thousand dollars a month as salary from the consulting business.

As for the bulk of the money, which remained securely stashed in two safety-deposit boxes at the Bank of Ossining, I thought about searching for worldwide banks for one in which the money could be laundered and returned to me in large sums. In the meantime, I would just sit on it.

At home in the evening at my condominium in Croton, I would close and lock the sliding glass door that led out to the deck off the living room. In my bedroom, I always left the sliding glass door open about a half yard while I slept. Although my condo had adequate heating and air conditioning, the sounds of the railroad and the Hudson River lulled me to sleep. Also, during the spring, fall, and cool summer days, a nice pleasant breeze came in off the river.

One night, after returning from New York City and falling into a fitful sleep, a strange noise awakened me. Not knowing exactly what woke me up, I lay quietly in bed, listening. Someone or something had entered my bedroom, searching slowly through various drawers in my dressers and desk.

Several years ago, I had purchased a small Beretta Model U22 Neos Semi Automatic Pistol with a silencer. The pistol had a special hiding place under my mattress, close to where my head rested on the pillow. With deliberate caution, I retrieved the weapon from its hiding place along with a flashlight from my nightstand. Sitting up and turning on the flashlight, I pointed the weapon at a small, dark figure rummaging through my dresser drawers.

"Hold it right there, I have a gun pointed at you." My voice, although I was nervous, remained flat and demanding.

The small figure in dark clothing froze in the beam of the flashlight.

"Please don't shoot me," a boy's or woman's voice pleaded.

I turned on the lights of the room, which were controlled by a panel near the head of my bed. There stood a woman I guessed to be in her mid twenties. She had dressed herself in a tight black outfit and wore a black knit cap. She had her hands raised over her head. Whoever she might be, she had one hell of a nice figure, with nice-sized tits and a wonderful ass, at least as much as I could see of it.

"What the fuck are you looking for?" I demanded to know.

"Just some jewelry and things." Her reply seemed to be more of a sarcastic response than the meek one I expected.

"Well, you're not going to find anything here," I said, holding the pistol with a steady aim. "Now sit down while I phone the police."

"I'm leaving now," she said, walking toward the sliding glass door that exited to the deck.

"One more step and I'll fucking shoot you." Being dead serious, I held my aim on her. She continued to walk toward the door.

Pop! The round hit a lamp just in front of her, shattering it with particles of glass spraying on her clothes. She stopped cold.

"Fuck, are you crazy?" she asked.

"You keep going and you'll find out just how crazy I am." I was emphatic, the tone of my voice increasing in volume, denoting my determination to stop her from leaving.

"Maybe we can work something out, like, what can I do for you?" This came as a curious response.

"What are you talking about?" My curiosity began to provoke some sexual fantasies.

"How about I give you a blow job," her unexpected but receptive reply.

"I don't need any fucking blow job," I retorted. "I can get one whenever I want," I lied.

"Maybe something else would please you." She knew she had hit a nerve receptor and probed for a positive outcome. Without a question, she excited my sexual desires and needs, Christ, my fucking needs. I hadn't seen a shape like that on a girl in a long time, if ever. It was a very pretty girl who stood in front of me, offering sex any way I wanted it. She had a round face and olive skin, with cropped, black hair, which I could see as she removed her cap.

"I'll tell you what, why don't you get undressed, while I think about what we could do," I said, and she began to strip.

Several years ago, a rash formed on my skin and a doctor at the veteran's hospital diagnosed it as dry skin. He told me to rub Vaseline on my skin after bathing. Since then, I always kept a jar of it next to my bed and another in the bathroom. In all the years with Janet and in my short relationship with Raquel, anal sex never came up. Several guys I served with in the Corps talked about how great it was. Like fucking a virgin, they said. Maybe now had come the time to find out.

While my sweet young friend undressed, I slathered some Vaseline on my erect dick.

"What now?" she snapped. Shit, who was in charge here?

"Get down on all fours," I instructed. I started to feel a little guilty about my plans to violate this girl. The advantage here might be considered unfair, however; she had been robbing my place, and she had volunteered for this. I kneeled down behind her, and Christ, what a fantastic girl. There before me, resting on all fours, was a beautiful hairless pussy with a nice asshole just above it. I began to get overly excited; I needed to calm down and think of something else. The first thought that came to mind had to be Maggie, the beautiful dog I shot. Shit, that almost terminated any sexual desire altogether. Back to the task at hand, I slid my dick up her ass.

"You fucking son of a bitch," she screamed so loud she could wake a neighbor. "You ass-fucker, my boyfriend will kill you when he finds out about this." She couldn't pull away from me, as I had a tight hold on her. "Wait, wait a fucking minute," she demanded.

"What the fuck do you mean, 'wait a minute?'" Who was fucking who here?

"I want to rub myself," she, almost in anger, responded.

"Rub yourself, what are you talking about?"

"I want to rub my pussy; you're sure not taking care of it," she said, so I stopped for a few moments while Sweetheart adjusted herself.

"Okay, now," she instructed me, as she obviously had taken charge at this point.

Never had there been anything so tight and hot on my cock, those guys were absolutely right; this had to be one of the best fucks I ever had. One problem, though, the head of my dick apparently pressed against the internal wall of her ass caused the ejaculation to be very difficult. Not really a significant problem, as the obstruction only prolonged my pleasure. She came at least three or four times before I finished even once. After almost one whole minute of ejaculation, I flopped down on the carpet of my bedroom. My pretty new friend rolled over and into the crook of my arm, cuddling close to my body. We lay quietly for several minutes, not speaking.

Finally, I spoke softly. "You can go whenever you want." No reply, she had fallen into a sound sleep. The pistol sat on top of my bed. No relaxing or sleeping for me, I could not take any chances, and for some reason I couldn't quite fully grasp I didn't want to wake her.

Two or so hours later, she stirred and woke up. She stared at me, apparently not aware of where she was. Eventually she remembered, sat up, and said, "Mind if I use your bathroom?" She spoke in a very sweet voice, which resonated with certain fondness I began to feel for her.

"No problem, it's right over there." I motioned. She got up, gathered her clothing, and went into the bathroom. Nothing in there could use as a weapon, I assured myself. The shower ran for over half an hour. She came out looking refreshed. Her hair was still wet; I guess she couldn't find the hair dryer.

"All set?" I inquired.

"Yes." She came over and gave me a hug and a kiss.

"You can use the front door if you like," I told her.

"No, some of my things are out on the deck. Thank you, though." She exited the way she came in.

Swish, bang, thank you ma'am; not even a name. I went over, locked the sliding glass door, and returned to my bed for a good night's sleep.

The next morning turned into a late one for me, as I woke up at seven thirty instead of six. A breakfast of scrambled eggs, buttered toast, bacon, and coffee sure hit the spot. I ate on the deck, which jutted out from my living room. The sun came up in all its glory, shining off the Hudson River with a bright sheen like the sun on an ice pond on a crisp winter's day. Some billowy cumulus clouds floated on a clear blue sky. I reflected on the night before. Could life be any better?

The rest of the day I devoted to cleaning up my apartment, making sure everything was in order for the next contract. Afterwards, a necessary prolonged visit to my parents, where Mom, in particular, expressed her annoyance with my not staying in touch. I assured her and Dad that from this point on, I would phone them at least once a week to let them know everything was okay.

The next contract now became my focus.

Chapter 15

Enough relaxation and enough sex (well, maybe enough sex for now). My major concentration had to be on a new contract. Philadelphia, Pennsylvania, was as good a starting point as any was for the next assignment. I looked again at the first referral on the list provided by Alice. Phoning from anywhere near Croton was not a good idea; no sense in leaving any kind of trail.

Continuing to use John Murdock's ID for now didn't present a problem. Using the fake identification in north New Jersey, I purchased an old Plymouth. From there I headed for Philadelphia. Just north of the city, I found a strip mall with a mailbox store. As before, two large mailboxes were rented for the month.

Once settled into a cheap motel just north of Philadelphia, I called the first individual on the list. Barbara Somers answered the phone on the third ring.

"Hello."

"Is this Barbara?" I asked, trying to be as soft spoken as possible.

"Yes, this is Barbara." She actually had a very sexy voice, but for the moment, that was of no concern to me. "How may I help you?"

"This is Bill, I was referred to you by Alice Goodhue," I said, feeling her out. "Do I have the correct Barbara?" I continued to speak as softly as possible so as not to alarm her in any way.

"Oh my god, yes," she said as the sexiness disappeared, being replaced by excitement, "but this is just not a good time to talk, can I phone you back in an hour or so?"

"You can't call me, but I can call back in an hour and a half if you wish," I said, continuing to maintain a flat voice. In my estimation, it's best not to show any excitement one way or another to the contact.

"Yes, but please phone me at a different number," and she provided me with a new phone number and hung up.

Shit, calling multiple times from the same location violated one of my doctrines. Taking a drive around Philadelphia, the city of brotherly love, which has one of the highest murder rates in the country, brought me to a park that overlooked the Delaware River. The city used to be upscale, with many businesses and some large manufacturing corporations. Many banks and brokerages had had a significant presence in the city center.

South Philly became notorious for gangs, killing, drug trafficking, and prostitution. During the 1970s, south Philly started to be gentrified, as affluent businesses and individuals recognized the historic value of the apartments and brownstone homes of the area. Upscale stores and restaurants soon followed, and the homes and buildings in the area dramatically increased in value.

Unfortunately, the rest of Philly went into a steep decline. White flight emptied much of north and central Philly. Businesses moved out of the city center and the overall infrastructure deteriorated. Unions were unwilling to give in to the declining conditions and demanded more money. Throughout the '80s and early '90s, the city stagnated.

In the mid 1990s, things began to change. Banks and white-collar businesses began to revitalize the city center. New glass high-rise office buildings appeared; the murder and crime rates began to fall precipitously. Philadelphia became the place to work and live.

The park I sat in, where the Delaware and Schuylkill rivers merge, is a busy place, and had excellent lighting at night. Numerous couples walked hand in hand or sat on one of the many benches, enjoying the cool evening breezes coming in off the rivers. Several had brought blankets and were lying on the ground in passionate embrace. Life went on, and evidently was even being made, as some of the couples with blankets moved in unison. They probably had no home to go to or couldn't afford a hotel or motel. More probably, they were here because their parents wouldn't condone such activity at home.

An hour and twenty minutes had passed since I had first called Barbara Somers. It was time to phone again. Using the cell phone I previously purchased, I punched in the new phone number she had provided me. She answered on the first ring.

"Hello, is this Bill?" The sexiness had returned, and she obviously knew how to lure men, at least over the phone.

"Yes, this is Bill. How are you?" I asked, trying to appear friendly.

"I have been waiting for your call ever since Alice told me of the wonderful work you did for her. I was hoping you would phone sooner, but I suppose you have other business to take care of." She seemed to have calmed down quite a bit since our previous conversation.

"Yes, I had a number of personal items to attend to before contacting you." I paused for a moment. "I prefer to concentrate on the business at hand, rather than having loose ends interrupting my thoughts. How can I help you?" inquiring of her needs.

"My husband, Steve, is my problem." She was prepared to fill in all the details. "Although he has provided a wealthy home for his family, he has been a philanderer, a drunk, a drug abuser, a wife beater, and a wife rapist. This has gone on for more than fifteen years, and I have tolerated it. However, just six month ago I found out that he is molesting our two young daughters, Tricia and Jean. I always felt that I could put up with his getting drunk or high on drugs and beating and raping me, at least until the girls were old enough to fend for themselves. Finding out what he'd done to Tricia was devastating. Then Jean informed me that he was molesting her and forcing her to suck him off.

"I have detailed everything in a letter as Alice advised me to do. The letter and one hundred thousand in unmarked hundred dollar bills are ready for you. I hope that is enough, two hundred is all I can afford; I have one hundred up front and one hundred when you have finished him off, just let me know where you want it sent to." She began to sound frantic again. Given the situation with her husband, being frantic was totally understandable.

"I will take care of Mr. Somers for you. As soon as I have your letter and down payment, a plan will be formulated and carried out when conditions permit. The one hundred up front and one hundred upon completion is sufficient for this contract." I gave her the address of the mailbox store, stating that she should not be the one to deliver the package. I asked her to find someone trustworthy to deliver it for her and not to let that person know what the package was for or what was in it. She agreed, and said the package would be delivered the next day.

The next day, a Saturday, I parked the car in a strip mall not far from the mailbox store. Through the course of the day, the store had very little business. Several people went in and out of the store. Just before nine that night, when the store was due to close, I went in. The first box, as expected, had nothing in it, the second contained a large package and a nondescript manila envelope. I took both to my car and setting them on the passenger seat, I took out the scanning device to determine if any electronic tracking devices were in the envelope or package. None were.

I drove back to the motel on a circuitous route, taking four times as long as a direct drive would take. Throughout the drive, as became my practice, I kept an eye on the rearview mirror to see if anyone had followed me. Evidently no one had, so eventually I returned to the motel and parked close to my room.

Once in the room, my attention turned to the envelope. Mr. Somers proved to be quite a character. He had been a football star in a local high school and had gone on to play at a small midwestern college. There, he became the star of the team, a big fish in a small pond. He met and married Barbara, a cheerleader (no surprise there). After college, Steve had a short, mediocre career in the NFL, bombing out after two seasons. However, he did have name recognition.

The Somers did not actually live in Philadelphia but had a large home in an upscale suburb named Lafayette Hills. Steve had joined the Acer's Golf Club, a private club situated not too far from their home. Being a former NFL player, he became well known in the community and was elected to an active position on the town board. Steve also attained a significant role on the police commission. Barbara wrote that she had tried on a numerous occasions to report Steve for beating and raping her but to no avail. Steve's influence with the police department negated any appeal on Barbara's part for justice, not even for their daughters.

Barbara Somers did not stand alone in her hatred of her husband. Steve, a crass, bellicose blowhard, thought he had a way with women—any woman. Most people disliked him but were afraid to show it. He used the admiration some men had for him to push people around and frequently engaged in sexual assault on women in the community. More than one husband would have gladly put a bullet in him, if they had the opportunity and the courage to do so. Steve didn't limit his exploitations to women of his own age group, but frequently went after girls in their late teens and early twenties. Once he seduced them, he would take them to a motel where he engaged in all forms of sexually deviant behavior.

He obviously fit my criteria, a total piece of sociopathic shit that needed to be dealt with. Normally, reservations about being a judge, jury, and executioner would affect my decision, but I could think of no reason this guy shouldn't be dealt with. Only the serious planning with a detailed checklist had to be completed before the contract would be carried out.

The next day, I rode around the community of Lafayette Hills, searching for the best location from which to take my shot. The downtown area of the village is rather small, consisting of only three or four cross streets with office buildings, restaurants, and retail stores. There were six or seven modern office buildings, and some were fourteen to fifteen stories high. A shot could not be made from any of these. Interspersed around these building were smaller office buildings that were five to seven stories tall. None of the smaller buildings had any form of security, night or day, although most of the buildings were locked up after nine o'clock at night. Two or three of the newer, larger office building had reception areas at the main entrance to screen anyone not having business in the building.

The building where Steve Somers maintained an office was one of the taller office buildings. His personal office was located on the fourteenth floor of a fourteen-story building—nothing like the executive suite. Steve parked his car in a reserved spot, located in an attached three-story private parking garage at the rear of the office building. Being the big shot, he also frequently parked directly in front of the building, taking up a metered parking space where he never put in a dime. Guess he had a little arrangement with the meter maid.

Diagonally across the street from Steve Somers' building, sat an older six-story office building. Most of the offices in this building were occupied by small businesses: insurance agents, manufacturing representatives, and some of the less successful attorneys who scratched out a living from the more unsavory elements of the city.

Much of the information I gleaned about the city and its inhabitants resulted from my research at the city library. Reading through old copies of the city papers proved most helpful in identifying characteristics of the community. Several articles were found concerning Mr. Somers. While in high school, he twice had been accused of raping a cheerleader, a different one on each occasion. After a brief hearing before a local trial judge, all charges were dismissed. I guess his sporting influence had some sway over the city even then.

Returning to the city, after his limited NFL career, the community greeted him with a parade down the main drag. He always remained the golden boy of Lafayette Hills. It didn't take long for him to get into trouble though. Within two years of his return, on multiple occasions he was arrested for drunken and disorderly conduct. Each time the same judge let him go on his own recognizance. Some of the articles indicated that he frequently got into fistfights with a jealous husband or boyfriend, though there were no further details.

Two years later, he again stood accused of raping one of the Acers Golf Club's female members. These charges, like the previous ones, were also dismissed. Shortly after, there were several other accusations of rape but nothing came of them; most of the information appeared in the back pages of the paper and then disappeared altogether. One could only surmise that the women and their husbands gave up reporting anything on this guy.

In the '70s, '80s, and early '90s, the city, like Philly, went through hard times. Unemployment rose and a lot of dissent over the Vietnam War grew between the generations. Then the city underwent a dramatic change with new businesses coming in and the subdivisions developing on the farmland surrounding the community. Jobs became plentiful and the economy boomed.

Steve's employer did well and much of the new business was due to Mr. Somers's name recognition.

As I assessed the area, two of the buildings in particular were determined to be suitable as a good base for a sniper shot. Not finding security in either of these buildings, I had no trouble wandering through each one, making drawings and making notes as I proceeded. Access to the roof was not a problem in either building, as both had back stairwells and elevators that went directly to their roofs.

The similarity between this contract and the one in Houston, Texas, struck me as being almost identical, which was very disconcerting. However, that job had worked out quite well. Do what you know best, right? That experience had provided me with some skills, skills that could be readily used in a similar situation.

Two of the elevators in two of the buildings were hydraulic lifts and the third building, a cable lift. All doors of the elevators in all the building had special key openings. Only a maintenance person or fireman could open the elevator door with a special key. This proved to be a necessary precaution to prevent anyone from opening the elevator door when the elevator car was not present. Two of the buildings had exterior fire escapes at the rear of the building. The third had interior enclosed fire stairs.

The buildings had been constructed in the '30s, '40s, or early '50s and were made of reinforced concrete. The elevator and the rear stairway of each went to the basement. The basement had some storage areas, but its primarily purpose was for the heating and air-conditioning systems. It appeared that the air-conditioning had been installed in the 1970s. Apparently, window units had provided air conditioning prior to that. The airshafts in the front section of each building were located just off the main staircase. The windows were small but provided good visibility of State Street and the front of Mr. Somers's office building.

With all that information, I returned to my motel room located just outside the business district of the village. To determine the best vantage point for taking out the target, one Steve Somers, a matrix listing the best and the worst elements of each of the buildings would satisfy my criteria. Finally, I ranked each quality from one to ten, one being satisfactory and ten being the best possible option. Included in the ranking, negative numbers indicated when an element, potentially, could result in an unacceptable exposure or situation.

Careful consideration had to be given to every aspect of each location. After entering the numeric quality of each element of the individual building, adding the columns gave an overall total, which I recorded at the bottom of the columns.

Two buildings, one north of Steve's building and one south of it, sat diagonally across State Street. The one to the south, a six-story, older brick building, offered a somewhat better exit plan. The building had an open lot in the back, which backed up to a four-story municipal parking garage. On the north side of this building sat a newer-masonry, fourteen-story office building. On the south side sat a five-story brick building with a men's clothing store at the grade level and offices on the upper floors. This building, diagonally across the street and to the south of Steve's building, presented the best possible selection.

A return visit would provide a complete reassessment of each criterion, positive or negative, of the building, especially the means of escape, as a minimum of three exit methods were required to meet my basis needs. Going out the way I came in, as usual, presented the best exit strategy, since it would attract the least attention. Going to the roof and down the fire escape at the rear of the building proved to be my second best escape route. Entering the elevator shaft and taking the service ladder to the basement was an unlikely consideration, as the basement area provided no concealment opportunities. Taking the stairs to the roof and rappelling to the courtyard in the rear of the building was potentially a useful option, but involved too much exposure. The last option, to throw a grapple hook over to the building just to the south and use the roof access door to exit to State Street also involved too much exposure. What happened after I shot Steve would dictate which method would be best.

For some reason, this contract just seemed bothersome. The similarities between the last job and this one proved particularly troublesome. Perhaps my previous experiences were jading me, or perhaps the longer one was in this business, the more a growing sense of confidence would lead to a significant error. Becoming error prone definitely would result in being caught or killed. Be that being as it may, a commitment had been made, the money was in hand, and therefore the contract would be completed. How could it be otherwise? This poor woman and her daughters were exposed to a deviant that would destroy their lives if left unchecked.

The next day I went to the airshaft, observing all the activity on State Street, especially the entrance to Mr. Somers's building. This being a Thursday, for some reason, was the day for Somers to park on the street in front of the building. Unfortunately, every other day he parked in his reserved spot in the parking structure to the rear of the building. This, of course, meant that the only day a shot could be taken from this location would be on a Thursday.

There was no way of taking a shot in the parking structure, and all other methodologies had been researched and eliminated. One possibility to consider, use a handgun and shoot him in the garage, either as he parked his car in the morning or as he left in the afternoon. This method, however, took training and practice, which I did not have and was not my forte, and I disregarded it as impracticable. Next Thursday would be that contract-fulfillment day.

To exercise additional caution, a return to Philly became necessary. I parked my car, or more accurately John Murdock's car, in a long-term parking lot and took the shuttle to the airport where I rented a new car from Aztec Car Rentals. Once back in Philly, I rented an upscale hotel room for the night. On the way to my room, I asked the bellhop about a nice "date" for the evening. He assured me that one could be provided.

Around seven thirty, there came a gentle knock on the door. Opening the door, a very attractive brunette presented herself as Janet, my date for the night. She purred her name. Shit, anyone but Janet. But what the hell, this certainly seemed to be a much different Janet.

"Come on in," I purred right back.

"Mind if I use your bathroom to freshen up?" she asked.

"No problem," I said, motioning toward the bathroom.

In anticipation of things to occur, I stripped to my shorts. About fifteen minutes later, lovely Janet emerged from the bathroom. She now wore a very sheer negligee.

"Man, you are a good-looking woman," the only mumbled comment coming from my otherwise drooling month.

"What would you like from me, John?" She still purred away.

Christ, I couldn't believe it, I just couldn't think of words that would be meaningful in this situation. Keeping my mouth shut made a lot of sense.

"Why don't we hop into bed and see what comes up?" she laughed.

In bed, we embraced and mauled each other for a while, finally stripping the rest of our clothes off. I was all set for a good sexual encounter when someone knocked on the door, not a little pit-a-pat knock, but one that almost knocked the doors off its hinges. Shit.

"Who is it?" I demanded.

"Hotel security," a very gruff man's voice responded through the very secure door.

"What do you want?" I demanded to know.

"We need to check your room, sir," a muffled response. "Prostitution is not allowed in this hotel."

"There's no prostitution here," I said, indicating my annoyance in my voice.

"Just the same, sir, we need to check." The male voice came a little louder and more forceful.

"Hold on just a few minutes while I phone the front desk to check you out," I instructed.

"I'm sorry, sir, but they are not informed of our activities." The man's anger increased in decibels.

"If they're not aware of your activities, then you're not getting into this room," I exclaimed, matching his decibels. "Anyway, if you are in fact hotel security, then you should have a master key."

"You son of a bitch, you open this fucking door right now," said the voice, no longer muffled. "That is my wife, Janet, and there is no way you're having sex with her." He now pounded forcibly on the door with his fists.

Janet jumped up, grabbed her clothes, and headed to the door to open it. What the fuck was going on here?

I jumped into my shorts and grabbed my Glock pistol from the nightstand drawer. Keeping the pistol handy always was a precautionary step I took. Janet opened the door and her husband, or whoever the fuck he was, came barreling in, heading in my direction.

Shit, I couldn't shoot this son of a bitch; it would raise all kinds of problems. An investigation would be undertaken by the hotel security and by the Philly Police Department, an investigation that would surely peel back my cover and disclose my true identity.

Seeing the pistol in my hand, Janet's rather large husband stopped cold. "Fuck," rolled out of his startled mouth, his eyes glued to the Glock.

"Just one more step and you will make lovely Janet a widow, and she'll have to earn her living by fucking everyone in town." These bastards, along with the bellhop, were obviously running a scam. The bellhop provided the lead, Janet the bait, and her loving husband the strong arm. It probably worked in the past, but it wasn't going to work this time. Too bad the police couldn't be informed, but that would only result in a lot of questions I couldn't answer.

"Get the fuck out, and take your honey with you," I hissed, trying not to raise my voice too much, not that it really mattered.

They withdrew, without any of my money, closing the door behind them. Once they were out, I packed my bags, put them into the trunk of the rental car, and I headed out of town. The hotel bill had been paid in advance so I had no worry there. Too bad that the shithead bellhop had received a nice tip for providing me with a date for the evening, a date with a burly husband who wanted to punch my clock for anything of value in my possession.

Staying away from Philly seemed like a good idea, but I needed to pass my time relaxing somehow. Still, spending another few days onsite where the contract would be fulfilled might be a good idea. The only problem had to do with my becoming too well known by occupants of the office building. To develop more vital information, I sequestered myself in the airshaft from early morning, before many of the various businesses opened, until late afternoon, when most employees left for the day.

The building selected for the base of the operation had virtually no security; the front doors were always unlocked. The elevator shaft had apparently been installed when the building was built; however, the elevator car itself appeared to be much newer. The car probably had been updated in the past ten to fifteen years. The elevator car lift used a hydraulic telescoping shaft, not a cable operation, meaning there would be a small or no elevator shed on the roof. The telescoping shaft itself, an older type not replaced with the refurbishment of the elevator, was much larger than on newer versions. The shaft housing the elevator, a very dark, foul smelling enclosure running from the roof to the elevator pit in the basement, had no illumination of any type. The maintenance ladder could not readily be seen on any given floor when the elevator door was opened with the special key. This I determined by staying late one evening to continue checking out all possible concealment areas in the building. The more I familiarized myself with all aspects of the building, the better my chances were of getting away without detection.

On Thursday, the day for the planned contract mission, I left the rented car at the motel and I took an early bus to the city center. I went to my selected position on the fourth floor. There, I dressed in black coveralls, blackened my face, and retrieved the equipment, water, some peanut butter crackers, my weapon system and scope, various tools, an elevator key, fifty feet of rope, a sports jacket, and other items I had hidden away in the airshaft. From my pack, I withdrew the tape with Gino Francotti's fingerprints and hair strands. Two of the fingerprints I transferred to the top of the windowsill with the addition of a thumbprint to the bottom underside of the sill. Additionally, two of his hairs were placed on the windowsill. Securing myself in the airshaft, everything was set for Mr. Steve Somers's final day.

Chapter 16

The day seemed unusually long, probably because I was concerned about having to take out Mr. Somers in such a populated area. My previous contract, because of the urban location, had resulted in a number of problems. The similarity between this site and the previous one, including the building and the whole scene, greatly troubled me. Others might find the likeness a bonus—same setting, same plan, all practiced and successfully completed. For me, it could portend a disastrous outcome. Dwelling on it only heightened my nervous state. The most had to be made of this situation; I needed to relax and prepare for the task at hand.

As on previous Thursdays, Steve Somers parked his car in front of the building and sauntered inside. As he opened the front door to enter the lobby, a young girl happened to enter at the same time. Steve at first seemed to be polite, holding the door open for the girl, but as she passed him, he gave her a slap on the ass. Man, this guy had some nerve. Whatever his relationship with this girl, he had no right to openly degrade a woman, any woman, in public.

Steve did not leave at five or five thirty as he usually did. At six, I began to get nervous. Perhaps he left through the back of the building, on a date or on some unexpected business. At six twenty-two, he emerged. I moved my sights on him, deep breath, let out slowly, held my breath, and squeezed the trigger. Bam, the round launched toward its prey.

Of all the fucking places in the entire fucking world, this had to be the one time I jerked a shot. Not since qualifying with a pistol in Quantico, Virginia, had I jerked a shot. Instead of hitting Steve Somers in the head as planned, the bullet hit him in the lower neck at the shoulder level. He rolled around on the sidewalk, screaming bloody fucking murder, and drawing all kinds of attention.

With deliberate patience, I sighted in on his head, breathed, squeezed, and hit the target just below his right ear, blowing out the top of his skull. Five or six people who had crowded around Steve were looking up and pointing in my direction. Others were facing the building or by the curb throwing up their lunch. Several police officers appeared, running down the street. Shit, talk about *déjà vu*; just like the last time, I had to move fast.

There was obviously no chance of going out the way I came in. Going to the roof would make too much noise and would not provide sufficient time to set up the rope to repel down the back of the building. Also, attempting to go the basement of the building, would just take too much time. The elevator remained the single viable option. Having the presence of mind, I left the fingerprints, hair, and a spent bullet casing at the scene of the shooting. After which, as fast as my ass would move me, I headed to the elevators.

With the elevator key, which I had purchased at a locksmith specializing in providing hardware for building maintenance personnel, I forced the doors open and entered the elevator shaft. With all my gear, including the rifle and scope strapped to my body, I jumped from the elevator door opening to the maintenance ladder, accomplishing this while ensuring the elevator doors closed behind me. Landing hard against the ladder, my grip was tenuous at best. Because of my perspiration and residual oils left on the ladder rung, my grip started to slip. My hand clasped the rung with every bit of strength I could summon, but to no avail. The upper portion of my body began to plummet the four or five stories to the basement pit of the elevator shaft.

As I started to envision a painful crash on the concrete floor below, my left leg felt like someone wanted to tear it from my body. My torso swung around and collided with the elevator shaft wall. Desperately, I tensed every nerve and muscle in my body, preventing me from crying out in pain.

My left leg had saved my life. Call it providence or just plain everyday luck, my left leg somehow had gotten wedged between the ladder and the elevator wall. At this point, I had no time to contemplate my good fortune; in considerable pain, I pulled myself upright on the ladder and positioned my body behind the ladder against the wall, completing the movement just in time, as the elevator car rose up from the first floor level. My left hand did not fully clear the elevator car as it passed me, resulting in four knuckles getting skinned. At first, I thought my hand had been broken, but despite the considerable pain, I could move all my fingers and flex my wrist. I gave passing thought to the possibility that forensics could discover the scrapped skin and possibly access a record of my DNA.

Close examination of my left leg determined no bones to be broken. I would undoubtedly be bruised and in pain for the next few days, but I had no plans to be traveling anywhere, at least for the next four or five days. No planned travel, however if by chance the searching party now making its way through the building discovers me, there would be travel to unwanted destinations.

The elevator car stopped on the fourth floor, and several men could be heard running and hollering instructions.

"Check the offices. Check the men's and women's rooms. Check the stairs. Check the airshaft. Reinforcements are on their way." Apparently, someone in authority gave instruction to whatever group had entered the building.

There was no way I could know how many were in the building searching for me. Shit, reinforcements? This could be serious; this would end my short-lived and extremely dangerous career. Someone else would have to take out the shits who fell through the cracks of our legal system. If by chance I survived, this definitely would be my last job in a populated city setting. On any future contract, the environment would have to be favorable to the utilization of my training, skills, and experience—such as my first contract, that of Dr. Able, which had easy accessibility in a remote area with exceptionally positive concealment. The remoteness of the area accommodated multiple avenues of egress. Any future contracts had to have those attributes; anything beyond that would require serious contemplation.

Despite the pain in my left leg, hand, and wrist, I decided to climb up a few floors and anchor myself to the maintenance ladder somewhere between floors five and six. Soon thereafter, I could vaguely see, through small openings in the elevator doors, spotlights on the building plus the distinctive sound of a helicopter flying overhead. People could be heard scurrying about the halls and stairways, opening and closing doors. Stomping feet on the roof, banging on the elevator doors, elevator cars going up and down, this undoubtedly would prove to be a long, spine-tingling, and interesting night.

Below, the elevator doors were opened, lights shined, in and the doors slammed shut. Soon, the door on floor five opened and a light shone in and searched around the walls of the shaft.

"Over there, over there," someone shouted, and the light illuminated the walls around me.

"Come on out of there, or I'll shoot," one of the men hollered.

Shit, this was it. I froze behind the ladder and waited for the bullet to hit me. Sweat beaded on the back of my neck and trickled down my spine. Soon, my forehead broke out in a profuse sweat, which ran over my eyes and down my nose, dripping off the end. The sweat stung my eyes so I closed them tight, both to release the pain of the sweat and to block out the pending discharge of a pistol. My sweating hands gripped tighter to the ladder and my body began to shake uncontrollably.

Bang! The weapon fired, and I braced for the inevitable, the end of my life. A zing and another zing as the bullet bounced off the far wall and then off the wall to my right. Pain suddenly penetrated my right shoulder. Then a distant dull thud could be heard as the spent round fell on the top of the elevator car. The elevator car had stopped at the floor just below. I held on despite the pain. The bullet had hit the opposite wall and ricocheted, grazing my right shoulder before falling.

"Man, that's just an indentation or something, there's no one in there," one of the men exclaimed.

"That fucker is long gone. Let's get the hell out of here," one of the searchers said to the other. They apparently paused, trying to determine what to do next. "You know that fucker should receive a medal and be given a hero's parade down Main Street, not hunted like an animal." The first continued his talk.

"Jesus, Bill, watch what you say; how the fuck can you say that anyway?" the second admonished the first.

"That fucking Steve Somers mistreated the shit out of woman. He seduced Ralph Goldman's daughter, took her to the Lane Motel out by the train station, and repeatedly raped her. They couldn't do shit to him, because she just turned eighteen and was a consenting adult. Man, that is just one case; he has done it over and over and gotten away with it," he concluded, followed by a long pause.

"Yeah, I guess you're right, but we can't do shit about it." The second man spoke almost so I couldn't hear him. "I heard the chief say his wife had accused him of molesting his daughters. They couldn't do shit about it because he's in tight with Judge Anderson." The elevator doors slammed shut. I guessed the search had ended, at least for now.

Listening to these two guys gave me a totally different perspective on my choice of being a selective assassin. Perhaps the idea of following my dream, in fact, had been the correct decision. There are many people out there who have been given a raw deal by the law and have no recourse. My helping out just a few might bring some justice. That chance discussion, overheard a few minutes before, brought a sense of pride to me.

By morning, things had calmed down considerably. There was still some activity in the building, but apparently the search teams had departed and the forensic teams were busy at their task. I had nothing to do but wait, and the wait could be a long one. As soon as the workers began to return to their jobs in the building, it would be time for me to consider leaving. Strapping myself to the ladder allowed me to rest and even have bouts of occasional sleep. Unfortunately, not expecting to be secluded for such a long period of time, I'd brought an insufficient amount of water or food. The blood had coagulated on my right shoulder and caused any movement of my right arm to be quite painful. Despite the pain, care had to be taken not to allow any of the blood to get on the wall or ladder.

After two days, the forensic team completed their search for evidence, and the worker bees were allowed to return to their labs. Leaving at this point was not a good idea. Everyone entering and leaving the building would be carefully checked and undoubtedly documented somehow, either with a register or photo or both. This would go on for a few days, and then the daily activity would return to normal.

Staying in my position for more than a week became physically difficult but necessary. My legs, arms, back, and the rest of my body ached from being in the same position. Perhaps moving would relieve some of the pain.

On Saturday morning, the elevator car rose to the sixth floor. Once there, the doors at the basement level opened and someone entered the elevator shaft and began to climb up the maintenance ladder. How high would he go? He passed the first and then second, third, and fourth. Soon he started to pass the fifth.

What an extremely lucky decision I had made to move to the pit of the elevator shaft. The previous morning, very early around two, I made my way down the ladder to the basement where I got some fresh water. No indication of my presence could be left anywhere. My wound was cleansed and dressed as carefully as possible with the few first aid supplies that were in my pack; then I returned to the pit of the elevator shaft.

The pit, an extremely dark hole at the bottom of the elevator shaft, had six four-foot high, large metal springs. I surmised that the springs were to cushion the elevator car in the event of a failure in the lifting mechanism. Being a pit, it was littered with all kinds of debris, especially oil from the hydraulic system; at best, it was very uncomfortable place to hide. The odor of the fluid permeated my clothing and probably my skin. Not a very pleasant scent, but I guess things could be a lot worse. The pit also provided more freedom of movement allowing me to move my legs and arms.

Very early the next Monday, a business day as usual, I decided to take a chance. Leaving the rope and some other items in the elevator shaft, I forced the doors open. Gingerly and painfully, I crawled out of my dark home. In one of the bathrooms, I removed the coveralls, revealing the dress pants, shirt, and tie I had concealed underneath. I washed my face, shaved, and in general cleaned up as much as possible under the circumstances. I stood for a while looking at myself in the mirror. At least ten years had been added to my face, not to mention how sore my body felt.

The coveralls, packed with shaving gear, the rope, and any other effects, were retrieved from the elevator pit and rolled together in a tight neat ball. I pushed up a loose tile in the ceiling above me and placed the ball of personal effects into the space. After putting on the sports jacket I had packed with my other gear, which was made of a rather expensive material that did not readily wrinkle, I looked like a local businessman. My rifle and pistol were in the attaché case I had designed especially for just such a situation.

I hid in a basement storage room until ten o'clock and then emerged and took the elevator to the first floor. I walked out of the building into the daylight without a limp or any other motion that would portray the pain that racked my body, especially my left leg. Walking a few blocks from the building, I boarded a city bus that took me within a few blocks of the motel where the rental car had been parked.

Once the bus dropped me near the motel, I went straight to my room, but instead of lying down like my body demanded, I fetched the keys for the rental car and went on a little excursion. This being a necessary precaution to determine if the car parked at the motel for extended period of days had raised any suspicions. A two-hour drive around the countryside seemed sufficient, as at no time did there appear to be any vehicle following me. Along the way, I stopped at a pharmacy in order to purchase first aid supplies for my leg, shoulder, and any other scrapes.

Back at the motel, I had a nice, long, hot shower, paying particular attention to the deep gash from the bullet and my black and blue left leg. After the hot shower and bandaging the wound, I slept for almost eleven hours. The next morning, I devoured an unhealthy breakfast of steak, three eggs scrambled with fried potatoes, my just reward. Along with my sumptuous breakfast, I read a copy of the local newspaper. No front-page news about the shooting of a hometown hero last Thursday on State Street. In the back pages, the dirt came out. The killing appeared to be a professional hit. Steve Somers was found to have many enemies in the city of Lafayette Hills, many of whom confessed they were quite happy he no longer lived among them. The killer or killers had done the city a service by eliminating such a disreputable individual. Some of these people expressing their gratitude for the killing were even prominent citizens of the city.

The investigation team found some good forensic evidence, but an undisclosed source would not say what evidence had been discovered. The killer apparently fled the building on State Street soon after committing the crime, leaving no evidence of how he escaped from the city. The police assumed the killer departed the city within an hour of the crime. The investigation still was ongoing, and the paper would pressure the police for results.

Finishing the breakfast and packing up the newspaper, I headed back to the motel for a day of rest. Although the room smelled and the bed was not what I would consider as being in the least bit comfortable, it provided welcome rest for the time being. Frequently being awakened by thumping and moaning from the adjoining rooms, obviously from midday sexual liaisons, really didn't bother me that much. Let them enjoy themselves.

On Wednesday, I packed the car, paid the motel bill in cash, and then made my usual last stop at the mailbox store, all completed within a half hour. As on previous occasions, the first box stood empty, and the second contained a letter and a package. I informed the clerk that the mailboxes would no longer be needed and gave him a little tip before leaving the store. The package and letter were scanned for any hidden tracking devices, and none were found. I threw them both over to the passenger seat; there would be time later to look at them in detail.

I drove to the long-term parking where Murdock's car was parked. There, all my belongings were transferred to the Plymouth and the rental car returned to Aztec Rentals. Interstate 95 runs north and south along the eastern seaboard. I picked up the route just north of Philly and headed toward Croton. In north New Jersey, I sold the car at a loss—but who cared. The Path, a subway train running from New Jersey to New York City, provided transportation into New York City, followed by a short subway ride to Grand Central Terminal and a train to Croton.

Once settled in at home, I had time to open the letter and then the package. In the letter, Barbara thanked me for what I had done and especially thanked me for her two daughters. Although she would be receiving a great deal of money from Steve's estate, at the present time she had little discretionary funds. She said she put fifty thousand in the package and would send me more in the future if I would provide an address. No way, Jose.

Well, the big shot sports hero had been taken out, and the rewards were numerous. The money, as usual, I placed in the safety-deposit box the next day. The balance of this day would be total relaxation.

Chapter 17

Before leaving Philly, I picked up a copy of the *Philadelphia Enquirer* with the thought of perusing the news portion once I returned to Croton. Of particular interest had to be any articles about Steve Somers. All the way back on page ten of the news section, I found a small article about a man being shot in the suburban community of Lafayette Hills, Pennsylvania.

The article covered a well-known, local, former football player—a town hero who had briefly played pro ball. After a stint with several NFL teams, he retired from football to become a successful local insurance salesman. The article went on to state that his wife and two daughters, Tricia and Jean, survived him; it was a very brief article, the extent of which covered no particulars of how he died or why he might have been shot.

Having some idle time, I decided to read the rest of the news section. Most of the articles were local news, nothing of note. Near the end of the first section of the paper appeared a human-interest story that seemed to be worth reading.

It was longer piece, a human-interest article about FBI agent Brianna Crawford-Taylor and a new program she had designed to identify and profile possible serial killers throughout the country. Brianna was an accomplished individual.

Brianna Crawford-Taylor was an accomplished individual, having grown up in the black slums of Philadelphia with only a mother to raise and support her. Brianna's two brothers had died at a young age as a result of gang warfare in the apartment complex where they lived. Her mother, Justina Crawford, a drug addict, alcoholic, and a prostitute, ultimately straightened her life out and concentrated on raising her daughter as best she could. She worked two or three jobs in order to provide a decent home for the child. The loss of her two sons seemed to only strengthen her resolve that Brianna would receive the best education possible and ultimately escape from the projects, the slum, drugs, and gang warfare.

As early as middle school, Brianna demonstrated a gift for mathematics and computers. Despite being the only girl in the computer class, she proved to be by far the most knowledgeable student. With the little money Justina had available from washing dishes, flipping burgers, making beds, and her other jobs, she managed to set aside funds to purchase Brianna a desktop computer. Soon Brianna devoted all her waking time to mathematics, the computer, and complex programs that she wrote, most of which she had learned through online Internet training.

In addition, Brianna soon learned how to take a computer apart, add hardware, and make repairs. By the time she became a junior in high school, she had designed and built her own desktop computer using materials purchased online. Many of her fellow students were after her to help them either repair their computers or to build a new one.

Brianna's abilities with computers were only a part of her knowledge base; she also excelled in math, physics, and chemistry. In every subject in high school, she always placed at the top or near the top of her class. By her senior year, Brianna had taken advance placement courses in preparation for college. At graduation, she had three full scholarships. With considerable thought and evaluation, she elected to go to Georgia Tech and major in computer science.

After three years at Georgia Tech, she graduated with honors and ended up with offers of positions at nine or ten different corporations, all well-known national and international corporations. Influenced by the untimely death of her two older brothers who were killed in gang violence when she was a young girl, after some deliberation, Brianna accepted a position with the Federal Bureau of Investigation. She was sent to the Quantico, Virginia, training facility and then to the main headquarters in Washington DC.

At FBI headquarters, Brianna found herself in a rather boring job where she sorted through statistics. She soon realized that the agents with the most interesting positions had law degrees. Taking advantage of the generous educational opportunities offered by the FBI, she returned to college, attending George Washington University and earning a degree in law in two years. She continued her education by achieving an additional undergraduate degree in psychology, also from George Washington University.

With her added knowledge, she returned to the FBI and was assigned to the Criminal Profilers Division. Approximately four years with the profiler section of the FBI left Brianna highly regarded. Her program analysis was instrumental in capturing and successfully prosecuting over twenty serial killers. One particularly significant case was regarding an interstate truck driver, Grey Strong, who picked up prostitutes at various truck stops, strangled them with their undergarments, and dumped their bodies at remote sites along the Interstate highways.

The death of a prostitute is not considered to be a high profile case, especially if those murdered were from lower-income families. And when families report females members missing, if the missing woman is a known prostitute, not very much police time will be devoted to tracking down her whereabouts, or if her body is found, tracking down her killer. All the women that Grey Strong, the serial killer, had murdered were known prostitutes. Other than a brief line in a local paper about their death, little else had been said or done. Local law enforcement generally lacked the resources to pursue the killer or killers of prostitutes who hung around truck stops located within their jurisdiction.

Brianna's computer program accumulated and sorted most of the articles from the various local newspapers, identifying similarities in the methods of the girls' deaths and the way their bodies were disposed of. Similarities in the way each girl was murdered raised a red flag to the possible existence of a serial killer. The compilation of the information by Brianna's program proved to be a reliable source in tracking down and capturing Grey Strong. As a result, Brianna received a special commendation from the head of the FBI as well as accolades from her boss and her fellow agents.

Brianna decided the program had some shortcomings and needed improvement. As a result, she had been working day and night, modifying various aspects of the program. A particular concern revolved around many of the smaller cities providing accurate and up-to-date information. Her current program had not picked up articles of critical information from the back pages of newspapers in smaller cities and communities throughout the country.

In recent tests, the program performed better than expected, and it identified at least six possible serial killers currently at large. Two were known to law enforcement agencies, but the other four were killers who murdered in various areas of the country. These killings were so scattered that until Brianna's program made the connections, no single agency had compiled sufficient data to identify them as multiple killings by the same individual.

One such connection that was particularly intriguing was the similarity found in three killings that used the same method to carry out the crime and yet were committed hundreds of miles distant from each other. All the killings were thought to be by a professional hit man, possibly one trained as a sniper in the military. In the most recent killing, in Lafayette Hills, Pennsylvania, some evidence had been recovered, namely three fingerprints and four hairs. With the information on these three murders, plus information on several other killings that the program had identified, the FBI hoped it would be able to zero in on serial killers around the country.

The article concluded that through the research of newspaper achieves, Brianna expected the program to identify numerous cold cases. Additionally, several other countries had expressed an interest in the program, Great Britain among them.

Seeing this lengthy human-interest story in the newspaper made my socks curl around my toes, metaphorically speaking. All my thoughts focused on this woman and her program, a program that zeroed in on me. My main concentration must now be on how to exit this little business before I made a serious blunder and ended in prison or the grave. Just dropping out and leaving the business now would leave too many loose ends, loose ends that could lead to me. Again, my thoughts turned to Ernesto Philipino and Gino Francotti, the head honcho and his enforcer, respectively. At least the evidence uncovered by the FBI in La Fayette Hills, Pennsylvania, pointed to Gino. Apparently, the little scenario I planned and executed now began to fall into place. I had a long way to go before the plan would actually accomplish my intentions, there being many pitfalls ahead.

I packed a small overnight bag and took the train to New York City. Spending a few days in the city to unwind and contemplate the situation in which I had put myself, proved to be a good idea. Perhaps a date could be arranged. I checked into one of the city's less upscale hotels and asked the bellboy if he knew of any woman that might like a date for the evening. He assured me he knew of several and would send one to my room every half hour so that I could decide which one would be best for the evening.

A warm shower, a change of clothes, and everything was set for the first girl. She showed up about ten minutes after I finished getting dressed and ready for the evening. Patricia was quite attractive and effervescent. A lovely girl, one you might call "nicely stacked," she certainly had me frothing at the mouth. But with due respect to the other girls, I took her name and said I would phone her later.

Three more girls showed up over the next hour or so. All were quite attractive and friendly enough but Patricia had made a lasting impression on me. At about eight, I gave Patricia a call and she picked up on the second ring.

"Hello." What a pleasant voice to get my hormones really roiling.

"Hey, it's Oscar," I said, having destroyed all documents related to my good friend John Murdock. "Would you like to come back up and keep me company for a while?" I couldn't exactly purr into the phone and sound manly at the same time, but I tried any way.

"I'll be right there," she said, and she hung up. Within five minutes, there came a soft knock on the door, when I opened it there stood Patricia in all her well-stacked beauty. Man, my excitement began to pique just thinking about a roll in the hay with her.

It must be a routine, as she excused herself to use the facilities while I prepared myself for any eventuality. When she reappeared not much remained to the imagination, and I just about let go before we even got into bed. We had sex and did everything possible, at least everything that, to the best of my knowledge, is recorded in any sex manual.

At two in the morning, I woke with a start. Patricia had left and left with most of the money in my wallet, a few hundred dollars. In retrospect, I guess it had been worth it. Initially, the thought of making a little phone call to her crossed my mind, but what the hell, a few hundred wasn't even a drop in the bucket for me anymore. Luckily, most of the hundred and fifty thousand had been deposited in my bank the previous day. Patricia would have really hit the jackpot if she found that stashed in my hotel room.

Hanging around in New York City is fun; there was so much to do, though of course it would have been more fun if someone shared the experience with me. Perhaps in time, when my adventures as a hit man ended, there would be someone to share things with. While in the city, much of my time was devoted to eating. Little Italy, Chinatown, Rockefeller Center, and hot dogs at the street vendors were all included in my gastronomical tour.

After several days of being a tourist, it came time to take the train to Croton. Doing a reverse commute is always fun. All the commuter trains coming into the city are packed but the ones going back out are sparsely occupied; in my case, the passenger car had one lonely occupant, me.

Finally getting home brought somewhat of a sense of relief. A hot shower and a few hours of rest were in order. Around eight thirty I woke to a dark home, one in which a feeling of being out of place occurred to me. Trying to acclimate to the surroundings took a few minutes. Shit, this was my home and feeling out of place just didn't set well. With some effort, I located the switch to the lamp on my nightstand and turned it on. The glare of the light startled me. How unusual; for some reason, I had become a stranger in my own home.

After putting on some sweats, my old Marine Corps stuff I cherished, I liberated a Cohiba cigar from its hiding place in the cigar humidor and poured a shot of Jack Daniels over a short glass of ice. Now feeling a little more comfortable with my surroundings, I headed for the deck off my bedroom. Sitting in a comfortable lounge chair, I looked out over the Hudson River, watching what appeared to be a tanker passing under the Tappan Zee Bridge, making its way north to some unknown destination. I lit up the cigar and settled back for a pleasant late evening repose.

Not fifteen minutes into my leisure there came a totally unexpected banging on my front downstairs door. Shit, probably Janet, I had forgotten to phone her, damn it. I took my sweet-ass time going downstairs, knowing that a confrontation lurked behind that door. Looking through the peephole,

I saw a gray-haired woman wearing glasses and a night coat. What the fuck did she want? She proceeded to bang on the door with some object I couldn't make out, but I assumed the old bitty had a cane.

I slowly opened the door, afraid of being attacked by this old fart.

"Can I help you?" I asked in a rather perplexed tone.

"You the one stinking up the neighborhood with some foul-smelling smoke?" she demanded to know.

"I'm afraid I don't know what you are referring to," I responded, hiding the cigar behind my back. Shit, being intimidated by this old goat didn't sit too well with me, but intimidated I definitely was.

"I'm talking about some cigar odor that is whisking from your upper deck into my bedroom; that is what I'm talking about." She stared at me through her thick-lens glasses. "Don't you pretend you don't know what I'm talking about; I can smell that garbage you're smoking from here." The old fuck had a sensitive sniffer.

"Look, miss whatever your name is," I said, starting to feel a little embarrassed for trying to deceive her, "this is my home, and if I want to smoke on the rear deck of my bedroom there is no rule that I know of that says I can't. Go close your doors and windows; I'll be finished in an hour or so." I slammed the door, but that didn't stop her from yelling.

"I'll talk to the association about this," she screamed at the top of her old-age lungs. "You're not getting away with polluting everyone's air." After a few minutes of haranguing me, she left.

Back to the upper deck for some serious drinking and yes, smoking. When the hell had she moved in? The last I knew a young couple lived there and they smoked, drank, and fought like cats and dogs with each other. All told, they had been really nice neighbors.

The next morning I had to bite the bullet and turn on the telephone answering machine. As expected, several messages from Janet. To my surprise, Janet actually sounded pleasant.

"Oscar, you promised you would stay in touch, and I haven't heard from you. Please call as soon as you can." Each message came across about the same, very pleasant. What was going on there? Four more came from Mom and Dad, again admonishing me for not staying in touch as I had promised. Mom in particular had become concerned about my frequent disappearances—long disappearances without any explanations.

I phoned Mom first; after all, she is my mother. "Hi, Mom, it's me. Sorry I haven't been in touch, but business recently has been very demanding." What a bullshit line to give to your mother, but what else could be said? Mom, I've been busy shooting people?

"Oscar, I'm your mother, and you worry me. Why don't you let us know where you're going, and what keeps you away in such secrecy for long periods of time?" In Mom's way, she was being sweet but stern. "I have trouble enough getting to sleep at night without having to lay awake worrying about you." This comment is Mom's ace card. Her not being able to get to sleep at night because of me always struck a nerve.

"Mom, I'm really sorry, I promise that in the future things will be better." This being a really lame excuse, but what else could one say to his mother? Mom hung up, apparently still angry with me. In the next few days, I would go over and patch things up. Meanwhile, I had to bite the bullet and call Janet. The office seemed the most logical place for her to be at this time of day.

"Good afternoon, this is Wylton Systems, how may I direct your call?" This receptionist, the same young girl who was there on my last visit, actually seemed to like her work and demonstrated a desire for professionalism, one that had been lacking in the previous few receptionists.

"This is Oscar Wylton; can I speak to Janet please?" I couldn't remember Janet's last name to save my ass. That jerk she married really had been one roaring asshole.

"Just a moment please, I will let her know you are on the line, Mr. Wylton. I will place you on hold until she picks up. Good afternoon, sir." She put me on hold, after showing a great deal of courtesy before hitting the hold button.

"Oscar, I'm so glad you called. We have a few problems you can help us with. Do you have time to stop by so we can go over them?" Jesus, talk about turning over a new leaf, and there was that "we" again. My antenna feelers came out in a defensive mode; she definitely had some plan cooking.

"Yeah, hi, yes, I can come by in about an hour. Okay?" It wasn't difficult to be nice to Janet when she showed her pleasant side. However, her new pleasantness really concerned me, as she had been such a wretch before. Why had she all of a sudden become so sweet? I hoped she didn't have designs on me and a resurrection of our defunct marriage. Man, I would have a hard time dealing with that.

On the way, a stop at a local deli for a tasty ham and cheese sandwich with a cold beer to wash it down would fulfill my hunger needs. After picking my lunch up at the deli, I headed for the Croton Yacht Club, which is an ideal spot to eat lunch. Looking out over the river and seeing ships, motorboats, and sailboats passing by always proved to be very relaxing. I reflected on my youth, when summer breaks from school provided leisure time for sailing and swimming. Sailing on the Hudson River, with just the wind whistling by and the water lapping against the hull, always provided a very romantic and relaxing repose. Most of the time, one of my many girlfriends would join me. Too often, though, they would get nervous about the boat tipping, especially when a good gust of wind came up, but we always found other ways of rocking the boat.

At Wylton Computer Systems, the receptionist expected me, so straight to Janet's office I went. Janet provided tight hugs and hard-pressed kisses to my cheek, but I tried to ignore the overly affectionate greeting, not showing any interest in spit swapping. She seemed a little disappointed that we didn't kiss and embrace passionately, but maybe that just came as a figment of my imagination. Of particular note was the fact that she had lost a considerable amount of weight and seemed to have firmed up her physique. Not that I had any particular interest in Janet's body shape; I just made a mental note.

As usual, several customer files could not be located either in the hard files or in the computer files. It took me all of twenty minutes to complete a search and correct the problems they were experiencing. I returned to Janet's office from my old office, which still had Freddy's name on the door.

"Janet," I said, trying to keep the conversation limited to business, "haven't you hired anyone to manage the computer systems here?" I stood in front of her desk without sitting down, ready to bolt out the door as soon as the situation permitted.

"Well, sort of." She looked up, probably wondering why I didn't sit down for a nice little chitchat. "A young man who just graduated from Croton Harmon High School comes in a couple of times a week. He is taking computer courses at New York University and is pretty sharp," she said, filling me in on the latest effort to find a reliable systems expert. I just hoped she didn't have more of an interest in his body than his mental capabilities with computers.

"I was hoping you would come back and assume your old position." Her hair had definitely been colored. She quite obviously had made an effort to improve her appearance. "The company could sure use your knowledge, particularly when it comes to handling customers. Because of Fred's incompetence, we lost about twenty percent of our clients. I know that if you returned we could work together to build the business back up." She displayed a pleading, tearful, and desperate need for help. In my mind, I questioned whether this search for sympathy applied solely to the business or included my loving return to a dysfunctional marriage. Shit, I hate it when women resort to tears and begging. Next, she'd offer a blowjob or something else. I really needed to get the fuck out of there.

"Janet, I promise I'll return," I said, staying focused on my plans, "as soon as some business deals are finished. I am deeply obligated to my new business and there is no way of just walking away." Well, not everything had to be true.

"I guess." A sort of pause for effect followed; Janet knew how to manipulate things, no question. "I understand and will be as patient as possible." Her demeanor had clearly changed, as had her appearance. "Just please stay in touch as frequently as you can." She actually seemed to be genuinely sincere. I suspected she felt I owed her, but definitely not to my way of thinking.

"I promise to do better from this date forward." I also responded in genuine sincerity.

She invited me over for dinner with the kids, including a movie on their new HDTV with a Bose surround system. This, in a way was like old family night. After I safely tucked each of the kids in bed, as swiftly as possible I headed for the door. This was an obvious attempted to make a clean break, but unfortunately, I didn't get away with it.

"Oscar." She stopped me in my tracks less than halfway to the door. I should have moved a little faster. "Can you stay for a little while so we can talk?" She had a whimper in her voice.

"Okay." Now what? We sat near each other in the living room. Waiting for Janet to get around to speaking whatever she had on her mind became increasingly stressful, the extended silence was deafening. Fortunately, after five or so minutes, she began to speak.

"Oscar, I know I didn't treat you very well in breaking up with you and initiating a divorce"—she sure got that part of it right—"but I felt you were leaving me and the kids alone to fend for ourselves. That is all over and in the past. I have been hoping we could arrange to see each other more often and especially have you spend more time with the kids and me. Do you think you could find that in your heart?" Could this possibly be a proposition or what? What happened to the free blowjob? Talk about pulling on the heartstrings, shit.

"I don't know," I said, needing a lot of diplomacy here. "Janet, the breakup and divorce jaded me as far as marriage and family life are concerned. Give me some time and space to see how things work out. Can you give me four or six months, please?" Damn, my conscience worked against me. Why should I be the one feeling guilty?

"Okay, Oscar, we'll wait and let you decide how to handle things." We? Where the fuck did *we* come into it? Talk about laying a guilt trip on someone. Janet still had her old manipulative ways and that really pissed me off.

"I better get going, I promise to stay in touch," I said, and out the door I went before any tears or more "wes" developed.

Back at my castle, a pleasant, relaxing evening on the deck would sooth away the troubles of the day. Fortunately for my aged neighbor, no fresh cigars were to be found anywhere in my apartment. A cold glass of Jack and a contemplative evening—a late evening—'til almost dawn I sat on the upper deck, just outside my bedroom. It interested me seeing all the tankers, freighters, and barges either pushed or pulled by tugboats, that made their way up or down the Hudson River throughout the night. For some reason, they aroused images of far-off ports with strange-sounding names and beautiful and willing women with no strings attached.

At three in the morning, enough was enough, so I staggered to my bedroom and flopped on the bed, not bothering to change into pajamas. Who needs them anyway? The sun beamed its way into my bedroom after piercing the eastern sky. The glare and warmth slowly penetrated my thumping head, rousing me. Jack is good, but too much of any alcohol is not good for the next day.

Going out for breakfast entered my foggy brain as being a good idea. I packed a few things and drove to the local duck pond diner, as it is known, where just about everyone in Croton had at least one or two meals a week. I consumed my usual order of scrambled eggs and steak with home fries with plenty of black coffee. Feed a drunk coffee, and you have a wide-awake drunk. Go figure, although it seemed to work for me.

Driving southwest would take me to Pittsburgh, Pennsylvania, in about six or seven hours. About fifteen miles northeast of Pittsburgh sits the small community of Aspinwall, where I exited the freeway. Turning on to Route 28 and driving around the town for a while, I found a small strip mall. In the mall, as became my custom, I found a cell phone outlet where three phones were purchased. The phones were not activated, and I did not give my correct name or any personal information to the sales assistant.

From Aspinwall, I drove through Pittsburgh to Wheeling and then south to another small town named Moundsville. It took over an hour to find a cell phone store but I located one just south of town in a strip mall. An additional three phones were purchased; again, no activation, no correct name, and no personal information were provided.

Near Wheeling, I found a motel, kind of a dump but all I needed was a good night's sleep. In the morning, I drove back to Pittsburgh and found a decent hotel to be my base. After checking in and lounging for a few hours, I went out and took a walk to a local mission that had an advertisement in the yellow pages of the phone book. Sure enough, some fifty or sixty souls lay about or stood around, probably waiting for a free meal.

I spent several days in my room at the hotel. I ate all my meals in the room and let my hair and beard grow. After a week, my hair had grown to an unkempt shoulder length and significant beard stubble covered my face. Phoning the front desk, I informed them I would be out on business for a few days but wanted to keep the room. Paying in advance held the room for the next couple of weeks.

Chapter 18

Dressed in some old stained and unwashed clothing, I made my way out the back door of the hotel and headed to the mission. Not far from the mission, I encountered four obviously homeless men. They demanded all my money and valuables, which, of course, I had none, other than some small change. Since my response was not to their liking and they considered me an intruder into their territory, a severe beating became my initiation into the local homeless society. The little change taken from my pockets I had intentionally put there, just in case such a situation arose.

I guess there is sort of an unwritten code among the homeless not to get involved in fights between other homeless people and not attempt to break them up, as a number of people stood around giving witness to my beating but not helping. The only positive thing to come out of the beating was the sympathy of a significant number of the other homeless people.

After the beating came to an end, one man in particular came to my rescue: Ralph Christenson, an amiable man around my age, though it was hard to tell given the wrinkles around his eyes and the gray hair on his face. He led me into the mission and found a nurse who looked over my wounds and decided they weren't life threatening—painful, but not life threatening.

Christ, in whose judgment? I thought to myself. Shit, my body was racked with pain. The good nurse gave me a few pills and instructed me to lie down in the dormitory the mission provided for the homeless. Ralph stayed by my side throughout the day and into the night.

The next day turned out to be a bitch; it felt like I had been in at least twelve rounds with a champion heavyweight fighter. That day I spent hanging around the mission and getting to know Ralph. He had been a star football player for one of the Pittsburgh high schools and had gone to college but didn't finish. He tried out for several professional football teams and actually earned a place on a Pittsburgh Steelers farm team. He endured the pain, which mostly resulted from playing football, by consuming alcohol and taking drugs. He primarily consumed alcohol since, unlike drugs, which were prohibitively expensive, cheap beer could be purchase just about anywhere.

Ralph had married his high school sweetheart and they had three children, two boys and a girl. Ralph trained and worked as a plumber ultimately, becoming a partner in a successful plumbing business. The money went to his head, and he launched himself into gambling, drinking, extramarital affairs, and drugs. For a number of years his plumbing partner tolerated him not showing up for work or showing up drunk, but finally had enough so he dissolved the business. Not long after Ralph's partner closed the business, his wife divorced him and threw him out of the house, which she received in the divorce settlement.

Eventually, Ralph spent every cent he had, but with no prospect of work, he ended up on skid row, as the area around the mission is known. He hadn't seen his wife or kids in the last ten years. He spent his days in search of another fix or another drink, preferably a six-pack since it would last most of the day, provided he nursed it. He had tried everything to kick the alcohol and drugs, but nothing worked. His only income now came from social security, which he had the mission keep in an account so he wouldn't be mugged or spend it all on alcohol and drugs. The mission would provide him a small weekly stipend, which for the most part went for beer.

As my intent for being here was to borrow—using the word rather loosely—Ralph's identity, I pretended I had no idea what social security was or what a card even looked like. When Ralph produced his card to show me, as usual, I memorized the information. I then went into the bathroom at the mission and wrote the information on a piece of paper. The paper was pinned to my undershorts, which had been arranged for that purpose. What luck, only three days and I had the necessary information to launch into the next contract.

I hung out with Ralph for the balance of the week. At the end of the week, when most of the homeless were sleeping, I made a very quiet exit from the mission's dormitory. With my appearance, getting into the hotel could be a problem. Being a real smart-ass, I had squirreled away some money in the bottom of my right sneaker beneath a little flap in the heel I had carved with that intent in mind.

With the money, I bought a razor, shave cream, and some shampoo at a nearby drug store. By early morning, I had located a consignment store where a decent pair of shoes, trousers, and a shirt were purchased. With a few coins left of my squirreled away funds, I went into a small bathroom at the local bus depot. In the bathroom, a shave, and a change of clothes were sufficient to get me back into the hotel.

After a good night's rest and a couple of nice expensive meals, I headed to the Department of Motor Vehicles. Getting a license in Ralph's name proved much easier than anticipated. Back at the hotel, I spent the day relaxing and watching movies on the widescreen HDTV in my room. At four in the afternoon, I took out one of the cell phones, activated it, and called the next number on Alice's list.

"Yeah, who the fuck is calling on this phone?" came the gruff accented response from a male voice on the other end.

"This is Bill," I kind of stammered into the phone.

"Who the fuck is Bill and how did you get this number?" the accented voice demanded to know.

"Alice gave me this number." I became very perplexed. Who had Alice put me in touch with? Who spoke on the other end? I had expected a woman to answer the phone.

"I don't know no fucking Alice, and if I fucked her I don't remember her." Alice must have given me the wrong number. "I fuck a lot of women, so don't fuck with me." This guy sure had a limited vocabulary. He also had a strong accent, Italian being my best guess.

"Sorry to have bothered you, sir." I started to disconnect.

"Wait a fucking minute," he continued in his laconic tone, "you the fucking hit guy?" This guy's language just about overwhelmed. Shit, marines didn't use the f-word that much.

"Yeah, this is Bill, the hit guy." I spoke softly yet distinctly, in contrast to his tone.

"No fucking shit." He really knew how to charm people. "Do you know how fucking long I've been waiting for your fucking call?" He became livid and spoke with an even deeper accent that I almost found impossible to understand at times.

"I had other business to take care of," I said, continuing my soft but forceful tone, "my last contract had to be fulfilled. What can I do for you?" I needed to be absolutely firm with this guy. He sounded like a Mafioso or some other mob character. Care had to be taken not to get involved in any criminal activity.

"Well, I got a fucking job, or contract as you call it. When the fuck can we meet?" He demanded a response that didn't sit well with me, and I wanted to test the waters a little more.

"I don't meet with anyone," I said, holding my ground not to divulge to anyone my identity. "All my contacts are through arrangements controlled by me. That is the only way I operate. If those terms are not acceptable, we can conclude our conversation and move on." Staying firm, and controlling the conversation, were essential, that's for fucking sure.

"Okay, how the fuck you want to handle this?" He began to mellow out, there must be an important job he wanted done.

"I'll need to know what the job is so we can agree on a price." I began my instructions, there could be no deviation. "Once we have established the ground rules, I can let you know when the job will be done," I said, trying to be as detailed as possible while disclosing nothing about myself or how I operated.

"The fucking contract is for two million, one million up front, and one million when it is fucking done." That sure perked my interest. "Is that sufficient to get you off your fucking ass and moving?" What a sweetheart. Shit, this guy went from mean to mellow to mean in less than a minute. The money made my eyes almost pop out of my head—two fucking million. Man, that made my mouth water. What the hell could be worth this kind of money, and did I want to get involved with it?

"I need to know more about the contract," I said, buying time to set things up. "I will phone you back tomorrow night at the same time and give you instructions on how to deliver the money and as much detailed information on the contract, or hit as you call it, as possible. If I cannot fulfill the contract or decide not to do it, all the money will be returned to you. Is that agreeable with you?" I asked, hoping for a positive response.

"Fucking A." That apparently meant yes, but it was anyone's guess. "I'll be fucking waiting for your call tomorrow night. You don't have to worry about no fucking taps on this fucking phone, just so you fucking know it's safe." This information I could use, but why did he indicate such a concern for his fucking phone? I pressed the red disconnect button on my cell phone. My warning antennas were up; perhaps I should walk away from this, but two mil? Only time would tell.

Setting up a drop for the dossier and the down payment, I used the same method employed on the past contracts, as this method had proved useful as a way of exchanging funds and information without risking the disclosure of my identity. A mailbox store, one just north of New York City in Westchester County, would provide me sufficient protection. A mailbox operation in New Rochelle, an arbitrary choice of locations, served as the drop and pickup point. As before, two very large mailboxes were rented with instructions to the clerk that any mail coming into mailbox one, be moved to mailbox two.

Having made the necessary arrangements for the mailboxes, I drove to the suburbs of Philadelphia to make the phone call to my new client, whoever he might be. No sense taking any chances on having the phone call traced by some of the client's henchmen. I did decide to use the same cell phone, something I hadn't done before.

"Yeah, who is it?" came the recognizable gruff voice.

"This is Bill, phoning as promised on Monday," I replied.

"Hey, no fucking shit, I've been waiting for your fucking call. So is everything set up to give you the fucking money and the fucking information you wanted?" Man, this guy had a really pleasant personality.

"Yeah, the money and information is to be dropped at a mailbox store in New Rochelle. Once I have had the opportunity to assess the information, I will let you know if I can do the job for you." I gave him the address of the mailbox store in New Rochelle.

"Fuck, why can't you just come by here and pick up the fucking money and information?" This guy sure wanted things his way.

"What is your address?" I said, being sly, as having his address would possibly identify him.

"My offices are on the fortieth floor at 222 Broadway in New York City," he instructed. "Just ask for Ernesto Philipino when you come in." Shit, Ernesto Philipino. What a stroke of luck; now I had his identity.

"I can't go to such a public location; there just is too much risk of disclosing my identity. Just follow my instructions so I can evaluate the information," I said, standing my ground, which became increasingly more important.

"Fuck, okay, I'll have one of my guys drop off the fucking packages tomorrow morning. When will I hear from you so I know I'm not fucking being ripped off?" One mil obviously made him a little nervous, and with a million in jeopardy, who could blame him?

"I'll phone you tomorrow afternoon and let you have a preliminary assessment," I said, trying to calm him down.

"What the fuck is a preliminary assessment?" Ernesto demanded to know.

"I will read through the information you provide and determine if the hit is feasible," came my succinct reply.

"Fuck, okay, I'll talk to you tomorrow, but just be aware, if you fuck with me, I'll come after you." This was a very serious comment, not made lightly; even though I considered myself in deep cover, Ernesto possibly had the resources to track me down and destroy my life, including the lives of my ex-wife and my children.

"Okay, tomorrow." I closed the cell phone, disconnecting the call.

At seven fifteen the next night, I picked up the package and envelope from the mailbox store. Both the dossier and the package of money were scanned for any tracking devices; none were found. The drive back to Croton without a doubt proved to be an extremely nervous one, as I had no idea what to expect from this new contract. There existed the real possibility of my being followed by one of Ernesto's henchman. The question, in my one-million-dollar-soused brain: did I have, without the one million, the necessary skill and objectivity to undertake a contract for the Ndranghetas and bring it to a successful conclusion, without getting myself killed? Could this be more than I could handle? The relatively large package of information had to contain at least two hundred pages. Once at home in my Croton condominium, a thorough reading of the contents might dissolve my worries.

Before going to my apartment, a stop at the diner for dinner would satiate my hunger, as I hadn't eaten anything since the previous night. While waiting for my meal, an old high-school friend recognized me and came over for a chat. We talked about what we had done since leaving Croton Harmon High School. James, my friend or acquaintance, hadn't really left Croton. Once he graduated, he married a girlfriend from high school, and followed in his father's footsteps building a very successful local painting business. We gradually ran out of things to say and parted, promising to stay in touch. It's good to have a little reminiscing to pass some idle time. My dinner arrived, and I quickly devoured it in silence.

At my condo, I opened the first package, a relatively large box, and there, in front of me, lay one million dollars in hundred dollar bills. Have you ever wondered what a package of ten thousand one hundred dollars bills looked like? I had never thought about it before but there it sat in a very nice attaché case right in front of me, one million dollars. I considered opening one of the packages and throwing it in the air like you see in the movies or on TV. Better not indulge myself until the contract had been completed, and then a private little party would be in order.

The second package contained approximately two hundred pages, typed, and with a number of diagrams and maps. To my amazement, extensive and extremely private details of the Mafioso and the Ndrangheta were disclosed in the dossier. I had no idea why Ernesto had permitted such detail to be sent to a person outside the two organizations. My only assessment was that this information had been compiled for some hit man within the organization. From this point on, any dealings with Ernesto had to be handled with extreme caution. The next eight to nine hours were spent reading through all the information provided by Ernesto and his associates, with some of the more important sections read multiple times to ensure I had a thorough understanding of every aspect of the target's operation and his home. Home didn't adequately describe this fortress, a well-designed, well-maintained, and well-manned fortification.

Angelo Lambrascha, known as The Don, or the godfather, of New York City, also controlled all the surrounding areas including Westchester County, North New Jersey, Atlantic City, and the southern portion of Connecticut. For years, the Mafioso and the Ndrangheta got along, no known bad blood existed between them; however, Ernesto wanted to expand his operations into the outer boroughs of New York City, namely Brooklyn, Queens, and Richmond (Staten Island). Angelo stood in the way. Numerous efforts at negotiations had been made without success. Angelo would not budge.

Ernesto had met with the other Ndrinas, or the family bosses who control all of the Ndrangheta organization. He had made numerous trips to Calabria, Italy, soliciting the approval of the other Ndrinas, all of whom agreed he should expand his operation. Most had cautioned Ernesto to avoid getting into open warfare with the Mafia in New York City. Ernesto concluded the only way of accomplishing his desired expansion without confronting the Mafia was simply to remove the blockage, to take out Angelo.

In this regard, several attempts had been made on Angelo's life, all of which had failed dismally. To date, five of Ernesto's best men had been killed and another six captured and sent out of the country with no prospect of returning. No one remained in his organization he could trust to carry out the hit. At this point, Ernesto did not even trust any of his lieutenants. No one else in the Ndrangheta was willing to undertake the contract.

The reason for their reluctance became quite clear as details unfolded as I read through the package. Angelo had an estate near Lake Placid, New York, a small city located in the Adirondack Mountains. The estate, an almost impenetrable fortress, was designed, constructed, and managed under the direction of several former FBI and CIA agents, hired specifically to provide protection for Angelo.

The grounds were surrounded by double chain-link fences. A dirt path behind the two fences provided both ATV mounts and foot patrols to guard against any intrusion. The fence, located two hundred yards from Angelo's home, formed an almost Berlin-wall effect. Inside the dirt road and circling the property were all kinds of devices used to sense any movement or even any unusual sound.

Angelo's home, a large brick building with an attached six-car garage, sat alone among forty-plus acres of forested land. Whenever he left the estate, on extremely rare occasions, he rode in an armored vehicle, accompanied by at least four other vehicles carrying armed personnel. Because of the mix of the vehicles, one could not determine which car or SUV Angelo rode in. Before any of the convoy left the compound, a complete sweep of the three-and-a-half-mile-long driveway and adjoining land had to be undertaken to ensure the area was completely safe and free of any intruders.

The estate sat approximately one and a half miles south of Lake Placid (the lake, not the city). The only paved road anywhere near the estate was New York State Route 73, which lay three miles to the east. The driveway into the estate could not be easily identifiable from Route 73, being just a dirt logging road leading off the highway. The seclusion, in a sense, was a plus for me—the more secluded, the better.

This would be an extremely difficult contract to fulfill but, shit, two million, how could I turn this down? The entire next day I spent going over every detail of the information provided by Ernesto. The plans covered every technical aspect of the property, including the builder's architectural drawing of Angelo's house. The basement area and the area over the garages were used strictly for security operations. The rest of the house, a very well-equipped home, was strictly for Angelo and his staff.

In addition to having the security force, which numbered about fifteen, there existed a household staff. The staff consisted of a personal assistant, several attractive maids, and a very competent chef and several kitchen assistants. Personal rooms for each of the staff were provided in the home. The security members had individual rooms in the basement. The rear of the basement actually sat above ground, so most of the rooms occupied by the security force had a window looking out on the grounds to the rear of the building. The operations center occupied the front portion of the basement, below ground, and had no windows.

By any stretch of the imagination, Angelo would be an extremely difficult target to take out. Angelo had built a fortress and manned it with the best security money could buy. Penetrating inside the fence had been proven virtually impossible by my predecessors, who badly bungled the job. The previous would-be assassins had employed a commando approach of breaching the fence and attempting to blow up the house. They got as far as inside the outer fence before being shot dead. Any movement inside the protected area would quickly be recognized and eliminated. This, apparently, is what happened to Ernesto's commandos when they made attempts in the past to take out Angelo. Such attempts also alerted Angelo and his staff of some unknown organization trying to assassinate Angelo. These attempts only caused the security staff to improve the fortress.

My first inclination: walk away; the prospects here were just too great for failure, and the odds of completing the contract and getting away clean definitely were not in my favor. Looking at the one million in one hundred dollar bills sitting next to me on the couch had the usual mysterious effect it has on most people. It warps and fries your brain, and mine was definitely in the deep fryer.

I got one of the cell phones from my bedroom. Not knowing if the location of the activation could be traced, I got in my car and drove south for almost eight hours. Outside of Washington DC, I activated the phone. Since it was too early in the morning to phone Ernesto, I found a local diner just off the 95 and partook of a nice leisurely breakfast while reading the *Washington*

Post. Perhaps there might be some more information about Brianna, the FBI woman agent, but nothing could be found anywhere in the newspaper.

The day had a heavy mist, one of those east coast days that promised to be off and on light rain, mist, and fog. At ten in the morning, I phoned Ernesto and gave him the good news, so I thought.

"Yeah, who the fuck is this?" Could I expect less from Ernesto?

"It's Bill, I've completed the assessment of the target," I said, launching into my prepared speech, "and have concluded that I can fulfill the contract." I was being as brief as possible, not wanting to get in any protracted conversation with this guy.

"Holy fucking shit." Without a doubt, this had to be Ernesto. "What the fuck do you do, buy a new phone every fucking time you call?" He must monitor every phone call received, possibly recording our conversations.

"Yes, to protect my identity, I use a different phone each time," I said, being somewhat reluctant to answer in the affirmative. "Anyway, I can do the contract for you." Trying to keep this guy focused.

"Well, at least that is good fucking news. How soon can you finish this up?" Did this guy have a mellow side? I doubted it. His breathing resounded very heavily into the phone; he probably had his morning glass or two of wine or maybe one of his lovely women was under him taking care of his morning sexual needs.

"Although I haven't had the opportunity of actually reconnoitering the site"—I shouldn't have been using two-dollar words with this guy, it only begged for trouble—"the contract can be feasibly completed within two months." This being my best guess.

"Two fucking months, two fucking months?" he bellowed into the phone, "Jesus fucking Christ what are you doing, renting a fucking tank? I figured two fucking weeks. Two fucking months is too fucking long, my fucking grandmother could complete this contract in two fucking months." Now he actually screamed into the phone, as if the increased volume would make a difference. There remained no doubt in my mind of how it would be to work directly for this arrogant fuck. Regardless of how deviant his underlings were, I felt a brief sense of sympathy.

"If you want me to do this job," I responded in a very controlled voice, "if you want this job done right, and you want it successfully completed, it has to be on my timetable. Otherwise, I will return all the money to you and we can part company. Are we in agreement on the timeframe?" Be firm, mother fucker, or you'll join all the previous hit men.

"Fuck. Fuck. You fucking come highly recommended, but two fucking months. Shit, my fucking dead aunt could take this guy out in two fucking months," he launched into a tirade.

I let things hang, not responding to his outburst, waiting for him to make up his mind.

"Fuck, okay, two fucking months, but keep me informed as to your activity, so I know how you are progressing." Fucker actually began to calm down, big surprise there. Now we were getting somewhere.

"There will be no communications during this operation since such communications could give away my position," this being a fundamental, non-negotiable, restriction on my part. Any phone talk or other communications could easily be picked up by the security force in Angelo's compound.

"Man, you could be long fucking gone," his voice, now at an even tempo, "gone with my fucking mil in two fucking months." He continued to press, but there would be no further negotiations.

"Sorry, but those are the terms of the contract. I cannot risk being detected." Continuing in a very flat tone of voice, "This is for your benefit as well as mine. Any communication picked up by Angelo's men would be traced from me to you."

"Okay. O fucking K, in two months I expect to fucking hear from you or I'll have you fucking hunted down and castrated, and fucking believe me, I will have you hung by your fucking nuts." He remained nervous about his money, but I didn't blame him.

"If you don't hear from me in two months, it's probably because I'm dead. I'll start the operation tomorrow." I hung up.

The return drive to Croton continued in a dreary day, with the light fog and misty rain adding to the monotony of the tires whining on the roadway. Falling asleep at the wheel became a major concern, so much so that a little side trip to Atlantic City would provide a good diversion.

Atlantic City as a whole has never quite regained the luster of the '30s, '40s and '50s. Gambling casinos are primarily along the boardwalk. Once you walk a few blocks in from the boardwalk, the city is somewhat depressing. But hell, I just wanted to drop some cash. Not wanting to elicit undue attention, I decided to distribute my cash between three different casinos along the boardwalk. After losing five or six thousand, I decided to call it a day.

Christ, not in my wildest dreams would I ever have considered dropping so much money so nonchalantly at gambling. One fervent goal, of my otherwise mundane life, is to select several financially struggling families and secretly funnel a significant amount of money into their bank accounts. Maybe ten randomly selected families, their culture, color, religion, ancestry did not matter, just their financial situation, their need for cash, and their being a well-structured family. The problem, first and foremost, was the IRS and how to get around the agency's requirements on traceability of all funds greater than ten thousand dollars. Something to think about, but for now put it on the back burner for future reference.

Walking a few blocks in from the boardwalk, I found an excellent seafood restaurant. The area seemed a little seedy, but the restaurant proved to be outstanding. Maybe the Gulf Coast of the United States offers some exceptional seafood; I'd never been there. From my perspective, the best seafood to be found anywhere in the United States is along the Eastern Seaboard. Several friends who have traveled a little more extensively than I have informed me that California seafood just isn't comparable to the East Coast. My recent trip to California had not provided me with sufficient time to put that theory to the test.

At about six o'clock, I headed north to Croton. Having had my fill of coffee, I was now really wired from the caffeine, I drove out of Atlantic City and turned north on the Garden State Parkway. Shit, the fog and the drizzle had gotten worse, and it sure made driving a fun task, if you consider driving in fog and drizzle fun. A normally three-hour drive ended up taking closer to six, but better to arrive late and alive than not at all.

Before getting too involved with this new character, a little more research on the Ndrangheta, particularly more detailed information on Ernesto Philipino, and his enforcer, Gino Francotti, would better prepare me in dealing with them. If I wanted my plan for diverting fault to these characters to work, instead of me being in the FBI's cross hairs, a more in-depth understanding of the Ndrangheta organization had to be compiled and analyzed. From this point on, whatever next, and hopefully last, contract I take on would have some evidence left at the scene implicating the Ndrangheta and with Gino in particular.

I spent several days at the New York City Library going through archives of New York daily papers along with in-depth analysis completed by various well-known local writers. From this seemly endless trove of data, I developed a number of facts and a few assumptions.

Ernesto Philipino's wife, Juliana, no longer the beauty she once had been, had now become a bitching, complaining, and demanding pain in the ass. Of course, Ernesto had never been a particularly great husband either, with four or five young woman located around the state of New York, several in Atlantic City, New Jersey, and, to keep things in the family, a couple in Calabria, Italy.

Juliana had a brother, Frank Valicina, whom she adored but who Ernesto held in great contemp. Juliana nagged Ernesto day and night to give Frank a job in one of his enterprises. Juliana had no real understanding as to what type of businesses Ernesto owned or managed; only that he was very successful.

Ernesto finally relented and gave Frank one of the pizza parlors in the Brooklyn borough of New York City.

Through research at a branch of the New York City libraries in Brooklyn, I turned up information on Frank Valicina. Archived on the computer system, there stood Frank Valicina in a front-page photo from a Brooklyn weekly paper. The photo showed Frank and some of his pizza business associates standing in front of Frank's Pizzeria. Frank's Pizzeria had an ideal business location on the north side of Atlantic Avenue between Crescent Street and Euclid Avenue. Atlantic Avenue and Euclid Avenue are two of the main drags in Brooklyn.

For several weeks, I kept track of Frank's movement. Generally, he would show up at the pizza joint at ten in the morning and open by ten thirty. On Wednesdays, he religiously, showed up at nine in the morning, went into the store, came back out, locked up, and carried a small cloth bag to the Brooklyn Bank. The bank has a branch at the intersection of Atlantic Avenue and Euclid, just a short distance from the store.

On the third Wednesday of my monitoring Frank's movements, I followed him to the Brooklyn Bank. The decision to follow him proved fortuitous, as Frank made an error in filling out a deposit slip for his personal checking account. He discarded the deposit slip into a wastebasket near the table used by bank customers to fill out various banking forms.

After Frank left, I sauntered over to the table and pretended to fill out a form, which I wadded up and tossed into the basket Frank had discarded his error deposit slip in. Acting like I had made an error in discarding the form, I looked into the basket and found Frank's slip. I took it from the wastebasket and held it in my hand until I left the bank.

Taking a short subway ride over to Manhattan, I went to my a savings and loan bank, a branch of the Bank of Ossining where my saving and checking accounts were, and arranged for a deposit in varying amounts of one hundred, one fifty, two hundred, etc. to be deposited into Frank's checking account. The deposits had to be completed every Wednesday around nine forty-five.

Having had success using the library system to identify Frank Valicina, I went to the New York City central library in Manhattan. Additional information on Ernesto and a number of his so-called associates, who were really his lackeys, were found in the newspaper achieves. The files included photos and the business locations of each lackey.

By identifying and tracking some of Ernesto's henchmen, a restaurant and bar just south of his office building appeared to be their hang out. Puglisi's Steak House, an upscale Italian restaurant, proved to be a hangout for both the Mafioso and Ndrangheta. Using some eavesdropping equipment, purchased at a specialty shop in New York City, I concealed a functioning iPod/listening device/recorder in my pocket, providing me with ability of listening to and recording various conversations. Employing this method, albeit a dangerous one, I developed a significant amount of information on Frank and Ernesto's dislike of him. This information would prove quite valuable.

Chapter 19

The next day, I loaded the car with some equipment and clothing. From my apartment, a short drive to White Plains Airport brought me to my first destination of the day, the long-term parking lot. I parked my car and took the shuttle to the main terminal. Using Ralph Christenson's identity, I rented a car from one of the local car rental companies. Once my luggage and equipment had been safely stored in the trunk, I began my drive to Lake Placid, New York.

The drive north on the New York State Thruway and then north on the Quickway (a section of the New York State Thruway running from Albany to the Canadian border) to the Adirondacks is actually a spectacular drive. The scenery, especially in the Adirondacks, is breathtaking. Rarely is there any heavy traffic, not even going through the populated areas of Albany, New York, the state's capitol. I had lucked out with a beautiful sunshiny day filled with magnificent soft blue skies interrupted by high-rising cumulus clouds that settled on the peaks of the Adirondack's tall pine trees. What more could one ask for? Maybe a million and three-quarters dollars stashed away in safety deposits at the Bank of Ossining. Shit, what if a fire occurred at the bank? Man, I'd be one poor motherfucker. What a dumb thought causing me to momentarily neglect the beauty around me.

A modern, expansive resort hotel located on the shores of Lake Placid would be my temporary home. The resort rested on the shores of Lake Placid just south of the city, a good location for my purpose. This being off-season, early September, the rates weren't astronomical, not that I really cared. The resort provided, swimming, sailboarding, sailing, and camping; these activities were what piqued my interest in the resort, in addition to its location. You could camp on the opposite shore of the lake or on any of the small islands that dotted the lake itself. Sailing and camping were all I needed to accomplish my research of the area and, in particular, Angelo Lambrascha's estate.

The drive up had taken more than eight hours, so bedtime would come early. In the meantime, a little stroll around the area provided a restful break before retiring to the resort for the night. The sun had begun to set over the opposite shore of the lake. The sky turned a unique red and gold with a greenish hue. The clouds added to the perfect picture by exhibiting mounds of red and pink interspersed with shades of gray. Christ, was I starting to mature in my old age or what? The diversion provided time to clear the cobwebs out of my brain, and now onto the business I came here for.

The next day, I rented a small twelve-foot sailboat from the resort hotel. Some smart-assed kid wanted to show me how to sail before he would let me take the boat out. It took me all of ten minutes to convince him of my sailing skills, especially after picking up a strong breeze and setting the boat almost on its side. I imagine he was anxious to get back to the dock so he could clean his shorts out. Small lake sailing is a far cry from Hudson River sailing or ocean sailing, which I had become extensively experienced at.

The resort had provided a fairly decent map of the lake and the surrounding area. Using the map, I charted a course for the opposite shore of the lake to a point that would bring me close to Angelo's fortress. Once on the other side of the lake, I tied the boat to a tree and started to make my way through the forest in the direction of Angelo's estate.

Moving through the forested area with its dense undergrowth proved to be extremely difficult and time-consuming. Luckily, I'd left the resort early in the morning, so there would be sufficient time to complete the task of scoping out the area surrounding the fortress and returning to the resort before sunset. The location of Angelo's property was approximately six miles from the lake. Using a GPS to guide me through the woods, which included some rock-climbing, I was able to travel about one mile per hour. This pace would allow little time to scope out the target and return to the resort but I had no other choice. If my trek took too long, I would notify the hotel of my delay by using one of the cell phones. This had to be a last resort situation, using the cell phone would possibly alert the security at Angelo's. On the other hand, having a search party come out from the resort looking for me wouldn't do either. I had to press on and set a time limit, a point at which turning back was the only option.

I quickened my pace, covering the next mile in about forty-five minutes. My conditioning now paying off, as the next two miles were completed in a total of one hour. On a flat plain in the forest, the anchor fence came into view approximately five hundred feet in front of me. In my judgment, I could not approach the fence any closer than the five hundred feet. A search for a good hide became the next important step in my plan. After an hour of searching, I concluded just too much time had been devoted to this task. Just settling on any position for a hide would not satisfy my criteria, a good hide provided the necessary concealment needed to avoid detection. I knew from my training that diligent attention to detail would result in survival. Over an hour later, an excellent site had been located. I actually borrowed into it to ensure full concealment from every angle, 360 degrees. The GPS coordinates were accurately recorded on my little map and stored into the GPS memory chip.

Getting back to the sailboat and returning to the resort before nightfall required some added physical effort, but I had to make it happen. At three in the afternoon, I started the trek back. As it took more than four hours to get to the location, not counting the hours spent searching for a hide, going back would get me to the shore around seven. The sun would set at six thirty-two, although it would be light out until maybe seven o'clock. At least I knew the terrain and utilized the GPS memory chip to retrace my path back out, hopefully cutting a half hour of more off the return trip.

Things were going pretty good until I almost reached the lake. Some grunting could be heard in the direction of the lake. I couldn't slow down and start avoiding every sound that came up. I took ten more paces and there in front of me stood a brown bear, his beady little eyes scanning over me. Shit, what to do; what had I read about confronting wildlife? Do not run is at the top of the list. Make yourself appear as large as possible, extending your arms out from your body and spread your legs quickly flashed through my mind.

I followed these rules to no avail, this fucker just wanted to chow down on me, no question about that. The urge to run overwhelmed my emotions, but I needed to keep my cool and stand my ground, as shaky as my ground might be. Mr. Bear sauntered over to have a closer look at his dinner and maybe take a little nibble to see if it fulfilled his hunger needs. One thing for sure, his meal now shook like Jell-O, not to mention my clothing had become saturated with sweat, accompanied by some urine making its way down into my left boot. He sniffed my leg and worked slowly up my body until we were face-to-face. He sniffed my face for a few moments, gave my nose a lick, and dropped down and sauntered away.

What, I'm not good enough for you, Mr. Bear? Maybe you can find some berries that are more filling. Remaining poised, I kept my arms outstretched until my furry friend sauntered out of sight. Funny, I had the Gluck with me most times when I ventured out, but being concerned about running into someone of authority during my journey precluded me from including it on this trip. Just as well, killing a bear didn't particularly appeal to me; besides, it is a violation of New York State law; brown bears are a protected species. Nothing about brown bears killing humans, I guess that is okay.

The encounter with Mr. Bear took almost a half hour off my schedule. However, a nice evening easterly breeze had come up on the lake, which propelled the sailboat in record time back to the resort. By the time I had docked, secured the boat to the dock, and stowed the sails, the sun had set and dusk slowly fell over the lake.

Returning to my room, I reflected on my day and my encounter with the bear. This unquestionably would be a very difficult project that required a great deal of thought and planning. In retrospect, perhaps more than two months should have been proposed initially to Ernesto. It just seemed to me I hadn't allowed sufficient time to complete the contract. For the next three hours, I outlined a plan, making definitive notations of every possible action needed to complete it. Two major hurdles existed. First, the double chain-link anchor fence. Any attempt to shoot through the fence could result in the bullet being deflected and not hitting the target. Second, Angelo rarely left the building, and when he did, he always rode in an array of six bulletproof cars surrounded by a security force. The array of six vehicles made it impossible to determine which vehicle Angelo rode in. To add to the complexity, the security staff would frequently make runs with just the six vehicles without Angelo in any of them. In addition, I had no way of knowing when he would be leaving the compound.

By morning, a plan began to germinate in my overtaxed brain. As I envisioned it, the fences could be taken out by two RPGs (rifle propelled grenades) fired in quick succession. The first would blow a hole through the outer fence and the second would blow a hole in the inner fence. Now that a path had been cleared to the main house, the next question remained on how to penetrate the brick and mortar construction of the house. Angelo rarely, if ever, went outside the large home. No daily walks, no flower gardens to maintain, to the best of my knowledge and in all the data provided by Ernesto, nothing would bring him out of his fortress.

Christ, just getting two RPGs would be a major task. On top of that, some method of penetrating the walls of the main house had to be devised, and knowing exactly when the target would be in range, appeared to be almost impossible. When I had been a scout/sniper in the Marine Corps, some new technology was in development. A fifty-caliber rifle had been used successfully on a number of occasions to take out targets at least one mile distant of the shooter. The fifty-caliber round could penetrate six inches of steel, so unquestionably it could penetrate eight plus inches of masonry. More intriguing and of great concern to me was the development of a radarscope that could see through a cement block, bricks, and structures of similar construction.

So my problem was how to acquire a fifty-caliber rifle along with at least six fifty-caliber rounds designed to penetrate masonry. In addition, two RPGs had to be purchased, fully loaded and ready to go. Shit, just child's play, anyone could pick up this equipment on any street corner in New York City. Bullshit. This would take a lot of imagination, not to mention research and extensive travel. I definitely wouldn't find this equipment anywhere in the United States. Then the question arose as to where this equipment could be purchased.

Once back in Croton, various possibilities of locating and purchasing the equipment raced through my mind. Somewhere in Central or South America appeared to be a good place to start, definitely high on my list. The Middle East, where there so much turmoil existed, had to be considered. Pakistan, India, and Bangladesh came to mind. But just thinking about these developed no definitive plan. What approach should I use? The Internet popped into my mind, almost anything could be found online; I just needed a clandestine search engine so any search could not be traced back to me.

Tossing and turning in my bed and not solving the problems robbed me of a good night's sleep. Just as I dosed off, there came a tap on the sliding glass door leading to the deck off my bedroom. Had some fucking woodpecker decided to drill into the glass door? Tap, tap, a little louder this time. Shit, not bothering to turn on any lights, I got up and went, very cautiously, to the door. The moon shone brightly on the river and the surrounding landscape. Just outside my door on the deck stood a small figure who looked to be completely dressed in black.

Who the hell would this be at this hour? I slid the door open, and the figure darted into my bedroom.

"Just hold on a fucking minute," I demanded. "Who the fuck are you?"

"Why don't you turn on the light by your nightstand so you can find out who I am?" said a familiar voice, but not one I could immediately identify. Following her instructions, I turned the light on.

"Jesus Christ, I don't believe it, what the fuck are you doing here?" I demanded to know, my total surprise evident in my voice. "Didn't you have enough of me the last time you were here?" Despite my remarks, I tried to be soft-spoken.

"You know, big guy, you're not the bad ass you think you are," the tone of her voice enticing me, so inviting. "Actually, you're not such a bad man, as men go, that is. I kind of like you, plus the business I am in doesn't allow me to make any lasting relationships. Since you seem to be a guy on the go, I thought maybe we could share a superficial relationship, one that would relieve our tensions, that is, without having to spill our guts out to each other. Anyway, I kind of like the way you took command and took advantage last time, even though I had a sore ass for a few hours. What do you say, shall we link up occasionally?" The sexiness of her voice caused my ole johnson to start to rise. Jesus, what a proposition, and one I just could not refuse. Such a relationship would be ideal. No strings of any kind, super.

"You know," I said, faltering a little in my response, "what's your name? That sounds like a really doable proposition; I'll go for it, no strings." A rather hasty response, however, I sure didn't need any time to think this through.

"Just call me Sabrina, I already know your name is Oscar." Shit, she already had a leg up on me, metaphorically speaking, that is. What else did she know about me that perhaps I didn't want shared?

"You've evidently been reading my mail," I observed.

"Not really," she said, looking straight at me with beautiful brown eyes, "I saw your name on something last time I stopped by. I'm really not a snoop, except when I'm going about my business, of course. What do you say we get busy right now by taking a nice hot shower together?" She started stripping down as she headed toward my bathroom, obviously no reply required.

"Shit, I always have hated showering alone." I followed her lead.

The next few hours consisted of sex like I'd never experienced before; this girl, Sabrina, proved to be an answer to any man's dream, she absolutely trumped any previous relationship, bar none. I knew this sex dream would soon end, and I would wake up in a pile of goo. There couldn't be a single position or method of a sexual act that we did not engage in. By three in the morning, we both were so exhausted from our labor of love that we fell asleep, on the floor, fully engaged in each other's arms.

At ten fifteen, the golden rays of the late morning sun cast through my open sliding glass door. Sabrina had left sometime during the early morning hours. I never got to thank her for our lovely evening. It seemed a good idea, though, to check my valuables to see if anything might be missing or disturbed. I found everything in place and my wallet as I had left it the night before. The Beretta, I found it where it had been hidden; still in place under the mattress where accessing it took seconds. Great, a fantastic new relationship with no strings. What more could a guy ask for?

It dawned on me that this fantastic relationship had been established on Sabrina's terms, not mine. She could come and go as she pleased, but what about poor old me? What if some afternoon or evening I had a strong craving for some physical action? Where, oh, where would Sabrina be? I would have no way of contacting her. There is an old saying, "Don't look a gift horse in the mouth, you might not like what you find." She was definitely a gift horse and no way would I ever look in her mouth. I might stick my tongue in and wiggle it around but actually looking in her mouth, no way.

With recreational activities taken care of, I had to get back to the project at hand. The little diversion was probably good for my psyche, as with all the concentration that had been put into the planning of this project, a headache had begun to throb in my demented brain. The sex with Sabrina relaxed me, so assessing the problems with the project proved to be a little easier.

An Internet search appeared to be the best approach. However, it could not be performed on my computer or anything tied to my identity. To be safe, a random drive into America's heartland would take me away from my home and my computer. I drove east on U.S. Interstate 70, exiting at number 107 and driving south on South Hamilton Road until I reached Eastland Mall. Cruising around the mall, I eventually found an Internet café. Using my good friend Ralph Christenson's identity, several hours of computer time with online capability were acquired.

Finding a source for contraband military hardware, as expected, was not an easy process. Just going to a widely used and popular search engine and typing in fifty-caliber rifle would probably bring some local FBI agent storming into the café. To my amazement, a Barrett M82A1 is legally sold in the United States, although not all states allow its sale. Purchasing one in the United States would entail all kinds of record checks, so that idea had to be discharged out of hand. My first thought: look at some other country's Web pages and work from there. The only problem with this approach was, I didn't speak or understand any foreign language.

The only logical approach, I hoped, was to type in a search for arms dealers in Brazil, which to the best of my knowledge, is a country engaged in selling large and disparate military hardware. At least in the jumbled files of my overtaxed brain I had some recollection of reading about arms dealers in Brazil. It seemed like a good place to start anyway.

Success! A name came up in Niteroi, Brazil, a city of half a million people located across the Baia Da Guanabara (The Bay of Guanabara) from Rio de Janeiro, Brazil. Just a point of interest; a nine-mile long bridge, the longest in Brazil, connects the two cities.

Señor Murilo Barbosa lists himself, in English no less, on the Internet as a military hardware provider that can accommodate just about any requirement. Damn, could this be so easy? Contacting him cold, either on the Internet or by landline phone, would result in dismal failure. A face-to-face meeting would be a professional technique that posed a greater prospect of success. I figured it best to fly to Rio de Janeiro and somehow meet face-to-face with Mr. Barbosa. In order to accept any shipments into the United States, some fictitious business with a real corporate seal, an IRS tax number, and a legal address needed to be established. A legitimate passport and a visa for Brazil also had to be obtained, all using good ole Ralph Christenson's identification.

First step: setting up a fictitious corporate business. Not a problem since Wylton Computer Systems provided considerable experience in establishing a corporation. Shit, that reminded me to phone Janet and Mom; I had to get on that right away. Janet seemed kind of distant and said that everything was going all right with the business and at home. The kids would like to see me and spend a little time together, all doable. I would go by tomorrow. Mom and Dad were fine and thanked me for checking in, asking if I would come by for dinner, which sounded fine to me, so Mom would set a date.

The papers for the business I had drawn up and processed by a law firm in New York City, which incorporated my business in Connecticut. I rented a small office space in Bridgeport, Connecticut. Also, some furniture and equipment, including computers, office phone system, and other paraphernalia, I obtained through a rental agreement, so the office appeared like a relatively successful small business.

Hiring a receptionist: definitely necessary to the illusion of a successful, functioning business. The only problem with hiring a secretary was how would she at least appear to be busy doing something? Maxine Brothton, the first and only person interviewed, accepted the position as secretary receptionist. She was rather young, in her early twenties, and sort of attractive, though that didn't matter. I gave her a key and told to open the office from nine and close it at five daily, except weekends and holidays. Some mail might be coming in, just open it and file it that is all, over and out. I would be traveling, for the most part, and would phone in on a regular basis to see if any problems cropped up.

Before flying down to Rio, I stopped by Janet's, my old home, to spend some time with Emma and David. Emma and David, as usual, were excited to see me, with plenty of shrieking, squealing, hugs, and kisses. Janet had prepared a big cookout in the backyard, family style. She dressed in a lovely print blouse and tight white shorts. I had to admit that she started to look much more attractive. Janet wasn't as warm and huggie as on the last time we were together. Just as well, it made me feel a lot more comfortable.

After eating, we all sat around, played games, and had a lot of laughs. The evening stretched into night, but it wasn't a problem since the kids didn't have school the next day. David went to bed first around eleven, and he begged me to come and tuck him in, which, of course, I did. The conversation that he launched into before saying good night definitely unnerved me.

"Daddy, when are you going to come back and live with us?" the excitement evident in his voice. "Mommy said as soon as you finished up some business, you are going to come back, and we would be family again," the volume of his voice growing louder toward the end of his sentence.

The shock of the question took a few seconds to sink in. How could I answer this question without either encouraging him or, just the opposite, letting him know there were no prospects of my returning to the family situation?

"Daddy has some very important business to take care of before we can consider being a family again." My voice soft, hopefully to ease him to sleep, "When the business is finished, we can talk about getting together as a family. Can you keep that among us men?" Shuck and jive, what else could be done?

"Okay, Daddy, I'll wait for you and keep it just between us men." He smiled up at me, accepting my explanation, sleepiness creeping into his voice as his head lay over on the pillow.

I kissed him and said goodnight. That damn Janet was being her old manipulative self. How could I get out of this one? She probably even had my parents thinking everything would be rosy again. Shit.

Janet and Emma were waiting for me in the living room. Sitting down, I scowled at Janet, and I'm sure she got the message. Emma's turn for bed and she asked her daddy to tuck her in. I didn't want another third degree, but I can't say no to my children.

"Daddy, Mommy says you might come back and live with us when you finish your business, will you *please*?" She looked up at me with pleading blue, moist eyes. This was heart-wrenching manipulation, damn it; wait 'til Janet was confronted with this.

"Let Daddy finish up his business in a few months, and then we will see about getting together, okay?" She seemed satisfied.

Now on to Janet, for the confrontation, but she foiled me. That sneaky fuck went off to bed. She left a note apologizing, saying she was just too tired to say goodnight. If I had a good set of balls, right back to the bedroom I would go, but of course I didn't, my nuts were little shriveled peas.

The next day: off to Rio de Janeiro, Brazil.

Chapter 20

The flight to Rio de Janeiro proved to be long and tedious, but a few pretty stewardesses made for a more relaxing trip. The flight arrived late at night, after ten o'clock, which didn't leave me time to rent a car and familiarize myself with the area. Staying in Rio instead of trying to make it over to Niteroi definitely proved to be the best option. A cab driver recommended a very upscale hotel in downtown Rio that turned out to be an excellent choice. Sleeping into the late morning and having a very leisurely breakfast of Brazilian steak, eggs, home fries, and coffee was definitely a good way to start the day, especially the Brazilian steak.

Before checking out of the hotel, the concierge arranged a rental car for me. The hotel also arranged for my stay in Niterio at one of their sister hotels. Driving around Rio provided a good snapshot of life in Brazil, at least in Rio de Janeiro, Brazil. The concierge had marked on a map, sections of the city to avoid, as they could prove dangerous, primarily to foreigners. For the most part, traffic moved freely, a nice change from traffic in New York City. The nine-mile-long bridge connecting Rio de Janeiro to Niteroi is a pleasant drive across an incredibly beautiful, deep aqua blue Baia da Guanabara. Many ships could be seen heading out to sea or coming into one of the many harbors, wharfs, and piers that dotted the bay. The import-export business has increased dramatically in the past ten years, as Brazil has grown to be a significant financial power, particularly in South America.

The mid-morning sun glistened off the water giving off various shades of yellow from a deep golden tone to a brilliant bright reminiscent of daisies or similar flowers. At the far end of the bridge, a tollbooth loomed ready to devour large amounts of my Brazilian *reals* (Brazilian dollar equivalents). To my pleasant surprise, the toll came to twenty *reals*, in U.S. terms, about ten bucks. Ten bucks to cross such a magnificent structure. The Baia Da Guanabara Bay Bridge is one of the longest and highest bridges in the world, the bridge being close to nine miles long and close to three thousand feet high at the highest span.

Niteroi is a wonderfully beautiful city with a smooth transition from the architecture of old Brazil to the modern glass museums that the city is noted for. The city overlooks Baia da Guanabara, with breathtaking views of the bay from my hotel room. The first day I spent getting checked in and acclimating myself to the hotel and the surrounding area. A walk down Rua XV de Novembro brought me to the building where Mr. Murilo Barbosa had his office.

In the lobby of the building, I found several directories indicating the floor and office of the occupants. To my surprise, one of the directories presented everything in English. Additionally, an individual passing though the lobby informed me that roughly sixty percent of Brazilians speak English. This unquestionably was good news, as I had no idea how to speak or understand Portuguese, the principal and official language of Brazil.

According the directory Mr. Barbosa occupied offices on the sixth floor in what appeared to be a double suite. Noting that no guard or receptionist maintained security at the lobby level, I decided to take an elevator ride to the sixth floor. The building, a modern structure with expensive furnishings included very expensive carpeted hallways, the kind of carpet you sink to your ankles in. carpeted hallways and thick, elaborately carved mahogany doors on each office throughout the building. I found Mr. Barbosa's suite situated right as you exited the elevator. Waiting another day, however, I considered prudent, as the time would provide me the opportunity to acclimate myself to Niterio and allow me time to prepare for a potential audience with Mr. Barbosa. How I would introduce myself and how best to approach asking him to provide me with weapons without particularly disclosing their likely use?

That afternoon I spent in several of the museums, which are interspersed about the city. The best known is Niemeyer Complex, which overlooks the bay. The buildings are contemporary and they featured modern artists of Brazil. In keeping with the modernist architecture of the building, most of the art within the buildings tended to be contemporary, which was not necessarily my cup of tea. Although I preferred more traditional forms of art, I did find the paintings and sculpture appealing. After completing my trip through the city, a nutritious meal at a recommended restaurant topped off the day.

My second day in Niteroi I planned to be strictly business, with a hoped for a face-to-face meeting with Mr. Barbosa. Just in case he agreed to see me, I had to ensure my fingerprints were not left on any articles in his office. From my luggage, a small bottle of super glue was removed and a small portion applied to each of my fingertips, taking care not to touch anything until the glue dried. Somehow, it didn't seem to portray an astute businessman to be walking around with various articles stuck to his fingers or his fingers glued together. Prior to my morning shower, all body hair was shaved off, save my dick area and my scalp. My head hair I cut as close to the scalp as possible without appearing to be some kind of skinhead or other related gang affiliate.

Since no effort had been made to schedule an appointment, a strong possibility existed that he would not even give me an audience. Entering his office through the large mahogany door brought me into a spacious reception area. I found the reception area, a large anteroom, to be expensively furnished with Italian leather furniture and original works of art; oil paintings hung on the three interior walls, and several pedestals displayed bronze statuary. The remaining wall, a windowed outer wall of the building, was furnished with a series of large glass windows framed in what appeared to be very expensive drapery.

A girl who looked to be in her late twenties sat behind a large mahogany desk. She looked up from her work, typing some information into a computer located on her desk. She spoke to me in what I thought to be Portuguese. Whatever, I couldn't decipher a word.

"I'm sorry, I only understand English," I said, staring at her with a blank look on my face. "Do you speak English?" I asked with a kind of I-hope-so look.

"Yes, I'm sorry. I speak several languages." She had a very pleasant, almost comforting voice, ideal for a person in her capacity. "How may I help you?" In addition to her lovely voice, she was quite beautiful. She wore a business suit, which partially concealed her ample breasts; there apparently was no blouse underneath. The front of her suit jacket opened just enough to display her cleavage. She had long black, shiny hair that hung over her shoulders on either side. Her eyes were a very soft brown like none I had ever seen before. They were most inviting, especially to a horny fuck like me.

"I am sorry," trying to conceal my effort not to look down her blouse, "I do not have an appointment, but I was wondering if Mr. Barbosa might take a few minutes to talk with me," I asked, slightly awkwardly but definitely in my best, practiced business intonation.

"And your name, please, sir?" Shit, she obviously had been instructed to always be strictly business, "and the purpose of your business with Mr. Barbosa?" She remained very pleasant. Probably thought I would prefer to spend my time looking inside her business jacket, looking at her tits, rather than seeing Mr. Barbosa.

"My name is Ralph Christenson," I said, starting to focus on the purpose of my visit, "and I am here to purchase some specialized equipment Mr. Barbosa may have." Continuing my strictly business composure suppressing the desire to somehow jump this lovely girl's bones and engage in unrestricted sexual gratification.

"Just a moment, please," she said as she turned in her chair, "while I ask Mr. Barbosa if he will see you." She got up and walked through a door just behind her desk.

Strange, I thought, no interoffice communication, or perhaps the young woman wanted to speak privately with Mr. Barbosa. Whatever, I just hoped Mr. Barbosa would consider seeing me.

Not knowing how long it would take, I sat on one of the Italian leather chairs and picked up a magazine to thumb through. To my surprise, the magazine was an American published magazine. The seemingly ubiquitous American publication *People,* I began to thumb through reaching only page two when the young woman reappeared in the door she had exited through.

"Mr. Barbosa will see you in a few minutes," she said with a very fetching smile that made my heart take an extra couple of beats, "he has a few business details he needs to finish up first. May I get you something to drink or eat? Perhaps some Brazilian coffee?" she asked politely, and maybe a little Brazilian pussy to go along with it.

"Yes, thank you, I would like some coffee, if it isn't too much trouble." Brazilian coffee is rich with excellent flavor, much stronger than any coffee available in the United States. She left the room through another door and returned shortly with a tray of coffee and some little sweet biscuits.

I continued to thumb through the *People* magazine, drink coffee, and munch on the biscuits, taking care not to leave any fingerprints on the magazine or coffee cup. Fortunately, the super glue appeared to be working. Approximately twenty minutes later, the door behind the woman's desk opened and a gentleman in his late forties or early fifties emerged.

"Mr. Christensen," he looked over at me, "would you like to come in?" He addressed me in a very pleasant and deep masculine voice.

"Yes," I replied, getting up from the chair and approaching Mr. Barbosa, who held the door open so I could enter his office. Once his office door closed, he extended his hand in a firm but friendly handshake. His office, considerably larger than the reception area, had an unobstructed view of Baia da Guanabara through floor to ceiling plate glass windows. The furnishings, carpeting, woodwork, and window drapes all appeared to have been selected and installed by a professional decorator, all right out of *Architecture Magazine* or some other upscale source. The walls were adorned with many original paintings, some by Brazilian artists and many others by internationally recognized artists. He sat behind a large mahogany desk, situated so he had a commanding view of the city and bay while still facing his guest or business associate.

Mr. Barbosa is what one might expect of a successful South America businessman, a short stocky man with black wavy hair and piercing brown, almost black, eyes. He dressed in a business suit, undoubtedly a very expensive one; under his jacket, he wore a white, French-cuffed shirt and a soft, muted red and gray striped tie.

"How may I help you?" he asked with a pleasant smile as he tilted back in his large dark red leather arm chair.

"I am looking to purchase some specialized military hardware," I answered in a very short, clipped sentence direct and very businesslike.

"I see," he studied me very carefully, "but what brings you to me in particular?"

"I conducted a search, looking for military equipment dealers who might have these particular items in their inventories." I wanted to convey that I was a person of trust and knowledge.

"And what type of equipment might that be?" He seemed a bit standoffish, which indicated he might not be particularly interested in doing business at all with me. Perhaps, however, he employed this method to ferret out prospective clients, at least ones he considered untrustworthy or devious; after all, this is a very dangerous business. Unfortunately for me I fell in the devious classification, just hoped my cover held up.

"Specifically, I am looking for two RPGs, a fifty-caliber rifle, a radarscope, a Barrett M86A1 scope, and night vision goggles with both infrared and light enhancement capabilities," I answered. "With the fifty-caliber rifle some specialized ammunition will be needed," adding to my growing list.

"Very interesting." He nodded. "But I doubt if I carry such equipment in my stock. Normally my business is with purchasers who require significant inventories, not individual items. I sincerely doubt if I can be of service to you." He sat up in his chair but did not get up from it, a very positive sign.

"Perhaps you can recommend another military hardware provider who sells this type equipment." I wanted to explore every possibility with him, not just give up. "Maybe someone who deals in individual items." I grasped for straws, hoping he would loosen up a little or at least share some of his business knowledge with me.

"Why don't we go to lunch and talk a little more. Perhaps once we know each other a little better we can talk business." His offer surprised me, definitely more than I had hoped for; had he broken the ice a little? A small prayer passed through my mind and across my lips, my sacrilegious mind.

For lunch, which more accurately might be considered an early dinner, we drove across the nine-mile bridge spanning Baia da Guanabara (Guanabara

Bay) to Rio de Janeiro. Rio is a very modern city on the south side of Guanabara Bay and it has many very modern high-rise buildings. The restaurant Murilo selected sat at the top of one of the highest building in Rio, the JW Marriott Hotel.

Mr. Barbosa evidently frequented the restaurant often as the maître d' immediately escorted us to what undoubtedly would be considered the best table in the restaurant. The table placement provided a one hundred and eighty degree commanding view of Copacabana Beach. The hotel actually sat on the beach, one of the few on the Atlantic Ocean side of side of Av. Inf. D. Henrique, the main street along Copacabana Beach.

As soon as we sat down, a waiter placed a drink next to Barbosa and handed me a menu. Without even looking for a menu, Murilo began to address the waiter as one would a servant, frequently raising his voice. He spoke in Portuguese so I had no way of telling what transpired. Following his instructions to the waiter, Murilo turned to me.

"What would you like to drink?" he asked me in a very pleasant voice.

"Jack Daniels on the rocks," I requested in a pleasant tone, unintentionally offsetting Murilo's rather terse instructions to the waiter.

He turned to the waiter and instructed him to bring my drink immediately, at least I assumed "Pronto," meant right away.

"If you haven't had Brazilian steak on a skewer, I highly recommend it." Murilo Barbosa said, leaning across the table and speaking in almost a hushed tone. I guess he reserved his bellicose outbursts for the little people like the waiters.

"That sounds good to me." I smiled across the table at Murilo. "Usually I like my steak medium rare, and any type of vegetable would be fine," I said, responding in a normal voice and tone.

"Good, good," Murilo said and then turned and instructed the waiter.

"Mr. Christenson, it is Mr. Christenson, right?" His questioning about my name somewhat unnerved me. Did he know something about me that I didn't want him to know? "You are here to purchase some specialized equipment for a project that needs to be completed in the United States?" He sounded like he had something in mind. "I believe we just might be able to supply your needs. In order to complete our deal, it would be best if you came to my home, located just north of Niteroi. I will give you a map and instructions on how to get there." The ice definitely had been broke; hopefully the equipment I needed was located at Barbosa's home, although somehow that seemed like a strange place to warehouse military supplies.

We fell into small talk for the remainder of the meal. As for the Brazilian steak, I enjoyed the tender and distinctive taste, a flavor possibility due to the way it was prepared, and I considered it nothing less than superb and easily superior to any consumed in the United States.

Following the meal, we remained at the table for a while, more or less feeling each other out. It seemed obvious to me, from the manner in which Murilo had directed our conversation, that he intended to pry my true identity out of me, however, his efforts were without success. But, perhaps my desire to conceal my identity only made me a little paranoid. His comments and questions regarding my education and where I currently lived, did leave me with the notion that he wanted to delve into my personal background. The thought that he did not accept me at face value, I found very disturbing, but for the moment, I would have to overlook it.

Nothing I touched during the meal would have my fingerprints on them, the super glue doing its job. The only possibilities for detection of my DNA, something I could do nothing about, were my hair and saliva. An astute individual could pick up a sample of either and use it to trace my background and identity. Provided Murilo had the resources, which without a doubt, he did.

After lunch, Murilo provided me with a map and detailed instructions on how to get to his home. He indicated its location in an exclusive residential area north of Niteroi. We agreed to meet the following day at about eleven o'clock.

The next day, the trip north from the center of Niteroi City to the residential area proved to be a very relaxing drive. The roads were modern, four-lane freeways that provided quick access to cities and towns in central and northern Brazil. Murilo's home was located on Avenido Bolivar, which turned out to be a street running through a very wealthy area of large estates on either side of the wide boulevard. As I drove, to my left, an eight-foot brick wall with iron spikes along the top seemed to stretch for over a mile, until finally a large iron gate appeared. A rather elaborate sign on the gated entrance indicated it to be The Barbosa Estate.

Driving into the entrance and stopping in front of the large iron gate apparently alerted an armed guard, who appeared out of nowhere. He addressed me in Portuguese, and obviously, I didn't have a clue as to what he said.

"My name is Ralph Christenson and I'm here to see Mr. Barbosa," informed him of my purpose for being there.

He looked at me a little perplexed and said something like, "Uno momento, señor." He disappeared through a small door in the gate, returning after a few minutes motioning for me to enter, which I cautiously did.

The drive up to Murilo's home was impressive; a paved road, wide enough to accommodate two large trucks passing each other, wound through some densely wooded areas, ultimately opening onto a large area of a well-manicured lawn. The very large home sat on top of a hill overlooking Niterio and Guanabara Bay. The house, constructed in a Spanish architectural motif, probably had over ten thousand square feet of floor space.

Another armed guard met me at the front of the home and escorted me into Murilo's spacious living room where I made myself comfortable while waiting to see Murilo. The furniture consisted of large, and for the most part, Italian leather chairs and couches. I had just reclined in one of the leather couches when a very attractive girl in her mid- to late-twenties appeared from nowhere. She had dressed in a revealing short skirt and a deep-cut blouse that showed most of her ample breasts.

"May I offer you something to drink, Señor Christenson?" she asked politely, while leaning over in front of me, fully displaying her breasts, including the nipples. For a few moments, I lost my thoughts, because of a sudden urge to fondle those beautiful succulent orbs.

"I ah, ah, would like a Bloody Mary. Do you know how to make a Bloody Mary?" in my very best stammer.

The girl smiled, well aware of the effect she had on me. She continued to lean over in front of me to sustain the effect, finally replying, "Yes, Señor Christenson," in a soft, slightly accented voice, "I do know how to make a Bloody Mary and any other drink or provide any other form of entertainment you may desire."

Shit, she gave me such a hard-on, so much so I had to move around to accommodate my erection without it becoming obvious. This girl was wise, at least wise about her effect on men, being well aware of what my movements were about.

"I will be right back with your drink"—she straightened up, the fantastic view of her tits gone—"and you might want to consider what you would like to do while you are waiting for Mr. Barbosa. Mr. Barbosa is busy with a conference call and will be tied up for about an hour or so before he can see you." She smiled and left the room through a large open hallway. Five or ten minutes later, at least enough time for my dick to soften, she returned carrying a tray with my drink and some crackers and a soft spreadable cheese.

With her back to me, she leaned over and set the tray on the coffee table just in front of the couch where I sat. Leaning over raised the short skirt she had on, displaying her well-proportioned, firm, round ass. Needless to say, my erection returned with a vengeance. Again, I began to move in order to free my dick so my shorts wouldn't prevent it from becoming fully erect. Of course, the pretty girl, the cause of my dick's discomfort, had turned around and observed my movements.

"Is Señor Christenson having some discomfort with his big cock?" she asked with a smile. She sat next to me on the couch, pressing her breast against me. "Perhaps Lana could help you get more comfortable?" she said as she placed her hand on my knee and began to rub my leg, slowly moving up my thigh.

I'm not one of the slick guys who always has an answer for everything when he's with a girl. You know the one who never has any problem in picking up a girl for the night and knows exactly what to say in all circumstances? A ladies man is what best describes them. Whatever they are, I'm definitely not of that character. In this situation, as usual, all that came out of my mouth was some slightly unintelligible stammering.

"I ah, yea, ah, that would be nice, ah, yea." Shit, it would be fantastic. She undid my belt, the button at the waist of my trousers, and unzipped my pants. Of course, Ole Johnny, my dick, knew exactly what to do and sprang through my shorts in full display for all to see; well, Lana and me anyway.

Within seconds, Lana removed her blouse and skirt and stood completely naked in front of me. Some beautiful female bodies have been displayed to me in the past, but Lana, at this moment, just had to be the best endowed that my lust-filled eyes had ever seen. She pulled my shorts and pants off and helped me remove my shirt. She straddled my legs, sat on my lap, and pressed her breast in my face. Without hesitation, I began to suckle her nipples. Lana moved her body up slightly, inserted my dick into her, and began to move up and down.

Her up and down motion gradually increased. We were both moaning in extreme pleasure until we climaxed together. At least, I thought we climaxed together. Some women fake the climax in order to make the man feel like he is a great lover.

We remained together on the couch for several minutes until the liquid of our lovemaking began to leak out of Lana and down my crotch and onto the Italian leather couch. Lana got up and removed a warm, moist towel from the tray she had brought in and began to clean me up. Wiping the towel over my cock and crotch, plus her being that close, excited me so my erection returned to life. Lana kissed it and began to fondle my nuts. She ran her tongue up the erection and then started to suck on me. It didn't take long for me to cum again. She swallowed, got up, and handed me my drink.

"I think this is what you had requested, Mr. Christenson," she said smiling at me.

"Yes, thank you very much for the drink," I replied. Taking a big gulp or two, I sat the glass down, retrieved my clothes, dressed, and sat back down on the couch, which Lana had wiped clean.

"I will see if Mr. Barbosa can see you now," Lana said as she dressed and left the room through the open hallway.

Some thirty or so minutes later she returned and said Mr. Barbosa now would see me. We went down the hallway Lana had just come through. As with Murilo's office, the walls had original works of art on both sides. I judged the works to be mostly by Brazilian or South American artists. At the end of the hallway, we went through large double doors and into Murilo's spacious office. One side of his office had one large window, providing a panoramic view of Niterio, Rio de Janeiro, and Guanabara Bay. The wall behind his desk was made of a rare South American wood with the other two walls covered in a fabric. Numerous original paintings graced two walls, in addition to statuary placed in a coordinated fashion about the office. A small wet bar sat to one side behind Murilo's large desk.

"Good afternoon, Mr. Christenson." He stood up and offered his hand, which I grasped with a firm but friendly handshake, "I expect you had a pleasant reception by my assistant." Of course, now we were well into the afternoon, despite the fact that the meeting had been scheduled for eleven that morning.

"Yes, thank you," I smiled, fully aware that he had intentionally planned the reception, "my reception was most pleasant. As a matter of fact, if such receptions are customary, I plan on many more visits to Brazil."

"I'm afraid other businesses in Brazil do not offer such a reception." He sat in his large leather chair behind an enormous mahogany desk. "But let us get down to our business. You are looking for two RPGs, a fifty-caliber rifle with ammunition, a radarscope, night vision goggles and a Barrett M86A1 scope, is that correct?" he inquired in a business-like tone.

Murilo Barbosa came across every bit a businessman. He dressed in a pin-striped business suit, most likely Italian or English, although Brazil has some excellent tailors. His shirt was a pale blue silk, with a slightly darker blue-striped tie.

"Yes, and the fifty-caliber ammunition must be able to penetrate at least eight to ten inches of masonry." I nodded, being in accord with his statement.

"The two RPGs, night vision goggles, and the fifty-caliber rifle with the required ammunition are stocked here in my warehouse; they would run approximately thirty thousand total. However, the Barrett and radarscope has to be acquired from Eastern Europe." He motioned with his hand, pointing in an easterly direction. "The Barrett is quite expensive, at least sixty thousand U.S. dollars, the radarscope I am not familiar with but will locate one for you, possibly another sixty thousand." He continued, "Do you still want to proceed with the purchase?" Apparently, he had become concerned with my ability to pay for such a weapon. A grand total of one hundred and fifty thousand U.S. dollars, considerably less than what I had expected.

"Yes, I want to proceed. However, there is a problem in payment, not that I don't have the funds. The problem is the funds are in cash and presently in safety-deposit boxes in the States," I said, informing him I had no difficulty in meeting any financial obligation, however, hoping my disclosure of the limited access to funds did not break the deal.

"That will not be a problem," he smiled, almost a knowing smile, "since I have accounts at our bank in New York City. Also, the delivery of the weapons can be made directly to your business in the United States. This would relieve any concerns you might have with U.S. Customs or with acquiring an import license," Murilo added.

"That is very convenient for me," I said, showing my satisfaction with his proposed arrangements. "I have fifty thousand U.S. in cash with me to make a down payment and the balance can be deposited to your account in New York City. Will that be an acceptable arrangement for you?" Things were moving along very smoothly.

"Appears everything is all set," Murilo remarked as he rose from his chair. "My business is conducted on a personal basis only, no contracts or written forms. Is that acceptable to you?"

"Yes, a handshake is fine." I got up to conclude our business with a handshake. Everything seemed all set as far as I was concerned. We shook hands across his desk and proceeded to the living room for a drink to seal the deal. Outside we could hear the sound of several large vehicles, along with the shouting of orders, to what sounded like some kind of paramilitary organization. Lana came running into the room, very excitedly saying something in Portuguese. Murilo jumped up, sending the glass with his drink shattering to the floor. He went behind the bar and began to search through the drawers, finally producing a flashlight and two pistols. He handed one of the pistols to me and instructed me to follow closely behind him.

What the fuck could possibly be going on? Were the police or some other organization after me? If so, why would Murilo be concerned about it, and why would he want to protect me?

Chapter 21

We wound our way down a hallway and through a large kitchen to an obscure door at the back. Murilo entered a code into a number pad next to the door; as the locking device activated, the large metal door swung open. Murilo motioned for me to follow him. As the door closed behind me, all I could see was Murilo's silhouette produced by his flashlight beam playing on the walls, floor, and ceiling as he moved along in front of me. The silhouette seemed to be slowly sinking; in the nick of time, I realized Murilo had been descending stairs. My realization prevented me from taking a painful plunge down a short flight of stairs, about a ten- to fifteen-foot fall. Grabbing the handrail broke my potential fall into the dark abyss that disappeared before me.

Murilo's silhouette proceeded along what appeared to be a concrete tunnel; I followed close as possible, without stepping on his heels. Fifty yards or so into the tunnel, we heard the distinct opening of the door we had come through, apparently having been forced open by our pursuers. A few moments later, I could hear the distinct sound of bodies and weapons falling down the stairway, the one I had almost fallen down. The sound of the falling bodies was followed by swearing, as apparently whoever had fallen down the stairs struggled to get up.

Unexpectedly, we heard the discharge of weapons as bullets came flying all around us, bouncing off the floor, walls, and ceiling. I instinctively threw myself, very painfully, onto the concrete floor. Murilo's silhouette disappeared as the flashlight, that had produced the silhouette, fell from his hand and crashed on the concrete floor. Moaning came from the direction I had last seen him.

The weapon firing continued in short bursts every few seconds. The pistol Murilo had provided for me was still in my hand. Although my knuckles had been skinned during the dive to the floor, the pain had to be the least of my worries, as I had maintained a tight grip on the pistol. Watching where the flash of the rifle muzzle came from, I took careful aim and fired. A cry of pain and the sound of the weapon and a body falling to the floor assured me I had hit my target.

Exercising caution, I crawled to where I last saw Murilo.

"Murilo," I called softly.

"Over here, I've been hit," he responded, evidence of his pain indicated by the tone of his voice.

Shit, this situation put us both in significant danger. The sound of other armed men descending the stairs warned us of the danger that could befall us if we didn't get our asses out of the hallway. After crawling some ten feet or so on the cold concrete floor, I located Murilo. "Are you okay?" I placed my right hand on his shoulder in an effort to communicate my concern.

"I've been hit in the right shoulder, not seriously, it's just painful at this point." He spoke in a hushed voice, almost a stammer, indicating his pain had increased. "We need to keep moving, the police will be coming through the tunnel pretty soon." His words came in a staccato, as if each word spoken produced more pain.

To slow the police's advance, I fired several shots from my pistol in their direction. Some obviously found their mark as cries of pain and the sound of bodies and weapons falling to the floor could be heard. Using their automatic weapons, the police continued to fire in short burst. Fortunately for us, they aimed too high. Taking careful aim at the point of the last muzzle flash, I squeezed off two more rounds. At least one of the projectiles found its mark, as another falling weapon and body along with considerable swearing came from the direction of my shot.

The burst of weapon fire from the police, or whoever the pursuers were, ceased. Either some or all had been wounded, or they were engaging in a different tactic.

My eyes had adjusted to the darkness and just enough ambient light existed so that I could see Murilo lying on the concrete floor about six inches from me. He lay on his back, holding his right shoulder with his left hand. Crawling around him, I located the flashlight but decided not to turn it on, as it would give our adversaries a clear target to shoot at. For the time being, I suspected, they were busy dealing with wounds and injuries. Murilo struggled to his feet, and he began to feel his way along the left wall of the tunnel with me close behind him, making our way away from the police.

About fifteen minutes later, I bounced off Murilo who had walked very painfully and with full force into a large metal door; this obviously and unpleasantly had to be the end of the tunnel.

"I have to turn the flashlight on for a few seconds," he seemed to be dealing with the pain a little better, "to see the code lock for this door." He grabbed my shoulder and waited for me to pass the flashlight to him.

I handed him the flashlight, but he couldn't hold it and enter the code at the same time. "Hold the light so I can see what I am doing," he instructed in a flat voice with no evidence of pain. Holding the flashlight on the code lock for a few moments allowed Murilo to open the door. We could hear running and shouting in the tunnel behind us. We hurried through the open door, making sure it closed securely behind us. The door, a very secure one made of heavy metal and with several large dead bolts, similar to a bank vault safe door, would be virtually impenetrable by the group following us.

Now standing in total darkness, I had no awareness of Murilo being close by. Proceeding slowly forward and feeling outwards, I encountered another concrete wall. "Murilo, are you there?" I whispered.

"Stay where you are until I turn on some lights," he cautioned from a distance to my left and a bit ahead of me. Several minutes later, the soft glow of mercury vapor discharge lamps began to penetrate the darkness. The sudden brightness of the lamps, as they came up to full intensity, caused my eyes to react as if camera flash bulb had gone off in my face. For a few minutes I stood still to allow my eyes to adjust to the brightness and for the spots in my eyes to diminish.

As my eyes adjusted, I found before me an enormous underground chamber with stores of armaments of every description. There were fifty-five millimeter howitzer cannons, racks and racks of RPGs, rifles, pistols and ammunition. There also appeared to be several light tanks and three or four Humvees, along with a number of military trucks. In my judgment, there had to be enough weaponry to supply a small army.

Murilo stood twenty feet from me, near a large electrical switch panel.

"Let's go to my office"—he grimaced as he spoke, indicating the pain had increased in intensity—"where there are some first aid supplies. Perhaps the wound can be attended to until I can get to my doctor." Although he obviously suffered considerably from the pain, he walked quickly toward the office space just to the left of the door we had just entered. I followed close on his heels. He had a large office, modestly furnished with an oversized wooden desk, a small wet bar, and some drawings of military vehicles on the walls. The walls were painted a light olive green, the ceiling a light color, and the floor a light grey asphalt tile. Various pieces of furniture were randomly placed around it, including a couch and two overstuffed chairs. He sat in the chair behind the desk and proceeded to look through the drawers.

"Ah, here it is," he exclaimed, pulling a box from one of the bottom drawers of his desk, "my first aid kit for just such an event." He sat the large plastic case on the desk and popped it open. Murilo motioned for me to come over and assist him, which I did willingly. He took several bottles out, one of which contained some type of pain medication. From a bar to the right of his desk, I retrieved a glass of water and handed it to him.

Murilo removed his shirt, revealing a jagged wound in his shoulder. Close examination indicated a ricocheting bullet had hit him. The bullet, still visible, had to be removed. From the first aid kit, I pulled out what I assumed to be forceps and removed the bullet and then cleansed and bandaged the wound. Throughout the entire procedure Murilo had remained stoic, not even a whimper or a moan, although in my perception the whole process had to be one of great pain.

"Feel okay?" I asked.

"Yes, the pain medication is beginning to take effect so we can conclude our business." Under the circumstances, this statement surprised me.

"Aren't you concerned about the police or army or whoever the fuck it is that attacked your home?" I asked in a rather perplexed manner.

"Oh, that; that's nothing." He leaned forward on the desk I guess to relieve some of the pain. "That goes on all the time, just some army officer or politician who hasn't been paid off. This is also a method they use to extract a lot more money from me." He seemed to shrug off our little episode, as if such a life-threatening scenario could be considered a little episode. "I'll take care of it later. For now, let's agree on our business. For fifty thousand U.S. now and the balance of one hundred thousand to my New York City bank, I'll provide the weapons you asked for, delivered to your office in Connecticut. Is that agreeable?" He lounged back in his chair, studying me.

"Normally I wouldn't enter into such an arrangement without some references from well-known associates." Murilo held an unflinching stare at me as he spoke, possibly trying to observe my reaction to his comment. "However, I pride myself on my judgment of people, and I find you to be a straightforward, honest, and trustworthy individual. I hope my judgment is a correct one, only time will tell."

"The terms, as you have explained them, are completely agreeable to me," I replied. From around my waist I removed a money belt strapped on early that morning. "There is fifty thousand here and the rest will be placed in your bank account in New York. As an aside, is it possible for me to launder some money through your bank? That is, can I open an account and deposit a considerable amount of cash and set up a checking and savings account there?" Perhaps I pushed things a little, as a conviction for laundering money anywhere in the Americas brings severe prison penalties.

"Our business is all set." He smiled across the desk at me, obviously pleased with the outcome of our negotiations. "Yes, you can launder your money; I will provide you a contact at the bank who will arrange everything for you. Let's take a look at the fifty-caliber rifle and the RPGs." He got up slowly and walked toward the door to his office, obviously still in considerable pain.

"Murilo, if you're in pain," I said, showing concern, "you should sit. I can look at the equipment later."

"Better if I keep busy." He opened the door to leave the office. "It keeps my mind off the pain. Let's go," he instructed as he walked toward the racks of weapons.

I followed him out of the office and down one of the aisles of equipment. Each row numbered and every shelf with a number and letter to keep track of all the equipment stored there. I became very impressed with the organization and the cleanliness of the warehouse. We walked down a long row of shelving and then made a right turn, after which Murilo began to scan the shelving, looking for a specific location. Finally finding it, he reached up and pulled down a rather heavy box.

"Let me help you with that," I called to him. He stopped and waited until I had a firm grip on the box, transferring most of the weight to my shoulders and arms. Slowly, we lowered the wooden box to the floor and opened it so I could see the contents. A fifty-caliber rifle coated in CLP, grease like substance in which weapons are stored, lay neatly packed in the box. Lifting it would only get large amounts of oily substance on my hands and clothing. I did check the bolt action and chamber, though, to ensure the weapon operated properly and appeared to be new. Satisfied, I closed the box up and with some difficulty placed it back on the shelf.

"Looks good to me," I advised Murilo. "Will this be the one sent to my office in Connecticut?" I asked.

"Yes, I try to let my customers look at the actual equipment before it is sent to them," he said. "Let's go look at the RPGs." He continued to walk down the main aisle of the warehouse.

"These are not armed, but will be shipped to you with all the munitions you have requested," he remarked as we walked toward the far end of the warehouse. "While we are at it, I will also show you all the various ammunitions we have available for the RPGs and the fifty-caliber rifle." He wanted to assure me that all my requirements would be met, an assurance that increased my trust in Murilo.

About halfway down the aisle, he turned right into a narrow passage between two high metal shelves. He began to look at numbers, which were clearly marked on each shelf. Murilo paused and climbed up on a shelf to retrieve a wooden crate. Once we lowered the crate to the floor, he opened it to show me the RPGs. Two of the weapons were packed in the crate along with several rounds of ammunition.

"Are these the items you had in mind?" he asked. I kneeled down in order to make a close examination of the weapons and the ordinance. While in the Marine Corps, I received instructions on the RPG and had several opportunities to fire them. The two RPGs in the crate were similar to the one the Marine Corps had trained me on.

"Yes," I said as I got up and looked over at Murilo. "These are exactly what I have been searching for."

On the shelf, opposite the rack with the RPGs, were several metal containers of fifty-caliber ammunition. Murilo showed me a number of rounds that would penetrate twelve to eighteen inches of masonry. I picked out two cases containing ten rounds each and added them to my request.

"This should complete my requirements," I assured him.

"Good!" he exclaimed. "I will have everything sent to your Connecticut office, including the scopes. Unfortunately, the scopes are not in my inventory but will be acquired from my East European connections. Let me show you out so you can return to your hotel."

"My rental car is at the front of your home," I said, showing concern over the possible presence of the police. "Is there any way it could be brought to me?" I asked.

"I will have my driver take you to your hotel and have your car delivered to you later today," he responded.

"I hope everything will be alright with you regarding both your wound and the invasion of your home." I candidly expressed my concern with his situation.

"Not to worry, my friend," he said, showing a broad grin. I guess the drugs had really taken affect. "Even as we speak the individual or individuals responsible for the forced entry of my home are being harshly dealt with." Murilo started walking toward the near side of the warehouse.

We exited a side door where a car and driver waited to transport me back to the hotel. I thanked Murilo for his time and courtesy. As Murilo shook my hand in departing, he informed me. "As this may or may not be of useful information to you in the future, however I think you should know anyway," he paused momentarily to reflect on what he was about to tell. "I have conducted business with your CIA for many years and have useful contacts with them. I would never disclose any of my business dealings with you to anyone without your authorization; trust me on that. If ever you were in need of a contact, please do not hesitate to contact me."

For a few moments I did not respond to his disclosure, as it somewhat set me back, an unexpected disclosure that required an intelligent response, as there was a strong possibility Murilo was testing me. "That is very gracious of you to provide me with such sensitive information. Given my business, there may undoubtedly be situation where such a contact could prove very useful. You are both an excellent source for specialized equipment and undoubtedly a reliable source of vital information. Possibly some of my future requirements will be in need of such a source. Thank you once again from your friendship and for conducting business with me, in particular, for providing a source for my almost insignificant needs." We finished up with some small talk, and then I relaxed in the back seat of one of Murilo's limousines as his chauffer drove me back to my hotel.

Once back at the hotel, I relaxed for a while in the luxurious comfort of the hotel room until late in the evening, when I ventured out for another Brazilian steak dinner. The next morning a hotel employee delivered the keys to the rental car. By noon, I had packed my bags and booked a flight out of Rio for that evening, headed to New York City.

Returning to Croton for a little rest and relaxation produced some unpleasant surprises. First, of course, were some nasty phone calls from Janet. Surprise, surprise, although she certainly had a right to be angry, since I had not stayed in touch as promised. I am somewhat fastidious about the arrangement of my apartment, especially the organization of my desk and the items on it. Several items I kept on top of the desk had been moved. And it was obvious someone had been rummaging through the files and other items in the drawers.

A slow walk around the apartment showed that there had been no forced entries. Sabrina did not have a key. The only one with a key to the apartment other than Mom and me was the superintendent. In a highly agitated mood, I phoned Julius, the superintendent of the apartments.

"Julius," I said, trying hard to be pleasant, "were you in my apartment in the last few weeks?" I wanted to know.

"I'm sorry, sir, but who is calling, please?" he asked courteously.

Shit. Probably would have been a good idea to identify myself. This took some of the wind out of my sails.

"This is Oscar Wylton, in unit 4B," I replied, a little more softly.

"Oscar, man, no way." He became immediately defensive, but probably had cause to be. "I wouldn't go into your apartment without getting your permission. Is there a problem? Do we need to call the police?"

"No need for the police," I insisted. No need to have them poking around in my apartment. The Croton Police Department is an excellent force, as far as small town police operations go, I have the highest respect for them; however, in this particular circumstance, there was no need to have them involved, nothing appeared to be missing. "Nothing is missing as far as I can tell. It's just that some of my things have been moved around. I'll check with my former wife and my mother. Maybe they were here for some reason. And thanks, Julius, I appreciate your keeping an eye on things around here." Sheepishly apologetic for inferring he might have been in my condominium, I hung up.

Fortunately, I didn't keep anything in the apartment that could tie me to my current business. The Beretta, the only weapon I kept in the apartment for protection, still remained safely stored safely under the mattress in the bedroom. Had someone put a trace on me and now checked out my comings and goings? This could be a major issue. If Janet had a private investigator following me around who had stumbled on my current occupation, it would put me in deep shit.

Several other possibilities existed. Sabrina might be checking me out, but why? If she followed me and discovered my secret life, it also would put me in the brown muck. A real long shot, my mom or dad might have checked up on me. But why would my mother and father be checking out my activities? At least if my parents had somehow discovered my illicit activities, they would only question my ethics and expect me to stop.

Having just spent the last thirty-six or so hours flying and driving without any sleep, all I wanted to do is hit the rack. Discovering the identity of whoever might have rummaged through my personal stuff could wait until I rested. Although it was only two in the afternoon, sleep came quickly.

The next morning I woke with a start. Something had disturbed me, but I couldn't tell what. I looked over at my clock; it was ten thirty, hopefully in the morning and not at night. The aroma of coffee percolating floated through the air of my apartment. Believe me, it smelled especially good. Probably my old maid neighbor preparing for a day of confrontation, she only needed a subject to pick, someone to vent her anger on. One thing for sure, it wouldn't be me, probably the super, poor Julius.

A shave and a long hot shower prepared me for a day of relaxation. I had nothing planned, just an easy day of exactly that, nothing. As I emerged from the bathroom with only a towel wrapped around me, there in all her beautiful glory stood Sabrina.

"What the fuck!" I managed in total surprise. "How did you get in here?" Despite her gorgeous appearance, I stood irate and almost naked. This type of surprise didn't sit well with me. My privacy had been compromised and it just wasn't something I appreciated.

"Just thought you might enjoy a nice breakfast," a beautiful smile graced her almost perfect face. "Maybe a romantic afternoon of chasing each other around your apartment, no holds barred," she cooed.

Sabrina wore a cream-colored silk blouse that revealed the hardness of her nipples. The tight brown pants she wore didn't conceal any of her voluptuous figure. Shit, talk about turning into a bowl of jelly; I melted right before her eyes. In recognition of the beauty that stood before me, my dick became erect. With only the towel around my waist, it soon became obvious to Sabrina the effect she had on me. Before I could react, she grabbed the towel and stripped it from me. I don't like being totally naked in front of anyone, it kind of strips away your dignity, but what the fuck was I going to do, cover my dick with my hands like some kind of sissy?

"Well, now, what do we have here?" She whistled as she stared at my manliness. "I don't believe I have seen anything so amorous since our last encounter," she said with a knowing smile followed by a disarming little chuckle. "Do we have time for some fresh coffee before we take care of your little problem, or maybe I should say your big problem?" Obviously, she had to suppress outright laughter.

"I would like to put something on. That is, if it's okay with you." I tried to regain some composure.

"Of course, I will wait for you in the kitchen. I honestly couldn't expect you to sit for an hour eating breakfast and drinking coffee with an erection like that one, totally exposed."

As I turned to walk into the bedroom, she gave me one helluva smack on my ass. I actually winced in pain, but fortunately, my face had turned away from her so she couldn't see my reaction.

Once dressed in sweats and socks, I went into the kitchen where a big smile, a big strong hug, and a full open-mouth kiss greeted me. Even though I harbored some suspicions that Sabrina somehow gaining entrance to my apartment without a key and without leaving any telltale signs of a break-in, I put it in the back of my mind. It seemed the most plausible decision under the circumstances.

In addition to a hot cup of coffee, Sabrina had bought an assortment of cinnamon rolls, donuts, and danishes. I sat down and selected a rather large cinnamon roll to go along with the coffee. Sabrina sat opposite me and picked at a donut, obviously having no intention of finishing it. In addition to her physical activity like climbing into people's second story apartment, she maintained her beautiful figure by eating healthy. I should practice the same discipline, but not until I had consumed the cinnamon roll.

We started the rest of the day with oral sex, me on her and then her on me, followed by, to my surprise, anal sex, which she seemed to greatly enjoy. The day became more amorous with unusual closeness that I hadn't previously experienced with Sabrina. Actually, the closeness bothered me, as I had no time to devote to a relationship. We fell asleep in each other's arms only to wake up at ten at night by the sound of my phone ringing. In poor judgment, I answered it.

"Hello?" I spoke softly and dumbfounded into the receiver, trying to shake the sleep from my brain.

"No fucking shit, you actually take the time to answer your fucking phone." How about that, good ole Janet had returned to her old self, a bitch. "Any chance you might explain your absence and not keeping your commitment to phone me?" Talk about a wet blanket on the party, Janet really knew how to spoil a good fuck, although I think she was pretty adapt at that when we were married.

"Sorry, I was in a situation where a phone call could not be made; actually I was out of the country on business," I said lamely, hoping it would pacify her for the moment at least. No way.

"Listen, you asshole, your children think you have totally forgotten they exist." Ah, the kids, that always made me feel guilty, and she knew it. "If it isn't too much to ask, could you please arrange your busy fucking schedule so there is some time for Emma and David? You don't have to worry about me; I will take care of myself." Maybe she had some justification to her anger, but she could've been a little more diplomatic.

"I promise that tomorrow I will be over to spend time with Emma and David." I honestly did feel guilty.

"Don't fucking strain yourself," she hissed. "They will be home from school at three o'clock and will be expecting you. Don't keep them out late; the next day is a school day. Maybe they can spend this weekend with you." She slammed the receiver down, evidently hoping she had punctured my eardrum.

Sabrina said she had some nighttime business to attend to and would be in touch with me later. She left by the front door so that she wouldn't have to disclose how she had gotten in. With all the physical and amorous activities that had taken place, I had totally forgotten to ask how she had entered my apartment. Also, I wanted to know if she had been in the apartment in the last week or so, something that we would have to have a meaningful discussion about in the near future, I promised myself. Once again, with the unusual closeness of this encounter I had forgotten to get a phone number, address, or some means of contacting her. Oh well, when the need for sex arose I would be plainly out of luck, shit.

The next few days, as well as the weekend, were spent with my children, enjoying movies, amusement parks, picnics, and physical activity. On Saturday, Janet surprised us with a backyard cookout. The kids hadn't pressed me at all about getting back together as a family, perhaps Janet informed them that it wasn't in the cards. Surprisingly, she made no effort at showing any affection toward me. Initially I had some discomfort in being together as a family but as the day and evening progressed, I began to relax.

Janet, however, had continued to improve her appearance. Saturday, the day of the surprise backyard cook out she dressed in tight white shorts and a snug yellow blouse that displayed some of her finer aspects, namely her ample bosom. She certainly had started to take care of her appearance. *Good for her*, I sincerely expressed in my thoughts.

Chapter 22

On Monday morning, I wanted to—and unconditionally had to—get to work. Having the FBI possibly on my ass presented a serious problem, but to have the Ndrangheta, namely Ernesto, on my ass, just didn't fulfill my lifetime ambition, mainly, staying alive. A phone call to Ernesto Philipino to keep him in the loop had to be made as soon as possible. As had become my custom, a location distant from Croton or from the target location in Lake Placid was needed, which I considered a necessary precaution so that my movements could not be traced. This time, sunny Florida became my destination. Once settled in a motel in Tampa, Florida, I placed a call to Ernesto.

"Who the fuck is it?" Ernesto was in his usual blustery mood.

"It's Bill," I said in my usual somber tone of voice. "I just want to keep you informed as to my progress," I stated flatly.

"No shit," he spit into the receiver, I could hear the spittle hit the microphone section of the phone, "and what pray tell are you fucking informing me of?"

"That progress has been made." Why the fuck had I bothered to phone him? "That is as much as I am willing to tell you." Straight to the point, no further comment required.

"Send me a fucking love letter when you think you've fucking completed the job." He slammed the phone down. I frankly didn't give a shit how he felt. The million lay very nicely in my safety-deposit box and the contract would be completed as agreed, or—. I didn't want to contemplate, "or."

Before proceeding, I went to New York City and located the bank Murilo had recommended. One hundred thousand, the balance of the payments on the weapons, I deposited into his account. With the individual Murilo recommended, I deposited another fifty thousand in addition to opening a savings and checking account. My true name or social security number were not required, just an account number that could be used any time to write checks, make withdrawal, or to deposit funds.

Another ten thousand I used to open a business account for the Connecticut shell operation. At this point, depositing all my funds in the New York City bank made no sense. I didn't know anyone there or have any information of substance about the bank. Putting all the funds in one pocket could lead to a significant loss if something unforeseen happened.

Once all the New York City business had been completed, I took a train to Bridgeport, Connecticut, where a car and an apartment had previously been rented using my Ralph Christenson alias. Driving for a few minutes from the apartment into downtown Bridgeport brought me to my Connecticut office. Maxine was all excited because some wooden crates had arrived the day before and she had signed the receipt. She wanted to know if she had the authority to sign for them. Of course, I assured her. It surprised me, however, that Murilo completed the shipment so quickly. The only items missing were the two scopes, which had to be shipped from some place in Europe.

I had to have the scopes to the complete the plan. However, for the time being it would be best to move the equipment to the chosen site, a little at a time. There was a paradox to contend with, as moving all the equipment at one time would certainly raise suspicions but making too many trips could also raise suspicions. I judged that a maximum of three trips could be taken without raising any local interest, in the Lake Placid area.

The first trip, take the fifty-caliber rifle and the fifty-caliber ammo to the site. The crates were large and bulky too much so to put into a car. I returned the car to the rental company and exchanged it for a small pickup truck to accommodate the crate. Maxine helped me load the crate into the bed of the truck.

"Jesus, Ralph," she exclaimed while trying to hold up her end of the crate, "this is awfully heavy. What is in it?" She, as usual, dressed in business attire, which made me feel a little guilty about her having to help me.

"Look, Maxine," I said in a pleasant but instructive voice, "part of your responsibilities here are not to ask questions, and also not to tell anyone, including your boyfriend or family, of any of the activities of this business. Can you do that for me?" This is the first time my instructions to Maxine took a stern inflection in my voice, more of an employer to an employee tone. I didn't particularly like talking down to Maxine, but this point had to be emphasized.

"Yes." She looked down, embarrassed for asking so many questions. "I'm sorry, Mr. Christensen. I will keep my mouth shut. I can't tell you how much I enjoy working for you. I guess I was just getting curious, that's all." She seemed genuine and I hoped she showed her true self.

"The name is Ralph. No Mr. Christensen, okay?" I smiled at her, trying to make her feel more comfortable.

"Okay!" She smiled back, evidently relieved that I really didn't direct any anger toward her.

With the crate loaded in the bed of the pickup, I started my drive to Saranac Lake, which would be a long drive. It was absolutely critical that I arrive there in daylight, unload the crate, and transport it to the hide. Distracted with the need to arrive at the destination in as little time as possible, I didn't keep an eye on the speedometer. Somewhere just north of Albany, New York, flashing red and blue lights appeared in the rearview mirror. What other exclamation could there be other than, "Oh fuck!"

In the side mirror, I could see the state trooper approaching the truck with that "I got you, mother fucker" gait of theirs. It really pissed me off but I couldn't do anything at this point except be as polite as possible, and just maybe he would let me go with a warning.

"Good afternoon, sir," he said in a stern but friendly voice, "how are you today?" That fucking fake greeting of theirs, how the fuck did he think I felt, being ticketed for speeding?

"Fine, officer," I said, returning his friendly greeting. "Is there a problem, sir?" I could be just as fake.

"Can I see your driver's license and registration, sir?" he asked, reminding me of my fucking drill instructor in the Marine Corps. This is probably what they do after they get out of the Corps, become troopers so they can wear the smoky hat strapped to their heads. They wear it with that forward tilt giving them a mean ass look. Always had it in some poor recruit's face while chewing his ass out, yeah they had plenty of practice to be pricks when they were in the Corps.

I handed him my license and the registration for the vehicle.

"Mr. Christensen, you were doing eighty-five in a seventy mile an hour zone, for which I will have to ticket you." No fucking shit. "Mind telling me what you are carrying in the crate in the back of your truck?"

Now, perhaps this would fuck me real good. What the fuck could I say, a crate of oranges?

"Just equipment I was sent to deliver to Lake Saranac." I hoped he would accept that as an explanation.

"Mind if I have a look?" He motioned toward the truck bed.

Now I might be fucked royally; however, if you were smart and planned ahead, wouldn't you be prepared for any situation you could think of? Forgive me for taking a bow, but I am smart (at least sometimes, anyway). Before leaving the office, Maxine made a fake shipping document, which I adeptly presented to the state trooper. He glanced through the document and seemed satisfied.

"Sign here for the ticket, Mr. Christensen." He handed me the ticket on a little clipboard. "Drive within the speed limit as posted, sir, you should observe the beauty of our Adirondack Park."

After signing the ticket and putting my copy in the glove compartment, I waited until the trooper finished his paperwork and drove away. The stop had cost me maybe fifteen minutes or so, which wouldn't adversely impact my arrival time in Lake Placid.

Just south of the village of Lake Saranac is an old logging road, which provided limited access to the location of my hide. Using the logging trail, I drove into the wooded area as far as possible, without alerting the security at Angelo Lambrascha's estate.

Maxine hit the nail on the head: the crate weighed at least seventy pounds, but I managed to get it up on my shoulder and started the difficult journey to the hide. The hide, located roughly one and a half miles from where I had parked the truck, required a significant amount of stamina and strength to haul seventy pounds. Although, I was in good shape and the terrain was relatively flat, carrying a seventy-pound dead weight soon sapped my endurance; as a result, the hike took almost three hours.

One eventuality that had to be considered while in the woods; I had no desire for a repeat encounter with Mr. Bear. Although, I had safely tucked the Glock in a holster under my left arm and under my light jacket, the sound of a weapon being discharged would surely result in some investigation by either Angelo's security or possibly the local law enforcement. Using the Glock with a silencer to kill a bear would leave an unexplained carcass in the woods for someone to discover and ask questions about. Shooting and burying the bear would take forever; I just didn't have that much time to waste. I could only hope that the bear, or any bear, would not appear and investigate me as a possible evening meal.

By the time the crate with the fifty-caliber rifle had been safely stashed in the hide and camouflaged, darkness began to envelop the forest. I walked back to the truck in the dark, as a flashlight could not be used for fear of alerting someone to my presence, a real bitch to navigate the forest in daylight, at night, almost impossible. More than once, I stepped into a hole and fell on my ass. On a couple of falls, my clothing was torn by sharp branches, resulting in some painful gouges into my legs, arms, and chest.

On the drive out of the area I kept the truck's lights off so as not to raise any suspicions. The total trip in, including driving the truck, parking, carrying the crate and concealing the rifle, took about six and a half hours. The trip out had taken over four hours. Once on the highway I could relax and enjoy the trip back, however, having been awake since early morning, plus the rigors of lugging the equipment to the hide sight, there existed a strong possibility of my falling asleep while driving.

Arriving at the small village of Keene, just southeast of Lake Placid, I stopped and found a small motel to spend the night. If I thought this would be a pleasant night of blissful sleep, the locals had other plans. From the time I landed on the hard, smelly mattress, until my tolerance had been exhausted, at about three in the morning, there continued to be banging and moaning from the rooms to either side of me. It sounded to me like every one-night stand within a fifty-mile radius had to happen at this particular motel on this particular night.

At five in the morning, the sounds from the room to the right were unnerving. Evidently the man, whoever he might be, didn't care for the woman he had with him. From the noise coming from the room, he unmercifully kept beating the shit out of the woman. A phone call to the front desk only elicited a sharp, "Mind your own fucking business."

I simply could not accept this; no guy had the right to use a woman as a punching bag. Putting on my trousers and shoes, I went next door and hammered on the door.

"What the fuck do you want?" came the surly shout from the man inside.

"Just want to talk to you for a moment, if you don't mind," I shouted back.

"Go the fuck away, and mind your own fucking business," a woman's voice exclaimed.

Go figure, Sir Galahad had been put in his place, and it would be a long time before I came to the aid of a damsel in distress again. No reason remained in trying to get any sleep, so I checked out.

Conveniently, just across the road from the motel, sat the local village diner, where I had supper the night before in a smoke-filled atmosphere of truck drivers and rude waitresses. Might as well have breakfast there, I thought.

"Heard you had Big Fred McNulty as your neighbor at the hotel," the waitress said as she half-smiled at me. There appeared to be some sarcasm in her remark.

"I guess so," I replied with disinterest, blowing it off as just some local gossip.

"He and Mabel, the night waitress, get into it a couple times a week." She continued to smirk at me. "Don't know why she puts up with his shit, he must give her one good fuck, that's all I can figure." I continued to peruse the menu, showing no particular interest in getting into a conversation with her, especially about any Big Fred McNulty or Mabel the night waitress.

"I'll have the steak and eggs with white toast and coffee," I said, showing my disinterest by not responding to her diatribe on Fred and Mabel. "Keep the steak medium rare if that's possible." It was a seldom-achieved request, but I made it anyway.

Just as the waitress turned to take my order to the kitchen, a rather large and husky mountain man came crashing through the door of the diner.

"Oh, oh, here's Big Fred loaded for bear," I heard the waitress whisper.

"Where's that mother fucker who was banging on my fucking door while I made love to Mabel?" he roared as he glared up and down the diner.

Spotting me, the only stranger in the room, he headed in my direction. This guy was at least six foot four and two hundred thirty pounds of mostly muscle. I just hoped that some of that muscle remained between his ears. Shit, I had no way out except through the front door or the kitchen, both of which were on the other side of Mr. Big Fred.

I really didn't want to have my body parts rearranged. At least I could prepare myself for the inevitable, so standing seemed the expedient thing to do at the moment.

Misjudging Big Fred initially almost landed me in never-never land. Instead of bellowing in my face as expected, he led with a telegraphed right hook. My Marine Corps instincts came to my rescue. I dropped down low to avoid the punch and caught Mr. Fred just below the beltline with my right shoulder. As I straightened up, Fred's momentum from the punch carried him forward. As I raised my body and shoulder, his forward motion and my lifting caused Mr. Fred to go into sprawling ass over teakettle spout, a perfect summersault ending with a thumping crash to the tiled floor of the diner. He landed so hard the building shook. I wheeled around, ready for a return engagement, but Big Fred lay moaning on the floor, poor soul.

Thinking it best to depart the scene as quickly as possible, I left a twenty-dollar bill on the table, bid a fond adieu, and headed out the door. Driving out of town, a police car and ambulance passed me, on their way to the diner I assumed, with sirens blaring and the pedal to the metal. I wondered how far I would get before the local constable chased me down and arrested me for assault. Making it to the Interstate without being stopped, raised my confidence that the police were not in hot pursuit. At least I didn't have to keep my eye on the rearview mirror. One thing for sure, Keene would be off my places to stop and rest or eat.

Arriving back at my office in Bridgeport, Connecticut, by mid-afternoon permitted some time for planning what next to transport to Lake Placid. In an effort to exercise some caution, I returned the pickup truck to the rental agency with the intent of renting a completely different one the next day. Maxine had cleaned things up in the office and had prepared coffee for me. She also went out and bought some cinnamon rolls, which I absolutely love—so much for maintaining my girlish figure. She sure was a sweetheart, and she would make a good wife for some lucky guy. I sincerely hoped that the guy that she ended up with was as thoughtful and caring as she was.

The next day, with a different pickup fully loaded, I headed back up to Lake Placid. This time driving slowly had to be the order of the day. Arriving at the logging road by midday, I checked both directions for any oncoming traffic. As none appeared, I drove the truck into the logging trail, as quickly as conditions would permit, no sense damaging the truck.

The initial problem of the day: just too much stuff to carry in one trip, the load had to be broken into two manageable lots. The first trip in with the RPGs proved to be a slow slog, and it took over three hours in and almost two hiking back out. One satisfaction, the round trip time had been significantly shortened. The final trip in with the remaining equipment, scope, and ammunition actually even took less time. However, the return trip required a great deal of covering my tracks. Leaving any telltale evidence would surely develop some unwanted investigation.

Although too much time had passed to logically attempt a drive back to Connecticut, even though I had become extremely tired, stopping anywhere near Keene just couldn't be a consideration. I did harbor some morbid curiosity as to what had really happened to Big Fred. Maybe Mabel could nurse him back to health. Go figure.

Just before the Interstate is the small town of Underwood. The town pretty much consisted of a gas station, a motel, and diner. Seemed like a good place to rest, while driving I had started to nod a little and didn't want to get into an accident. Smashing into a tree just didn't enter in the scheme of things.

I checked into the motel and then headed over to the diner. Much to my dismay, the waitress turned out to be the same one who had served me at the Keene diner.

"Well, well, look at who has stopped in to eat." She seemed sarcastic; however, I chose to ignore her commentary, just as long as she didn't head to the phone to call the local sheriff.

"I just want to get some dinner and head out, okay?" I tried to be as firm but pleasant as possible.

"You know, you sure did that town and Mabel a big favor, knocking the stuffing out of Big Fred like you did." My ears perked up. "I think they would've given you a parade if you had hung around for a little while. Ole Fred's been a pain in the ass for years, ever since he was a big high school football star. Everybody has always sucked up to him; time had come for someone to knock him on his big ass. Thanks, honey, from all the folks in Keene." She smiled in appreciation, the disclosure of Big Fred being the town bully and my being an unintended hero, sure could have knocked me over with a feather.

"I'm kind of sorry," sort of a lame comment by me, being I really felt no sorrow for Mr. Fred. "Hope I didn't break any bones or anything like that," actually expressing a bald-faced lie, as I honestly hoped his head had fractured. The way that guy treated women, he needed someone to straighten him out.

"Shit, honey, you fractured his skull. He's been in the hospital ever since you decked him. Let me get you something on the house, honey. What will it be?" She had her order pad out, ready to write my request on it.

"A medium rare steak, French fries, or preferably home fries if you have them, coffee, and some toast is all I want," I replied.

"You got it, sweetie, home fries and all, coming right up," she said as she walked away.

No shit, I fractured Big Fred's skull. Not only that, but apparently I turned out to be a local hero. That night I slept like a baby; at least the adjoining rooms weren't being used as hourly love nests.

The next day, back in Connecticut plans were made for the next trip to Lake Placid. Once there, I would put in motion the completion of the most difficult contract I had ever undertaken to date. I returned the pickup truck to the rental company and obtained a small compact car from the same rental company. The only deal with the car, it had to be dropped off at the company's office in Saranac Lake, a village ten miles northwest of Lake Placid. With the trunk of the car loaded with my backpack and some other gear, I set off for Lake Saranac, New York.

Once the car had been dropped off, a bus took me to Lake Placid. That night I rented a room at one of the upscale hotels in Lake Placid. After finishing a meal of local trout with all the trimmings, the remainder of the evening was spent in front of a large fireplace with a good cigar and some Jack Daniels on ice. This might be my last night of freedom or of life.

The next day started early with a five o'clock breakfast and a walk to the local boat rental dock. I explained to the agent at the boat rental company that I wanted a small outboard motor for a few days to go camping on one of the islands. He said Moose Island or Buck Island offered some excellent campsites. I nodded, loaded the boat with my gear and supplies, and headed out on the lake.

The solitariness of the boat trip across the lake provided some respite to what lay ahead for me. I spent the time reflecting on my life: what did my present situation represent, was I doing the right thing, would there be a next week or next month for me? No answers came to mind. Most people, for sure, would consider me nothing more than a criminal, a cold-blooded killer. Perhaps they are right. This life had come too easily, certainly more time could have been devoted to finding work in the computer field; something would have eventually turned up. The decision came too readily, like something I actually aspired to. The unemployment merely provided the excuse, all without careful consideration as to the consequences. This would be my last contract, though, after this, I would devote myself to my children and perhaps a new love interest.

Angelo's property lay to the northwest side of the lake, secluded deep in the woods of the Adirondack Forest. He must have had real pull with someone in order to obtain such a large piece of land close to the forest preserve. Virtually nothing else, no homes, lodges, or businesses existed within miles of his property.

I beached the boat and walked through the woods to the hide where all the equipment previously had been stored. The distance from where the boat had been beached on the lake to the hide measured approximately half a mile, and I deliberately left a trail from the boat to the hide.

The next two days were spent observing the building where Angelo was said to be living. Through the radarscope, a significant amount of activity could be seen throughout the home. Every morning at precisely seven thirty, a meeting occurred in a large room near the center of the home. A rough count of some eight or nine individuals were of particular note; a single individual, who had been observed descending a stairway at six o'clock and then sitting as if having breakfast in a dining room, or what I assumed to be a dining room, evidently was the big man himself, Angelo Lambrascha.

At the conclusion of his breakfast, he moved into a large room, which obviously was a meeting room, as this is where all the various members gathered each morning. This person always sat at the head of the conference table. When he arrived in the room, everyone stood up and when he left, everyone stood again. Everything confirmed that this individual had to be Angelo, the target.

After the morning meetings, this individual went to a room, a study or library, and sat for a considerable period of time, actually most of the day. He spent his time there working on a device, which any good educated guess determined to be a computer. At seven at night, the individual went from the library back to the dining area and sat down to a leisurely meal. Several servants, or what I considered were servants, did not sit or interact with the individual other than placing items on the table and later removing them. From there the individual, Mr. Lambrascha, went to an area where he reclined in a chair and read either books or magazines. At nine thirty, he rose from the chair and ascended the stairs, reclining in what obviously had to be his bed, as he remained there through the night.

The others in the building, approximately fifteen people from what I could make out, launched into a daily routine right after the morning meeting. They all seemed to have specific duties. The kitchen and servant staff had rooms just off the kitchen. A chauffeur had several rooms over the garage area. The rest of the staff had rooms in the basement area of the building, which I couldn't see into through the radarscope, as they were below ground level.

The individual going up and down the stairs, eating meals in the dining area, and conducting the meetings must be Angelo. I had to take my chances on his being Angelo. Whoever it was, he was sure to be dead in a day or so. For four days, I checked out the routine to ensure no noticeable deviation occurred; Angelo proved to be a man of habit and a man of schedules.

Finally comfortable with the routine, I went down to the lake where I had beached the boat. There the empty boat was launched, the motor started, set to slow forward, as slow as possible, and headed to graze the northwest shore of Moose Island, the island furthest from my location. If my calculations were correct, the prevailing winds of the lake would carry the boat around the island and cause it to be beached somewhere on the northeast shore. At a slow speed, it should take close to twenty-two hours.

I climbed out of the boat and walked backward, ensuring my foot prints were visible in the soft earth of the path, to the hide. Once in the hide, the weapons were set for the task at hand. From my backpack, I took out Gino's fingerprints and the bottle of his urine taken from the restaurant in New York City. The fingerprints were pressed on each of the weapons in a random manner so that they appeared to be accidentally left by Gino. The urine I sprayed against one of the trees some distance from the hide but close to the trail so that it appeared to be left naturally.

At the bottom of the hide, a trench eighteen inches deep had been dug, into which I dropped the crate containing the fifty-caliber rifle. Next, I withdrew the rifle from the crate and placed it on a tripod that came with the weapon. The tripod had to be set firmly into the ground and the rifle had to be as level as possible for an accurate shot. My plan: take Angelo out as he started up the stairs at nine thirty at night.

By seven fifteen, everything had been set to my satisfaction. A continuous review rolled through my mind as I tried to address every possible scenario and plan how to respond to it. Some cheese, peanut butter, and crackers washed down with water from my canteen helped pass the time.

At nine o'clock, I began my watch, confirming that Mr. Angelo was keeping to his rigid schedule. From time to time, throughout the day, similar checks had been made with positive results; he maintained his schedule.

At nine thirty, the image began to approach the bottom of the stairs. I had a window of opportunity for only a few seconds. RPG one away, RPG two away, aim, breathe, fifty-caliber round one away, load and breach number two, aim, breathe, trigger, two away, load, and breach number three, aim, breathe, trigger, number three away, load and breach number four, aim, breathe, trigger, number four away, all within less than thirty two seconds. Now the real fun would begin.

Chapter 23

I looked through the radarscope but couldn't make out anything from the smoke and debris. Looking through the scope up the stairs and into the bedroom, I saw no evidence of anyone having ascended the stairs or having entered the bedroom. My best estimate, only a one tenth of one percent chance that Angelo would be at the next morning's meeting. He had to be in the rubble and debris at the foot of the stairs.

I put the fifty-caliber rifle in the crate and covered it with dirt, leaves, and twigs. The tripod was flung back down the trail toward where the boat had been, as far as my strength would permit. The two RPG launchers, also flung down the trail some distance beyond the tripod. I dropped into the hide and pulled my camouflage suit over me so that no one standing within a foot of me would see only leaves and twigs.

My activities were just completed when two men came crashing through the underbrush carrying bright flashlights. They were within a few feet of the hide just minutes if not seconds after I had concealed myself.

"That fucking son of a bitch had to be in this area somewhere," the individual obviously in charge said to the other. "Our asses are in deep fucking trouble, we have to at least find this son of a bitch." He continued, almost as an after-thought.

"Quit standing there talking, keep looking around, he can't be far," commanded one of the other men, evidently the one leading the charge.

"Shit, Al, look at this," the first individual called out. "It looks like a tripod or something, probably used to support the weapon he used."

The other had moved down the trail away from the hide.

"Fucking Christ, here is a rocket-propelled grenade launcher." It sounded like the first guy again; I guess he moved out in front of the others. "He must be heading down the trail toward the lake," came a voice farther away. My ruse evidently was paying off; at least that is what I thought.

"Get the fucking dogs, we'll catch that fucker before daylight," said the first voice, the one that sounded like he was in command.

Shit, dogs brought back memories of Maggie.

Within twenty minutes, I could hear dogs barking and heading in my direction. They would probably head to my hide. What to do? Fifteen minutes passed and the dogs were on the trail and headed right for me.

"Hey, Bill, over here," one of the dog handlers called out, "the dogs have found something."

The men gathered around the hide, shining their powerful lights into it and began to pull back the cover.

"This is where he took the shots from," the lead man exclaimed.

Prior planning saved my ass once again. From my perch way up in the tree, I watched carefully every move made by the search party below me. One of the dogs went over and began to sniff the tree where Gino's urine had been sprayed.

"Hey, look at this," the dog handler called out, "the guy took a leak against this tree," he concluded.

"Have forensics get a sample if possible," the boss man instructed, "to see if we can identify our killer."

Killer? That partially confirmed the success of my plan. Forensics? What the hell would a forensics team be doing out here? Shit, these guys were extensively prepared and undoubtedly had a complete lab on the premises.

Soon the search party began to work its way down the trail I had left, leading them to the lake. Within minutes of their departure, a helicopter could be heard overhead along with a two hundred thousand-candlepower searchlight. I started to have some serious afterthoughts of the killing I just carried out. Was Angelo in fact the person who Ernesto claimed him to be? Or perhaps he might be a federal witness or some other kind of individual being protected by federal agents? My ass could be in some serious trouble.

For now, my main interest had to focus on how to get my ass out of this situation. First, using the method of moving from tree to tree, successfully used previously, I moved several hundred yards from the hide location. In the new location, I moved as high up in the tree as possible and applied straps around the tree and myself to secure my body and equipment to the tree. Once secured, exhaustion enveloped my body and mind, causing me to fall into a deep sleep.

At six in the morning, helicopters woke me as they flew low over my perch in the tree. Just in case they possessed infrared cameras, I had taken the precaution of wearing a suit that would conceal me from such devices. Below, men were walking in a search line similar to ones used at any crime scenes, looking for evidence. Shit, this area probably had been completely closed off as a crime scene, and guess who the sad ass criminal was? I still had sufficient water, cheese, and crackers for about two days, and I calculated I could last maybe two or three more before some exit strategy had to be finalized. Otherwise, my rotting corpse would be found in the tree a few years hence.

Things died down after sundown, a very good indication that the search was nearing an end. I could also see and hear numerous vehicles leaving the compound and not returning. By the afternoon of day two, everything seemed to be unusually quiet, almost too quiet. The only sounds I could hear were from the village across the lake. Occasional sirens, whistles, and clanks of some kind could be heard from the village, but nothing closer than that.

To be safe, I spent the next two days in my perch, getting increasingly sore from the confined position. Finally, time came to move on. For more than a thousand yards, I moved from tree to tree in the dense forest, dropping to the ground in a very remote area of the Adirondack forest almost a mile from the hide. From there, a hike over the mountain to Saranac Lake brought me back to civilization.

Every law enforcement agent in the area must have been on the lookout for anyone emerging from the woods, so great caution had to be taken with every move. Just outside the village, I found a small lake where I bathed, shaved, and changed into some leisure clothes I took from my backpack. I buried my pack and all the paraphernalia I no longer required, deep in a hole situated in the Adirondack Forest Preserve, where chances of its discovery was as remote as a three-dollar bill. From there, I worked my way into the village and blended in with the town's people and tourists.

Hanging around anywhere in this area, especially overnight, would be inviting trouble, taking a cab anywhere, also a bad idea. Saranac Lake is a fairly large village, about six thousand plus some two or three thousand tourists. Trailways Bus Company has a small terminal in the village, so I opted for a bus ride out of town. There were two buses running each day except weekends, one at seven in the morning, which had already left, and one at four in the afternoon. I purchased a ticket for the four o'clock bus, which would take me southeast to Albany, New York.

Finding a seat on the bus, not a problem, very few people were traveling that day. Sitting in a seat with no one next to me, I settled in for the trip to Albany, which would take some three or so hours. As the bus moved away from the terminal, I began to relax, and being quite tired, I dozed off.

After thirty minutes or so of travel, the bus stopped, and I woke with a start. Why had the bus stopped? Looking out the window, the answer became obvious. We were stopping in Lake Placid, apparently a scheduled stop.

Panic began to set back in. There were police all over the place as they checked the passengers getting on to the bus, obviously, in search of someone, unquestionably me. Shit, the guy the boat had been rented from could give the police a description of me. The police undoubtedly had a sketch in their hands and checked it against every passenger boarding the bus.

Sweat began to form on the back of my neck and trickle down my spine, adding to my uneasiness. I sat trapped like a rat in a corner with nowhere to go. The police officer holding a paper in his hand, probably the sketch of me, began to board the bus. I could feel the cold steel of the handcuffs tightening on my wrist, the barred cell door clanging shut, as I awaited my destiny as a prisoner for life. Since I had taken out a big cheese Mafioso, my life in prison would last all of twenty seconds, if that.

To my surprise and deep relief, the police officer only stood at the front of the bus and looked back along the aisle. Apparently satisfied that the killer had not boarded in Saranac Lake, he exited the bus and motioned for the driver to continue his trip. The driver closed the door, started the engine, put it in gear, and started his drive to Albany.

A woman in her late forties, maybe early fifties, sat in the seat next to me even though there were many open seats on the bus. She seemed pleasant enough and had on perfume I didn't find offensive; actually, it was rather fragrant. After traveling for ten minutes or so, curiosity got the better of me. I turned to her and introduced myself as Ralph.

She replied, "Hello, my name Sara, and I'm on my way to visit my grandchildren in Binghamton, New York." Sara had a very pleasant grandmother voice, "I live in Lake Placid and have spent my entire life here. This is such a wonder community, I just love it here."

"What was all the activity with the police back there?" I coyly asked.

"Oh, I heard some mafia guy got shot up across the lake the other day." She looked over her glasses at me. "Someone said that the guys protecting him were close friends of Jim Naybor, our police chief. Whoever it was that killed the mafia guy rented a boat from Earl down at the boat dock. Earl says he's rented a lot of boats, and he doesn't really remember who the guy was or anything about him—could even be a girl, I suppose.

"My boy's a policeman in Binghamton, been there for, oh, twelve or so years. He's a good boy, married to Francis Coply. She came from The Lake, too. We call Lake Placid 'The Lake' around here, you know. Anyway, when my son, Billy, graduated from the police academy, there weren't any openings at The Lake, so he got a job in Binghamton.

"I go down every week to visit with them. They have two wonderful children. Jessica, she's the oldest, and Billy Jr., he's a big boy just like his dad and his grandfather. Bill Sr. passed away a few years back and I sure do miss him."

The only part I really cared about was what the police were looking for.

Confirming that the Mafia guy, in fact had been killed, came as especially good news. Now I could relax and listen to Sara go on and on and just nod and nod.

From Albany, I took a train to Grand Central Terminal in New York City and then boarded a train to Bridgeport, Connecticut.

While in New York City between trains, I went to my bank, the Brazilian bank, and withdrew twenty thousand dollars—in tens and twenties. Not having any way of carrying that much cash, I had purchased a hard attaché case before going to the bank. On the train ride to Bridgeport, I kept a tight grip on the case. Arriving in Bridgeport long after dark and having no personal transportation available, I decided to take public transportation, a bus to the apartment previously rented.

On the ride aboard the bus, I kept my tight grip on the case. At each stop, a number of people would get on and off the bus, mostly minorities. I do not consider myself a prejudiced person, believing everyone has a right to the freedoms provided by the United States and a right to become a citizen of the United States, provided the immigrant follows the legal processes. Serving in the Marine Corps had exposed me to all colors, ethnicities, and cultures. I found everyone to be of equal intelligence, with a desire to live in a country offering freedom. Minorities were especially committed to laying down their lives to preserve the freedom they and their families have come to enjoy in the United States. This particularly applied to Hispanics, even though in the country with only a green card, without question had volunteered for some of the most dangerous missions. I was proud to have served with them.

As we approached my stop, in addition to the driver and me, there were only two other people on the bus. I pulled the cord to signal the driver that the next stop would be mine. As I got up to exit the bus, out of the corner of my eye the motion of the other two riders indicated they were getting off at the same stop. Carrying so much money on me, and my overly paranoid protection of the attaché case, no doubt provoked suspicions of its content. To heighten my concern, the neighborhood in which I had my apartment was a middle-income residential area, and, to add to my paranoia, it was a section of the city without streetlights.

Walking toward the apartment, I could hear the distinct sounds of shoe leather hitting the concrete sidewalk behind me. It would be indeed unusual for these two Hispanics to live in this section of the city. As usual, whenever conditions permitted, safely tucked under my left armpit was the quick-draw holster containing the Glock. The silencer for it had been placed in my right pocket, possibly not the best location, however, readily accessible. Continuing to walk, I removed the silencer and the pistol, screwing the silencer on, doing all this while trying to hold the briefcase tightly under my left arm.

As my walk took me past a heavily wooded lot, I picked up the pace, hoping not to be accosted while so close to an area of such seclusion.

"Hey, amigo, what's in your case, my friend?" came the voice of one of the men behind me, probably the larger of the two.

I stopped and turned to face my adversaries, as this would better position me to deal with the situation, having them come up from behind and blindsiding me didn't particularly appeal to me.

"Believe me, my amigos, there is nothing of interest to you in my case, just some business papers, pens, pencils, and a calculator," I replied forcefully, having the assurance of my superiority in this situation, a superior position provided by the Glock. Otherwise, I'd be shitting bricks in my pants.

The two who had gotten off the bus at the same stop as I did stood separated about seven feet apart from each other and some ten feet from me. The bigger of the two did all the talking. He stood about five foot ten or five eleven and had a husky build. I would not like to tangle with him physically. The other, shorter, perhaps five foot five to five six with a slight build, seemed almost frail. I could kick his ass without raising a sweat.

"If that is the case, me amigo, you wouldn't mind showing us what you have there, now would you?" A definite arrogance and a chuckle in his voice; the motherfucker just wouldn't back down.

"I strongly advise both of you to move on and leave me alone. Let me go to my home without any further discussion." I remained emphatic. I had no desire to kill these two men. They could have a family, children to support. Softening my approach, I said, "Look, I have a weapon and will use it to protect myself, do you understand?" the tone of my voice being more conciliatory, although it was definitely not my intent to be cooperative or in any way signify a weakening in my position. "I cannot and will not show you what is in my case; it is none of your business. Now, please, and I implore you, please move on." I did not consider myself a killer and had no desire to become one.

It didn't work. "Oh, amigo, we can't just walk away and not know what is in the case, the case you seem to be protecting." His voice laced with sarcasm. "It must have something of value or you wouldn't be so protective of it and so reluctant to let us have a look inside of it." The larger of the two continued to do all the talking.

"I am not bullshitting you, I have killed before and I have no hesitation in killing both of you; just move on and leave me alone," I hissed. I had never hissed before, but hissing now seemed necessary.

The smaller of the two gave me the impression he wanted to leave, but the other said something to him in Spanish and he stopped; but he did continue to exhibit a nervousness with the situation.

"Why don't you do as your friend wants and just leave?" I implored him.

"No, no, amigo, my friend does not want to leave; he wants to see what is in your case. He knows it must be of great value or you wouldn't hold it so tightly to your body." He glared at me through the darkness. Only a light from a window further up the street and behind me reflected in his eyes. "Why don't you just set it down and walk away so there will be no trouble."

Shit, maybe giving them the money was the best option, but I just couldn't let go. Leaving the money for them would cause me some deep emotional anguish, an anguish that would affect my sleep and my self-respect. I couldn't do it. Why wouldn't these idiots just leave, walk away? I pulled the pistol into view and fired a single shot between them. The ricochet awakened the night and it certainly awakened my advisories. The little guy moved down the block faster than a jackrabbit. I had never witnessed a person move so fast; he was out of sight within seconds. The big guy moved a little slower but responded with a slow gait in the direction of his friend. He definitely recognized the danger that was obvious in this situation.

I swallowed hard and noted my hands were shaking. None of the kills made while in the Marine Corps or as a hired gun in civilian life were face-to-face with the two exceptions of Paul McCarthy and the goatherd boy. The boy I was compelled to kill at close range or jeopardize the entire mission. Paul McCarthy was a longer shot, but still inside the boundary of my comfort zone, my comfort range being in excess of one hundred yards. All the rest had been long-range and impersonal. One thing, though, I deserved a pat on the back for keeping my cool and not taking these two guys out. Christ, what a mess that would have created.

What the fuck would I have done with the bodies? Suppose I hadn't decided to arm myself—they would have kicked the shit out of me and taken the case and the money. No sense reflecting on what could have happened, it was time to get to the apartment so I could pack and get out.

Within the hour, I had packed everything, placed it all in the trunk of my car and headed to downtown Bridgeport and a decent hotel. A Jack Daniels on ice at the hotel bar and a good night's sleep would relieve my jangled nerves. Being over-tired, I slept until ten the next morning. After checking out, a short drive brought me to the office of my phony company. Maxine sat attentively behind her desk in the reception area.

"Hi, gorgeous," I greeted her with a big smile, "How would you like to go and have a nice expensive breakfast, like at the Hilton or the Marriott? " Both hotels had restaurants on the top floor. Maxine seemed a little shocked initially but took a few minutes to gather her composure.

Maxine, a brunette with soft brown eyes and somewhat of an attractive figure, was not a knockout but had a sparkling personality that made her appear much more attractive. She always dressed professionally, usually wearing a white blouse that buttoned all the way to the neck and a full-length skirt and high heels. I'm sure she took the shoes off when she sat at the desk, but I had no way of telling; she always sat close to the desk so her feet were never visible. She, without a doubt, had front office appeal.

"That sounds good, Ralph, but what is the occasion?"

"When we get to breakfast, I will fill you in on all the details," I said, smiling at her with that "I know something you don't" look. "You ready to go?" I asked.

"Just need to freshen up a little, if that is okay." She jumped up from behind the desk and headed to the bathroom at the rear of the office.

"Always keep your date waiting, huh?" I called after her. "Sure, go ahead, I'll wait for you in my office." It gave me a chance to look around and see if any mail had come in.

Looking at Maxine as she returned from the bathroom, now that I had started to relax a little, my sexual urges were beginning to surface. Still, there could be absolutely no intention on my part of making a pass at her or giving a second thought to a sexual encounter.

The Marriott is located in the center city of Bridgeport, a few blocks from the office, so we drove there. Parking in the hotel garage only took minutes. Several other people had entered the elevator with us, so neither of us initiated a conversation, just looked around and waited for the elevator to stop at the fourteenth floor. A maître d' seated us, without any wait, at a very comfortable table with a panoramic view of Bridgeport and Long Island Sound.

Deferring to Maxine to order first, as it seemed the polite thing to do, the waiter and I waited as she perused the menu, finally deciding on an omelet, orange juice, and coffee. Naturally, I ordered my favorite—steak and eggs—with my usual fervent request for medium rare and a side of white toast dry. To wash it all down, a couple of cups of coffee.

With all the preliminaries out of the way, it was time to give Maxine a little update. "Well, what will it be, good news first or bad news first?" I asked, breaking the silence.

"Oh, there's bad news?" She looked a little forlorn, her eyes falling to the plate in front of her.

"Well, yes, I am sorry but the office is going to be closed. The contract for which the office had been opened for has been completed," I said, putting it as softly as possible. Her feelings were definitely hurt, which became obvious in her eyes as she stared at me in disbelief. For a few moments, I thought she might burst into tears, but she seemed to gain her composure and sat up straight in anticipation of the good news.

"And if that is the bad news, what is the good news?" she asked very softly with almost a crackling in her voice. Shit, this proved to be more difficult than expected, but hopefully the next part of my task would be pleasant for both of us.

"The good news is that you are going to receive a cash bonus," I said, some excitement manifest in my voice. "There is a strict edict that goes along with the bonus and it is very important that you comply with it," I continued, trying to contain my excitement and at least appear stern. "Think you will be able to follow the instructions religiously?"

"I guess that depends on what the rules are." Good response from Maxine.

"Today, Maxine, I am going to give you twenty thousand dollars in cash. The rules are that you cannot spend the money on extravagant items, you cannot put the money in a bank, and you should spend a little at a time so as not to raise any suspicions in regard to the money. Can you abide by those rules?" I carefully instructed her. "The reason for these caveats is that the money comes from a top secret military operation, which can never be disclosed to anyone." A little bullshit never hurt.

"Oh my god, yes," she really perked up, almost jumping out of her seat. "Oh, this is so wonderful, I just can't believe it, and I've never had that much money at one time. I have just a nice secret place to keep it and will take out a little at a time. I just can't thank you; I don't know what to say." She obviously appreciated the little gift.

"That is not all," I said, trying to contain some of her enthusiasm. "If you abide by the edicts, in six months there will be another twenty thousand. Okay?" Kind of dumb to ask if it was okay, it just seemed to roll out my head and off the end of my tongue; go figure.

Maxine looked dumbstruck and couldn't put together two words of appreciation. As a giver, it made me feel especially good; making someone like Maxine so happy brought me great pleasure. She just nodded.

Maxine came across as a bright, bubbly, very kind person; however, my take on her was that she would never achieve any great success. She lacked the motivation to improve herself through education or similar endeavors. The forty thousand promised her plus another sixty I will surprise her with in the near future would provide her with a descent nest egg, albeit all not accessible at one time. That amount of money should provide her a reasonable source of discretionary funds for a small purchase, something in the three thousand to five thousand dollar range. My biggest worry, a boyfriend or husband comes on the scene is informed of the nest egg and wants to spend it all right away. They could end up in a real bind with the IRS trying to explain the source of so much money. But that no longer concerned me.

Our food arrived at the perfect time. I decided to change the subject. It would ease up on the silence that had cloaked the table and our breakfast since the initial excitement over the bonus had past.

"You know, Bridgeport is a pretty interesting city," I said in a lame effort at initiating a conversation. "General Electric, at one time had a fairly significant manufacturing operation here. Too bad they closed down and sold off the product line," I commented.

"My dad worked for General Electric for more than twenty years," she picked up the conversation, "and then all the sudden, one day they let all the employees know the business was closing down. That had a dramatic effect on the city and on our family in particular. Dad remained out of work for over two years, and when he finally found work, his wages were about half what he had been making with GE. He became sullen and came home drunk most nights," she came off a little remorseful, probably a poor choice of subjects. "Weekends he would spend with his buddies, also former GE employees, grumbling about how shabbily they were treated and how the union only contributed to their situation. They would sit and drink away the weekend, usually not even returning home Saturday nights. Probably for the best for mom, since dad treated her like she had caused all the problems." Maxine came to life, too bad I hadn't selected a different subject.

"You know, Maxine, things are changing for the better in Bridgeport." I said, trying to improve on a poorly chosen topic. "You have a new mayor who is bringing in businesses, mostly computer-related businesses. You should find work in one of those new companies, with your capabilities you would go far." I didn't want to say a glowing letter of recommendation would be forthcoming since the business had been closed. Specifically, there could be no trail of any kind leading back to me. Fortunately, Maxine did not pursue the subject.

We finished our breakfast in a leisurely manner with idle discussions about family and what plans we each had for the future. Mine, of course, were fabricated. Back at the office, I gave Maxine the twenty thousand in hundred dollar bills. She left in tears, happy tears, although with sadness about having to leave. I assured her that we would stay in touch.

All the office furniture and equipment including several computers, all of which I had purchased from the rental company, the business now donated to a local private school for underprivileged children. They were more than happy to send over a truck to pick everything up. Within a day, the office was completely closed and the lease terminated. The car, which had been purchased in Ralph's name, I sold at a local car dealership at a substantial loss; so what's new there.

Chapter 24

Deposits had been continuously transferred from my New York Brazilian bank account to Frank Valincia's, Ernesto's brother-in-law, savings account in Brooklyn. I don't know if Frank ever even looked at the account, he probably thought the account was overdrawn. His wife, Juliana, Ernesto's sister, had her own account and wouldn't bother with Frank's account; therefore, she had no knowledge of the deposits.

I had to extricate myself from this business; since all the building blocks were just about in place, it made sense to begin the process now. To start, a recent printout of Frank's savings account had to be produced; I had to pull the information up and print it out on a computer system that could not be traced to me. To accomplish this I went to a computer café in New York City and rented time on one of their computers. To rent time on a computer, photo identification must be presented to the clerk, therefore ole Ralph once again came to my rescue—or actually his driver's license with my picture on it did. Since I already had Frank's account number in my possession, all I would need would be a password, Frank Valincia's password.

Going to his bank's Web site, his account could readily be accessed using the account number; however, the account could not be opened without a password or PIN (Personal Identification Number). Coming up with a PIN could be a problem, but some thought as to how Dino's mind worked would help. He and Juliana had a daughter, Missy, who had been born on July 8, 2001. A long shot would be the PIN 782001 or some permutation of those numbers. Unfortunately, there are one million possible combinations to this series of numbers. The selection had to be some logical combination. Punching in 782001 did not work, so I tried 100287, no luck, and then the European method of writing dates, 872001, and his account opened up. Jesus, what a long shot, I should be playing the Lotto.

I made a copy of the savings account information and copied it to a spreadsheet on a separate page. The page showed Frank had made deposits to his account on the same day he made deposits to Ernesto's business account. The deposits to Ernesto's business account were supposed to be the proceeds from the pizza business, all of the proceeds, period. I signed out of Frank's account and wrote an e-mail to Ernesto's office that read, "You might find your brother-in-law's savings account interesting," nothing more.

The next day I started hanging out at Puglisi's Steak House to see if there were any discussions regarding the information e-mailed to Ernesto. The following week, bits of conversations could be picked up regarding a meeting Ernesto had with his lieutenants at his Saranac Lake estate. Putting together the tidbits of information, gained over several weeks, I was able to develop a reasonable understanding as to what had transpired at the meeting. The eavesdropping provided vital information to me since it confirmed that Ernesto had been the person who contracted me to take out Angelo.

A meeting of Ernesto's organization was held several weeks later at his Saranac Lake estate and attended by Ernesto, his secretary Margaret Benzio, and accountant Joey Shapiro. As Ernesto instructed, all his lieutenants Joseph (Joe) Balgazi of the Connecticut operations, Bill (Fatso) Flugazy of North New Jersey operations, Benjamin (Bingo) Latorino of Staten Island operations, Anthony (Big Tony) of Westchester, New York, operations, and Dominick (The Don) of Rockland County, New York, operations were present. In addition to the local bosses (lieutenants), each boss had an entourage of henchman, chauffeurs, and female "assistants." The last person at the table was Gino, the enforcer who sat to the right of Ernesto.

Once everyone had situated themselves around the conference table, and Cuban cigars and a drink of choice were passed out, Ernesto, in his inimitable way addressed the group.

"You fuckers aren't here to just fucking relax, smoke, drink, and fuck your girlfriend, you're fucking here for fucking business. Do I make myself perfectly fucking clear?"

All nodded in silent agreement.

"The first fucking order of business is to discuss how you are going to expand your territory. Angelo is no longer in our fucking way, so it is fucking time to expand into other fucking areas. Joe, let's fucking start with you; what the fuck are you going to do?" Ernesto stared at Joe, who sat just to Ernesto's left.

"Well, I had assumed something was up with the disappearance of Angelo so I started moving some of my gambling people into lower Connecticut along with a number of my more dignified girls to attract the well-heeled crowd." Joe wanted to be pretty sure he met Ernesto's expectations.

"I hope to fuck you're moving fast before Angelo's fucking organization recovers and begins to protect their territory," Ernesto reprimanded Joe.

And so the day went, one after the other going into some detail as to what they were doing to expand their individual areas of business, none of which pleased Ernesto.

The meeting dragged on, with Ernesto berating each of his under bosses. They were all idiots, none of the under bosses ever met Ernesto's unreasonable expectations. He demanded that they each increase their businesses by forty percent within the next six months or he would replace each and every one of them. "Replace" meant do away with; they would meet an unexpected demise. Gino's function would be to enforce Ernesto's directives by eliminate those who didn't perform, a role Gino relished.

The next day Ernesto had another very important subject to discuss, one that he demanded remain a secret within the organization. Anyone who violated the secrecy code would be eliminated from the organizations.

Ernesto led off, "That fucking no-good fucking brother-in-law of mine, Frankie, has been fucking stealing from me. Gino, I want that fucker exterminated."

"No problem, boss, I'll work out a plan and take care of it." Gino had all the confidence in the world he could kill Frank without there being any traceability to him or Ernesto's organization.

"Na, fuck. Na, that's not the fucking way it's going to go down, Gino. I'll tell you how the fucker is to be taken out, you fucking *capisce*?" Ernesto glowered at Gino.

"Fuck, boss, I've always worked things out on my own, haven't I? I've always been successful, no one ever finds any clues traceable to me or the organization," Gino asserted, the wrong thing to do with Ernesto.

"You fucking do what the fuck I tell you to do, or someone else will do the job, *capisce*?" Ernesto spat out his words.

"Ah, yeah, okay boss." What else could Gino say?

"What I fucking want you to do, is to get a bolt action 30-06 caliber rifle with a scope, *capisce*? I've rented a fucking apartment on Atlantic Avenue between Autumn Avenue and Crescent Street. The fucking apartment is on the sixth floor on the front of the building overlooking Atlantic Avenue, giving you a good fucking view of Atlantic Avenue. My fucking stealing brother-in-law walks along Atlantic to get to his fucking, that is, *my* fucking, bank. I want you to take him out. I don't want my fucking sister to think I had anything to do with his death, *capisce*? This way it looks like a fucking serial killer took the fuck out." Ernesto completed his detailed instructions.

"Yeah, I'll get it done, Mr. Ernesto, as you have instructed, the job will be done. Will I receive my usual fifty grand for this job?" Gino Francotti wanted to be certain he had the usual assurance of a contract for fifty thousand dollars.

"Yeah, but I want to know the fucking day and the approximate time you're going to do that fuck in—and then the fifty fucking gees as usual." Ernesto swiped his hand as if to dismiss the question.

The meeting broke up and everyone retired to the downstairs living room with its large fireplace and comfortable seating. Waiting there for them were their girlfriends, drinks, and fresh Cuban cigars.

I also decided to keep an eye on developments in Lake Placid since Angelo Lambrascha had been eliminated. Both the *Lake Placid News* and *Saranac Lake News* had Web sites. Some information detailed on the front-page of each of the papers in particular concerned me. The story of Angelo's death graced the front pages of the local newspapers for several weeks, such a killing in their territory brought much controversy, especially the disclosure of a big shot crime boss living amongst them.

Also, according to the article, Briana Crawford-Taylor, the FBI agent who had developed the computer program for identifying serial killers nationwide, had come to Lake Placid as a continuing aspect to her investigation. Briana was considered an integral member of the FBI team investigating the murder of Mr. Lambrascha.

Her new program was more effective than originally thought. Without question, four killings were attributed to the same person, as the same DNA and fingerprints had been found at several of the locations, including the most recent: the masterful killing of a mafia boss, Angelo Lambrascha, near Lake Placid. There now could be no doubt that this individual must be a trained, skilled assassin.

The killing near Lake Placid especially pointed to a highly skilled assassination, since the Don had the best protection money could buy. This killer had penetrated one of the most thoroughly secured private areas in the United States. Not only had he or she completed the assassination, but had escaped totally undetected. This took a unique person, a person with exceptional training and experience, possibly a former U.S. Army Ranger, a Navy Seal, or a Special Forces trained individual.

The investigation near Lake Placid had disclosed some detailed information. Of particular interest, the killing in Houston, Texas, where an individual of interest, a John Murdock, had been staying at a hotel located near where the killing took place. A trace on Mr. Murdock revealed that he had a New York driver's license that had been issued to him in Elmira, NY, a short time before the killing of the Don took place. The New York DMV indicated Murdock had just received a license from California. At Houston police's request, a police officer from Elmira was sent to the address provided by Mr. Murdock, however he no longer lived at that address, having moved out over a month ago. A thorough forensic examination of the property turned up nothing of interest. Too many families with pets had occupied the property.

Unfortunately, New York did not keep details about the California license other than that it had been issued in Los Angeles. A check with the Los Angeles, CA, DMV disclosed four hundred sixty John Murdock licenses had been issued in the LA area. The logistics in attempting to trace down so many John Murdocks would be a daunting task requiring many man-hours, with a limited potential for success. The LAPD did not have the resources or the time to search for each to confirm their authenticity. The FBI sent several agents to Los Angeles, and the LAPD provided a printout of all John Murdocks in their files. This proved to be a dead end, in addition, no other useful information resulted from the local Lake Placid, New York, police investigation, and no John Murdock had registered at any of the hotels or motels in or around the city.

Having developed essential information on Gino Francotti and Frank Valincia, the missing piece was Ernesto. What were his plans for Gino and Frank? Information on Gino and Frank had been developed by spying, eavesdropping on Ndrangheta's conversations at Mama Rotino's, and research at the local libraries and through computer Web searches. In order to uncover additional information on Ernesto, I would devote most of my evenings having dinner, mostly two- to three-hour dinners, at Puglisi's Steak House eavesdropping on various conversations.

To acquire the necessary information would take some time. For one thing, I had no idea what nights Ernesto went to Puglisi's or where he sat once he arrived at the restaurant. Over several weeks, I determined that he frequented Puglisi's three times a week on Monday, Wednesday, and Friday. He always arrived about the same time and always sat at the same table in the back of the restaurant. This routine made it easier for me to eavesdrop on him. To conceal my eavesdropping, an MP3 device had been modified to listen in and record his conversations while it still functioned as a music player.

Ernesto, like all good mafia dons, had informants. One night, several weeks after the Saranac Lake meeting, Ernesto had dinner at Puglisi's with a person I identified as an intermediate. An intermediate is a person who had a contact at the FBI, as the contact in the FBI could never be seen talking with Ernesto. Over the course of the dinner, Ernesto, on at least three occasions, instructed his informant to tell the agent about the planned killing of Frank. Ernesto specifically instructed the intermediate that Gino had to kill Frank before they shot Gino. Only with this agreement would Ernesto disclose the location and time of the planned shooting. Several dinners at Puglisi's later, Ernesto learned from the intermediate that the FBI agent had agreed to the terms of the proposed contract.

On one of my visits to New York City, I transferred three hundred thousand dollars from the Bank of Ossining to the Bank of Brazil, the

Brazilian bank Murilo had recommended. During each of my visits to the Bank of Brazil, my contact had always been a Senor Gomez—this contact per Murilo's instruction. I found Senor Gomez to be very rigorous, insisting he be addressed as Senor Gomez, no first name or any informal conversation. He always took the cash and gave me a receipt. On the first visit, he set up a savings account and a checking account. I always had a perception of mistrust in dealing with him. The three hundred thousand would be my test of Senor Gomez's integrity, including the testing of the Bank of Brazil's integrity.

My next project: I planned to follow Gino to see what his plans were. On several occasions, he led me to a fourteen-story apartment building at 310 Crescent Street in Brooklyn. This, I discovered to be very close to Frank's Pizzeria, so it naturally confirmed for me that Gino's target had to be Frank Valincia. Obviously, my devious plan had taken root, and Ernesto was not pleased with his brother-in-law. Nothing is ever certain, so being vigilant and assessing Gino's moves and preparations seemed, at this juncture, the most logical approach for me to pursue.

Employing my methods, I tracked Gino to the sixth floor of the building, apartment 625. The entrance to the apartment sat at the front center of the building, right across from the elevator and a stairwell. The stairwell had a fire door at each floor, which provided me easy access to each floor. The building had a security entrance, but the lock apparently had been broken some time ago, so anyone could walk into the building directly off the Atlantic Avenue.

Somehow, I had to gain entrance to the apartment to see what Gino might be carrying in the attaché case he had with him each time he made a trip to the building. Just down the hall from the apartment was a janitor's closet, full of mops, brooms, and cleaning paraphernalia. The closet would provide me an excellent location to observe the hallway and the front door of the apartment. Since Gino apparently had a schedule, which he religiously abided by, he would arrive at the apartment building at ten o'clock sharp every day and leave at precisely two thirty in the afternoon. One day provided me with an opportunity to obtain a copy of the apartment's key. While hiding in the janitor's closet, I watched as Gino opened the door and go into the apartment. To my surprise, he left the key in the door and the door ajar.

Thinking quickly, I took a pad and pencil out of my pocket, carefully removed the key from the lock and made a trace of it, including the grooves on both sides and their approximate depth and wrote down the name of the manufacturer of the lock. I hurriedly put the key back in the lock, none too soon, as I could hear Gino walking across the wooden floor of the apartment. I did not have time to make it back to the janitor's closet, so a short walk across the hallway brought me to the elevators where a push of the button summoning the elevator. As I stood waiting for the elevator car, Gino came out and looked around, stared at me for a few moments and then went back in and slammed the door shut behind him. Could he have been suspicious of me? I had no way of knowing but he could not have seen much of my facial features, as the hallway only had a few 40-watt bulbs, which provided very little illumination.

The manufacturer of the lock proved to be Yale, which provided me some idea of the type of key that would be needed. At a hardware store in Croton, I picked out, from a rack of key blanks, six different Yale key blanks, all a close approximation to the drawing I had made at the apartment. The clerk asked if he could cut a key for me, which I pleasantly declined. With a little vise attached to the kitchen counter and some small files, I began the process of duplicating a key. After five and a half hours, there in front of me were six possible key fits for the apartment lock.

Going to the apartment on Atlantic Avenue in Brooklyn late at night, greatly reduced the chance of encountering Gino. The last train out of New York City to Croton is at two in the morning, so the best time to gain entrance to the apartment would be around midnight. That way, I could determine if anything in the apartment would aid me in my effort to entrap Gino and still catch the last train out to Croton. The subway entrance, a mere two blocks from the apartment, provided easy reliable transportation to Grand Central terminal and my ride home. Unsure of the neighborhood around Gino's apartment, I hurried so as not to be followed or accosted by any unsavory characters. Even with the Glock securely under my left arm, defending myself in the city would only bring questions, questions I didn't particularly care about answering.

In order not to raise any suspicions, I took the stairs up to the sixth floor instead of the elevator. The elevator, being old, made a hell of a lot of noise when operated. Once on the sixth floor, I carefully opened the stairwell door. Just down the hall were two lovebirds making out under a dim light bulbs. After a half hour or so the elevator started up; the door opened on the sixth floor and then it closed followed by the elevator decending, I assumed to be the first floor of the building. Peering out of the stairwell door, the lovebirds had departed.

At the door, I fumbled with the keys, trying one after the other. On the fifth try, the key slid into the lock, but it would not turn. The sixth key had to be it or there would be no chance of searching the apartment. I slid it into the lock, and it seemed to have some give but didn't turn. I tried moving the key in and out of the lock, turning it with each try, and just when I was about ready to give up—click—the deadbolt opened. I entered the apartment, closing and locking the door behind me.

There were no lights in the apartment, but my flashlight provided sufficient illumination. I moved cautiously through the living room, walking very carefully so as not to alert neighbors, particularly the ones just downstairs, below this apartment. Once through the living room and into the dining room, there, by a window overlooking Atlantic Avenue, sat a small fold up chair and a box containing a Springfield 30-06 with a scope. On close examination, the weapon was a newer model than mine was, a Nikon 5-20x44 Monarch with a scope attached, which was also a different type. Any thoughts of exchanging the weapon only briefly crossed my mind. Undoubtedly, Gino would detect the difference almost immediately.

I started back across the dining room to the living room when a small shaft of light from the hallway cast its way across the living room floor. Had I forgotten to close and lock the door? A shadow moved in through the light and the door closed. "Fuck!" the only thought I could generate. I worked my way back across the dining room and into the kitchen where I waited for whatever would happen next.

A powerful flashlight came on and the beam penetrated the darkness of the room. The beam slowly worked around the room and came to rest on the chair and the rifle by the front windows. The individual took breaths in rather short gasps; he sat down on the chair with his back to me. From the attaché case, he removed some boxes and sat them on the floor, after which he sat straight up, fumbled in his pocket, and withdrew a pack of cigarettes, drawing one out and lighting it. He sat and enjoyed his smoke for about twenty minutes and then got up and walked out of the apartment, quietly closing the door behind him and locking it. I could hear the deadbolt lock engage.

Deciding to be very cautious, I waited an hour and a half before venturing out of the apartment. No one appeared in the hall, so I took the stairs to the first floor and left the building. Making my way to the subway station along a deserted Atlantic Avenue late at night is an experience in itself. Infrequently a car would pass or an individual would be hanging out on a street corner or at the front of one of the apartment buildings having a smoke. Several times couples holding hands passed on their way somewhere. The city really isn't the scary place some make it out to be; I guess you have to live here in order to really appreciate it.

New York subways at night run less frequently than they do in the daytime. As I stood on the platform, only one person stood nearby waiting for the train. On the subway train trip to Grand Central Terminal, I encountered a number of hard-looking unsavory characters, but none bothered me or asked for money or cigarettes. They seemed mostly intent on getting somewhere, either to work, home, or somewhere else.

By the time the subway train stopped at Grand Central Station, the last train to Croton had already departed. The police enforce a law not permitting anyone to hang out in the station when trains are not running, so the terminal is closed down from about two thirty to five in the morning. This time also provides time for the janitorial staff to clean the public areas of the terminal.

While waiting for the first train out, I found a small coffee shop near Grand Central. My time whiled away eating pie, drinking coffee, and reading the early edition of the *New York Daily News*. The small narrow shop had only bar stools and a counter to sit at, no booths or tables. Several other customers came and went, only two or three like me were in not hurry, also apparently waiting for the morning train.

The five thirty express to Poughkeepsie, New York, arrived in Croton at six fifteen. Since I parked my car in the lot at the Croton station, my trip home took only a few minutes, getting me home by seven and ready to hit the sack by seven fifteen. At least that had been the plan. On entering my apartment, who should be there waiting for me but Sabrina. She had made herself at home and lounged in the living room, watching something in Spanish on the TV. Unfortunately for me, I was a little sensitive when it came to Sabrina, and I didn't want to sacrifice the close relationship we had by demanding how she got into my apartment. Christ, free sex ruled my side of the relationship.

"Aye," I mumbled.

"Hi, Oscar, how go the wars?" She certainly displayed a cheerful nature.

"Really beat," was my rather depressed response. "I've been up all night so just a shower and bed for me."

"No problem, handsome." She continued her cheerfulness. "You get some sleep and I'll have a nice meal for you when you wake up. Also, if you're a really good boy, there might be some other things to do after we eat. Sound okay to you?" She sure knew my hot buttons.

"Sure, see you in a little while," I answered with as much amusement in my voice as I could muster.

After showering, drying, and a little primping, I lay down in my bed and soon fell fast asleep. Several hours later, I woke with a start to a warm body against my backside and a friendly bare arm around my chest.

"Hi," she said. I rolled over and there was beautiful Sabrina, totally naked. I stripped off my shorts and wrapped my arms and legs around her. We kissed passionately. Coming up for air, she said, "Thought we should do our little things before we eat." Her breath had a pleasant mint aroma; I hoped mine wasn't too offensive. "Is that all right with you?"

I grunted and began to caress her body, planting kisses on every single part of her.

Jesus, sex with this woman came utterly without bounds. After our little thing, which wasn't a thing and definitely wasn't little, we fell asleep in each other's arms—so much for eating after sex.

Chapter 25

The next day when I woke, Sabrina was nowhere in sight, which was just as well since serious business had to be taken care of. My Springfield 30-02 rifle, along with the scope, sat in an attaché case, which had been safely concealed in the trunk of my car. Retrieving it from my car and thoroughly checking out the rifle and scope to ensure every detailed part functioned properly, gave me some comfort. On a recent trip to the Catskill Mountains in upstate New York, I had fired the weapon, now it was part of my plan not to clean the weapon. Knowing at least my equipment would work as planned provided some sense of security. With nothing seemingly left to chance, I returned the attaché case with the weapon and scope to the trunk of the car.

Back upstairs, I made a phone call to Janet. She picked up on the second ring.

"Hi, it's me," I said as pleasantly as possible.

"Oscar, so happy to hear from you," she actually sounded sincere.

"Just wanted to check in," I said, showing some concern for my family and the business, "and see if everything is okay."

"Everything here is fine." She certainly sounded perky this morning. "But the business sure can use your knowledge and time. Any idea on how soon you will finish up your secret life? Devoting your full time to this business, I am confident, will again make our little computer system grow and prosper." She continued being very pleasant, sugarcoating every word.

The little "our little computer system" came totally out of the blue and definitely uninvited. I had no intentions of returning to "our" business. Some serious reservations as to what Janet might be up to began to crowd out what should be my complete focus. My total mental concentration should be on Gino, and the plan to divert all the evidence of a serial killer directly to him. Very simply, I could not let Janet's little references of *we*, *us*, or *our* conflict with the plan—time to move on.

"I think in another week or so," I answered, trying to reassure her without making a serious commitment to a specific date, "depends on how things go, but I will keep you informed. Tell the kids I said hello." I wanted to conclude the conversation on a good note and move on.

"Thanks for calling, Oscar." Surprisingly, she hung up without any further questions or admonishments.

Her attitude toward me, and definitely my attitude toward her, seemed surreal, almost a premonition, like something foreboding might occur in the near future. I was getting melancholy; could this be a forewarning? This feeling could not be allowed to consume me, and any thoughts of death or trauma were forced from my mind.

I phoned my mother to let her know everything was okay. She wanted to know when Janet and I would be getting back together. I ducked the question by changing the subject quickly and gave a cheery good-bye, promising to phone again in a week or so.

I dressed in a business suit with a nice white shirt and tie. Looking very professional, I parked the car at the Croton-Harmon Railroad Station, and with the attaché case in hand I boarded the train to New York City. Once in the city, a short subway ride took me to Atlantic Avenue in Brooklyn, where I walked the two blocks to 310 Crescent Street. About nine thirty, I walked up the stairs to the sixth floor.

I couldn't see any evidence of Gino being there, so hiding in the janitor's closet was, decidedly, my only logical option. The risk of using the stairwell could result in an encounter with one of the building's tenants, who might question the purpose of my being the building. From all appearances, the closet hadn't been used in years, and with an unencumbered view of Gino's apartment door and the elevator, it definitely provided me an excellent place to hide. Keeping the door slightly ajar, I could maintain constant surveillance of the hallway in both directions, the door to the stairwell, the elevator door, and the door to Gino's apartment; what more could a guy ask for?

Once in the closet, I put the rifle together, mounted the scope, and placed the attaché case behind the brooms and mops. The weapon had been fired recently in upstate New York; if I was successful in exchanging my weapon with Gino's, any subsequent inspection of the weapon would confirm it had been fired. This element of my plan, a critical part, could determine its success or failure.

No sooner had the weapon been assembled than a shot rang out, and then another more distant shot. I bolted from the closet, fully expecting to see Gino running from the apartment, but nothing. Very cautiously, I went to the apartment and pressed my ear to the door, nothing, not a sound.

I took the key out of my pocket and opened the door. On the floor by the window, Gino lay motionless. Approaching his body slowly, I could see a pool of blood oozing out by his head.

Quickly, I grabbed his rifle, pressed his hands and fingers to my rifle, and left the apartment, closing the door behind me. My actions were none too soon, because as I ducked back into the janitor's closet, the elevator door opened and four or five men ran out.

"Check all the apartments," the apparent head agent instructed, "he could be in any of the apartments that front on Atlantic Avenue. Check all of them," he sternly instructed the others, who began pounding on the apartment doors on the north side of the building. At several, there was no response, including the apartment Gino lay dead in.

"Find something we can force these doors open with." The head guy hollered out to the others. "There," pointing in my direction where I remained hidden, "looks like a janitor's closet, there should be something in that closet we can use to force these doors open with."

Holy shit, this was the end for sure. I hid Gino's rifle with the scope behind some brooms, mops, and other junk in the corner where the attaché case lay hidden. In the other corner, a large standpipe, a water pipe for the sprinkler system in the building, ran floor to ceiling. Climbing on top of the sink, I wedged my hand and foot behind the pipe and pressed myself against the ceiling of the closet. Fortunately for me, as this was an older building, the twelve-foot ceiling provided some concealment. I had secured myself, half of me behind the standpipe, when a sudden a cramp hit my left leg. A fucking charley horse, shit, now what? I had such extreme pain; I bit my lip to prevent myself from crying out or even moaning. Hanging on, just enduring the intense pain, was all that could be done.

The door started to open when a different voice could be heard, "Hey, Mr. Peterson, the superintendent is on his way up with a master key, he should be here in a couple of minutes." The superintendent of the building had keys to open the door.

"Tell him to fucking hurry it up," the boss, Mr. Peterson, said, showing his impatience. "We don't have all day to fuck around here," he growled, "that son of a bitch could be long gone if we continue to fucking dawdle our time away here."

Slowly, I straightened out my left leg, gradually relieving the pain. Once my leg began to relax, I lowered myself back down to the floor and peered out the small opening of the closet door. The door opened just enough so I could see the hallway and apartment door. They had opened Gino's apartment and everyone went in except one man who stood guard outside the door, I guess the big boss didn't want any tourists strolling through the crime scene.

"We finally got the son of a bitch," Mr. Peterson yelled in what sounded like a voice of victory. "We've been after this fuck for months, not a single lead until today, and we got the fucker." He continued in the same elated voice; I wouldn't be surprised if he was doing a jig by Gino's body. "Tell McMurray that was one hell of a shot. The NYPD should give him a citation."

Could this finally be the conclusion of my sojourn into a very dangerous, secret life as an assassin, my deadly and unorthodox life as a wanted man? The current indication could be deceptive, I had no positive assurance that the end had actually arrived. I could only pray this could be the end, and my life would return to normal. The only ones with a clue as to what my life consisted of for the past year or so were Raquel in California and Sabrina, and in reality, neither of them knew very much.

The next few days, all of the New York papers were filled with the news of a shoot-out in Brooklyn. According to the papers, FBI Agent Briana Crawford-Taylor, the lead agent on this case, had her office located in a suburb of Philadelphia. As the lead agent, she directed two agents in the New York area, Agent Chicaralli and Agent Peterson. Agent Chicaralli had been keeping Crawford-Taylor abreast of developments. The serial killer, the one they were trying to track for months, was contracted to take out an owner of a pizza parlor in Brooklyn, New York. Peterson and Chicaralli had arranged for two sharpshooters from the New York City Police Department. Peterson acted as a spotter for one and Chicaralli for the other.

Unfortunately, Chicaralli did not spot the shooter until after he had killed the pizza parlor owner. The muzzle flash of the serial killer's rifle disclosed his position, Agent Chicaralli witnessing the flash, directed the NYPD sharpshooter to the window location. With a single shot, the NYPD officer, a Bill McMurray, took out the serial killer.

Everything had checked out, according to Agent Chicaralli. The rifle checked out as the one used in three of the previous killings and the fingerprints, taken from the previous killings, definitely proved to be those of the now-dead serial killer, Gino Francotti. Samples of blood, skin, and hair sent to the NYCPD laboratory for DNA analysis should produce results in the next two days. Without a doubt, they had a lock on this case and it could be filed away.

Senior Agent Briana Crawford-Taylor initially had some reservations about everything coming together so conveniently. She advised Agents Chicaralli that it just didn't make sense that this individual would be careless enough to leave so much incriminating evidence, especially for an alleged mob hit man. However, she could not refute what had been found at any of the crime scenes—solid evidence produced by the diligent research of the crime scene investigation units. Several days later, the laboratory results on the DNA were in and matched to that of Gino Francott.

I had spent five hours in the janitor's closet waiting for things to settle down. The crime scene investigators had come and gone and the medical examiner had come and gone. Now the coroner arrived to remove the body. I prepared to bail when a distinctive, though unidentifiable sound could be heard in the hallway. Looking out, I could see the fucking janitor vacuuming the rug in the hallway and he headed straight in my direction. I couldn't logically explain my presence in his closet.

Gino's rifle could not be disassembled and placed in my attaché case, so it and the case had to be left behind for now, and I planned to return later that night to pick them up. Right now, my problem was how the fuck to get out of the closet without the janitor seeing me. I had no magic tricks up my sleeve. Once again, I crunched myself up into the corner by the ceiling, using the standpipe to hold me in place, and expecting any minute to get another charley horse.

As expected, the fucking cramp in my leg returned with a vengeance, the pain grew almost unbearable. Sweat soaked my body and ran like a river down my face and my back. The janitor opened the closet door and peered inside as if he had never seen the place before. Once he had the lights on and started removing mops or brooms, the rifle and paraphernalia would be visible. No question that once he saw the weapon he would summon the boss and my goose would be cooked. He fumbled around for a light switch but, not finding one, he grunted something to himself in Spanish and then closed the door. Jesus Christ, I am one lucky son of a bitch—sorry, Mom.

I'm really not sure who my guardian angel is, but he or she clearly worked overtime on my behalf. Twenty minutes later, I left the closet and the building without the rifle. Hanging around New York City is always a pleasure. I rented a hotel room in one of the small off-Broadway hotels. At the hotel, while I showered and cleaned myself up, my shirt went to the laundry and my suit to the dry cleaner, all back within an hour. There is so much to see and do in New York. On this particular day, a trip to the top of the Empire State Building helped pass the time. A nice long supper at Mama Rotoni's, a celebration dinner, closed out this chapter of my life.

I sat in the back as usual and ordered a bottle of Chianti, a really good vintage, the most expensive on the menu. While waiting for the wine, I perused Mama Rotini's extensive menu, six pages of outstanding Italian cuisine. The waiter came back and I ordered cioppino, a very good Italian seafood dish. He left with my order, and I leaned back in the plush cushions of my booth and enjoyed a really fine wine.

To my right, out of the corner of my eye, there was some movement, so instinctively I turned to see what distracted me. Two very large Italians, at least I assumed they were Italian, stood staring down at me, both dressed in expensive business suits, gray shirts, and dark gray ties. I guess I had missed the memo on what to wear for this occasion.

"What the fuck do you want here?" the smaller of the two growled at me, the smaller one being only being a measly six foot two and probably 210 pounds.

"Just a nice meal," I replied, somewhat mystified by the questioning.

"You fucking come in here all the time," spittle flew from his mouth as he enunciated his heavily accented words, "trying to listen in on what is being said, you fuck." He slicked his black, gray-speckled hair back as he spoke. The big shit just stood there, expressionless, probably waiting for the word to punch my lights out. "You a fucking reporter or a cop?" He growled in a deep baritone voice.

"I'm sorry," I was hoping the bubble in my ass was a fart, as shitting my pants would definitely spoil the wine and my dinner, "but I really just come here because the meals are so good. That is all." My heart started to race. What did these guys know? Had someone been following me? "If you don't want me here, I will gladly leave." Shit, was I whining or begging? This was the one time I came here just to enjoy a meal and thugs jump me.

"Just listen to this, fuck," the little shit continued to emphasize his importance while the big lug with the ugly face, a broken nose probably from a fight, just stood behind him and smiled, "if we catch you listening in on any of our conversations, we assure you, you won't be listening to anything again. *Capisce?*" He turned and walked into the big guy, mumbled something like "Get the fuck out of my way," and they both walked away.

Fuck, who could enjoy a meal after that? However, the aroma of the food was so enticing I forced myself to eat. I had to admit the timing of my little encounter with little and big thug had occurred at a fortuitous time for me. If it had been on any previous occasion at Mama Rotoni's my eavesdropping equipment might have been discovered. I raised a glass of wine to toast my guardian angel.

Now I had to watch my back. On the subway trip back to Brooklyn, I changed trains four times, looping back and forth, just in case someone followed me. Finally back at 310 Crescent Street, I went back up to the sixth floor and retrieved Gino's rifle, breaking it down as much as possible and then stuffing it into a canvas athletics bag I had purchased for that purpose.

The train ride back to Croton gave me the opportunity to reflect on my life for the past year or so. What had I accomplished, had I made any positive contributions to society? For centuries, men have gone to war, putting themselves in harm's way, many of them dying in the process. Some are briefly remembered for their heroics, others merely perish. No matter, as a group they are remembered at least once every year on Veteran's Day, an almost insignificant measure of gratitude for the men and women who gave their all to the preservation of freedom.

What I had done in Bosnia and in Afghanistan might be considered heroic by citizens of the Western world, but not by Serbians, or to the mullah I had encountered on the trail in Afghanistan. To them, I killed in the name of capitalism. No one, other than some high-ranking individuals in the United States, knew of my and thousands of other warriors' contributions to our society. Only files, buried away somewhere in the Pentagon, were a recognition of our valor. Life would go on, as it should. That's what we sacrifice for, what we put ourselves in danger for.

But the greater question now was if what I had done these past months had made any positive contribution to society. To me, the answer might be a resounding yes, but what of others? The individuals I had killed were villainous people; they had managed to avoid prosecution in this country, either through their contacts or because they had acquired considerable wealth to protect themselves. I didn't really have the answer. I rested my head on the window and watched the Hudson River pass by.

Epilogue

Several weeks later, Ernesto instructed all his underbosses to attend a meeting at his Saranac Lake estate. As he always did, Ernesto showed up with his entourage of servants, maids, and a chef—a new chef since Ernesto could not keep the same one two weeks in a row. He had a penchant for being overly fussy about his food, and when it wasn't prepared to his liking, he invariably threw it at the chef—dish and all. The chefs would run as if their lives depended on it, and they probably did, given Ernesto's reputation.

The underbosses preferred not to attend these meetings but had no choice. Unlike the chefs, they could not just leave. The only way out for them was feet first in a very expensive casket, along with all the pomp afforded a deceased member of a royal family. At least four hearses (for just one body), six to eight flower cars, and an unending line of Cadillac limousines with every member of Ernesto's organization had to be present, no questions asked.

The usual group of Ernesto's staff attended with his supposed secretary, Margaret Benzio, who never took a note in her life. She clearly displayed her assets, always wearing a low-cut blouse or dress to reveal her more-than-ample breasts. Her skirts were so tight and revealing that nothing could be left to the imagination. Of course, she never bothered with a bra; it wouldn't allow her nipples to show through. Joe Balgazi, Fatso Flugazy, Big Tony Mendoza, and The Don Pulchisi, along with their henchmen and "secretaries," also were in attendance.

Missing from the meeting, of course, was Gino Francotti, as he had been buried several weeks prior. The usual funeral had all the fanfare, with a line of black Cadillacs and Lincolns that stretched for three miles. The eulogies at the cemetery went on for close to four hours. Ernesto wanted Gino's funeral to be "big time." Gino's death brought a newfound reputation to the organization: one that enforced its own rules.

The day after Gino's burial, they held the funeral for Frank Valicina, which had to be at least as splendid as Gino's to placate any doubts Ernesto's wife, Juliana, might have about Frank's untimely death. She couldn't understand why some serial killer would just up and kill Frank, but there it was in all the papers. Fortunately, Ernesto never disclosed any of his business dealings to Juliana, so she had no idea that Gino had been a part of Ernesto's organization. After several weeks of denial, she seemed satisfied with the serial killer explanation.

The meeting got underway with Ernesto's usual tirade about the incompetence of the individuals in his organization, particularly the underbosses. He had expected an increase of at least 40 percent from each of the areas in their control. With Angelo Lambrascha out of the way, the underbosses should have expanded their operations into adjoining sectors that had previously been under control of the Angelo Lambrascha's Mafioso organization.

"You are all fucking *stupido*." Ernesto stood at the head of the table, hammering on it with both fists. "Can't fucking run a simple fucking business that is handed to you on a fucking silver platter. *Stupido, stupido*, every fucking one of you," he ranted.

Big Tony Mendoza made a serious mistake.

"But, boss," he pleaded, "we only recently started expanding our operations into the Angelo's areas; there just hasn't been enough time to really make any significant gains."

Ernesto picked up one of the heavy, rectangular glass ashtrays that sat in front of him and flung it as hard as he could at Tony's head, striking him on the left side of the temple just above his eye. Blood began to pour out of the wound. One of his henchmen handed him a hanky, which Tony applied to the wound. The hanky quickly saturated with blood. The henchman retrieved some ice from the service bar at the back of the room, a small towel from the washroom, and handed Tony the towel with the ice in it, which Tony applied it to the wound, stemming some of the blood flow.

"Fucking, *stupido*, looking for stupid excuses," there could be no satisfying Ernesto. "You all have had plenty of time to expand your fucking operations. I'm going to replace every fucking one of you. I'm tired of your fucking bullshit." Ernesto stood with his hands flat on the conference table, glaring at the underbosses, his face red with anger and his eyes filled with fire as he gazed down at them.

A sudden pop, followed by a noise similar to gravel falling on the wood floor sounded somewhere behind Ernesto. He seemed to move back, like he wanted to sit in his chair, however the momentum of his body pushed the chair away from him; his outstretched arms slowly lowered, and his head came down with a sickening thud on the heavy wood conference table. His body slowly slid back, landing in a grotesque clump on the floor between the table and his chair.

For fully five minutes, no one spoke, moved, or even looked at each other. Complete stillness pervaded the room, not even a motion of the heads or hands of the group appeared noticeable.

Finally, Dominick Pulchisi, who sat to the right of Ernesto, rose from his chair and gingerly walked around to where Ernesto lay. He prodded Ernesto's body with his foot, fully expecting Ernesto to jump up and assault him. Ernesto's head lulled over, and Dominick could see a red hole in his forehead, blood slowly oozing from it.

Dominick walked back to his chair, picked up his glass of scotch, and raised it up.

"Here's to Ernesto, long may he live," he said with a laugh.

Everyone in the room joined him, raising their glasses and repeating, "Here's to Ernesto, long may he live," after which they all laughed.

"Let's all go downstairs and enjoy a fine afternoon with good food, drink, and especially good company. Send the cleaning crew up here to take out the trash," Dominick instructed.

As they filed out, Dominick put his arm around Big Tony Mendoza's shoulder and said, "You know, Tony, I think that's the best fucking one and a half mil we ever spent."

About the Author

Charles E. Wilcox was a combat marine who served with the Second Marine Division. He graduated from the University of San Francisco and went on to earn an MBA from University of Phoenix. Previously employed in plant operation management and contract negotiations, he currently lives with his wife, Rita, in Dana Point, California.